by C.C.S. Jones

Paperback ISBNs 979-8-9918586-7-0 / 979-8-9918586-4-9
Hardcover ISBN 979-8-9918586-6-3
Hardcover (with dust jacket) ISBN 979-8-9918586-9-4
Special Edition ISBN 979-8-9918586-8-7
E-book ISBN 979-8-9918586-5-6
Library of Congress Control Number: 2025901244

To my children,

who inspire me every day and remind me of the beauty in dreaming big. May you always believe in yourselves and know that you can achieve anything you set your mind to.

☉☽ CHAPTER 1 ☾☉

My legs felt like they were wading through wet concrete, every step heavier than the last, but I kept moving. People jostled past, their faces a blur of excitement, and the stadium lights bore down, too harsh. Was he still following me?

I glanced over my shoulder, but the crowd shifted again, swallowing any chance of spotting him. My fingers tightened around the tray, the plastic cups groaning like they were seconds from surrendering. Perfect. I'd volunteered for the drink run without thinking it through—classic me, always first to help, last to realize what I'd gotten myself into. Now here I was, balancing this wobbly tray like it carried my last ounce of dignity.

My pulse thudded in my ears, drowning out the music and laughter rolling through the stands. This was supposed to be the perfect kickoff to summer, but it felt more like I'd wandered straight into an episode of *True Crime Confidential.* And if anyone was destined to stumble headfirst into trouble, it was me—undisputed queen of clumsy missteps and inconvenient timing.

I slipped past a pack of football players, the tray still upright, drinks still intact, and there he was—impossible to miss. The same guy from the gas station yesterday, the coffee shop this morning, and the parking lot earlier tonight. Everything about him set my nerves on edge: the too-perfect features, like he'd stepped out of a Renaissance sculpture, and that stare…

He lurked by the concession stand, like tailing me was his full-time job, half-hidden behind a group of cheerleaders. His blond curls caught the floodlights, practically haloed, but there was nothing angelic about the way his eyes pinned me in place. He didn't move. He just… watched.

I wasn't imagining it. I *knew* I wasn't. I could already see tomorrow's headline: "Jessa Whitley, 17, dirty blond hair, brown eyes, last seen carrying overpriced sodas before disappearing into the night." Yeah, no thanks. Not happening.

I slowed, torn between options. Confront him? Pretend he wasn't there? But before I could decide, he was gone. One second he was watching me, and the next, all I had were spiraling thoughts and a growing pit of dread twisting somewhere deep in my gut, staring at the spot he'd been.

Safety in numbers… I needed to find my friends. My purse strap slid off my shoulder, and I hiked it back up with a silent prayer that my asthma would sit this one out. Samantha was halfway up the bleachers, her phone glowing as she laughed at something Dawn said. The drumline pounded a steady beat, a rhythm that screamed freedom and summer nights.

Naturally, fate had other plans.

My foot snagged on something, and I pitched forward with all the grace of a collapsing Jenga tower. A poor freshman dove out of the way, his eyes wide with horror as I flailed for the railing, clinging to the tray like it was a life raft.

My fingers closed around the handrail, and the world flickered. The stadium dissolved. A crushing wave of freezing salt water slammed into me, icy and relentless. I gasped, my chest locking up as the cold dragged me under. Flames erupted, blistering heat roaring through the water, out of place and terrifying. Fire and water collided, each sensation searing, impossible to make sense of.

And just like that, I was back.

The stadium lights blazed too brightly, the crowd's roar hammered through my skull, and the tray of drinks was done for—drenched across me in a sticky mess. I staggered, my lungs fighting the telltale squeeze of an oncoming asthma attack, heart racing like I'd been yanked through two worlds at once.

I blinked, gasping for air, as the crowd came into focus. Everyone stared. Phones raised. Screens glowing. The humiliation burned hotter than the flames I'd just imagined.

My heart still pounded, my face still burned, but I plastered on a shaky smile and reached for the scraps of my dignity. If I didn't salvage this, I'd be a hashtag by morning.

"Hey, Jessa, practicing for a wet t-shirt contest?"

Brian. Of course. He was *that* guy—clueless, tactless, and perpetually convinced he was the funniest person in the room.

I shot him a glare sharp enough to slice steel. "Wow, Brian. Congrats. You've officially peaked." Flicking some of the sticky drink in his direction, I turned on my heel and bolted, abandoning any hope of catching up with Samantha.

Remnants of soda clung to my arms, the sour-sweet smell of it making me queasy. All I wanted was one night, just one, without drama. If it weren't dodging Zach and his new girlfriend, it would have been stressing over finals or enduring Dawn's relentless campaign to replace me as Sam's bestie. Couldn't I catch a break?

I ducked into the shadows beneath the bleachers and dumped the tray into a trash bin, the metal clang echoing my frustration. Hidden from the crowd, my composure cracked. Embarrassment burned hot under my skin, but the terror from whatever hallucination I'd just experienced overwhelmed it. My breath came in short, ragged bursts as I fumbled through my purse for my inhaler. With two pumps, the cool rush of air steadied my lungs. The lingering taste of albuterol sat on my tongue as I shoved the inhaler back into my bag, my hands still trembling with leftover adrenaline.

But the relief was short-lived.

Across from the crowd, by the concession stands, a flash of white-blond curls stopped me cold. Blondie. He was there, staring straight at me. Again.

Before I could move, Sam rounded the corner, stepping right into my line of sight. "Hey, what's going on?"

Her face was a mix of concern and confusion, her gaze sweeping over me, searching for answers, and I wondered how much of my latest disaster she'd witnessed.

I forced a grin, shaky and unconvincing. "Tripped. No big deal." It wasn't a total lie, but it felt hollow.

I thought about telling her. About Blondie and how he seemed to be everywhere, like a bad penny I couldn't shake. But when I glanced over her shoulder, the spot by the concession stand was empty.

He was gone.

Maybe I was imagining things. Maybe the stress of the last week of school had finally caught up to me.

"Sam!" Dawn Yeung appeared behind Sam, her timing as perfect as her salon-fresh hair. She barely spared me a glance, her focus zeroed in on Sam like I was invisible. "Weren't we finding Mike?"

Sam's brows knitted as she turned back to me. "You're sure you're okay?"

I forced a shrug, ignoring the knot in my stomach. "I'm fine. Go with Dawn. We'll catch up tonight."

She hesitated, torn like always. Sam had this way of wanting to make everyone happy, even the people who didn't deserve it. It made her an easy target for people like Dawn, who saw her kindness as something to exploit.

Reluctantly, she trailed after Dawn, but not before tossing one last glance my way. I forced a quick wave and a casual smile that didn't quite reach my eyes. As they vanished into the crowd, I exhaled slowly, letting the tension ease—at least a little—while my thoughts raced in a direction I couldn't stop.

This night had overstayed its welcome, and it wasn't over yet. A bunch of us had planned to hit Charlie's Diner in Midtown for pancakes and late-night gossip. Maybe the after-party could salvage things, maybe help me shake off this disaster. Assuming I could make it there without tripping over my own feet or, worse, running into my stalker again.

On the way home, I replayed the night in my head, trying to make sense of everything. The drowning, the fire, Blondie—it all blurred together, too surreal to believe. By the time I stepped through my front door, the end-of-year bash felt like a distant nightmare, but the tension in my chest refused to budge.

I ditched my sticky clothes and splashed cold water on my face, willing myself to reset before heading back out. The thought of food and neutral territory with friends was enough to keep me moving. I needed a win, even a small one.

Charlie's Diner was already buzzing when I arrived. The place never closed. A haven for high schoolers, truckers, and insomniacs mingling under the glow of fluorescent lights and the steady hum of old ceiling fans. The greasy scent of bacon and coffee greeted me as I walked in, a small comfort in a night that felt anything but normal.

Sam waved me over from a corner booth. She was with Dawn, Mike, and a few others, already deep in conversation. My phone buzzed faintly in my pocket, and I glanced at it… a reminder I still owed my mom a text. And, of course, Charlie's was a signal dead zone.

"I'll be right back," I told Sam, holding up my phone. "I've got to let my mom know I'm alive."

Sam set her ponytail with a snap of elastic and slid out of the booth. "I'll come with."

We stepped outside, where the diner's neon sign bathed the sidewalk in flickering pink light. The humid air stuck to my skin as I typed out a quick message and hit send, hoping the spotty signal wouldn't sabotage it.

Sam leaned against the building, scrolling through her phone. "So, what's up with you tonight? You've been jumpy since this morning."

I hesitated, debating how much to share. "I think someone's following me," I said.

Sam straightened, her phone forgotten. "What? Who?"

"I don't know. Blond guy… keeps showing up—at the gas station, the stadium, everywhere. It's probably nothing," I added quickly, trying to dismiss the unease creeping up. "I'm just being paranoid."

"Jessa, that's not 'nothing.' You can't just brush this off. If someone's creeping on you, we need to—"

A crash from inside the diner cut her off. We both jumped, turning toward the window. The dim light made it hard to see much.

"What was that?" Sam pressed her hands against the glass, trying to get a better view.

Before I could respond, she crumpled to the ground.

"Sam!" I dropped my phone in panic and knelt beside her. My hands trembled as I checked for a pulse. Steady. Breathing? Fine. I shook her a bit. "Sam?"

My own breathing came in short, sharp gasps. What was I supposed to do? Call for help? Shake her awake? My mind raced, colliding with a hundred useless thoughts.

"Someone, help!" I screamed, scrambling to the diner's door and stumbling inside. I froze in the threshold. The scene before me wasn't just strange. It was impossible.

Every person in the diner had slumped over across the red vinyl booths, dead. Forks dangled from limp hands. Food scattered across plates. A waitress lay sprawled against the counter, her notepad still in her hand like a discarded prop.

The silence felt suffocating. Was this some kind of gas leak? Did the rapture come, and I'd been left behind? I took a shaky step forward, trying my best to control my already rapid breathing.

I jumped at a loud, guttural snore breaking the quiet. My gaze shot to the sound. Brian, sprawled across a booth, mouth open, snoring like a chainsaw.

I almost laughed, relieved, but the sound caught in my throat as my brain tried to process what I was seeing. They weren't dead. They were just… asleep?

I scanned the room again. "Hello? If this is some kind of prank, congratulations, you've officially freaked me out." The words felt flat, swallowed by the unnatural quiet.

Zach, with his tousled sandy hair and a jawline that could cut glass, stretched out over the table as though vying for gold in competitive napping. He barely stirred under my urgent shakes.

"Zach! Wake up!" I shook him harder. "Come on, joke's over…"

A shadow stirred near the back of the diner, coalescing into a man with dark hair that melted into the dim light. His eyes—yellow, piercing, and not human—ignited a low, twisting dread deep in my stomach.

"There you are," he crooned, his voice smooth and venomous.

A sharp buzzing erupted in my ears, drowning out everything else. Instinct screamed at me to run. Fear rooted me in place. His eyes glowed like a malfunctioning streetlight and his grin twisted into something feral, something *wrong*.

"Who the hell are you?" The words tumbled out, shaky and raw.

He just grinned wider, as if my hysteria was exactly what he wanted. The buzzing cranked up to eleven, digging into my skull like a swarm of tiny, jagged needles. I clutched my head, desperate to block it out, but the noise only grew, scattering my thoughts into fragments. My fingers fumbled in my purse for my inhaler, but it slipped from my shoulder and thudded to the floor.

I went to reach for it, hoping to snatch it and run, but his voice froze me mid-motion.

"You can't run, Jessa." His steps were slow, deliberate, like a predator savoring its prey. Every movement sent a fresh wave of terror through me.

The hell I can't. My body jolted into action, abandoning my purse, my inhaler—my literal nectar of life. My hip body-checked a table as I fled outside.

The street felt off. The air was too still, and the flickering streetlights cast distorted shadows that seemed to stretch and twist, like they were alive. I sidestepped Sam, still unconscious on the sidewalk, terror propelling me into the middle of the street. I spun in place, scanning the shadows.

"Help!" The eerie stillness swallowed my cry. No passing cars, no distant rumble of engines, no cicadas—just the faint hum of Charlie's neon sign.

A quick glance over my shoulder confirmed my worst fear. Yellow Eyes had stepped out of the diner, moving around Sam with unnerving calm, like he had all the time in the world. Panic seized me, and I ran—or tried to.

Pain shot through my bruised hip with every step, forcing me into a limping jog as my lungs burned, struggling to keep up. The night blurred around me. I didn't know where I was heading—only that I had to get away.

What was after me? My mind flashed through every horror movie I'd ever seen—vampire, werewolf, alien invader? Whatever he was, Yellow Eyes was gunning for me, and I was fresh out of wooden stakes, silver bullets, and alien-proof bunkers.

I knew I should keep running, but something deep within me, something I didn't fully understand, soared to the surface. My knees were jelly, my mind shouting, *What the hell are you doing?* But my body had other plans, bracing for a fight I had no business picking as I stopped and turned to face him. This was it. End of the line. I locked eyes with him, my heart hammering in my chest, wondering why I wasn't running for my life.

"Giving up already?" His voice dripped with mockery, savoring every second of my fear. Then he lunged, a blur of motion, his speed defying logic.

Without thinking, I blocked with my hands, every nerve on fire as I braced for the inevitable clash. My eyes squeezed shut, ready for the bone-crushing impact. But instead, my hands pushed something solid, and then...

nothing.

I opened my eyes, watching in confusion as Yellow Eyes flew backward down the hill, a look of shock mirroring my own. I staggered back and stared at my hands in disbelief. "What the actual—"

A whirlwind of dark smog slammed into me, knocking the air from my lungs as I hit the ground with a crack. The pain radiated through my back, stealing what little breath I had left. An icy, bone-white hand latched onto my shirt and yanked me up like a ragdoll.

I found myself face-to-face with a new terror, different from Yellow Eyes, more sinister, more terrifying. Sharp, searing pain followed, tearing through me like claws rending flesh. I tried to scream, but the sound was swallowed by the emptiness in my lungs. His face, pale as death, hovered inches from mine, eyes like bruised amethyst, cold, unfeeling.

As suddenly as he'd grabbed me, he hurled me across the street like discarded trash. The world spun violently, my head slamming into the pavement. Pain exploded—hot, merciless, blinding—and the world shattered into darkness.

☉︎☽ CHAPTER 2 ☾☉︎

The world swirled in smudged shadows and muted colors, my vision refusing to focus. But then, sounds began to creep in, piercing the haze.

"That was too close." A woman's voice, low and tense, tugged at the edges of my splintered thoughts, pulling me back to reality.

"Yeah," a deeper voice replied, calm but laced with frustration. "We had the element of surprise this time."

Every nerve in my body screamed as pain surged in relentless waves. Beneath it, a flicker of warmth stirred, spreading slowly through me. It eased the burn in my lungs, coaxing them into a steady rhythm and dulling the sharp edges of the pain.

Time felt slippery, moments blending in an abstract smear of sensations. The cold pavement bit into my scraped palms, a reminder that I was alive, though nothing about it felt real. Above me, a streetlight buzzed faintly, anchoring me in Midtown despite the alien wrongness of everything else.

"You okay?"

The voice startled me, forcing me out of the fog. I flinched, too exhausted to scream, and looked up to see a figure crouching nearby, his face half-hidden in the soft light. Definitely not Yellow Eyes. Definitely not the other ghostly figure either. Just my luck—another guy. Because clearly, they'd all been stellar company tonight.

Before I could muster the energy to respond, a girl stepped into view. My pulse spiked.

"Who are you?" I croaked, wincing at how weak I sounded.

"Calm down. We're not here to hurt you," she said, her tone more irritation than comforting. With her cropped silver top and cargo pants, she looked like she'd just stepped off the set of some edgy dystopian movie.

I glanced between them, my brain struggling to catch up. Words failed me, my tongue on some kind of personal strike. The guy sat on the pavement across from me, unnervingly casual, as if this were a beach bonfire and not whatever post-assault debrief it was turning into. Moonlight illuminated his wavy, hobbit-style brown hair and the look worked for him. They both looked around my age, but there was an edge to them—like they belonged to a world with sharper corners than mine.

"I'm sure you have questions," he said.

A laugh tried to escape me, but it came out as a hoarse grunt. He studied me with an intensity that made my skin prickle. Was it concern? Or something else? My instincts weren't screaming danger like they had with Yellow Eyes, but I wasn't ready to trust either of them.

"Do you speak?" the redhead asked, her impatience breaking through her earlier attempt at civility. I couldn't tear my gaze off the guy, though. His expression shifted, a flicker of something that looked a lot like recognition.

"Give her a minute, Cynthia." He stared at me, hard, like Sam when she was wrestling with a quadratic equation. "She did just come back to life."

"Do what now?" I pushed myself upright. "I was dead? I died?"

"You're okay now," he added, like it was supposed to be reassuring. It wasn't. The words only fueled the wildfire of questions igniting in my head.

"Who are you? What just happened?" Adrenaline soared as my breath edged toward hyperventilation.

Cynthia rolled her eyes, visibly over it. "Honestly, you'd think these transformations would come with a manual by now," she muttered, more to herself than anyone else. She glanced at the sky, as if expecting some cosmic intervention. "We don't have time for this. We need to move."

"Transformations?" My voice wavered as I staggered to my feet.

"Yeah, you're the new Potential," she sighed, as if that explained everything.

Somehow, my legs held, though they felt like they belonged to someone else. My hands, shaking and sticky with blood, looked just as foreign and my chest ached with the phantom reminder of asthma's grip. I eyed the stretch of empty pavement ahead, debating my odds at making an escape without collapsing.

Paul, now on my radar as potentially less creepy—though the jury was still out—offered a hand as he stood. He moved slowly, like he knew I might bolt. "Easy, don't panic."

"Don't panic? Right, because dying is just your average Saturday," I shot back, my sarcasm reaching new heights as the absurdity of the situation dialed up. "You just said I was dead… or almost died? Where's the guy who tried to kill me? And who are you? Start talking before I—"

"Before you what? Pretend you're an actual threat?" Cynthia snapped, her smirk practically a challenge.

Paul sighed. "Cynthia, enough."

Her bitch-itude was the least of my worries. Paul's hand brushed my shoulder, but before I could pull away, a warm zap burst through me, rebooting my lungs.

"Wait." I took in a deep, cleansing breath and met his gaze. "Did you just do that?"

His eyes dropped, a shadow of something like regret flickering across his face. "The threats are gone. For now."

"Threats? As in, plural?" My knees wobbled, but I forced myself to stay upright. When he stepped forward to help, I pushed him away. Weakly, but enough to make my point.

"We don't have time for this, Paul," Cynthia huffed. "They're about to wake up."

"They?" My friends? The town? I staggered back a step, glancing toward the empty street, half-expecting those glowing yellow eyes to come crawling out of the dark again.

Paul didn't answer, his gaze flicking toward Cynthia, unspoken tension crackling between them. The blood on my hands was real, the throbbing in my skull too fresh to dismiss. I'd been thrown across the street—maybe killed—and now I was *alive* again. Somehow.

"She's right." Paul turned toward me, and for a second, the moonlight caught his eyes, flashing gold. Something ancient flickered there before it vanished. I blinked, wondering if I'd imagined it.

Sifting through my confused brain, I forced out a coherent thought. "Seriously. Who the hell are you guys?"

"I'm Paul," he said, his calm demeanor so at odds with the chaos around us it bordered on unsettling.

Cynthia shot me a look that could curdle milk, then rolled her eyes skyward. "And I'm Cynthia."

Clearly, I was dealing with experts in the art of vague answers.

"Great. Introductions over. Now, let's get you back to Charlie's." Cynthia started walking.

Charlie's. They knew where I'd been. Normally, I'd be freaking out about strangers tracking my whereabouts, but after tonight's parade of weirdness, it barely registered. "Did you make everyone fall asleep?" I asked, planting my feet. I wasn't moving until I got something concrete.

My headache pulsed behind my eye, and I winced, reaching to rub it. Paul touched my arm, a jolt of static sparking at his touch. I yanked it back, ignoring his startled look. I wasn't about to let his cryptic gestures throw me off.

Cynthia snorted and stopped to glance at me. "Hypnos," she finally said, tossing the name out like it was the obvious answer to my question.

It clicked instantly. Hypnos—the god of sleep. I'd been a Greek mythology nerd long before it was cool, if it ever really was, memorizing family trees while other kids were flipping through the latest manga. "The sleep god?"

Paul offered his hand again, but I ignored it. "Like I said, there's a lot to go over."

I waved wildly at the diner. "Are they okay? Will they wake up? They're not going to die, are they?"

"They'll be fine," Paul said, his voice steady but layered with urgency. "But we need to get you back to your group before someone notices you're gone."

As much as I wanted to keep pressing, a strange pull—like an invisible thread—urged me to move. Reluctantly, I fell into step beside them, unspoken questions crowding the silence.

Paul reached for my hand again, his persistence bordering on irritating, but this time he didn't wait for permission. His touch once again sent a zing of energy through me, leaving my skin buzzing. The rush was so sudden, I nearly tripped.

"We should clean this up," he murmured, grabbing the hem of his tan shirt and using it to wipe the blood from my hands. His movements were methodical, pressing between my fingers and following the lines of my palms.

"Uh, yeah. Sure," I muttered, thrown by his calm focus. It didn't match the escalating urgency radiating off Cynthia, who shot him a glare.

An owl hooted somewhere in the distance; the sound punctuated by the barking of dogs a block away. Cynthia's head snapped up, her eyes darting between me and Paul. "We're out of time."

Midtown was waking up.

Paul turned to me. "Hang on. This next part's intense, but trust me, okay?"

I narrowed my eyes, skepticism at full blast, but before I could argue, he scooped me up like I weighed nothing, cradling me against his chest and—

What the actual hell?

My brain short-circuited. One second, I was bracing for… I don't even know what, and the next, it felt like I'd been fired out of a cannon. Wind whipped past my face, stealing my breath. By the time my senses caught up, we were standing outside Charlie's.

My legs shook a bit when he set me down, and I clutched his arm to steady myself. Did we just… teleport? My thoughts raced, trying to grasp the impossible.

His hand brushed a strand of hair from my face, his touch almost absentminded, and I froze, torn between awe and disbelief. Who *was* this guy, and how much weirder could this night get?

The streetlights cast a muted glow over his features—strong, angular, and unsettlingly calm. His twilight-blue eyes fixed on mine with a look so piercing it felt like he could see straight through me. It was the kind of gaze that made you question whether you'd been missing something important about yourself all along.

"We'll talk soon," he said. The way he tucked my hair behind my ear should've felt invasive, but instead, it struck some unnamable chord inside me. Familiar, but in a way I couldn't explain.

"And when might 'soon' be?" I shot back, trying to mask the tremor in my voice. "Am I still on the hit list? What about my friends?"

"We'll be in touch," he replied. His hand skimmed my cheek, so fleeting it could've been accidental, yet it left a trace of something unspoken.

"Jessa?"

I spun around at Sam's voice, relief rushing over me when I saw her sitting up, dazed but alive. By the time I turned back, Paul and Cynthia were gone, their silhouettes swallowed by the night like shadows retreating into themselves, leaving me with more questions than answers.

"Who were *they*?" Sam groaned, rubbing her temples. "Please tell me that wasn't Mr. Creepy stalking you." She reached for our phones, studying them as if they might explain everything.

"Not sure." I stuffed my blood-stained hands into my pockets, trying to keep the evidence hidden. "You okay?"

"I guess? Did I… blackout? Why am I on the ground?" She slowly stood, handing me my phone.

"I'll explain later. Let's get inside."

We walked into the diner, and it took every ounce of self-control not to lose my shit in front of an audience. Everything was… normal. No food splatters. No overturned plates. No bodies slumped in booths. Instead, Charlie's bustled with casual chaos, like Yellow Eyes hadn't just gone full sleep-zombie on everyone and tried to add me to his count.

Conversations hummed, forks clinked against plates, and people scarfed down pancakes like this was just another midnight hangout. I swallowed hard. This wasn't possible. Either the world had gone mad… or I had. Right now, I wasn't putting money on reality.

☉☽ CHAPTER 3 ☾☉

Sam came out of her bathroom in her usual hoodie and leggings, collapsing onto her bed like the night had completely drained her. Her dad's condo had become my second home over the years—especially for sleepovers when we needed a break from life. The fold-out futon creaked beneath me as I shifted, nerves prickling at everything I hadn't said yet.

"You're doing that thing where you get quiet and weird," Sam said, pulling out an earbud and tossing her phone aside. "What's going on? And don't say 'nothing.'"

I hesitated, my hands twisting in the blanket. "Give me a second."

"Fine." She flopped back against her pillows. "But if you're plotting something, I expect at least a warning this time. Remember when you made me sneak into your mom's garage to grab the paint cans, and—"

"I said I'd warn you next time!" I shot back with a small grin, pushing myself off the futon and heading for the bathroom.

The harsh fluorescent light flickered as I closed the door behind me. I caught a glimpse of myself in the mirror—hair tangled, face pale, shirt rumpled—and tried to steady my breath. Sam and I had been through a lot together: the matchmaking schemes for her dad and my mom, late-night binges of K-dramas, endless planning for a friendship tattoo we never got around to. She was the one person I trusted completely, but this? This would test even her capacity for weird.

Splashing cold water on my face, I tried to organize my thoughts.

Hypnos. The purple-eyed killer. Paul and Cynthia. How did I even start to explain something that didn't make sense to me?

When I came out, Sam was still on her bed, scrolling on her phone. She looked up immediately, her expression shifting from casual curiosity to genuine concern. "Okay, now you're really freaking me out. Just say it."

I sat on the edge of the futon, my foot bouncing nervously. "You're going to think I've lost it."

"That bad, huh?" she asked, setting her phone aside. "All right, lay it on me."

I hesitated, my throat tightening around the words I needed to say. Swallowing a couple of times, I finally managed to push them out. "You remember Hypnos? From mythology class?"

Sam gave me a look, her brow furrowing like it always did when I dragged her into something questionable—like sneaking an extra slice of pizza and getting busted by the cafeteria monitor. "Yeah. God of sleep. Why?"

Right. Straight to the point. No need for a refresher.

"He was at Charlie's," I continued, "And he wasn't just *there*—he put everyone to sleep."

Sam blinked, her expression somewhere between skeptical and deeply concerned. "Hypnos, like, the actual Hypnos?"

"Yeah." My voice wavered, but I pressed on. "I saw him, Sam. He was the reason you woke up on the ground not remembering how you got there."

She let out a short, nervous laugh. "You're serious."

"Dead serious."

Sam sat up straighter, crossing her arms. "Why would a Greek god show up at a diner in Midtown to knock us all out? Was there an ancient prophecy about pancakes I missed?"

"I don't know!" My hands flew up, exasperated. "But it wasn't just him."

She blinked, the humor in her tone fading. "What do you mean?"

"There was another guy. Purple eyes, creepy as hell. He threw me— like, across the street. I hit my head."

Her mouth opened, then closed, like she was trying to piece it together. "Wait. What?"

"And then I think I died," I added, my voice small. "Or almost. I don't know. Paul and Cynthia showed up and… fixed me."

Sam's eyes narrowed. "Fixed you? How?"

"No idea!" My throat suddenly felt very dry. "They did something. It felt… weird. Like, electricity, but not painful." I swallowed. "And then they left. But you saw them, right? Leaving the diner?"

She nodded slowly. "Yeah, I saw them."

"None of this makes sense, Sam, but it *happened*. You were there."

For too many seconds, she didn't say anything. The silence hung heavily between us, broken only by the faint hum of the AC unit. I could almost hear her thoughts churning, the disbelief battling with the trust we'd built over years of shared secrets and ridiculous schemes. Her fingers tapped against the edge of her blanket, the rhythm uneven, like she was stalling for time to find the right words. Every second felt like an eternity.

Sam exhaled, rubbing her temples. "Jess, I want to believe you, I really do. But this is a lot. Like, a *lot* a lot."

"I know." My voice cracked. "I don't know how to explain it better. I just… I need you to believe me. Even if it sounds crazy."

She studied me, then ran a hand through her hair and nodded. "Okay. I believe you. I don't get it, but I believe you."

I exhaled the breath I'd been holding, relief trickling in despite the nagging fear that I might be losing my mind. At least Sam was willing to go along with me, even if she secretly thought I'd cracked. "Thanks."

She gave me a tired smile, like she wasn't sure what she'd just signed up for but was too loyal to back out now. "So, now what? We just go to sleep and hope the gods don't kill us in our dreams?"

I blinked at her. "I mean, you could've eased me into that thought instead of dropkicking me with it, but yeah, sure, let's go with that."

She snorted, rolling over to face me. "Okay, but seriously. Are we supposed to, like, prepare? Do we stay awake? Should we have a plan?"

The idea of planning anything felt like trying to build a spaceship out of bubble gum. I shook my head. "I don't know what comes next, Sam. But donuts in the morning would be a good start."

Her lips quirked into a small smile. "Donuts? Really? That's your big plan?"

"Hey, if I'm about to get smited or whatever, I'd rather go out on a sugar high," I shot back, pulling the blanket over my head. "You can't fight divine chaos on an empty stomach. It's probably, like, a rule."

Sam laughed, the sound a little less tense this time. "Okay, donuts it is. But if I wake up with a god sitting on the bed, you're explaining it to my dad."

"Deal," I muttered from beneath the blanket, hoping she couldn't hear the edge of fear in my voice.

The room fell into a heavy silence as I readjusted the blanket, suddenly too warm and restless to stay cocooned. The moonlight spilled across the floor in silvery patches, painting her room in soft, uneven shadows. I stared at the ceiling, willing my mind to slow down.

Sam's breathing evened out after a while, a gentle rhythm that should've been comforting, but instead it only amplified the noise in my head. I closed my eyes, forcing myself to try, but sleep dangled just out of reach—a cruel tease that brought no relief, only glimpses of calm that dissolved the moment I reached for them.

A sudden, ear-splitting clatter broke the silence, like an avalanche of tin cans tumbling down a metal staircase. My heart hammered, each beat echoing in my chest as I fumbled for my inhaler. It was useless—completely out of puffs from earlier. Images of Hypnos and his piercing yellow eyes flickered through my mind. He was coming for me. I was sure of it.

The sky erupted in an orange blaze, dragging my attention to the window. A fireball streaked across the night, its heat radiating through the glass. I tore off my blankets and stumbled toward the window just in time to see another fiery arc rip across the heavens. It felt like the world was raining fire. The earth trembled with each explosion, turning the outside into a terrifying battleground of light and shadow. Struggling with the stubborn, paint-chipped window, I finally forced it open. The acrid stench of smoke stung my throat and burned my lungs.

Was this the apocalypse? Dread coiled in my stomach, tightening with every breath. I turned to warn Sam, only to find her bed empty. This had to be a nightmare. It had to be.

A chillingly familiar sensation crawled through me, tugging at the edges of my consciousness, vivid, overwhelming, like a memory clawing its way to the surface. The stadium, the weird ocean and fire experience… the same haunting intensity.

Drawn back to the window, I stared helplessly as my town burned. Screams sliced through the night air, each one a dagger to my already frazzled nerves. There was something I should be doing, something critical, but the answer skittered just out of reach, mocking me.

Turning to escape, I froze. A full-length mirror loomed in my path. When had that been there? My reflection was gone, replaced by a man with cold, violet eyes and the faint outline of feathered wings.

The room burst into flames, the fire encircling me in a sinister, living dance. It fed on my fear, growing stronger with every hysterical breath. The man in the mirror dissolved, leaving only my reflection staring back. But the smile on its face... it wasn't mine. It twisted with hunger, hatred, and malice.

Through the inferno, a voice slipped into my mind—dark, sultry, and unfamiliar. "Amara," it whispered.

I snapped awake, my breath caught in my throat like barbed wire. For a split second, I expected the nightmare to spill into reality. My heart slowed slightly as I caught sight of Sam, still peacefully asleep, blissfully unaware of my torment.

Shakily, I forced myself upright and stumbled to the window. Sliding it open, I let the cool night air wash over my sweat-drenched skin. Richland slept undisturbed below, its quiet streets a stark contradiction to the nightmare I'd just endured. But it felt so real. Too real. My jaw clenched as frustration bubbled up. Of all nights to forget to refill my inhaler.

A faint scratch at the door pulled me out of my thoughts. My gaze darted across the room, past Sam's sleeping form, to a small slip of paper lying just inside the door. Samantha was the youngest of five, her siblings long gone, leaving just her and her dad. And her dad wouldn't leave notes under the door.

Crossing the creaky floorboards, I picked up the paper. Elegant script looped across its surface, the faint scent of something familiar rising from it. The déjà vu struck hard, leaving a strange mix of recognition and confusion in its wake. Somehow, I knew this handwriting belonged to Paul, though I couldn't explain how.

Meet me on the roof and we'll talk.
Yours Truly, Paul.

Biting my lip, I weighed the risk against the torrent of unanswered questions swirling in my head. One last glance at Sam confirmed she was none the wiser to my late-night rendezvous plans.

Slipping the note into my pocket, I moved quietly toward the door. It clicked shut behind me with a finality that made my pulse quicken.

Answers were waiting on the rooftop. I just wasn't sure if I was ready for them.

☉☽ CHAPTER 4 ☾☉

I had no idea what I was doing. Climbing onto a rooftop in the middle of the night to meet a stranger wasn't exactly my brightest idea. But the promise of answers tugged at me, along with the undeniable thrill of a hot guy's attention… not that I'd ever admit it. Besides, if I'd survived sneaking up here last summer on a dare from Sam's brother, how bad could this really be?

My legs ached as I climbed the escape stairs, exhaustion slowing me down. The night had been one giant cosmic joke, and if these gods were real, I had the feeling I was the punchline. The thought of Hypnos sent a shudder through me. What else from mythology was out there, lurking in the shadows? And more importantly, what did that make me?

The heavy metal door groaned open, revealing the rooftop in all its unsettling stillness. Paul stood not far from the exit, leaning against a massive air conditioning unit like he had no better place to be. Above him, the stars scattered across the night sky, their light dim against the city's haze.

"I wasn't sure you'd come," he said, hands buried in his pockets.

I forced a smile, hoping it didn't betray the nerves buzzing under my skin. "Well, meeting strange guys on rooftops isn't exactly on my bucket list."

He smiled, slow and disarming, and I hated how it pulled at parts of me I wasn't ready to unpack. It was like he carried a quiet force that made the rest of the world blur in the background. But then I thought about Cynthia, all sharp edges and murder-eyes, and whatever spell his smile had started to weave vanished. No way was I going to be her next victim.

Paul moved toward the ledge, his eyes sweeping across the city below. "You see things, right? Visions." Straight to the point. No buildup, no preamble. I could almost respect it if it weren't so disturbing.

"If by 'visions,' you mean nightmares that make me question my grip on reality, then yeah." I crossed my arms, trying to keep my voice steady. "How do you know about that? And what does it have to do with me?"

His eyes stayed on the horizon, giving nothing away. "When did they start?"

I stared at him, exhaling loudly. "I came here for answers, not to play twenty questions. Who are you?"

He finally turned to look at me. "I'm trying to figure out where to start."

I had the patience of a caffeinated squirrel, so I stomped closer, staying a good two feet from the edge, my stomach twisting just looking at the drop. "You leave me a cryptic note, drag me up here in the middle of the night, and now you're stalling? Forget it." I spun toward the door, ready to leave him and his mystery behind.

"Jessa, wait."

The sound of my name on his lips stopped me in my tracks. It wasn't just how he said it—gentle, almost reverent—or that he knew it. It was what it did to me. Something low and tantalizing unfurled in my chest, making me hate how easy it was to respond to him.

I turned back slowly, folding my arms as if they could shield me from the way his gaze seemed to peel me apart. "How do you know my name?"

Paul took a step closer, his movements deliberate, unhurried. "I do have answers," he said. "It just takes a minute to explain everything."

"That's convenient," I quipped, refusing to step back. "Especially for someone who clearly doesn't have a clue what to say."

"You'll get your answers. I promise."

"Right. As soon as you figure them out yourself, I'm sure." I shook my head, breaking eye contact just long enough for frustration to creep in and take hold. Turning again, I made for the door.

I barely got a step in before he was suddenly there, blocking my path.

My breath hitched as I stumbled back. One second, he'd been a good ten feet away, and the next, he was in front of me like Barry Allen.

"How did you—" I trailed off, my mind scrambling to make sense of it.

Paul raised his hands, a gesture of peace. "I'm not here to hurt you."

"That's what they all say," I muttered, trying to steady the frantic rhythm of my pulse. My arms tightened around me, a flimsy barrier against the storm of questions swirling in my head. "What are you?"

For the first time, something flickered in his expression. Regret, maybe, or hesitation. Whatever it was, it vanished before I could pin it down. "I'll tell you everything. But you have to trust me."

"Trust you?" I scoffed, the laugh brittle in my throat. "You just sprinted across the roof like The Flash, and you want me to trust you?"

His silence wasn't reassuring. He just stood there, eyes steady on mine, like he could outlast my skepticism. And damn it, there was something about the way he looked at me—focused, unflinching, like I was the center of some secret universe—that made me falter. Against all logic, part of me wanted to believe him.

But that part wasn't in charge. Not tonight.

"Did I really die?" The words slipped out before I could stop them, filled with doubts about all the craziness tonight had thrown at me. For now, figuring him out could wait.

He sighed. "Almost."

Not the answer I wanted. "Why are people... gods... trying to kill me? Are they really gods?"

"I was getting to that."

"Well, I don't have all night."

"People going to start looking for you?"

"Maybe." A lie, obviously. Sam and her dad were probably out cold, and part of me envied them for it. Sleep sounded a lot better than unraveling whatever *this* was.

I stared at him, willing him to say something that made sense. Anything. But his maddening calmness only fanned the flames of my frustration. The longer I stood here, the more ridiculous it felt—like I was waiting for a train that wasn't coming.

What was I doing? Chasing answers from some guy who might not even have them? The night's craziness reeled in my head: Hypnos and his piercing yellow eyes, the pale-faced killer who'd hurled me across the street, and Paul, who somehow knew too much but said too little. It was a twisted riddle with no solutions, and I was no closer to understanding any of it.

And then there was Sam. I couldn't risk dragging her into something so far out of our depth. I couldn't risk myself either, not for a bunch of half-baked explanations.

"You know what? Forget it." I threw up my hands, exasperated. "I'm done. If anyone catches me up here, I'm in a shit ton of trouble."

I turned toward the door, determined to leave him and his cryptic nonsense behind. But as I stepped around him, his expression shifted—tightening in a way that made me falter. A stark reminder that, despite his good looks, I didn't know him. Not really. My steps quickened, anxiety creeping in where irritation had been just moments before.

His hand landed on my shoulder—not rough, but firm enough to stop me. I spun, instinct taking over, and raised my arms defensively. Of course, my movements were as graceful as a baby deer on ice, and Paul easily caught my wrist.

"Let go!" I blurted, yanking back on instinct.

Just as quickly as he'd grabbed me, Paul let go, and guilt flashed across his face—faint, but unmistakable. When his hand pulled away, a jolt of electricity where he touched me set every nerve on edge. The sensation tasted like sweet champagne and smelled like honey, leaving a buzz in my head like the aftermath of one of Dawn's wild parties… a cocktail of freedom, love, power, and courage... almost intoxicating. But beneath it all was that nagging itch in my brain, like I was the only one left out of a secret everyone else was in on.

I took a deep breath, trying to steady myself as I looked at Paul. There was something in the way his face was set, in the way he watched me, that tugged at the edges of my memory. Then, it clicked. A photo from *Statues of the Gods: The Art of the Acropolis*, a book I'd read last spring, floated to the surface. I'd studied the image of Apollo, the golden boy of the gods, with his strong jawline and regal build, more times than I could count. The resemblance was undeniable, too precise to ignore.

No, it wasn't just a resemblance. It was him. I couldn't explain how I knew. I just *knew*.

The raw energy coursing through me began to fade, and I finally found my voice and stopped circling him. "Paul." My lips tightened, resisting the words that begged to escape, but the need to know overpowered my hesitation. "Paul, as in, Apollo?"

What if I was wrong? The urge to take back my words hit hard, imagining him laughing in my face, dismissing me as delusional.

But he didn't laugh. A flicker of sadness passed through his eyes. "You were a part of this once."

A nervous laugh escaped before I could stop it. "Part of what?" I backed away. Maybe he was the one who was crazy. But he didn't answer, just watched me, waiting for something to click in my mind. My gaze dropped to my bare feet, as if the answers might be hidden between my toes, then slowly traveled up the lines of his beige pants to his face.

"Part of *your* history?" I locked eyes with him, and a wave of disbelief washed over me, like the ground beneath me was shifting. This was madness. Greek gods were myths, stories—nothing more.

But then the night's terrors replayed in my mind: that piercing yellow stare, the scorching pain, and those impossibly fast figures who were anything but human. As crazy as it all sounded, I couldn't shake the creeping suspicion that maybe, just maybe, Paul was speaking some twisted version of the truth.

"What does any of this have to do with what happened today?" I demanded, backing up. He mirrored each retreat, closing the distance until I realized the door was now behind him. I shot a glance over my shoulder— the ledge of the roof was much closer than I'd thought.

"When did you start having visions?"

"No." The word cut through the air, fueled by the anger that had been simmering inside me. I planted my feet. "You haven't answered a single question I've asked. Why should I answer any more of yours?"

"Come on, Jessa. Think about what you know of me."

"Stop with the questions," I growled. "I'm done playing this game."

"It was a suggestion," he said, a faint smile playing at the corners of his lips, though there was an edge to it that made my skin crawl. The seriousness in his eyes clashed with his almost amused tone.

The nerve. I wanted to wipe that smug smile off his face, even if it did make him more attractive. But I couldn't ignore the persistent thought in the back of my mind: Apollo. Not that I ever expected to meet a Greek god in person, but he'd always been one of my favorites. Apollo, son of Zeus, god of light and sun, medicine and healing, music, and anything artistic. Great in archery and, being a god of truth, couldn't lie.

"If you're really him, prove it. Show me something unmistakable, something only a Greek god could do."

He stayed silent, his gaze unwavering, and it only made my frustration burn hotter. My patience was on life support. "Whatever," I muttered, brushing past him with more force than necessary. I was done with this exhausting back-and-forth. But as I moved to leave, a thought wormed its way into my mind, stubborn and unshakable.

"Wait." I paused and looked back at him, catching a fleeting expression on his face before it vanished. Putting my hands on my hips, I tried to steady myself. "You can't lie, can you?"

He nodded, confidence radiating off him. I envied that certainty. I'd give anything to feel that in control.

I stepped closer. "Then why aren't you answering my questions?"

"Because," he said. "I can't lie."

My brain scrambled to catch up. My mouth opened, but the "huh?" I wanted to verbalize stayed mute. The god of truth. The wind whistled between us, and I worked hard at keeping my voice level, but it dropped to a whisper. "So, what, you're trying to protect me from the truth?"

"Having an overwhelming amount of information dumped on you can be a hard pill to swallow." He stepped closer, too close. The wind played with his hair some more, whirling his scent around me, a sweet, earthy smell that reminded me of a sunny day at the park.

"I can handle it," I said, though it felt more like a challenge to myself than a statement of fact.

"I don't know." His response was simple, but each word landed like a punch, hollowing out the confidence I'd been clinging to. He sighed, looking at me, searching for something I wasn't sure I could give. "I promise I'll tell you everything, but right now, as cliché as this sounds, the fate of the world depends on those visions. I need to know what you've seen." He paused, a flicker of something close to a wince crossing his face. "You're sort of like an oracle."

"Say what?"

A hint of a smile tugged at the corner of his mouth. "An oracle. You know, people who see—"

"I know what an oracle is," I snapped. "Why am I one?"

"You're a Potential... the new Demi Guardian," he answered, his tone matter of fact. "It's sort of your thing to see the desires of the Underworld. Any plans they make, thoughts they think that have anything to do with mortals, and you get a heads up."

Demi Guardian? Underworld? Mortals? The words piled up in my brain, each one heavier than the last, like my thoughts were buffering on an overworked Wi-Fi connection—system overload.

Maybe he was right. Maybe I wasn't cut out for this. Any second now, I'll wake up. I pinched my thigh hard, but nothing happened. "Fine. Whatever, but if I tell you about these visions, I better get the truth."

"I promise."

A promise from the god of truth had to mean something, right? "Water. Lots of water, like I was drowning."

He shook his head, waving a dismissive hand, not meeting my eyes. "That's not a vision of the future."

"Okaaay." I closed my eyes, forcing myself to confront the latest "vision" that had overwhelmed me. The memory of the screams, the death, and that haunting figure in the mirror made my skin crawl. A cold sweat broke out on my neck. I exhaled slowly and looked up at Paul. "Richland. Up in flames. Now it's your turn."

Before he could respond, the roof door groaned open, the sound slicing through the night. Blondie stood framed in the doorway, his eyes cutting between Paul and me.

Trap.

My heart leapt to my throat, and instinctively, I stepped back. The heel of my foot hit the ledge, and momentum, gravity, and sheer bad luck did the rest.

The world tipped violently, and the sensation of falling consumed me. There wasn't even time to scream, just the sharp realization that I was going down.

Paul's hand shot out, locking around my wrist and pulling me forward with a force that jolted through my entire body. I slammed into his chest, the impact knocking the air out of my lungs. My fingers dug into his shirt, clinging to him as if letting go meant certain death. The world steadied, but my mind was still spinning, trying to make sense of how I'd just survived my worst fear.

"You okay?" he asked, his voice strained as he held me close, his hands firm on my back. I nodded weakly, though I wasn't sure if I was answering his question or just trying to convince myself that I was still alive.

His eyes searched mine, concern softening his features in a way that almost made me forget the terror still coursing through me. I forced myself to pull away, my breath coming in shaky gasps. "No. No, I'm not okay."

Hoping that maybe I'd imagined Blondie, I glanced over Paul's shoulder, but there he was, still standing in front of the closed door, his expression one of mild amusement, as if we were merely an interesting sideshow.

"Do you know him? Are you friends? Did you have him following me around?" My voice trembled, tinged with hysteria. Blondie began to advance, and I pointed firmly at him. "Stay!" I ordered, the word more a desperate plea than a command. "Paul, answer me."

His hands found my shoulders again, and with a gentle touch, he calmed my breathing, steadying the frantic rhythm in my chest. "Calm down. He's not an enemy."

I wanted to scream at him, to demand he stop messing with my body like he had any right to control my breath. How could he be so calm when I felt like I was unraveling? And why did his touch make everything inside me settle when I knew I should be losing it?

"Somehow, I don't believe you," I spat, the words thick with distrust as my instincts growling at me, tearing down every rational thought.

"She still has a strong connection to the past," Blondie said, daring to take a few more steps toward us before stopping again. I was startled to see the thunderstorm gray of his irises from this distance. Hadn't I needed glasses at my last eye exam?

I swallowed the fire scalding the back of my throat and pressed closer to Paul. I didn't want to trust Paul, but something about him—beyond the fact that he'd saved me—felt strangely familiar, like a half-remembered song or a dream I couldn't shake. "What past? What are you talking about?"

Blondie, being a total jerk, ignored my question and addressed Paul instead. "You were taking too long."

My small measure of trust was reaffirmed when Paul kept his hands on my shoulders protectively. "Appreciate your concern, but you should've waited."

No one felt obliged to fill me in on anything. I pulled away from Paul. "Who the hell is this?" I turned to my stalker. "And why have you been following me?"

The cherub-faced man bowed slightly. "You can call me Henry."

Right, just like I could call Apollo "Paul".

"Somehow, I have a feeling there's more to that name."

"She's a smart one," Henry teased, his accent a mix of American and something else. "Did she tell you?"

Again, bypassing me. I'd had enough of being ignored to last a lifetime. No, scratch that, to last an immortal lifetime now that I thought about it.

"Falling fire," Paul said.

I didn't like the frown creasing Henry's mouth. "Hephaestus?"

Paul shrugged. "Not sure."

I glanced between them, still not fully grasping the situation. "The god of fire?"

Paul ran a hand through his hair, piecing together some internal puzzle. Watching him think was like curling up in my mom's bed while she brushed my hair… a comforting, cherished memory. "Are you sure it was fire you saw?"

I shrugged this time. "I wasn't aware I should've been keeping a journal."

The most brilliant silver light I'd ever seen carved across the sky in a wide arc. Paul spun around and ran to the roof's edge, kicking up gravel behind him. The sudden shift in the atmosphere gripped me in place. "What is it?"

"Cynthia," Paul said, his voice tight. In a swirl of motion, his body evaporated into golden mist before disappearing altogether.

I blinked, trying to process what I'd just witnessed. Paul's vanishing act was a slap in the face, confirming that he really was a god. I briefly thought of Cynthia, his girlfriend. Seriously, Jessa? You're worried about a guy's relationship status when there are actual gods running around trying to kill you? Priorities.

A moment ago, he'd been solid, real, and now all that remained was his faint scent. Hugging my elbows, I watched the city below from a safe distance. Maybe if I ignored Henry, he'd disappear like Paul.

The wind whipped my hair into my face, and I pushed it back behind my ears, scanning the horizon for any sign of Paul or Cynthia. Who was I kidding, thinking I could spot them from here? But the nagging dread clung to me like a stubborn shadow. Something was wrong, and I couldn't shake the feeling that I was tied to it all. It was crazy to think Greek gods existed, but my mind was beginning to entertain the possibility.

I needed answers, and Paul hadn't given me much. Despite his stalker tendencies, maybe Henry would be more forthcoming.

"Where'd he go?" I asked, trying to sound casual, keeping my eyes on the city.

Silence. Relief washed over me. Maybe he'd vanished with Paul. But a glance over my shoulder proved otherwise. Henry stood by the door, hands in his pockets, as if he hadn't been watching me all day... and yesterday. "To help Cynthia."

"Thanks for that invaluable information," I muttered. "Why does she need help? Isn't she a god like him? Like you?" I appreciated that Henry kept his distance. After today, I was torn between wanting answers and wanting complete solitude.

"Yes."

I squared my shoulders. "Could you be any more cryptic? Seriously, you're as bad as Paul."

Henry grinned, his tone playful. "I wouldn't go that far, and we prefer 'guardians.'"

"Guardians? Like guardian angels or something?" I studied his profile, trying to match him with one of the statues in the book, as if I'd remember what they all looked like.

"Something like that."

"So, are they in trouble?" I asked, looking out over the edge again, wondering if Hypnos was lurking out there, or some other myth I'd written off as fiction.

"I wouldn't worry about them." His eyes narrowed, studying me.

I shifted uncomfortably. "It's Hypnos, isn't it?" His silence was expected. I scratched my ankle with my toes, irritated by the gritty dust on my feet. "Why'd he try to kill me?"

"You catch on quickly," he said, sounding almost impressed. "We're doing our best to protect you, but you're not safe. You should go back."

"So, what, you think I'm just gonna let some creepy stalker guy dictate my curfew now?"

"Believe me, it's not about curfew. It's about staying alive. But hey, do what you want. Just don't say I didn't warn you."

Who did he think he was, swooping in with vague warnings and expecting me to just roll over? There was something in his tone, something that bothered me more than I wanted to admit. The seriousness in his voice struck a chord, and it was hard to shake off. Still, I wasn't about to back down.

I took a step closer to him, my voice steady. "Why don't my friends—and everyone at the diner for that matter—remember anything?"

"It's just the way things work."

"Really? That's your answer? My best friend could come up with something better."

His expression darkened, and I couldn't help but worry about what a pissed-off god... guardian... whatever, might do. "You told her?" he snapped, closing the space between us.

I froze. Lie! "What are you talking about? Told who?" I couldn't let him suspect Sam knew anything.

"You can't bring mortals into this," he said sharply, a hint of spit hitting my face.

Clenching my fists, I met his gaze. "What mortals? I haven't told anyone anything."

His smirk was more cruel than friendly. "You've always been a horrible liar."

"What?"

The ground trembled beneath us, a low hum vibrating through the air. Out of the corner of my eye, the street shifted, the pavement seeming to take a shallow breath. Maybe it was my nerves, but after tonight, I wasn't ruling out anything. For a second, everything stilled—rooftop silent, the city below deceptively calm. I inhaled, trying to collect my thoughts, but they scattered like leaves in the wind.

Henry followed my gaze out to the streets, his eyes narrowing as if he saw something beyond the city lights. "I should go. You should get back to bed," he said, his tone betraying that he knew more about what was happening out there than he was letting on.

"No. I'm finally getting some answers. You owe me that much after stalking me all day."

He shook his head. "Stop talking to your friends, or something might happen to them. And not a good something."

"Was that a threat?" I asked, already deciding that if he so much as touched my friends, I'd find a way to make him regret it, god or not.

"No. Just a fact. Stay quiet. We'll find you when the time is right." He turned to leave but paused. "And stay away from Paul." With a puff of air and a swirl of white light, he vanished.

"Hey!" I shouted, dropping my arms in frustration. Alone on the rooftop, I hurried back to Sam's condo, chasing after the illusion of safety. I needed sleep—or maybe a complete mental reset. And above all, I had to make sure Samantha kept this whole mythical-gods-turned-real madness under wraps. I wasn't about to start babysitting the entire world, but somehow, it felt like the world had just dumped its problems in my lap.

☉☽ CHAPTER 5 ☾☉

The events at Charlie's had to have been a dream. After a full day of slipping back into the monotony of home life with nothing remotely insane happening I was starting to convince myself that someone had spiked my drink that night. Maybe it was a hallucinogen.

Still, there was this annoying little part of me, tucked in the back of my brain, that hoped it hadn't all been a fabrication. It was stupid. What was I even thinking? I could barely handle high school drama, let alone life-threatening chaos and cosmic conspiracies. But the nagging thought wouldn't leave me alone.

So, instead of trying to shove it away, I did what any irrational, sleep-deprived person would do—I threw myself into research. Hours vanished into the black hole of the internet. My desk became a makeshift pillow as I scrolled through forums, online libraries, and conspiracy blogs. But for all my efforts, the results were... pitiful. No hidden insights on Greek mythology, no obscure references to Demi Guardians, no whispered prophecies about Hypnos or why I'd suddenly be on his radar. And Paul? Nothing beyond what anyone already knew about Apollo, the golden boy of the gods.

When dawn crept through my window, I shut my laptop with a groan, no closer to unraveling anything. My bloodshot eyes felt like sandpaper, and my head swirled with more questions than answers.

The morning blurred past as I got ready for the Memorial Day parade, every step mechanical, like my body was on autopilot. Somewhere between fixing my hair and grabbing my gear, I made a video call to Sam, hoping she could help make sense of my research—or at least confirm I wasn't losing it. But she just stared at me, wide-eyed, like I'd recited the quadratic formula backward.

She didn't remember passing out at Charlie's. Didn't remember a single thing about Greek gods. And when I brought up Blondie, the maybe-stalker, her blank stare said it all: I was completely on my own.

After the parade, I resolved to shove the whole mess into the dustiest corner of my brain and focus on normal life. Sweaty, drained, and ready to collapse, I climbed onto the bus, hoping for a moment of peace.

Of course, public transportation had other plans. The seats seemed designed by someone with a vendetta against humanity and the air reeked of gym socks marinated in misery.

I glanced at the driver, a middle-aged man with a face locked in eternal disappointment. He leaned against the steering wheel, staring blankly ahead. I shuffled past him, dodging the stray backpacks and elbows that came with the territory. The chatter of tired students filled the bus, broken occasionally by bursts of laughter that made the Texas heat feel even more unbearable.

A familiar laugh yanked my attention to the back of the bus. There he was—Zach, my ex-boyfriend, legs stretched out as if the bus was his personal lounge. And on his arm? Ashlyn Morrison: student council president, cheer captain, homecoming queen in training, and the principal's golden child. She was everything I'd never wanted to be—until now.

"Dude, Whitley, move your ass!" Brian's voice barked from behind, jolting me out of my thoughts.

Samantha, a few rows ahead, glanced over her shoulder, her eyes wide with pity. Her expression said it all: *How are you going to handle this?*

Dawn, sitting beside her, darted a look between me and Zach, while Brian jabbed me in the back like I was personally responsible for blocking his path to salvation.

"Keep your panties on, Brian," I snapped, sliding into the seat behind Sam just to shut him up.

Brian hustled past, muttering something about trumpet cases and bad attitudes. I didn't care. My attention was pinned to the back of the bus, where Ashlyn twirled a strand of her perfect hair while leaning into Zach. My heart felt like it had been tossed into a blender set to puree, each beat shredding whatever scraps of dignity I had left.

Zach and Ashlyn. Ashlyn and Zach.

The thought looped in my head, relentless, like a bad song you couldn't shake. No matter how much I wanted to convince myself I was over him—truly, completely over him—hearing his laugh while Ashlyn practically purred in his ear was proof, I was anything but over Zach London.

I turned away, desperate for distraction. Anything but them. Leaning back against the seat, I closed my eyes, but it didn't help. The bus was a torture chamber on wheels. My knees jammed against the seat in front of me, and every bump in the road sent shockwaves up my spine. It was like the bus had joined forces with the universe to see just how miserable it could make me.

Okay, new plan: think about Hypnos. The god of sleep had tried to kill me, which, on the list of things to freak out about, seemed like it should outrank Zach and Ashlyn's public display of affection. Except… every time I tried to focus on Hypnos, all I could think about was the fact that he *wanted me dead*. How was that better? It wasn't.

My thoughts twisted and tangled, flitting between Paul and his cryptic energy, Henry's warnings, and Hypnos's terrifying presence. None of it made sense, and the harder I tried to piece it together, the more it felt like grasping at smoke. I shifted in my seat again, trying to find a position that didn't make me feel like I was sitting on a pile of jagged rocks.

Another burst of laughter from the back of the bus drew my attention. Ashlyn leaned closer to Zach, whispering something that made him grin. My stomach clenched, the air in my chest growing tighter with every second. It was stupid to care. I *knew* it was stupid. But knowing didn't make it hurt less.

"Jess?" Samantha's voice pulled me out of my spiraling thoughts. She leaned over the seat in front of me, her brow furrowed with concern. "You okay?"

I forced a smile. "Yeah, just tired."

Sam didn't look convinced. Her eyes were full of curiosity, like she was trying to peel back the layers of whatever I wasn't saying. But she knew me too well to press. With a slight shake of her head, she turned back to her conversation with Dawn, letting me stew in my own silence.

I sighed, pressing my forehead against the cold bus window.

No matter how hard I tried to ignore it, the truth gnawed at me: I was stuck. Stuck on this bus. Stuck in my stupid feelings for Zach. Stuck in a life where gods wanted me dead and my ex looked way too happy with someone else.

Fan-freaking-tastic.

The bus rumbled on, the steady motion doing little to settle my thoughts. I tried focusing on piecing together everything that had happened at Charlie's—the gods, the visions, the strange pull toward Paul—but the threads refused to untangle. It was all connected somehow; I just had to figure out how.

Then again, maybe I'd imagined it all. Yesterday had been unsettlingly normal, the kind of day that made you doubt your own sanity. Every time I'd tried dropping hints to Sam, she'd just give me that puzzled look, like I'd suddenly started speaking fluent Elvish.

I slunk deeper into my seat. The situation with Zach was my fault. I knew that, but it didn't make it hurt any less. We'd been high school sweethearts, the kind of couple people assumed would end up on one of those "childhood friends to forever" montages. Growing up as neighbors since I was nine gave us a shared history that felt unshakable. Zach wasn't into Greek mythology like I was, but he'd cared because I cared, which at the time had felt like enough.

But then Ashlyn Morrison, Miss Perfect Everything, had taken an interest in him. I didn't have to imagine what Zach saw in her; she was the picture-perfect alternative to all my flaws. Insecurity sank its claws in, and the tighter I tried to hold onto him, the more I convinced myself he was slipping away. Instead of trusting him, I'd imploded. I'd ended things before he could, as if beating him to the punch would somehow soften the blow. It didn't. And Zach hadn't wasted time moving on. Less than two weeks later, there he was—Ashlyn on his arm, proving my worst fears right.

Ashlyn caught my eye, flashing a smile as fake as her acrylic nails, her fingers wiggling in a little wave. I wanted to pull her fingers off and throw them out the window.

I turned away quickly, my pulse hammering in my ears. Dawn's chin appeared on the seatback in front of me, her expression somewhere between sympathetic and smug.

"I don't know what he sees in her," she whispered, shooting me one of those "this must suck" smiles. Dawn could be supportive when it suited her, but loyalty wasn't her biggest strength.

I shrugged, perfecting my not-caring act. "Who knows?"

As the bus pulled into the parking lot, my breath caught. Standing near the school entrance was a familiar figure with short blond curls. Henry. Hope flickered, I'm not crazy. But when I blinked, he was gone.

Vanished.

Figment of my imagination? Maybe. Or maybe disappearing into thin air was just another perk of the god squad package, assuming they were even real.

The bus groaned to a stop, and I followed suit, slumping in my seat. Whether Henry was real or just my imagination playing tricks, I wasn't ready to deal with it. Not now. I had more immediate concerns—like getting off this bus and pretending my life wasn't a disaster.

I stood, slinging my bag over my shoulder and pointedly not looking toward the back of the bus. I didn't need another mental image of Zach and Ashlyn cocooned in their little love bubble.

Stepping onto the pavement, I let out a shaky breath I hadn't realized I'd been holding. Solid ground. Stable. Comforting. Unlike literally everything else in my life. But stability lasted all of two seconds before the strap of my bag slid off my shoulder. Gravity did the rest, sending my water bottle and a mess of color guard silks tumbling to the concrete.

"Great," I muttered, crouching to gather the spill. Before I could grab anything, a hand swooped in, lifting the bag with annoying ease.

"Here."

I looked up, and there was Zach, holding my bag like it hadn't just betrayed me. His voice hit me with a strange mix of familiarity and hesitation, soft in a way I hadn't heard in months.

"Thanks." I took the bag and slung it back over my shoulder. Our fingers brushed for half a second, but it was enough to send a spark of nostalgia through me, deep and unwelcome in my chest.

We stood there, caught in this awkward moment where the noise of the parking lot faded into the background. His eyes met mine, and for a second, I almost forgot how much I hated seeing him with Ashlyn. Almost.

There was something in his expression—a flicker of regret, maybe? Or was I just imagining it?

The spell broke when I caught sight of Ashlyn near the bus, glaring at me like I'd just committed a cardinal sin by existing within five feet of her boyfriend. Her fingers drummed on her crossed arms, each tap a little warning shot.

"Zach, are you coming?" Her voice sliced through the moment, prissy and territorial.

Zach glanced over his shoulder, then back at me. "Yeah, just a sec." His smile was small, almost apologetic, but it didn't land. Too little, too late.

He jogged back to Ashlyn, who wasted no time looping her arm through his. Her glare never wavered, burning with silent ownership. I straightened, adjusting the strap of my bag like it could somehow steady the mess of emotions threatening to crack through the walls I'd built around them.

As they walked away, a hollow ache settled in my chest—a familiar sting of something slipping further out of reach. Something fractured, maybe even broken beyond repair. I shoved it down, refusing to let it get the better of me.

Shaking off the encounter, I headed for my car, my feet dragging like they hadn't gotten the memo to move on. Across the lot, Sam and Dawn sped off in Dawn's flashy red convertible—a gaudy, rolling testament to her parents' wealth. Their laughter trailed behind them, carefree and weightless, like they weren't tethered to the same storms I was.

Fumbling for my keys, I focused on the simple act of unlocking the car—anything to keep my thoughts from spiraling. The boy who'd just picked up my bag used to pick me up too—when I fell, when I doubted, when I needed him most. The memory hit harder than I wanted to admit, but I blinked it away, sliding into the driver's seat and snapping on my sunglasses, a flimsy shield against the glaring sun.

The engine sputtered, coughed, then roared reluctantly to life. A glance in the rearview mirror showed the parking lot emptying out, its silence weirdly fitting. The sun's warmth pressed against my skin through the windshield, sinking deeper than it should have. It felt steady, reassuring—like it was trying to tell me something. Suddenly, my mood lifted, a spark of optimism kindling in my heart.

The summer stretched ahead, and for the first time in a while, I decided to leave my personal baggage in the school parking lot and let myself hope for something good.

☉︎☽ CHAPTER 6 ☾☉︎

Normal. That was my mantra after everything the past couple of days had hurled my way. I stared at my reflection in the pink-framed full-length mirror, clipping my hair back into place. Totally normal. Completely forgettable. Nothing like the girl who might've tangled with gods two nights ago.

I sighed and gave the mirror one last look-over, silently daring it to show me someone less average. Still me. Still Jessa Whitley, just a collection of bad luck wrapped in questionable life choices.

"Jess! Mike's here," mom hollered from downstairs.

"Be right down!" I called back, smacking on some peach lip gloss and rubbing at the smudged mascara under my eyes. Normalcy. That was the goal. And band practice was my best shot at it.

In the kitchen, my mom perched on a bar stool, head bent over her phone, thumb moving at lightning speed. Probably texting the latest guy auditioning for the role of Boyfriend Number Three to become my new stepdad. Call me bitter, but with her track record, I wasn't holding my breath. Her golden curls were pulled back in a loose ponytail, as perfect as ever. I used to love her hair—until Ashlyn came along, proving there was room for exactly one blonde goddess in Richland Heights.

"Be in the garage, Mom." Singing wasn't exactly at the top of my priorities list, but it beat doom-scrolling through my thoughts.

She waved absently, barely glancing up.

Mike was already leaning in the doorway, the sunlight outlining his tall frame. His carefully groomed afro was on point, as always, and he greeted me with an easy grin.

"So, how was the parade?" he asked, falling into step as we headed to the garage.

"Good," I said, keeping it vague. Not technically a lie, but not the whole truth either. I couldn't help wondering how much Dawn had already told him. She and Mike had become inseparable since spring break, thanks to one of her infamous house parties.

"Yeah?" Mike slung his guitar strap off his shoulder and leaned it against the wall before making a beeline for the cooler. He grabbed a soda, the hiss of carbonation filling the silence as I checked the amp and mic setup.

"Yeah?" he pressed, his tone light but curious. "Because Dawn said—"

I groaned, cutting him off. "Let me guess. She gave you the full-color, overly dramatic recap?"

Mike winced. "Pretty much. Ashlyn sucks, by the way."

"Tell me something I don't know," I muttered, twisting the mic cord through my fingers. By the time school started, Zach and Ashlyn's nauseating PDA would be common knowledge. Maybe I'd write a song about it.

Mike chuckled and crushed his empty can like it owed him money. "Where's Lizzie?"

As if on cue, Lizzie's trademark squeal rang out, followed by the sound of her dad's car peeling off down the street. Before I could brace myself, she barreled into the garage, tackling me in a rib-crushing hug.

"Air, Lizzie. Air." I squirmed, laughing despite myself.

"Jessa! Okay, spill! How was the parade? Did you nail the routine? Any hot girls in uniform?"

I laughed, squirming in her grip. "Air, Lizzie. I need air."

"Oops! Sorry." She stepped back, practically bouncing on her toes, her green eyes sparkling with excitement. Her black pixie cut was spiked into perfect chaos, just like her personality. She was the human equivalent of a Red Bull chased with liquid adrenaline.

"Ready?" I asked, hoping to dodge the parade questions.

Lizzie whipped out her drumsticks with a flourish, spinning them like they were lightsabers. "Let's do this!" She darted to her battered drum set, hammering out a beat that was pure caffeinated chaos.

Mike adjusted his guitar strap and strummed a few chords to test the amp. I flinched at the screech of feedback, the sound slicing through the garage like an angry banshee. Shaking my head, I adjusted the mic. Our gear was trash, being broke high schoolers and all, but it held up for most rehearsals.

I tightened my grip on the mic, letting the anticipation of singing with my friends settle the ache left behind by Zach and Ashlyn's public betrayal. Even the simmering fear of gods with grudges felt distant in the moment.

"I missed you guys."

Mike winked and launched into the opening chords of *Purple Lies*. Lizzie grinned, blowing me a kiss before matching his rhythm with her sticks.

Then came the hum.

It started soft, blending with the amp's buzz, but it grew louder. My fingers tightened around the cord as I glanced at Mike, who was already looking at the amp.

His legs buckled and he hit the floor hard.

"Mike!"

Every sound vanished, leaving nothing but a throb pressing against my ears. I spun toward Lizzie, only to find her slumped forward, her face pressed against a drum, sticks dangling from her limp fingers. The hum was gone, replaced by that harsh, familiar white noise.

It was happening again.

For a split second, a twisted sense of relief washed over me—I wasn't crazy after all. But that relief quickly morphed into terror, every hair on my body standing on end.

Slowly, I turned, my breaths now rapid, shallow bursts. Hypnos stood in the threshold, his hungry yellow eyes pinning me in place. His grin stretched wider than it had any right to, sharp teeth gleaming. Every step a tap to a slow countdown I couldn't stop.

Move, Jessa. Move.

But I couldn't. My limbs were cemented in place, my hands curling to hide the tremors. Hypnos dipped his head as if readying to charge when a streak of gold slammed into him. The entire garage rattled from the impact,

Paul's hit careening Hypnos across the lawn.

"Don't move!" Paul barked.

Noted. I wasn't going anywhere. He disappeared into the lawn, followed by the sounds of guy fighting noises.

My brain couldn't keep up. Lizzie and Mike were still unconscious, the hum fading from the garage but glaring in my head like it had claimed real estate. I stood there, useless, panic needling at the edges of my brain, but anger—hot and irrational—burned it back. What was I supposed to do? Take on Hypnos? Yeah, right. But sitting here doing nothing? That wasn't an option either. I had to see. To know Paul had the upper hand.

I forced myself onto the driveway, my breath catching as an ominous ribbon of black smog twisted across the pavement. It writhed its way toward the two gods tearing into each other in a blur of impossible speed. For a fleeting moment, it hovered over them, almost like it was deciding… then it shifted. Toward me.

I stepped back as it glided closer, dark tendrils snaking over the driveway, condensing and twisting like a living thing. The air grew so frigid my breath escaped in wispy puffs, the chill settling deep into my bones. Certainty flooded me. A cruel, undeniable truth. This was what it felt like to be about to die.

The smog thickened, folding into itself until it solidified. The color drained from me as recognition struck. I couldn't forget my pale-faced killer from Midtown.

The god of Death.

To call him beautiful felt like an insult—like calling the sun "warm" or the ocean "big." His nearly translucent skin shimmered, catching the faint light like abalone seashells, shifting with an ethereal iridescence. Lavender eyes, framed by unfairly long lashes, locked onto mine with a force that scattered every coherent thought. His white hair cascaded past his waist, catching on the sharp angles of his jaw as he tilted his head, reminiscent of the heroic figures from one of those Chinese costume dramas—perfectly composed, yet radiating an untouchable, otherworldly allure.

A smile ghosted his lips, faint and knowing. It could've stolen my breath. If I had any left to steal.

Screw this.

I spun on my heel, bolting back into the garage, my only thought:

Run.

The door swung wildly under my grip, and—wait, did I just pull it clean off its hinges?

No time to think about that. I sprinted through the hallway, adrenaline and sheer terror propelling me forward. My mom was slumped at the kitchen bar, fast asleep, oblivious to the literal god of death on our doorstep. My lungs burned as I wheezed for air, but I couldn't stop. *The junk drawer.*

Skidding to a halt, I yanked it open, the whole thing flying out of its track and crashing to the floor in a chaotic rain of coupons, pens, and random crap.

I'm not going to die. I'm not going to die.

Dropping to my knees, I shoved aside a mess of batteries and rubber bands until my fingers closed around my literal nectar of life. The inhaler.

"It's pointless to try and run." His voice lanced through the room and I froze.

Death stood by the stove, his form pulling itself together from tendrils of inky black smoke, deliberate and theatrical. Unlike Paul's blink-and-he's-there routine, this was methodical—like he wanted me to see every unnerving detail of him solidifying. And judging by the cold malice in his lavender eyes, chatting wasn't on the menu.

A scream ripped out of me as I scrambled to my feet, the inhaler slipping from my grasp and clattering to the floor. My brain screamed to grab it, to breathe, to move, but my body had other plans—frozen, useless, a cruel betrayal at the worst possible moment. Of course. My asthma chose now to remind me I was flawed, wheezing and gasping as I faced the god who could probably snuff me out with a thought.

My knees hit the floor, my hand flailing across the tiles, desperate to find the inhaler without looking away from him. His laugh, low and guttural, slithered through the room. He reached out, his fingers curling absently through my mom's hair

"Don't touch her," I wheezed. My fingers finally brushed against the smooth plastic of the inhaler. I snatched it, sprang to my feet, and took a desperate puff. The air dragged into my lungs—a small, pathetic victory. Not enough, but better than nothing. "What do you want?" I forced out, trying to sound stronger than the useless mess I felt like inside.

Death paused, his fingers still twisting strands of my mom's hair. He tilted his head, sunlight glinting off his impossibly bright, unnervingly perfect hair. "Isn't it obvious?"

"But why?" The words wavered, but I swallowed the lump in my throat. Tears burned at the edges of my vision, but I refused to let them fall. I wouldn't give him the satisfaction.

My throat burned as I forced down the fear threatening to spill over. He stepped closer, every movement deliberate, calculated. I stumbled back, my eyes darting around the room for anything that might save me. A weapon, a distraction, divine intervention.

His fingers never stopped twisting strands of my mom's hair, the casual indifference in his touch igniting a spark of rage deep in my chest.

"Leave her alone!" My voice cracked, but the fury behind it was unmistakable.

Death's lips curved faintly, his voice thick with mockery. "And what exactly are you going to do? Kill me?" The laugh that followed was softer than a whisper, chilling in its simplicity.

Could I kill the god of Death? My eyes darted to the knife block at the edge of the counter. Without giving him time to react, I lunged for it, grabbing the first knife I touched and flung it.

Time dragged, each second an eternity, as the knife hurtled toward him. It struck with a sickening *thunk*, embedding itself deep in his chest. The handle wobbled, as if even it doubted what it had just done.

Death barely glanced down, his pale fingers curling around the knife's hilt. The slow, deliberate way he pulled it free sent a chill down my spine. Sunlight danced off the blade, clean and gleaming.

"Mortal weapons cannot harm me," he said, each word carrying the weight of inevitability. "But you should know that by now."

A tremor rolled through me, my body barely holding together under the weight of fear. How do you kill death? I forced my breaths to stay steady, even as his gaze locked onto mine—sharp, probing, like a cat deciding how much fun it could have with its cornered prey.

My eyes darted to the front door, which felt miles away, the distance expanding with every frantic heartbeat. Could I make it?

"He hasn't told you, has he?" Death's voice broke through my calculations, and I snapped my attention back to him.

"Told me what?"

His steps matched my every retreat, the space between us shrinking with terrifying ease. "What you are."

"What I—" My back hit the counter, and my breath caught.

"He's still trying to protect you."

"Who?"

"You know who," he said, his smile vanishing, replaced by something darker, more dangerous. "His loyalty will be his downfall."

Before his words even registered, he shifted—a dark, smoke-like blur—and reappeared inches from me. His fingers encircled my wrists, yanking them above my head with effortless force. The wall pressed hard against my back as his palm slammed down next to my face, trapping me. His body crushed into mine, all hard lines and chilling pressure. His invasive proximity was wrong, too intimate. My pulse thundered in my ears, but I managed to glare. "You are so not my type."

"Charming." His sickly-sweet breath brushed over my cheek like frost. I tried to jerk free, but it was like fighting a steel trap. His grip didn't budge, barely even acknowledged my struggle.

Beneath his dark lashes, blue flecks in his lavender eyes seemed to catch the light, pulling me in like a tide I couldn't fight. My thoughts blurred, the edges of my panic softening under the weight of his stare. His grip on my wrists tightened and suddenly, all I could think about was peace. The kind only the dead could know.

"I'm doing you a favor," he whispered, his voice weaving through the fog settling in my mind.

No. This wasn't right. My pulse stumbled as I tried to focus on the sensation of the cold wall at my back, on the pain in my wrists. Something to ground me, to pull me out of whatever this was. My breathing waned, faint but still mine. I almost thought I could resist.

But then, behind him, a black river glided toward a yawning tunnel. An old man stood in a small boat, his lantern casting a dim glow over the dead shuffling along the walkways beyond. The River Acheron.

"You're not supposed to be up there," the ferryman called, his voice familiar yet distant, like an echo carried on water. His red sash draped modestly over his too-thin form, the sight of him oddly comforting. I should have felt alarm, fear. Instead, I felt... secure. Safe.

"I'm not supposed to be up there," I murmured, the words slipping out unbidden, as if they belonged to someone else entirely.

He was right. It all clicked into place. "I should go with you." I felt light, gravity abandoning me. My skin tingled, a strange peace calling to me, buried somewhere in the depths of Death's eyes. Freedom. I could be free— just one step forward, and I'd be on the boat, the water rocking beneath me, the gentle splash of the bow lolling me.

"Come," the ferryman urged, his fingers almost brushing mine. Every ounce of resistance drained from me as I reached out toward his knobby fingers.

"Amara, no!" Paul's voice tore through the trance, ripping me free like a lifeline yanking me from deep waters. It wasn't my name, but I knew it was meant for me.

The River Acheron dissolved, slipping away like the remnants of a fading dream. The ferryman's lantern flickered once before winking out, and the spectral waters ebbed into nothingness. The stillness was absolute, as if existence itself had paused, suspended in a single fragile moment. Then everything came crashing back.

The stinging pulls of my hair, the icy bite of the air, and Death's complete disregard for personal space snapped me back to a reality I desperately wished I could escape.

"Let. Go!" I snarled, twisting against his grip. Something inside me surged—something instinctive, fierce, and unfamiliar. My wrist slipped free, and before I could even think, my hand lashed out toward his face.

He caught it mid-strike, his grip locking my fingers in place. "Foolish," he murmured, almost bored, before slamming my hand against the wall.

The crack of breaking bone reverberated through me, a sound so piercing it silenced every other thought. Pain erupted everywhere, shooting down from my broken fingers and seizing every nerve in its path. A scream from my throat more animal than human and for a horrifying second, I realized I may never use my hand again.

The room wavered, shapes blending and shifting as I fought against the blinding pain. His cold fingers still held me upright, his grip like steel shackles, but every part of me screamed to move, to fight.

Glass exploded behind me and Paul barreled through the window, shards cascading around him like jagged confetti. Hypnos followed in a blur of shadow, but Paul caught him mid-step, gripping the sleep god by the collar and hurling him across the counter. Dishes shattered on impact, narrowly missing my mom's motionless figure slumped against the bar.

A hot gust swept through the room, and from the silver mist, Cynthia materialized. Her expression was a mix of fury and precision, her presence commanding as she launched herself into the fight. But nothing could pull me from the crushing reality of my hand, hot tears spilling down my cold cheeks as I fought to hold back my sobs.

Through tear-blurred vision, I saw Death's eyes, swirling black with fury. My head buzzed, my lungs emptied with each desperate wheeze. Before the glass even settled, Death closed the distance, his mouth crushing against mine.

It wasn't a kiss. It was annihilation. A soul-deep freeze trapped me in place. Voices shouted, objects clattered, chaos erupted around me, but it was all ambient noise to the droning in my head and the salty-sweet taste filling my mouth. I tried to pull away, but he only pressed harder, his body pinning mine against the wall as he drained the life out of me. Drained my soul.

He wasn't just stealing air… he was taking me. Everything. Every spark of warmth, every fragment of who I was.

Something deep in me snapped, like a tightly wound spring breaking free. A force I couldn't name or explain fought its way to the surface. I wasn't ready to die.

I drove my knee upward, aiming for his groin.

He barely twitched, but the pressure on my lips eased just enough. Gritting my teeth, I poured everything I had into my arms and shoved, the motion fueled by something that felt both foreign and completely mine.

☉︎☽ CHAPTER 7 ☾☉︎

A rush of energy shot through my fingers as I sent Death crashing into the counter with a force that couldn't possibly be mine. What the hell am I? No time to figure that out. Cradling my shattered wrist, I bolted for the broken window and leapt out. As I landed, I couldn't help but glance back. Cynthia clocked Death square in the jaw, sending him hurtling into the refrigerator. For a second, I almost felt bad for the fridge.

Coughing and gasping, I stumbled to the massive oak tree in our front yard, trying to pull myself together. Pure survival instincts screamed at me to keep running, but I couldn't just abandon my mom, Mike, or Lizzie. Crashes thundered from inside the house, and the gods' voices carried on the wind, hurling insults like a bunch of enraged teenagers. If the situation weren't so deadly, I might've laughed at the absurdity.

Another window shattered, spraying glass like shrapnel. Hypnos followed, looking more pissed off than ever. Shit.

Fear tore through me, but I braced myself. For what, I had no idea. But that strength I'd felt earlier? It was back, fiercer than before. Fight. My body screamed at me to fight. Adrenaline pounded through me, smothering the pain in my wrist.

Silver arrows whistled out of the kitchen window, each one piercing Hypnos's back. He winced but barely slowed, charging straight at me. I screamed despite myself. He launched into the air like a predator, a ferocious grin spreading across his face. My body reacted on pure instinct, knees bending, legs coiled to launch me up to meet him.

But something else got there first. A white blur slammed into Hypnos, sending him crashing to the ground. Henry landed like an Avenger and kicked Hypnos across the yard.

"Run!" he barked, charging at the sleep god, his feet not even touching the grass.

But I couldn't run. My body wouldn't listen. This time, it wasn't fear paralyzing me—it was the need to protect. My mom, my friends… what would these gods do to them if they couldn't get to me?

"No!" Paul's scream thundered from inside the house. "Henry, stop Thanatos!"

Before I could react, he materialized inches from my face, seized my arm, and spun me like a disc. My shoulder wrenched free with a sickening pop. Wind tore at my body, hair whipped across my face, my stomach flipped, and he released me.

I screamed, hurtling through the air until a tree stopped me with a brutal thud. Something in my arm cracked. Pain exploded, radiating through every nerve. My scream tore from my throat as I stared at the jagged bone piercing through torn skin. Bile rose in my throat, the midday light blurring as dizziness threatened to drag me under, breaths coming in wheezing gasps.

"You had to make this difficult," Thanatos spat, his white robes drifting around him, immaculate despite his psychotic behavior.

I couldn't keep my eyes from the gruesome sight of my arm. The thick, metallic smell of blood filled my nostrils, and I heaved.

"Get away from her!" Cynthia launched herself through the air, tackling him with a battle grace I'd only seen in movies.

Paul appeared beside me, his hands gently cradling my broken arm. Warmth poured into me as his hands touched my skin. The golden glow surrounding him was hypnotic. My lungs opened fully, and I sucked in a breath so clean it felt foreign.

If it weren't for Paul's golden aura, I might have been fixated on the sight of my bone slipping back into place, the skin knitting together as if nothing had happened. But my focus stayed on him. Time seemed to slow as I absorbed every detail: the way his blue eyes shimmered, the radiance that made him seem ethereal, almost too beautiful to be real. I wished he'd say something, anything, to assure me this wasn't real. That it was all just some bizarre test or vision. But he wouldn't even meet my gaze.

A crash shattered the moment. Henry sailed through the air, slamming into the upper branches of the oak tree, and Cynthia's furious shouts erupted from the porch as she squared off against Thanatos, spewing profanities I'd never imagined coming from a Greek goddess.

Hypnos materialized behind Paul, and another scream tore through the air—shrill, raw, and ripped straight from my gut. Paul released my arm and spun to face him, but Hypnos was already moving.

The blow landed like thunder, Hypnos's fist colliding with Paul's jaw in a sickening crack. Paul went down hard. He rose, shaking off the hit, but before he got much further, Hypnos was on me. His hand clamped around my throat, crushing my windpipe with inhuman force. My breath vanished, stolen in an instant. My feet left the earth, dangling helplessly as I thrashed and clawed at his wrist. It was like trying to pry apart solid steel. My body jerked, twisting and flailing, but it wasn't enough. I couldn't breathe. I couldn't escape. I couldn't think.

"Try and push me now, bitch."

Oh, you did not just go there. Fury boiled in me, but the raw power coursing through my veins was uncontrollable. No focus, no way to channel it. My nails dug into his wrist, my kicks barely grazing his chest. This was it. This was how I died.

The thought barely formed before instinct took over. My fingers tightened around his wrist, squeezing with every ounce of desperation. His eyes widened, a sharp inhale betraying his shock. Holy shit, was I hurting him?

Hypnos roared and released me, stumbling back with disbelief carved into his features. He stared at his wrist, then at me and the air between us thickened with his fury, but something deep within me—something primal— rushed to the surface.

Before I could second-guess myself, I lunged forward and swung a punch straight into his face. The impact reverberated through my knuckles and Hypnos went flying, crashing into the side of my house with a resounding thud.

Paul streaked through the air like a comet, slamming into Hypnos before he could recover. The sleep god crumpled into a heap, out cold.

I stared at my hands, not even aching from the punch. "What the..."

"Watch out!"

I spun at Cynthia's warning. Thanatos charged at me in his smog-form. Cynthia and Henry were sprawled over two separate lawns, temporarily incapacitated. My mind raced as I searched for something I could use to defend myself with my sudden inhuman strength. Tree? No, Mom loved that tree. Hypnos? Too many limbs. Car?

I sprinted to my car, wincing at the thought of what I was about to do to my old clunker. My fingers curled around the driver's side door, and I pulled, not knowing what to expect but hoping the car would be a good enough weapon to take down Death.

The door ripped off. Not exactly what I had in mind, but I could roll with it. I swung the door with everything I had, the weight of metal screaming through the air. It collided with Thanatos's head just as he reached me, the impact sending a shudder up my arms as he flew back, crashing into the road.

My ears popped, disbelief and adrenaline rushing through me as I blinked. Thanatos was gone. I gasped for breath, searching frantically for Hypnos. He'd vanished too. The others ran toward me, all of them winded except Paul.

Cynthia reached me first, her hand firm on my shoulder as she looked me over for injuries. "You okay?"

I couldn't answer. Crimson blood stained her stomach, and I covered my mouth at the sight. Before I could look away, something caught my eye. Gold flecks mixed with her blood like glitter. My shock warred with a sick curiosity. How does that even work? I stared, mesmerized, as Paul placed a hand between the tear in Cynthia's silver shirt. The way he did it, so naturally, almost possessively, sent a prick of unease through me. My fascination with godly blood and flawless abs faded as I realized just how much I didn't know about these people... these gods.

Paul placed his hand on Cynthia's wound, and in an instant, it was mended. My anger swelled, hands trembling, tears building. I looked from Henry to Cynthia, and finally settled on Paul. "Are they dead?"

He shook his head.

"You owe me an explanation," I growled.

Cynthia glanced at me. A flicker of something—pity, annoyance, superiority—flashed across her face. I hated how she could make me feel so small, like I was a child who couldn't possibly understand the big, scary world she lived in. "You've been part of this longer than you realize, Jessa. This isn't the first time you've been caught in the middle of something bigger than yourself."

"What does that even mean?" I was sick and tired of them keeping me in the dark, sick of Cynthia's knowing looks and condescending tone. It was as if she enjoyed watching me squirm, like she got some twisted satisfaction from holding all the cards.

She just shook her head, her lips pressed into a thin line. "You'll remember when the time is right. They'll be waking up any minute," she nodded toward the garage.

I turned back to Paul. "I don't care about that. Tell me what I am. Why do I have cryptic visions? How can I pull a car door off like it's nothing? Is it part of being a Demi Guardian? Why the hell are two gods trying to kill me? What is going on?" I'd ramped up to yelling, knuckles white.

Cynthia blocked my view of Paul with a look I knew all too well. She didn't like me. At all. And for a second, I wondered if she wanted me dead too.

Paul stepped between us, probably sensing that if Cynthia threw one more condescending look my way, I'd be tempted to gouge her eyes out with my newfound strength just for the satisfaction. "I owe her some answers."

"Damn right you do." A little tension released from my body, and I loosened my fists. Henry and Cynthia exchanged wary glances before taking a few steps back.

Paul kept his eyes on me as he addressed them. "Mind doing clean-up?"

The two looked at each other one more time. I had to wonder if it was for my safety or his that they looked concerned. In a swirl of white and silver air, the two disappeared. The sound of glass fitting back into the open windowpane, the screech of metal as my car door was reattached, and the rustling of broken branches all sounded surreal. But the unreal was becoming common now, and I wasn't as freaked out by it as I probably should have been.

Paul placed his hands on my shoulders and looked down at me. Surprised by the sudden closeness and warmth of his glowing presence, I swallowed and tried to steady my breath. I realized then that I'd never seen him during the day before. The whole sun god thing must be why he carried that radiant halo around his flawless body.

He reached to push a strand of hair from my face but hesitated, his hand hovering before retreating back to my shoulder instead. "Are you okay?"

"No." My voice came out raw with anger and fear. "My mom, my friends… they could've been killed." Voice trembling, I held back the tears threatening to fall. I had to stay strong.

His expression softened, guilt flickering across his face. "I'm sorry. This isn't how it was supposed to happen. You should've been prepared for this."

"Prepared for what?" I snapped, my voice rising again, my emotions clawing their way out. "Gods trying to kill me? Weird powers I don't understand? A whole new reality I didn't ask for?"

I glanced away, unable to meet his eyes. My body was still trembling, and I hated it. Hated how vulnerable I felt. For some reason, I wanted to seem stronger for him, even though I barely knew him and had no reason to trust him. That thought alone made my chest tighten even more.

The sunlight framed him, catching the blue in his eyes, making them shine like sunlight on water. "Okay, you know Hercules, right?"

I snorted. "Seriously?" Of course I knew. He knew I knew. He was stalling. He chewed on his lower lip, nervous, but no other explanation came. Only a stare that told me I had to, once again, put the puzzle together. My brain sputtered and gave up. I shifted on my feet, the urge to bolt from him and his cryptic nonsense growing stronger with every second of silence.

His eyes wouldn't release mine, searching for something. Now I was the one nervous. The energy from his touch hummed through my body like an unshakable current. He was so intense it scared me. And too close. The scent of clover on his breath mixed with the cool press of his damp fingertips on my shoulder, making it impossible to look away.

"I'll do my best to explain," he said, his voice low. The pause that followed stretched unbearably, each second feeling like an eternity. "You're… sort of like the new Hercules."

My mouth opened, but no words came out. Hercules. As in *the* Hercules—Greek hero, half mortal, half immortal. A demigod. And I was a… Demi Guardian? Demi…

No.

No, no, no.

No way. I clamped my mouth shut, swallowing my immediate denial, and gave him a slow nod to continue. My legs itched to bolt, every fiber of me screaming to put some distance between myself and his words. But I stayed. Because as much as I wanted to escape, I knew there was nowhere I could go to outrun what he was telling me.

"Do you know who your father is?" Paul's question hit me like a cold wind, cutting through my defenses.

"No." The word slipped out before I could brace myself, and the deep, hardened scar of my fatherless past ripped open. I'd spent years burying the ache, trying to forget the revolving door of pretenders who'd swooped in, vying for my mom's attention but never stepping up to fill the shoes I'd desperately wanted filled. Needed filled.

The idea that guys weren't meant to stick around had become a fact of life, and it was that belief, I figured, that ultimately wrecked things with Zach. It was easier to blame someone else for your mistakes. I blamed my father for most of mine.

Paul's expression hardened, his lips pressed into a firm line, jaw taut with tension. Whatever he was about to say, I knew I wasn't going to like it.

"He was a god."

I blinked, sure I'd misheard him. "Say what?"

His thumbs grazed my neck, light and deliberate, igniting a ripple that shot through me like electricity. The warmth spread like fire, sinking into my skin, and for a moment, I forgot how to breathe. My pulse quickened, each beat deafening in my ears. It wasn't just his words that had me on edge; it was the way his fingers touched me, tracing invisible patterns as though he knew the effect it was having on me.

My mind raced to process his revelation, but his touch made it almost impossible to think clearly. What was it about him that did this to me? And why was I letting it happen when it was clear he was keeping things from me? My hands clenched at my sides, caught between the need to push him away and the magnetic pull that made me want to close the space between us.

Paul seemed to sense the weight of my silence, his tone softening as he treaded carefully. "Think about Hercules," he said, clearly trying to redirect me from the bombshell he'd just dropped about my father. "He was the first of your kind—a half-mortal, a demigod, put here to fend off the underworld and protect the mortal world from its threats."

Before I could respond, Cynthia appeared behind Paul, her hand resting on his shoulder with a proprietary air. Her cold green eyes locked onto mine, and a flicker of unease crawled up my spine. I instinctively stepped back, out of Paul's grasp, hating myself for how easily she'd driven me away. How could I not? She looked every inch the goddess she likely was—confident, radiant, and clearly holding all the cards.

Her lips curled into a smile that didn't quite touch her eyes, the kind of smile that spoke volumes without saying a word. It wasn't kind; it was victorious. She nodded toward the garage. Before I could process what that meant, Mike's guitar sprang to life inside, the discordant melody cutting through the tension like a buzz saw. Lizzie jerked upright in her stool, grabbing for her drumsticks and banging out a beat like her hands had a mind of their own. The sound spilled out into the yard, vibrating with an almost unnatural energy. It was jarring, eerie, and completely unlike any rehearsal I'd ever heard.

Paul leaned in, his whisper a featherlight caress against my frayed nerves. "I'll come back."

His promise sent a shiver skittering down my neck, but when I turned to respond, they were gone. Paul, Cynthia, and Henry had disappeared into thin air as if they'd never been there. The atmosphere buzzed with that prickling, someone's-watching-you feeling, and a realization hit me. Could they be invisible, watching me right now? The thought left me feeling exposed, like I should start charging rent for all the gods creeping on me. I'd probably never know privacy again.

I turned toward the garage, my mind scrambling to piece together a believable excuse for Lizzie and Mike. What could I even say about why I was out here instead of singing the opening notes of our set? By the time I stepped inside, the prickling sensation that told me I wasn't alone had faded, leaving only the echo of my own unease.

They were gone, but Paul's answers—and the impossible questions they raised—jingled in my brain like spare change in an empty jar. And the uneasy truth that my life had done a complete 180? Yeah, that wasn't going anywhere.

☉︎☽ CHAPTER 8 ☾☉︎

Rehearsal was better than expected, given that I'd nearly been killed by gods an hour earlier. Still, I cut it short with a half-hearted "not feeling it" excuse. Singing was usually my escape, but today, even that felt like too much.

Instead, I buried myself under the covers, trying to lose myself in *The Odyssey*. I wasn't sure which scared me more—the idea that this was all real, or that I was going crazy. The urge to call Sam and spill everything gnawed at me, but how could I explain what even I couldn't fully grasp? I hadn't lost my mind at Charlie's. They showed up here, destroyed my house, nearly killed me. It had to be real, right? But why didn't Sam remember any of it? I tossed the book aside and let out a growl of pure exasperation. Maybe I really did need to see a head doctor.

I ran my fingers over the cover of my old, worn book. I'd read it five times now. I never imagined my love for Greek mythology had logic to it.

"Come set the table!" My mom called from downstairs.

Rubbing my eyes, I let out a long sigh. My once-broken arm felt tight and sore but considering it had been sporting an exposed bone earlier, it wasn't doing too bad. I shuddered. Nope. Bad thoughts. Time to redirect.

Mom's idea of distracting myself sounded better by the second. Reading about a hero battling Greek monsters—eerily close to my own reality—was doing a terrible job of keeping my mind off things anyway.

My body protested with each step down the stairs, like I'd been used as a human stress ball and left with all the creases. After the beating I took earlier, it was a miracle I wasn't a pile of goo. The closer I got to the kitchen, the more Sunday night's lasagna teased my nose, the scent almost dulling my aches. My stomach growled like a caged beast, suddenly ravenous enough to rival a senior wrestler's post-tournament hunger.

Resigned to setting the table—silverware, napkins, and drinks all perfectly in place on our no-scratches-from-gods-brawling table—Mom and I took our seats, said grace, and dug in. I'd polished off half my plate by the time she'd barely made a dent in hers.

She sipped her tea, giving me that look that said she'd be asking questions. Nosy questions I had no intention of answering.

"You're uncommonly quiet tonight. Everything okay?"

I mumbled a half-hearted affirmative, conveniently finishing a large bite I'd just stuffed in my mouth. The lasagna was a bit saltier than usual.

"Are you sure? I was expecting some gossip or a play-by-play of the parade. All I get is a moody teenager?"

"Aren't teenagers supposed to be moody?" I asked around my bite, staring into my glass of tea, watching the ice crack under its heat.

"Excuse me for asking." She wiped some sauce off the corner of her mouth with a napkin.

Her red v-cut blouse and matching lipstick made me realize something. "You have a date tonight?"

She nodded with a bashful smile, trying to hide it behind another sip. "David."

The realtor, if I remembered. "What's this, number three now since April?" I smirked, wondering if she could take the same kind of heat. I knew she couldn't. She hated talking about personal stuff and I couldn't really blame her. I hadn't been the easiest daughter to deal with when it came to new men in her life.

Don't get me wrong, I wanted my mom to be happy, but I couldn't help but resent the parade of men vying for her attention—each one trying to outdo the last, like some twisted reality show where the prize was my mom's affection.

"Yes," she said cautiously. "So, I was thinking tomorrow after I get home from work, we could go clothes shopping?"

Glad we'd moved off the subject of me and on to clothes, I shrugged. "Sure."

The tips of my fork scraped the bottom of my empty plate, twisting the leftover sauce into thin, winding lines. Which god was my father? The question ate into my consciousness like acid. No matter how hard I tried to redirect my thoughts, they always circled back to that burning hunger for answers.

Mom sighed and clanked her fork on the table. "Jessa, what's wrong with you? You know you can tell me anything, I'm your mother."

Here we go.

I looked up from what were now four tomato-red rivers of sauce, running a hand through my hair as I shook my head. "Nothing, Mom. Really."

She wasn't buying it. I had to come up with something because the truth was, well... the truth. I dropped my gaze back to my plate, an odd compulsion driving me to finish what I'd started. Four rivers weren't enough. Sliding the edge of my fork down the plate, I carved one more, completing my work.

It would absolutely shatter my mom if she found out I was the only thing standing between her and a bunch of gruesome monsters she didn't even know existed. "I don't know, I guess it's the whole Zach thing."

She nodded, buying the bluff, though it wasn't entirely a lie. Her face softened, her eyes taking on that all-too-familiar motherly look of understanding.

"I know, honey, I'm sorry."

She really didn't know, but she was the last person I wanted to discuss relationship matters with, given her "stellar" track record. She offered me a sweet smile and reached over to pat my hand. I let her. "But you have to work on getting over him. You're going to be a senior. There are plenty of fish in the sea. And no one wants to date a moping, moody, depressed girl."

Trying not to narrow my eyes at her, I pulled my hand back to my empty plate and got up for seconds. "Thanks, Mom, I'll keep that in mind."

#

Security was the only word that fit the sanctuary of my bedroom.

The rock icons staring down from the walls and the sparkly beads hanging like a curtain in front of my window offered a comforting contrast to my otherwise completely spastic mood. Instead of trying to catch up on the sleep my body desperately craved, I sat on my bed for over an hour, replaying everything that had happened in the past three days.

From the moment I saw Henry trailing me, to the crazy visions, my first encounter with Hypnos at the diner, and my literal brush with Death, I tried to piece it all together. I wasn't ready to tackle the whole "my father is a god" issue—not yet. There was only so much my brain could take before it short-circuited. There had to be more to it than just this Hercules thing, right? Did I even want to believe it? And I still couldn't figure out why Sam had forgotten everything. I chewed on my lip, wondering if I should try telling her again. I needed someone to talk to, someone human.

My phone chimed with Lizzie's text tone, pulling me out of my thoughts. I swiped to open it.

wanna hang?

I sighed, typing back, **tmrw**

No way I'd be good company tonight. Her reply came almost instantly: **kk**

I tossed the phone aside and tried to lose myself in *The Odyssey*, hoping the drama of Odysseus and the Cyclops might distract me. I barely made it a paragraph before Sam's text broke through my fragile focus. Her message popped up on the screen: **swimming @ dawn's tmw?**

Fingers hovering over the keys, I typed back: **ns, shopping w mom**

I stared at the screen, the blue glow washing over my hands as I waited for her reply.

u ok?

ya

Lying over text was so much easier.

But Sam knew me too well for that. The phone started buzzing, and I flinched at the sound. Her name flashed on the screen, and with a reluctant sigh, I answered.

"Yeah?"

"Need to talk?"

"About what?" Translation: Yes. Yes. Yes. You've forgotten I had a stalker, that Greek gods are real, and that some of them tried to kill me.

You're the only person who might believe me—again.

I picked at the pink stuffed bunny in my lap, its once-plush fur now old and worn. I'd had it since I was a baby. Back then, it had been my shield, my comfort.

Sam sighed on her end of the phone. "I don't know. Zach, maybe? You haven't talked to me since this morning." She sounded a little annoyed. "And even then you sounded... off."

That's because you couldn't remember anything! I shrugged. "Just adjusting to summer, I guess."

That was about as true as my band winning a Grammy. I had to tell her. "You got a minute?"

"What's up?" This time, she sounded eager.

A knock on my door sent my stomach flipping. I stared at it a second, then glanced at my clock. Mom's date couldn't be over already, unless David blew it. I got up from the bed and headed to the door, wondering if I'd be consoling a broken-hearted mother again.

Sam continued, "Spill! Oh, and before I forget, I think you should hang with us tomorrow, get your mind off you-know-who."

Maybe hanging out wouldn't be the worst idea. Pretending everything was normal for a few hours could be a nice break from the whole "Greek gods trying to kill me" thing. But would it really get my mind off Bargain Bin Heartbreaker? Or just remind me how completely screwed up everything's become? I gripped the knob and turned it as I said, "Yeah, I'm sure I—"

Paul stood in my doorway, staring down at me through those frustratingly perfect, wavy bangs. My heart jolted—part panic, part... something else. His presence had that storm-on-the-horizon kind of energy: thrilling, sure, but terrifying because you didn't know what might get wrecked in the process.

"Um." My hand tightened on the knob as I muttered into the phone, "Sam, I'llgiveyouacalllaterbye." Ending the call, I took a steadying breath and tried to sound like I hadn't just lost all grip on rational thought. "You know, most people use the front door."

"Sorry," he said breathlessly, his hands fidgeting at his sides. "I… don't usually do this."

I raised an eyebrow, hoping it masked the sudden surge of unease.

"And what exactly is 'this'?" Sarcasm came easier than showing just how off-balance he had me feeling.

He smiled—disarming, of course, because life wasn't unfair enough already. It was the kind of smile that made Zach look like he was trying too hard. I hated how easily it short-circuited my focus, leaving me scrambling to remember that he wasn't here to charm me.

"Giving you some answers?"

Oh, because cryptic half-truths were just what I needed right now. I snorted. "No, really. What are you doing here?"

His eyes dropped to the floor, and a faint color brushed his cheeks. "I promise, all the questions will be coming from you this time."

I crossed my arms, trying to steady the restless jitters bouncing around just beneath my skin. There was something about him that made it impossible to settle, like my body couldn't decide whether to let its guard down or put every wall back up. My mind, unfortunately, was leaning toward the latter. He was hiding something—I knew it.

Still, he made it hard not to get distracted. I shoved aside the current of nervous energy I always felt when he was around. Cynthia would probably hand me a one-way ticket to the afterlife if she knew where my head was going right now. Seriously, why was I even contemplating... what? Getting drawn into his orbit when I still didn't know if I could trust him? Focus, Jessa.

And then I saw it. The pile of yesterday's clothes, including the undergarment kind, in front of my closet, the empty Twizzlers package crumpled on the floor, and the half-empty can of Dr. Pepper precariously perched on my nightstand. Panic flared, my cheeks going nuclear. Holy mother of God, had he seen that?

"Um, here, I have an idea," I said, voice an octave too high. I grabbed Paul's arm and steered him toward the window. Ducking through the curtain of rainbow beads, I yanked the screenless frame up and all but shoved him out. "After you."

He gave me a look, half amusement, half disbelief, like he was deciding whether to call me out or just roll with it. The faint smirk tugging at his lips made my stomach flip in the most annoying way. Without a word, he climbed out onto the slanted roof overhang outside. I followed, sticking close to the wall and as far from the edge as possible, before sitting beside him.

The humid summer air clung to my skin, but a soft breeze ruffled the edges of Paul's hair. The rough texture of the roof dug into my leg and somewhere in the distance, the Andersons' pugs barked like tiny alarms, their yips blending into the quiet hum of the neighborhood.

Paul leaned back against the siding, sitting cross-legged, his movements as relaxed as if we were lounging on a picnic blanket instead of perched on a rooftop. I didn't have to look to know he was watching me. I could feel his gaze as it stoking the familiar undercurrent pulsing beneath my skin. I focused on the star-dimmed sky instead, the haze of city lights washing out what should have been a brilliant display. The dimness matched my state of mind.

I wasn't sure if I even wanted to know the truth anymore, but the need for answers was relentless, digging into me like a thorn buried too deep to pull out. I tightened my arms around my knees, bracing myself. Whatever bombshell Paul was about to drop, it felt like it was going to change everything. Again.

☉☽ CHAPTER 9 ☾☉

My pulse hammered as I pressed against the house siding, every muscle tense with the familiar, irrational fear of toppling off the roof. I'd been here plenty of times before—back when Zach and I were inseparable, and this little rooftop was our shared escape. His room, just a yard away, directly faced mine. For years, our windows had been like a secret bridge between our worlds. Now that connection felt as distant as another lifetime.

Despite my fear of heights, I'd shoved it down every time, enough to keep climbing out here. Tonight, though? Tonight felt different. Maybe it was because the guy was different. Or maybe it was because my life had officially spiraled into some bizarre mythic fever dream.

Paul shifted beside me, his eyes landing squarely on my face. It wasn't casual. It was a stare. Intense. Probing. Like he was searching for something. My stomach twisted. Did I have something on my face? Great, just my luck to climb onto this roof looking like a walking pasta ad.

I rubbed my cheek with my arm, pretending to scratch an itch but hoping to wipe away any possible sauce smear in the process. "You swear you're actually going to answer my questions this time?"

His barely audible laugh made my nerves tangle in confusing ways. "Yes, I promise."

Was he laughing at my question? Or, worse, at the lasagna stain I was certain was smeared across my face? I pressed myself harder into the siding, the scratchy shingles digging into my legs as I sat crisscrossed. I couldn't decide which was more humiliating—Paul's laughter or the fact that I clung to the house like a scared kitten.

The faint hum of a car engine mixed with the chirping of cicadas as I tried to collect my thoughts. Where did I even start? It felt like I'd been handed a golden ticket to grill some A-list celebrity, only to realize I had, like, five minutes to ask everything—and zero idea what to say first.

"Hercules? Seriously?" My voice came out drier than I meant, more sarcasm than curiosity.

Paul didn't flinch but his lips parted like he'd answer, then hesitated, his expression calm yet unreadable. After a beat, he simply nodded, holding back the details like they were state secrets.

"How? Why?"

"To make the world safe for mankind," he said evenly, his gaze cutting into me like he was deciphering every flicker of emotion on my face. "Protection from those in the Chthonic who would rather see mortals wiped out."

Wiped out? The idea snagged in my brain, dragging with it visions of apocalyptic chaos ripped straight out of a disaster movie. I wanted to laugh at the absurdity, but Paul's tone—calm, certain, like he'd lived through it— made my chest tighten. Half of me clung to the hope this was some elaborate prank. The other half? About as sure as my mom's swiping on dating apps.

"Okay," I said slowly, "so I'm supposed to kill demons to protect the world?" When he didn't correct me, a flicker of pride sparked—only to be snuffed out by the weight of what it all meant. I swallowed hard, ignoring the urge to puke off the side of the roof.

Hercules. I was Hercules. The thought looped in my mind, tangled with flashes of the garage door ripped off its hinges and my car door torn clean away. My nails were a wreck, chipped from relentless picking. Paul's warm fingers wrapped over mine, stopping my anxious habit mid-motion.

The moment his skin touched mine, a quiet current hummed through me, like the world had tilted just slightly off its axis. His thumb brushed over my knuckles in a slow, deliberate sweep, leaving a trail of warmth I couldn't shake. I didn't pull away, caught somewhere between wanting to lean into the comfort it offered and questioning why such a simple gesture could feel so overwhelming.

Comfort. It was a feeling I hadn't let myself expect from anyone since Zach. The thought crept in uninvited, pulling my attention like a thread unraveling. Pressing harder against the house siding, I fixed my eyes anywhere but on the dizzying drop below.

Paul was nothing like Zach. Comparing them was laughable. Zach was a guitar riff from a grunge band—raw, fleeting, and gone as soon as the song ended. Paul? He was a symphony. Timeless. Composed. The kind of music that didn't just play in your head but rearranged the rhythm of your soul.

I forced myself to exhale, letting the tension in my shoulders loosen. "Sorry, it's just... this is a lot. I'm trying."

"I know. It's a lot to take in." He hesitated. "It's why I didn't tell you everything the other night. There's only so much a human mind can handle. Even if they might be half-mortal."

I winced. Half-mortal. "So, how? Why me? Why now?"

"There can only be one Demi at a time." He glanced skyward. "The last one died four days ago. There are Potentials out there, demigods like you, but they may never get their power or even know they're anything more than human. The Fates choose randomly. When one Demi dies, another is activated. It's… immediate. No warning."

My skin prickled, like someone had blown unexpectedly on the back of my neck. "And you just… wait for someone to, what, transform?"

Paul nodded. "We don't get a list of Potentials, and that's by design, so we scout for who may become the next one."

There were more like me? As strange as it was, the thought brought a flicker of comfort. If I got myself killed, at least someone else would be there to pick up the pieces. But my brain stuck on the idea of scouting. Memories of the gas station and the end-of-year bash at the stadium resurfaced. Scouting could easily be mistaken for stalking, right?

"Henry."

He nodded. "Henry was the scout."

"So which god is Henry?"

"Hermes." Paul's hand slipped away from mine, casual, but I couldn't help wondering if Hermes was a sore subject for him.

The name rolled around in my mind, and I recalled everything I could remember about the god of commerce.

"So, I'm the Demi Guardian..." The words felt foreign on my tongue. "Henry found out, and then, a few hours later, I'm being killed by the god of death."

Then it hit me—sharp and tingly, like smacking your funny bone on the corner of a desk.

"Henry," I said, my voice tight as the thought festered in my mind. Henry had spotted me. Then Thanatos and Hypnos found me.

I swallowed down the bitterness rising in my throat, trying to steady my voice. "Henry had to have told them. That's how they knew where I was."

Paul's jaw went rigid, the muscles shifting subtly as though he were biting back something harsh. "Henry found me, not Thanatos. It's how I got to you in time, before you…" His voice faltered, his gaze dropping to the ground a story below.

Before I died.

His hands flexed subtly at his sides, clearly uncomfortable with where this conversation had turned.

"Henry said you're called Guardians. Guardians of what?"

"Everything."

Vague, much?

"And you."

My heart tripped over itself, his words breaking through the steady front I'd been trying to hold. I stared at a hangnail, refusing to look at him. "You still haven't answered the 'Why me?' part," I half-mumbled.

"Because you've done this before," he said softly.

"You mean… reincarnation?"

"Something like that. Your soul has been recycled. It's usually a deciding factor when the Fates pick the next Demi out of the Potentials."

I licked my dry lips, trying to keep up. The wind wasn't helping. I wanted to know how we knew each other—because we must have. If my soul had been here before, he'd have known me. Maybe that explained the way he looked at me, the way he touched me.

"How many times has… my soul done this before?"

He couldn't hold my gaze, and he swallowed. I wished I could read him, understand what he was thinking. "This is the first time your soul has been recycled."

"Oh." The disappointment in his voice was subtle but unmistakable. Something was off, and I couldn't figure it out.

"What about Zeus?" I asked, desperate to shift the mood. "Can't he just, I don't know, threaten the naughty gods with a zap from his lightning bolt?"

Paul's face tightened. "My father turned his back on the human world a long time ago, leaving the gods to their own devices."

Oh. Right. Zeus was his dad. So much for lightening the mood. I might as well have asked him about his worst childhood trauma. Come on, how smart was it to be attracted to a god whose father ruled the sky? And speaking of my attraction to him…

"Cynthia. What goddess is she?"

Paul's lips curved into a smile, soft and almost amused, catching the faint silver glow of moonlight. It wasn't much, but it was the first hint of ease I'd seen from him all night. For once, I felt like I'd managed to steer the conversation out of the emotional minefield.

"Artemis."

It took a second longer than I'd have liked to piece it together. Artemis, goddess of the moon. *Oh God, I'm such an idiot.* Cynthia wasn't Paul's girlfriend—she was his sister.

The touches, the closeness… My shoulders loosened before I even realized it. Relief swept through me so fast I almost laughed. Of course, Paul wasn't with her. He was the god of truth. Disloyalty wasn't exactly in his playbook.

"I have one more question." That was a lie.

"Alright." His voice was quiet, eyes fixed somewhere distant.

"How do you do the poofing thing, and can I do it?"

Paul chuckled and I had a feeling it was at me and not the question. At least he wasn't upset anymore. "No. Only immortals, Guardians, can do that."

"Have you ever tried it with a demigod?"

He winced. "Not personally. There's always a chance the Demi might come back missing some vital parts or organs."

My giddy excitement deflated. "Well, that's no fun."

"No fun at all."

His head suddenly jerked to the side, his entire body going rigid. The sudden movement snapped my attention away from the quiet rhythm of our conversation. His expression sharpened as if he'd picked up on something I couldn't hear or see.

"What's wrong?"

He didn't answer right away, his eyes narrowing toward the horizon. "I have to go."

I straightened. "Wait, what?" The words stumbled out before I could process his abrupt shift. "Go where?"

"I can't explain right now."

"Seriously?" Frustration flared, the warm cocoon of our moment shattered. He couldn't just dump a truckload of existential drama on me and vanish into the night like some divine escape artist. "You're leaving me with all of... this?"

His expression hinted at regret, but the urgency in his posture remained. "I'll be back. We still need to talk about your training."

Training? What did training even look like for a demigod? Would I need a sword? Did demigods jog? Or was it more "lift this boulder" and "dodge that lightning bolt"? Before I could ask, he was gone. One second beside me, the next an empty space, colder and lighter, like he'd stolen some invisible part of the air.

A car door slammed shut below. For a second, I assumed it was Mom, back early from a disastrous date. But then Zach's bedroom light flicked on, pulling my attention to the window across the expanse and I momentarily forgot to breathe.

Zach.

My chest tightened, the sudden flash of his silhouette drawing memories I wasn't ready to deal with. Once, that light coming on would've been my favorite moment of the night—our signal to climb out and meet here, in this spot. Now, it just felt like a ghost flickering through a part of me I couldn't quite bury.

I blinked, trying to shake off the sting of nostalgia. The last thing I wanted was for him to glance outside and think I was sitting out here pining for what used to be. Zach's shadow moved closer to the blinds, and my pulse kicked into overdrive.

Nope.

My brain caught up to my reflexes as I scrambled on my hands and knees back toward the safety of my room. This wasn't just any climb back through the window. It was a tactical retreat. I threw myself onto the floor, sprawled out like I'd just evaded a sniper. My heart pounded like a bass drum in a rock concert against the cool floorboards.

What was I so afraid of? That Zach had seen me? That he hadn't?

My world was tangled up in gods and prophecies and truths I wasn't ready for. Yet somehow, the thought of Zach catching me sitting alone on the roof still stung in a way I hated to admit.

I closed my eyes, willing the ache to dissolve. Whatever Zach had meant to me, it wasn't this anymore. At least, that's what I told myself as I stared at the dust-covered floorboards. The roof still felt like ours, even if the world I once climbed up there to escape from had been replaced by one I could barely comprehend.

☉☽ CHAPTER 10 ☾☉

I cried myself to sleep that night. Everything was happening too fast, and even trying to talk about it didn't help. Samantha's blank reaction yesterday nagged at me, leaving me more confused than ever. The nightmares didn't help—each one jolting me awake in a sweaty, panicked mess. By the time Samantha's call finally woke me, I'd slept through the morning and well into the afternoon.

Thirty minutes later, I was stepping out of my car and meeting Sam on her porch, the sun warm against my bare skin. I wasn't really in the mood for swimming, let alone dealing with Dawn's bipolar friendship. But soaking up the sun? That was different. Next to singing, it was one of my favorite things. Don't confuse that with swimming, though. I hated swimming.

The clack of our flip-flops and the occasional drone of a car passing filled the silence. Twisting the cap off my Dr. Pepper, I took a long sip, letting the fizz cool my throat. I focused on the bubbles, doing everything I could to avoid thinking about the conversation I needed to have with her.

Sam finally blew out a sigh, the wind rustling her sheer pink cover-up, which didn't do much actual covering. "So, doing the shopping thing with your mom later?"

I groaned. "More like giving her a chance to interrogate me, but yeah." Hopefully, she'd work late. Not impossible in marketing, but I knew my mom. She'd put me first. Cool at times, but also kind of a curse.

"You've been acting a little off lately. Like last night. Bitchy move, by the way." Sam lowered her sunglasses, eyes locked on Andy Parson mowing the yard across the street.

I blinked. Last night? Oh. Right. I'd hung up on her mid-call when Paul showed up. "Yeah, sorry about that."

How was I supposed to start this conversation again? The same way I had last time? If only I could remember what I'd said.

Sam was still ogling Andy, her focus clearly elsewhere. I snapped my fingers in front of her face. "Focus, Sam. Bitchy friend here."

She pushed her sunglasses back up with a smug little smile. "What? He's cute."

"Sure, if you're into narcissistic gym rats."

"Whatever," she said, laughing. But she was grinning in that I-totally-care-but-won't-admit-it way. Sam had been my ride or die since junior high, pulling me out of my Zach-centric bubble and into the world of girl talk, venting, and questionable taste in guys. She made the chaos of high school feel a little less suffocating, especially after the Zach-astrophe.

"What?" I shot her a sideways glance.

"Can you try, for once, not to think about him? He's a jerk and deserves dealing with the hell that is Ashlyn."

I groaned. "Seriously, Sam, I'm fine."

"Whatever. You're so not fine."

We turned onto Dawn's street, where a lineup of shiny, overpriced cars gleamed in the driveways. Classic Dawn. No way was I parking my old clunker here to ruin her aesthetic. Another sip of Dr. Pepper saved me from replying.

"You know he isn't happy," Sam said, not looking at me as she pulled out her phone.

I sighed. "Texting Dawn?"

"Yeah, she's wondering where we are."

No surprise there. Dawn had zero patience whatsoever.

Sam's words rolled around in my head, and annoyingly, there was a lot of truth to them. Ashlyn and Zach had been going out for about two months, and I'd noticed a total shift in him. At first, I'd thought he was happy, but come on—what guy could be happy with an overbearing, prissy, control-freak of a girlfriend? The thought made me grit my teeth, but Zach wasn't exactly my top concern these days.

"Listen, I need to talk to you about something that happened at Charlie's," I blurted, unable to hold it in anymore.

Sam shrugged, her flip-flops slapping against the sidewalk as she walked. "Okay, spill."

"Well, um… you remember what happened at the stadium?"

Her eyebrows scrunched together, like she was searching through a mental filing cabinet for something that didn't exist. "You mean you almost rolling down the bleachers with our drinks?"

"What? No. Not that."

"Oh."

I sighed. "Anyway, do you remember anything else? Like, about a stalker?"

That earned me a raised brow. "A stalker?"

"Yeah. And you fainting at Charlie's?"

She stifled a laugh, bordering a snort. "Seriously? Oh, I've got to hear all about this." We were rounding the corner to Dawn's house now, and I already regretted bringing it up.

"Later," I muttered. The last thing I wanted was Dawn butting into this conversation. "We'll talk after."

Sam pouted dramatically. "So unfair. Teasing me like that! I totally need to hear about this stalker thing."

"Someone has a stalker?" Dawn's voice cut in before I could respond. "Or is doing the stalking?" She stood on her porch, sucking on a red Popsicle like she was auditioning for a commercial, music blaring from her backyard. Her sleek black ponytail swayed with her exaggerated lean against one of the white columns on her wraparound porch.

"No, neither," I said quickly. "It's a boring story." I waved it off, trying not to sound as irritated as I felt. "Are we late?"

Dawn arched a perfectly sculpted brow. "Yeah, um, prompt is definitely not your thing." Her straight, blindingly white smile practically sparkled. "Come on, I got everything set up out back."

We followed her through the sun-drenched foyer, the light bouncing off the polished wooden floors and reflecting through the arched windows. Dawn's swagger was in full force, hips swaying just enough to remind you she wanted her bikini-clad backside to be noticed. Sam pulled her cover up off and I followed suite, hanging my sundress over one arm as we continued our trek through her mini mansion.

"Nice bikini, by the way," Dawn said over her shoulder. "New, right?"

Nope. Had it since last summer. "Yep."

"Cobalt's a good color for you."

Sam shot me a look, and I bit back a laugh, knowing exactly what she was thinking. Dawn, forever the wannabe fashion influencer. The air was practically buzzing with the sound of her own self-importance.

Dawn's backyard was the kind of paradise only money—and Philip, her eternally sweaty gardener—could create. He waved at us while packing up his tools, his smile as greasy as the hair plastered to his forehead. Not exactly movie material, but Philip had always been nice, which earned him a solid spot in my good graces.

The rhythm of the bass pumping through the speakers began to chip away at my stress with every beat. Maybe this wasn't such a terrible idea after all. Good jams, an endless supply of Dr. Pepper, and enough strawberries to make my stomach hurt got me through the next couple of hours in total guyless bliss. Some of them were even stress-free. We painted our nails, belted out songs—Dawn's hilariously off-key—and took turns lounging by the pool. My "dip" in the pool was just me sitting on the steps, legs dangling in the water. Close enough.

Yep, girl time was exactly the medication I needed. Even if I couldn't completely stop thinking about Paul, Greek gods wanting to kill me, and the whole savior of mankind gig. Because, honestly, who can just forget something like that? Not to mention, the heebie-jeebies crawling up my arm like static electricity were a sure sign one of my god-friends was lurking around, probably enjoying the view.

Sam and I stretched out on either side of Dawn in wooden lounge chairs, sipping our drinks through straws like we were some high-class celebrities. The sun warmed my skin, and for once, I almost felt normal.

Until Sam gasped, whipping off her sunglasses. "Dawn, what is he doing?"

Dawn shielded her eyes, squinting toward the second-floor window where her little brother stood, phone in hand.

"Is he—oh my God, is he taking a picture?" Sam sat up straighter, her face twisted in disbelief.

I laughed. "Dude, your brother's a perv."

"Lee!" Dawn jumped to her feet, her voice a shriek. "I told you to stay invisible, you little shit! I'm going to find that stupid phone of yours and run it over with my car!"

Her speed-walking tirade, especially in that bikini, was too much. I busted out laughing.

"Jessa, that's so not funny! What if he plasters it all over social media or something?"

I shrugged and stood, wiping tears of laughter from my eyes. "So what? You look good in that little red bikini of yours. And don't forget, Dawn thinks cobalt is *so* my color." I rolled my eyes for emphasis.

"Where're you going?"

"Bathroom." I darted across the blazing patio, my feet barely skimming the ground to avoid third-degree burns. But my steps had a purpose, and it wasn't to pee. I was done feeling like someone was constantly breathing down my neck. This was not going to be the rest of my life.

I stepped into the half-bath under the staircase, locking the door with a click. "Okay, whoever the hell you are, show yourself." Dawn was clear on the other side of the house, so I didn't have to worry about her eavesdropping. For now, anyway.

I stared at my reflection, catching the slight red tint spreading over the bridge of my nose and cheeks. Crap. Forgot the sunblock again.

Nothing happened. My patience was about as thin as the hair left on my mom's boyfriend's bald spot. I sighed, flipping on the faucet and washing my hands with cranberry-pomegranate scented soap. I hated soap that smelled like food. The sweetness clung to my skin as I dried my hands on the mauve towel, irritation about to boil over. "Come on. I can *feel* you."

The air shifted, heavy and charged, making my ears pop. I flinched, even though I'd been waiting for it.

Paul leaned against the doorframe, his smile all amusement. "You asked for it."

"Still." I pressed my palm to my chest, willing my lungs to calm. "I don't think I'll ever get used to that."

The familiar grip of an impending asthma attack pinched my chest. He'd healed me before, but I wasn't sure how it worked—was it his touch?

Or would my touch work, too? Curiosity won out. Without overthinking it, I brushed my hand against his arm. Instantly, my lungs opened up, and it felt like I'd just breathed in the crispest mountain air, every inhale clean and full.

Paul's eyes flickered with something that looked an awful lot like desire before he quickly looked away, his face smoothing into that maddeningly unreadable expression. Reserved. Controlled. Like he was holding himself back. Did I always feel *fixed* when we touched? I wanted to ask, but the reason I'd stormed into the bathroom slammed back into focus.

"Why are you hounding me?" My voice carried more bite than I'd intended.

He tilted his head, clearly amused. "Hounding you?"

"Fine. Stalking me, then."

He let out a puff of air and crossed his arms. "I'm your Guardian." His voice was steady, but something flickered in his eyes—an emotion he was working hard to suppress.

"Paul, I can't live with someone constantly looking over my shoulder." I crossed my arms beneath my bikini top, mimicking his stance. His eyes flicked downward, just for a second, and a rush of awkward energy zinged through me. God or not, he was still a guy. I dropped my arms, hoping to salvage some dignity, but the twitch at the corner of his mouth only irritated me further.

"Is the world ending?" I asked, sucking in my cheeks to keep my irritation in check.

"No."

"Is Thanatos here?"

"No."

"Is a demon about to rip someone's heart out?"

"What? No." His push off the doorframe was fluid, graceful, but the set of his jaw and the fire in his eyes said he was battling something—maybe himself.

"Then why are you here?" The frustration in my voice edged higher.

He stepped closer, shrinking the space between us. A charge purred in the air, making it harder to breathe. The room suddenly felt smaller, and something I couldn't name stirred inside me. Heat, a pull to him, like gravity was working overtime.

"To protect you," he said, his tone low... different.

I swallowed hard, trying to ignore the swirl of emotions his closeness stirred. His gaze left my thoughts a tangled mess. "From what? Drowning in the pool? I'm a big girl. I can take care of myself around my friends."

His eyes shifted, his intensity faltering, and something flickered there in its place—pain, dull and unguarded, like an old wound torn open. He seemed far away, lost in something darker, something deeper.

He blinked, and it was gone. His features hardened, lips thinning as his voice dropped, firm but controlled. "You must start taking this seriously. I know it's a lot. Under normal circumstances—"

I cut him off with a sudden laugh. "Normal? What is normal about any of this?"

He didn't flinch, didn't even blink. "Under normal circumstances," he repeated, like I hadn't spoken, "you'd be trained at a steady pace. The truth would come in pieces, not all at once. But with Thanatos and his demons hunting you, we don't have that luxury. There's too much you don't understand."

"How am I supposed to handle this when no one tells me the full story?" I waved my arms wildly during my near-hysterical tirade, forcing him to step back. "I don't even know what I'm up against, or why some psycho god wants me dead! I'm just supposed to trust you? To go along with rules that make no sense and pray I don't screw it all up? Normal is gone. Safety is gone."

The tension in Paul's expression sharpened the golden glow beginning to circle his irises. My stomach twisted. What did Apollo look like when he lost his temper? Did I really want to find out?

"You think you're safe? You're not. He knows where you live, Jessa. Every night, every single night, we're fighting off his demons to keep you alive until you can do it yourself."

My back hit the wall, and I froze. His words, so matter of fact, stripped away the thin veil of denial I'd been clinging to. Demons surrounding my house? Images of slimy, grotesque monsters—part movie horror, part fevered imagination—flashed through my mind. My breath came in short gasps as the reality of it all closed in on me and I pressed a hand to my chest, trying to stop the spiral.

"I can't do this," I said, my voice shaking, betraying every ounce of fear I'd tried to bury. "I can't."

I shook my head, willing the panic away. "Jesus, I can't even breathe on my own!" I stumbled to the toilet, its mauve carpet-cover as ridiculous as my crumbling composure. Sitting down, I cradled my head in my hands, staring at the bathroom tiles. "I don't have anyone to talk to now. No one to help me deal with all this shit. You took that from me. My only chance at sanity."

Paul crouched in front of me, his movements measured as he leaned in just enough to demand my attention. "What do you mean we took your only chance at being sane?"

I snapped my head up, the motion breaking through the heavy tension in the cramped bathroom. "Oh, please, don't play dumb. I know you took Sam's memory. She doesn't remember anything. That's not fair!"

"You told a mortal?" Of course that was his first reaction. Not an apology. Not a shred of remorse. Just the accusation, abrupt and cutting.

"Of course I tol—"

His hands gripped my shoulders before I could finish, the heat from his touch searing hot. He didn't let go, crouched there, his golden gaze fixed on mine.

"Jessa, how careless are you?" Each word landed with heavy blame. "You can't tell mortals about this. *You* are made to handle this. You're a *demigod*. They're not. Their minds aren't built to comprehend this world or the dangers you face."

I laughed, sharp and bitter, rising to my feet so fast he had to step back. "You think I'm handling this? Seriously? Because from where I'm standing, I'm doing a freaktastic job." About to tell him where he could shove his no-telling-mortals rule, he cut me off.

"I can't... we can't protect you and all your friends. You have a new responsibility now, Jessa. I know it's hard to adjust, but you have no choice." Tension thrummed beneath every word. His fists clenched, knuckles whitening as his uneven breaths betrayed the effort it took to stay calm.

If my eyes could do the angry swirling golden mist thing his were doing, they'd be storm clouds by now. "There's always a choice," I said between clenched teeth, voice shaky.

"The only other option is death."

I wanted to go home and curl up in bed with my mom reading to me. I wanted to rewind time to before any of this, back when the most complicated thing in my life was figuring out how to avoid Zach at school. I needed some kind of promise that everything would be okay, that demons weren't going to break into my house, eat my mom, and kill me before I even had a chance to fight back. What had my life turned into?

I turned back to the sink and gripped the edges. Paul's hand settled on my shoulder, the warmth of his touch easing my frantic breathing. But it didn't calm the tangle of desperation clawing at the edges of my control, threatening to pull me apart piece by piece. His voice softened, a thread of gentleness breaking through his earlier frustration. "I know it's hard."

"Do you? You've never been in this situation. You're always the god, the one who knows everything, who's immortal, who can't be hurt."

My eyes squeezed shut, the pressure behind them building as I fought back tears. "I need someone else to talk to. Someone normal. Someone who can actually understand."

His hand fell from my shoulder, the loss of warmth sudden and stark. I looked up, catching his reflection in the mirror as he stepped back, his face hardening into that stony mask again.

"You can't," he said, his tone as stubborn as the expression on his face. "I'm sorry. It's too dangerous—for the mortal you tell, and for us. They become collateral damage in the end, Jessa. Is that small piece of sanity worth their life?"

I couldn't answer that question. Not here. Not now. The lump in my throat refused to let the words out, and I was terrified my voice would crack, betraying the tears I was barely holding back.

"Listen," Paul said, his tone gentler now. "You need space. I get that. I'll try to give it to you when you're with your friends. But I'll always be close enough to know if you need me. Always. If you ever need my help, just call me."

He paused, his eyes roaming my face for seconds that felt like an eternity. "And tonight… meet me on the roof. We'll start preparing you, properly this time."

Before I could respond, footsteps echoed down the hall, heading toward the bathroom. Paul vanished in a faint rush of wind, leaving behind only the charged air of his presence and the weight of everything he'd said.

☉☽ CHAPTER 11 ☾☉

Shopping with Mom used to be my escape—counting down to a near-limitless spree, feeding my inner fashionista. But now, it felt pointless, like playing dress-up while the world was on fire. The rituals we'd built over the years, our back-to-school hauls and weekend trips, felt hollow. Like I was grasping at something that wasn't there anymore.

How exactly does one train to be Herculean? Is there a crash course, or do I just start lifting cars? More importantly, would I even survive long enough to meet Paul tonight? That chat in Dawn's bathroom hadn't just left me depressed, it had cranked my paranoia up to level 3,000.

"Jessa, hun, yes or no?" My mom hung up a turquoise top. Her impatient glare made it clear she'd already asked this once.

I shrugged. "Yeah, it works."

"With these, you think?" She held up a pair of black strappy heels.

I nodded, but my thoughts stayed locked on the fight with Death in my front yard. It was only a matter of time before I'd have to face Hypnos and Thanatos again. It wasn't until then, replaying the images of those two freaks, that I realized they were brothers. Hypnos, with his black hair, yellow eyes, and sharp teeth, was the perfect foil to Thanatos, who looked like he'd stepped out of a Chinese costume drama, his alabaster skin gleaming and waist-length white hair flowing. The only thing they had in common was their ability to send a chill down my spine.

My mom stood inches in front of me, patience thinning. "Come on, Jessa. Try to be a little enthusiastic. This is our day!"

I rubbed my face with a sigh. "You're right. Sorry." Why couldn't I just enjoy this one day with her? Was it too much to ask for one moment to feel normal? I wished there were a way to balance everything—normal life, weird life. Like pineapple on pizza, there had to be a way to make it work.

Think positive, Jessa. I could do it. It would just take some getting used to. And my feet weren't even wet yet with my supposed badass abilities. Right. Good thoughts. The whole hopeless, depressed-girl thing wasn't really me, anyway.

I took in the outfit my mom had pieced together. "Yeah, I like that. And maybe with these earrings?" I flipped the earring tower on the glass counter and thumbed a pair of hoops with turquoise and black beads.

Her face lit up. "You sure you don't want to be a fashion designer?"

"Please, Mom. No college talk."

She laughed behind pursed lips, leading me to another aisle of clothes in shades of red. But then a sudden tug in my brain halted me in my tracks. Colors exploded behind my eyes as a vision overtook me, drowning out my current reality.

The River Acheron glistened black, its depths swallowing the dim orange glow of torchlight hooked to Charon's boat. The ferryman stood silent, guiding his vessel packed with restless souls toward their final destination. Whispers crawled through my brain, their voices tangling with the soft lapping of the water—pleas, urges, songs, all laced with anguish that sank deep into my chest.

But unlike earlier visions, this one felt different. Like a countdown.

The river shifted, morphed into a new river. Fire ripped across the waters, obliterating everything in its path. The river of Phlegethon. The earth roared open, flames and the dead pouring into the streets, chasing down humans until nothing remained but ash and echoes. Screams pierced through my skull, each one more excruciating than the last.

Through the inferno strode a bearded man, his towering frame unyielding against the frenzy. In one hand, he wielded a massive sword that gleamed in the firelight. Behind him, volcanoes erupted in violent rhythm, their tremors rattling the earth. At his waist, six pairs of glowing eyes blinked into existence, their glares slicing through the smoke like a warning.

My surroundings blinked back into focus, and I stumbled into my mom.

"Jessa, for heaven's sake, watch where you're going!" she snapped, steadying herself on a rack.

"Right. Sorry." I brushed past her to sit on a nearby shoe bench. My heart thundered, the vision's remnants scraping against the edges of my thoughts. This wasn't just some cryptic prophecy. It was a warning… a promise. The attack wasn't coming. It had already begun.

"Ma'am?"

The pointed tone pulled me back to reality, and I blinked up at the store clerk. "Ma'am, did you want to try something on?"

I shook my head slightly, refocusing. My mom stood in front of me, arms full of clothes, looking mildly exasperated. "Alright, try these on."

Oh, joy.

The next hour passed in a blur. I moved like a robot, trying on outfit after outfit for my new summer wardrobe, barely noticing what I was wearing. My mind replayed the images from my vision. The River Phlegethon, burning people, the towering man with the sword and those glowing eyes. I repeated them until the visuals seared into my brain. Pun intended.

Too many times before, I'd woken up from visions with only fragments left, but I couldn't afford to forget anymore. I needed to remember.

It wasn't until my mom pulled into the driveway and killed the engine that I finally came back to the present. She turned to look at me, and I sank further into my seat under her heavy gaze. That spectacularly effective mix of "you are such an ungrateful daughter" and "don't you love me?" was etched into her expression.

The silence between us felt heavier than I'd expected. Once, shopping trips like this were our escape—bonding over hideous neon leggings or debating the ethics of crop tops. Now, I was just going through the motions, nodding at clothes I barely saw, pretending everything was fine.

But it wasn't.

She was waiting for me to speak, but my voice caught, stuck somewhere deep in my throat. How could I explain it? That my life was no longer just mine to share. That the gods, demons, and responsibilities pulling me under made the world we'd built together feel impossibly far away.

The truth was, I was losing her. Losing us.

I stared out the window as the sky deepened to indigo, the last sliver of daylight clinging to the horizon like it wasn't ready to let go. Shadows stretched long and thin across the street, reaching through the trees like fingers trying to pull the day into night. A perfect picture of normal life. Too bad my ship had sailed, leaving me stranded on the shores of chaos.

Her hands gripped the steering wheel a little too tightly, her knuckles pale against the leather. The heavy silence in the car was like a clock counting down to something unsaid. Her lips pressed into a thin line, the faintest crease forming between her brows. Small signs I might have missed before but now seemed so loud.

She was still looking at me, her eyes questioning. And for a second— just one—I imagined telling her everything. But the thought of her face crumbling under the weight of my truth stopped me cold.

Finally, she unbuckled her seatbelt and grabbed her keys, never taking her eyes off me until she stepped out and slammed the door shut. The sound echoed like a final punctuation mark to all our unsaid words.

I exhaled slowly, willing the knot in my chest to loosen, but it only wound tighter. I buried my face in my hands, letting out a frustrated growl.

Maybe it was stupid to think I could keep two lives from colliding. But I couldn't seem to let go of the delusion.

☉☽ CHAPTER 12 ☾☉

That night after dinner, I escaped into my room before mom could barrage me with more questions. Everything was why. Why the mood swings, why the moping, why the ungratefulness. Blech.

I let out a long, meditative exhale, and tried focusing on tonight. Not sure what exactly to wear when one trains to be a demi guardian, I changed into my favorite pair of cut-offs, rummaging through my shirts to find a cute one. Sure, I was a little out of my league with Paul, but the guy, er, god, was hot. Not hot in the conventional sense, like Hollywood's boy heartthrobs, but classic. Sexy, like if Ryan Reynolds and Henry Cavill had a baby.

Frowning at Zach's old jersey hiding under a pile of shirts, I made a mental note to burn it before school started and snatched a pink sleeveless hoodie. I threw it on over a white tank and examined myself in the full-length mirror on my closet door. I needed to pluck my eyebrows but for now, it would do.

I ditched any sort of fashion accessory. The last thing I'd want was my ear to be ripped off thanks to demon claws getting stuck in a hoop. I pulled my hair up into a ponytail and slid my phone in my pocket. Did demons even have claws?

Socks and Converse shoes finished off the look for my first night of kicking demon ass. Positive thoughts. I would be kicking demon ass and not the other way around. Right?

Right.

I stared at myself in the mirror and laughed. This was beyond mental. I looked nothing like a demigod. I looked like a normal girl-next-door nobody. Maybe that was the point? Before my thoughts could get much further, the hairs on my arms sprang up. The effect rushed down the rest of my body. I turned, walked to my window, and pushed it up.

As I suspected, Paul waited for me on the rooftop. "Ready?" he asked.

"I guess." I climbed out onto the roof and crouched next to him. I was a little nervous about how to react around him after our conversation at Dawn's, or argument, or whatever it had been.

But Paul seemed just like the Paul that sat with me on my roof the night before: calm, relaxed, seriousness mixed with a hint of liveliness. "Your mom?"

I shrugged. "She thinks I'm brooding."

He perked up an eyebrow but didn't pry. "Have you had any more visions?"

So, he didn't plan on jumping right in with the training or what we'd talked about earlier. Fine by me, it worked wonders for my nerves. I sat next to him. "Actually, yeah, I did."

He turned to face me, giving me his full attention. "And?"

Suddenly, I felt a wave of nervousness, like I might say the wrong thing or that my visions weren't impressive enough. I swiped through the images in my mind, like scrolling through photos on my phone. "Fire seems to be the theme. I was in the River Acheron first, then Phlegethon."

I caught his subtle movement, a tenseness maybe, and it only amplified the need to say something important. I crossed my legs and scratched the black sandy stuff on the shingles. "Lots of the dead, Charon, and then fire."

Paul was somewhere else, his eyes distant, and his face hard. It would make my life so much easier if I could just plug into his brain and understand him and his world. It hadn't been the first time I'd caught myself wanting that. I cleared my throat and decided to keep going. "Fire took over the river, and then I saw earth. Volcanoes, more fire, screaming people. A man and a..." I stopped, because honestly, I had no idea what exactly it was I'd seen. "A bunch of glowing eyes." I flicked some shingle crumbs off the roof. "Any idea what all that means?"

Paul sat back and let out a sigh through his nose. "Fire and volcanoes usually symbolize Hephaestus."

"Right, the god of fire. But he's not an Underworld god?"

Paul shook his head. "Technically, no. But he's the only god we know who can destroy a soul. He did it once, a long time ago. Anyway, it makes little difference anymore where gods associate themselves. Anyone can choose to work for the dark powers of the Underworld. Ever since—" He paused, his gaze flickering toward the horizon as if the memory itself was too heavy to meet my eyes. "Since the Great Flood, everyone felt it their right to choose who they work with."

"The Great Flood?" I thought for a moment. "As in Noah's Ark?"

"That's one of the stories related to it, yes."

Wait. Noah's Ark? That wasn't history—it was biblical. Or mythical. Or maybe both? As if mythology hadn't already blurred into reality, now I had to wrap my head around biblical stories being part of this whole mess, too? And what was with this destroying-a-soul thing? I wanted more. I studied Paul, not understanding his sudden mood swing. His frown sent my chest tingling. Apparently, I didn't like seeing him upset.

"What do you mean destroying a soul? How many stories are there that I'm not aware of? And why did this flood change the way the Guardians do things?"

"Gods," he said simply. The word hung in the air between us, daring me to question it. For a moment, something flickered in his eyes—an emotion I couldn't quite place. His eyes stayed fixed on me, as though he wanted to say something he shouldn't. His body tensed, his shoulders stiffening, but just as quickly as the moment appeared, it vanished. His calm slipped back into place like a mask he'd worn too often. I watched him closely, wondering if that calm was real, or if, beneath it, he was just as conflicted as I was.

He cleared his throat and continued, "Not all of us gods are Guardians, only a select few that have sworn and proven their loyalty to the point of becoming mortal if it's broken. Me, Henry, Cynthia, and a few others. Because of this, when we're in mortal form, like I am with you now, we don't have our full powers. That's why your training matters, Jessa. We can only protect you so much."

This was all way over my head. My jaw clicked as I ground my teeth. "Paul," I started, hating the edge in my voice. "How am I going to learn all of this? It's like a whole new reality I have to figure out, and I can hardly grasp everything you're throwing at me."

"You said you wanted to know."

Not what I wanted to hear. "So, let me get this straight. Greek gods exist, but not all are like you, a Guardian. Guardians don't have their full godly powers, and as for the gods, some work for the Underworld, while others, what, stay neutral? Those associated with the Underworld want to wipe out the humans or destroy souls… whatever that means. Why? I have no idea. Because we're mortal? Hardly, that couldn't be it or else we'd have been gone the minute we, um, were."

Yeah, I had to sound like a blabbering idiot, but my head lacked that "it's time to shut up" switch. Talking it out made it somehow more logical in my head.

I let out my breath and kept going. "This Great Flood, or Noah's Ark, that destroyed most of mankind was spurred on by… the Underworld? Their first attempt to get rid of us? And after that, the rules changed and any god could be on any side, the whole good versus evil thing. And now Hephaestus has this plan to burn us," I paused, realizing I wasn't part of that 'us'. I wasn't human. I was only half of them. My heart flattened at that thought. "Them," I corrected. "Am I close?"

My heart bounced around in my chest at the smile forming on Paul's lips. He smirked, the corner of his mouth twitching like he was fighting back actual pride. "Not bad, rookie."

I relaxed my jaw. Paul's change in mood erased the intensity that had pinned me down a second ago. "So, what did I miss?"

Paul stood and dusted himself off. The breeze caught the collar of his black shirt. It wasn't buttoned all the way, showing the black cotton tee beneath. I'd never seen him decked out in black. His image did a number on my nerves. Dark worked for him.

"The Flood wasn't their first attempt." He gave me a sideways glance. "It was their first success."

"Oh." That was a little terrifying. But he didn't give me much chance to dwell on it.

"Ready?"

The training thing. I'd completely forgotten. I wanted to ask him more questions, feed my brain so it could grow with this new "I'm a demigod" life, but everything about Paul screamed to get off the subject.

"Right, yeah." I scooted to my window and got one leg in before noticing Paul wasn't following. He smiled a little and nodded his head toward the ground. My throat closed and for a moment, I felt like the roof ripped out from under me.

Shaking my head, I gripped the window frame. "No." Deep breaths. "You don't seriously expect me to jump down, do you?"

"First lesson," Paul said, nodding toward the edge of the roof again.

"What, to break a leg?"

"To see what you're capable of," he said. "Every demi is different. We won't know your strength, your limits, until we test them. This isn't just about courage. It's about unlocking what's already inside you. And we're running out of time."

Heights and I were not friends, and the thought of stepping off the roof felt less like a lesson and more like a death wish. "And if what's inside me is just, I don't know, normal?"

His face stayed deadpan, but his eyes carried the faintest spark of amusement. "You're not normal, and you know it. Stop stalling."

"I'm not stalling," I muttered. Demons? Fine. But jumping off a roof? I'd rather take my chances with a four-headed Cyclops. I moved my leg inch by inch out from the open window. "So how do you know I *won't* break a leg?" He just stared at me, his way of letting me work that out on my own. "You don't. Great."

Each step I took toward the edge of the roof felt heavier, like my legs were weighed down with lead. My brain hurt from focusing so hard on not slipping. If I was going to break my legs, dammit, I'd at least do it with some grace. Knowing Paul had the power to heal didn't make me feel any better about my possible outcome.

"We don't have all night," he said, his tone dripping with teasing authority.

I shot him a scowl, which only made his smile widen. "You're thoroughly enjoying this, aren't you?"

"Just a little."

I took a deep breath, let it out, and hoped some of my terror went with it. The patch of grass waited below, distant and unforgiving, making my stomach lurch as if I were already falling.

"I can't," I whispered.

The wind stopped brushing against my back, and I knew Paul had moved closer. His hands rested on my shoulders, and just like that, my anxiety began to dissolve. My chest loosened and my breathing steadied.

"Sure you can," he murmured, his lips so close to my ear that his breath tickled my skin. "Count to five."

His closeness stirred something deep inside me, a mix of unease and reassurance that made it impossible to focus on anything else. I clenched my fists, hating the tremble in my hands and wishing I could be braver—especially right now. Stupid fear of heights.

"I won't let anything happen to you," he said, his voice gentle, coaxing, like he was trying to draw a skittish animal out of hiding. His breath was warm against my ear, sending a ripple through my pulse and raising the fine hairs on my skin. There was something in his tone, an urgency that hinted this wasn't just about my jump.

I loosened my fists, letting his words settle in. If I couldn't face this, how was I supposed to face anything else? Taking a deep breath, I stepped to the edge.

"Ready?" he asked. "One, two, three…"

With a deep breath, I finished the count with him. "Four, five." I launched myself off the roof, the wind rushing against my face as I fell—terrified, hopeful, and slightly exhilarated.

☉☽ CHAPTER 13 ☾☉

The wind snatched my hair, and gravity sent my stomach whirling. The fall stretched on, each second amplifying my terror. For a fleeting moment, I panicked. What if the ground opened up to devour me? But then, with an *umph*, my feet hit something solid. I had squeezed my eyes shut sometime during my literal leap of faith and pried one eye open to look down.

Grass. My feet were on grass. Relief washed over me, then pride bubbled up, pushing aside the fear. "Hah!" I grinned, searching for Paul.

The wide alley between Zach's house and mine was quiet, shrubbery and flowers packed against the sides of the houses. Zach's house blocked the moon from shedding any light and I glanced back up to my bedroom window, half expecting to see my mom. Hopefully, she was still getting her reality TV fix for the night.

Paul leaned casually against the white lattice connected to Zach's house, arms crossed. Not sure when he'd made it down here, but it didn't matter. Thanks to my bedroom light, I was able to see one corner of his mouth curl up. "See?"

I couldn't help but eat up the satisfaction in his voice. I dusted my hands off on my shorts, bubbling with pride.

"So now what? We've already established I have superhuman strength." I flexed my muscles, the thrill of the jump swinging my mood into full gleedom. Especially seeing as I didn't fall into a heap of broken bones.

Paul shook his head with a laugh. He pushed away from the lattice and walked past me. "Let's see how fast you are." In a gust of air, he was gone.

"Wait," the rest of my words hung on my lips, my eyes catching the subtle far away movement of someone running. Damn, he was fast.

Pushing past the idea of feeling stupid sprinting down the sidewalk of my neighborhood for no particular reason, I ran. Part of me felt smug, chanting silently that it didn't matter if neighbors saw me because I was someone "special".

The gods must've heard my thoughts, because my lesson in humility gripped my lungs and crushed. I stumbled to a stop after three houses, hunched over, gasping for air. My fingers clawed at my chest, searching for relief that wouldn't come. So much for being superhuman.

Paul appeared beside me in an instant, his hands firm on my arm. A calming energy radiated through me, loosening the tightness in my lungs. The air rushed back, and I straightened slowly, embarrassment prickling my skin. I should be used to humiliation by now, especially after all the shit that had gone down the past few days. But no, this topped it all. Here I was, training to be a Demi Guardian, and I couldn't even run. Sure, it'd happened before around him, but things were different now.

Why couldn't Cynthia train me? She'd be much easier to fail in front of.

"This is stupid," I said, swallowing a cough and looking everywhere but at him. "What demigod can't run? Seriously, the second demons try and escape, I'm screwed."

He was about to say something, but I shot him a sharp look. "And I can't expect you to be shadowing me every second of my life, so no, that won't help, either." I walked away, flexing my fingers, hating that I hated myself.

Being smart, Paul gave me some distance until I got back to my house. I slumped down on the driveway, leaning against the bumper of my car. How was this supposed to work? Either I'd screw it up and watch the world burn, or I'd get replaced by a better Hercules.

Paul watched me, his hair tousled by the breeze, hands stuffed in his pockets.

"Afraid you'll catch my lameness or something?" I teased, forcing a weak smile. "Sit."

He looked puzzled for a second before grinning. "Yes, ma'am."

He sat beside me, elbows on his knees, his calm presence wrapping around me like a warm blanket. He really needed to wear black more often. Watching him, I forgot how useless I felt. My soul felt like it'd been set on fire—in a good way. He even smelled amazing, better than any cologne I'd ever sprayed on Zach during our shopping trips.

The moment didn't last. My brain, ever the killjoy, reminded me how far I had to go as a demigod. How useless I still felt.

"So," I picked at some grass growing in the seam between the driveway and sidewalk. "So much for the training, I guess?"

"What do you mean?"

I hated the queasy feeling sloshing around in my stomach. "Disappointed?"

He didn't answer, and with each second of silence that ticked by, my confidence spiraled further down a flushing toilet. I had to admit, even with Zach, I never cared this much about what someone thought of me. What bothered me more was that I didn't understand why. Yeah, he was a god and all or use to be—I remained confused on that detail—but every time he's around, my insides start some weird dance-a-thon, a mixture between queasy and pure excitement. I lacked any sort of control over it, and I hated that.

When I focused back on Paul, I realized he'd been staring at me. There was a hint of something familiar in his almost-smile as he finally answered my question of being a total loser in the demigod category. "No."

I stopped holding my breath. "Why?"

"There's more to being a Demi than running around slaying demons. So you can't run, doesn't mean there aren't other ways."

I rolled my eyes. "What, like flying?"

He shrugged. "Maybe."

Holy shit.

I imagined myself flying, the wind brushing through my hair, the warmth of the sun on my back. The image of soaring high above the ground, free and weightless, was almost enough to make me laugh. Wasn't I supposed to be terrified of heights? Somehow, the excitement of the possibility made me forget.

Twirling strands of grass between my fingers, I watched the Andersons through their bay window, eating dinner with the TV flickering in the background. "What else can Demis do?"

"It really just depends. You all have the strength factor. Some have had healing, others speed or breathing underwater."

"Really?" I sat up, my interest piqued. Suddenly, finding out what I could do didn't seem so bad.

"Really. Now, can we get on with this training of yours, or do you want to mope some more?"

"I'm not moping."

"Oh?" He raised his eyebrows in a way that said, then-what-are-you-doing?

I sighed. "Fine, maybe a little. But I'm done."

"Sure?" A smile tugged at the corners of his mouth.

"Yes," I said, a little less patient.

Paul stood and held out a hand. Reluctantly, I took it and let him pull me to my feet. He reached into his button up and pulled out two gleaming weapons. The polished silver caught the moonlight, scattering sharp beams across the driveway.

"Baby tridents?" I said, eyebrows raised.

He grinned, suppressing a laugh. "Close, but not quite. They're called Sais."

"Sais," I repeated, tasting the word on my tongue as I carefully took them from his hands. The cool metal hummed against my palms, a strange mix of adrenaline and power coursing through me.

"Here, let me show you how to hold them." Paul stepped closer, positioning himself behind me. His hands settled over mine, steady and sure, guiding my grip on the sais. The closeness sent a spark through me, leaving my breath uneven and my heart thudding in my chest.

"So, the pointy end—" I began, trying to keep my thoughts from scattering.

"—is the blade," he finished for me, his voice low and teasing in my ear. "And the non-sharpy end," he continued, his fingers adjusting mine with deliberate slowness, "is called the hilt. You'll want to hold it like this for balance."

I glanced up at him from the corner of my eye, expecting to feel irritation at his playful teasing. But instead, a smile tugged at my lips. His touch, the warmth of his body so close to mine, was intoxicating.

Paul shifted even closer, his chest brushing lightly against my back as he helped me adjust my stance. His hands adjusting mine, his touch sending a wave of something deeper than just heat through me—something that left me yearning for more.

"Keep your wrists loose," he said, his hands sliding down to adjust my grip again, his fingers skating over my skin in a way that made my heart stutter. "You don't want to be too rigid, or you'll lose control of the weapon."

"Right," I nodded, swallowing hard as I tried to concentrate.

"Let's try a few basic moves," Paul suggested, stepping back slightly. "Start with a simple strike."

He guided my arm in a swift, downward motion, the movement smooth and controlled. I mimicked the motion, feeling the sais slice through the air. The thrill of it sent a rush through me that was both empowering and a little addictive.

I glanced back at Paul, who watched me with that same mix of curiosity and something else I couldn't quite place. There was an undeniable charge between us, something simmering just beneath the surface. It was as if every touch, every glance, carried a hidden meaning, one I couldn't fully understand but couldn't help wanting to explore.

"So, like this?" I adjusted my grip on the sais and mimicked the move he'd just shown me, swinging one in a rounded arc. The motion wasn't as smooth as his, but holding the weapon felt liberating, even as I pushed through the awkwardness.

He smirked, eyes locked on mine. "Something like that."

I turned the baby tridents over in my hands, still trying to figure out how the hell these things were supposed to fit into my life, let alone my wardrobe. Before I could even begin to imagine it, Paul pulled out a leather belt with little... pockets? No, not pockets—sheaths. In one smooth motion, he wrapped the belt around my waist, his movements so fluid it felt like second nature. He pulled me a little closer as he buckled it, his hands resting lightly on my waist afterward, as if the gesture was instinctive.

"This sheath is for your sais," he said, like we weren't talking about weapons at all, but about something secretive… forbidden. His touch lingered just a moment longer than necessary before he stepped back, leaving a warmth in its wake that had nothing to do with the belt.

I tried to swallow the nervous flutter in my chest and cleared my throat. Okay, not baby tridents—sais. But I think I liked the term baby tridents better.

Paul broke through my semi-studious memory-storing. "You okay?"

"Yeah, fine. Just thinking."

He tsked. "Careful."

I laughed, an unexpected reaction. It felt good, like life was pouring through me. "You're funny when you want to be."

"I try. So, what's on your mind?"

You. Everything about you. "Stuff."

"Let's walk." And with that, we strolled down the sidewalk. It was some pretty unorthodox training.

I had to get my mind on something to think about other than the intoxicating scent and sight of Paul. I was such nerd. I couldn't help myself. I'd done the same thing with Zach. The thought stirred up unwanted emotions, feelings I knew would only make me cling to Paul more. Maybe that's what this was about... lacking a guy after years of non-stop cool boyfriend relationship thing I had with Zach. Man, Ashlyn sucked.

"So?" Paul watched me from the corner of his eye, arms behind his back.

Yeah, he definitely wouldn't want to talk about Zach. And why did I even think of that as a possible subject? My brain triggered an escape route. *Pick a subject, any subject!* The most pressing thought surfaced first. "My father."

He nodded, as if expecting the question. "Don't know."

I stopped walking. "What? How can you not know?"

He didn't stop, and feeling like an idiot, I jogged to catch up to him.

"Jessa, there are a lot of potentials out there, and, well, you really think we keep tabs on what the elders are doing?" He made a gagged expression.

Okay, it was kind of funny. I know I wouldn't want to know who exactly my mom was, uh, doing. I didn't need visuals.

"So how do we find out?" I hadn't expected to feel as disappointed as I did. My chest even ached a little.

All my life I'd gone without knowing who my father had been, and I learned not caring was the easiest way to get through it. Being so close to knowing, though, had me caring a lot more than I'd planned.

"Usually your abilities."

I curled my lip up. "Figures."

"Don't worry, tonight is about figuring them out." It felt good he had a plan for my training.

A beam of silver light shot up into the sky, splitting the quiet night. I jumped, my heart racing. Not something you saw on a casual stroll through the neighborhood.

Paul went rigid. "Cynthia." He stared hard at me, then the sky, maybe deliberating whether to bring me along or not. But how? There was no way I'd be able to keep up with him.

He spun to me, desperation in his eyes. I found myself willing to do anything for him.

"You're coming with me," he said.

"Wait, what?" My doubt bubbled up, but before I could protest, Paul scooped me into his arms. I yelped, and in a jerk, air smashed against my face, peeling back my eyelids as I tried forcing them shut. The deafening whoosh of air rampaged my ears, threatening to blow my brains right out of my head.

This travel arrangement sucked worse than a punch to the boob.

☉☽ CHAPTER 14 ☾☉

I'd forgotten how fast Paul could move—one second, I was standing; the next, the world blurred into streaks of color and rushing wind. I clung to him, struggling to hook my other arm around his shoulder, half-expecting the speed to rip me away.

Just as I managed to latch on tight, wondering if it was possible to strangle a god, everything came to an abrupt halt. The world spun around me, and it felt like my brain needed a moment to catch up with my body, the sudden stillness leaving me even more disoriented.

So much for my ponytail. My hair tumbled over my shoulders, the hair-tie lost somewhere in the sprint—or whatever the hell it should be called because sprint was hardly worthy. Paul wasn't even out of breath. He set me down gently, my sneakers crunching on twigs. I squinted up at the dark canopy of trees, trying to pinpoint where we were.

Something swished through the trees to our left, and we spun toward it. In the distance, a silver arrow shot through the branches, followed by a grunt. A loud thump echoed nearby, probably the target of the arrow falling into a heap. It sounded big.

"Stay here," Paul said, his tone clipped and protective.

"What? No," I said, grabbing his arm. "You didn't bring me here to stand around while you do all the work. I need to learn. Isn't that the whole point?"

His eyes searched mine and for a second, I thought he'd argue—but instead, he nodded reluctantly. "Fine. But stay close."

"Sure, right, of course." I fell into step beside him, the sais strapped to my hips making me feel like some kind of swaggering cowboy—only, instead of guns, I had ancient weapons. Both of us ducked low, poised to spring into action. "Not like I want to wander off while a bunch of bloodthirsty demons are on the loose."

He shot up a finger that pretty much said "shut up". I wrinkled my nose at him and followed his line of sight. Someone screamed, more a scream of annoyance than of pain.

Cynthia's red hair flashed through the brush. We walked under an opening in the canopy, and I recognized Addison Park.

"It took you like, three seconds to go five miles. You should run a marathon."

Paul either didn't hear me or ignored me. The moment an oversized figure lumbered after Cynthia, he vanished.

"Hey!" I shouted, but I was talking to myself.

I pushed through the tangled mess of trees and shrubs, moving one step at a time. Another arrow whistled through the air. With a sudden, almost unnatural clarity, I tracked its silver gleam as it sliced above my head and into the thicket behind me.

An opening in the trees revealed the park, empty and dark but for the moon and a lamppost nearby. The swings creaked, flying back and forth as if a heavy gust of wind had knocked them into action.

My heart plummeted through my shoes at the rush of footsteps behind and I spun. I choked on my scream and leaped to the side, landing on all fours. The ground trembled beneath each thunderous step as the giant barreled past, his thick skin glinting under the moonlight like oiled leather. The arrow lodged in his shoulder bobbed with every motion, but it didn't slow him. If anything, it seemed to fuel his rage.

Cynthia charged after him, her silver gown catching the moonlight as she fired more arrows. I couldn't decide what was more impressive: her aim or the fact that she was doing all this in a gown. Two, four, six stung the back of the giant before he flopped face first into the merry-go-round.

I rolled over and sat up as a low growl rumbled behind me in the trees. How many giants were there?

I scrambled back in a crab walk. Not fast enough. The ugly beast burst through the trees and stopped short at seeing me. He snarled. God, he was ugly. Droopy, thick lips, bulging eyes, gorilla-like arms. No claws. That was a plus.

I heard another growl behind me in the playground, and another somewhere in the distance. Droopy Lips opened his mouth and roared, blasting me with vomit-inducing breath. I gagged, trying not to barf. As I rolled away to get up and run, he charged at me.

Screaming, I abandoned rolling and jumped to my feet. He jumped at me. Instinctively, I caught him mid-leap and hurled him a few feet away. He landed on his side with a startled whine. I stared at my hands. A white-hot burning sensation had spread throughout my entire body. Strangely, it felt good.

Cynthia cried out. I whipped around, sprinting for her before I could register what was wrong. She threw her bow to the ground at the heap of a motionless giant and let out a ferocious scream that sounded part war cry, part unhinged fury.

"Stupid piece of Underworld dung!" she snarled, her words practically spitting venom. Spotting me, she blinked, her fiery glare turning my way. "Bastard took my arrows!"

I hesitated, unsure whether to laugh or keep my distance. "Uh… you sure told him."

"Not him, idiot." She kicked the unconscious giant like it had insulted her ancestors. "The other one."

I raised an eyebrow. "Dude."

"What? Do you see any arrows on him?" she snapped, gesturing dramatically at the arrow-less heap with both hands like it was obvious.

Right. Note to self: never get on Cynthia's bad side.

"Where's Paul?"

"Don't know," I said, wondering if I should be worried.

I turned as the earth trembled beneath my feet again. The rush of adrenaline made me grin, despite my panting. I felt fearless, indestructible, a total bad ass. This was beyond awesome. Crouching a little, I danced on the balls of my toes, ready to test out my strength again. If I could catch a leaping giant, surely, I could tackle a running one, right?

My toes dug into the soil before I pushed into a run. Cynthia hollered after me, something that sounded a lot like "what the hell are you doing?"

I ignored her, charging at Droopy Lips. His arms widened, fingers flexing as if he planned to smash me into pulp. A spike of fear sliced through me. Shit, what the hell *was* I doing? Too late now.

Centering the raw energy pulsing through me, I pushed it down to my legs and dove into the giant's chest. With a powerful *oomph*, I sent the demon on his back. Droopy Lips's arm swung around and flung me off. My back smacked the earth, a gust of air escaping my lungs.

I groaned and pushed myself up. Ow.

"You idiot!" snapped Cynthia. "You need the sais!"

I changed my mind about my training arrangements. I'd much rather deal with disappointing Paul than having Cynthia on my ass all the time.

Tearing through the trees came a third giant, carrying a familiar bag of arrows, Paul chased after him. I didn't have time to see what was about to happen. Droopy Lips was up and charging again. I got to my feet, my back achy but otherwise fine, and whipped out my baby tridents.

I waved them like fingers, provoking the ugly thing. "Bring it!"

I heard Cynthia laugh. Then, in my peripheral, the giant she'd shot down rolled over and got to his feet.

"I thought you killed it!"

"Only you can kill them, rookie!" Though she was screaming at me, her voice was happy, full of excitement like she lived for this kind of stuff.

Droopy Lips roared, his massive fist swinging toward my chest. I brought up my sais, but too late—his blow landed like a wrecking ball, hurling me through the air. Pain exploded in my ribs as I slammed into the park slide, the impact forcing every ounce of air from my lungs. Again. I slid down, my familiar wheezing drowning out all other commotion.

Paul appeared and pulled me up, his hands firmly on my forearms, his eyes searching mine. Instead of a lecture about my latest act of stupidity, he let his warm, healing energy flow through me.

Two seconds, tops, and then he stepped back and handed me my baby tridents I'd dropped somewhere in my flight. My fingers wrapped around the hilts, still warm from his touch.

"We can only stun them. You, however, can send them back to where they came from."

"I'm not very good at using baby tridents."

Paul seemed torn between laughing and being genuinely concerned about my intelligence. "Sais. They're called sais. And trust me, it'll come to you. You'll remember." His hand stayed on my shoulder, like he wasn't quite ready to let go. We both turned to look at Droopy Lips.

The demon growled, trying to get Cynthia out of his way to get to me. Cynthia yelled some profanities at us before being snatched and hurdled into the swing set.

This was it. No more choices. *Right now, I'm a demigod. Right now, I'm powerful.* I glanced at the sais in both of my hands.

Clueless, but powerful.

I pushed past Paul in a sprint. I reached Droopy Lips before he could snatch Cynthia again, the goddess tangled up in the chains. With a ferocious scream I didn't know I possessed, I swung the sais around randomly, hoping maybe one of my powers was knowing how to use these damn things.

Unfortunately, no.

After a few horrible swipes and narrow ducks from a giant fist, a blade finally stuck into Droopy Lips's side. A gurgling, hideous noise bubbled over his lips.

At the same time, the giant Cynthia had stunned earlier was up and on her. I couldn't spot the third giant. Cynthia's demon yanked swing chains apart and snapped them at her like whips. She did her best to block but instead, the chains wrapped around her arm. I didn't see what happened next.

Droopy Lips reared back, one fist poised to strike. I tried to stab him again with both baby tridents, but I wasn't fast enough. His fist swung around, hard.

A breath later, I realized my face wasn't crunched, not even touched. My eyes opened just in time to see Paul flying haphazardly through the air. Droopy Lips looked agitated, having missed his target. Somehow, Paul had taken the hit for me.

Paul flew into the canopy of trees. The other two giants charged after him. Cynthia screamed savagely, now effectively tied to the swing set, unable to free herself from the chains.

"Get me out of these things!" Cynthia shrieked, going ballistic, desperate to break free.

"I'm a little busy!" I shouted, slashing my baby tridents across Droopy Lips' leathery skin, carving through him like an overcooked brisket.

But it wasn't enough. His thick hide barely gave way under my attack, and his furious roar shook the branches.

Suddenly, a surge of energy rippled through me, raw and instinctive, as if I'd tapped into a well of power buried deep in my bones. My body moved on its own, fluid and precise, like it had been waiting for this moment all along. It felt... natural, but the realization sent a chill through me. What else was hiding inside me, waiting to be unleashed?

Droopy Lips lunged at me again, his massive fist swinging down. But this time, I didn't just react. I anticipated. My body twisted out of the way, the motion fluid and quick, like I'd done it a thousand times before.

"You don't understand! Paul! He needs help! It's night!" At first, Cynthia's words didn't make any sense, and I started to wonder if she'd hit her head a little too hard. But then my stomach twisted before dropping altogether.

A renewed sense of urgency rushed through me. I struck with both blades, each one finding a weak spot in his thick armor-like skin. The weapons felt like extensions of my own arms, guided by an instinct I hadn't known existed, as if my muscles remembered something my mind didn't.

He howled in pain, and I seized the moment. Dropping low, I swept my leg out in a wide arc, using my superhuman strength to knock him off balance. His massive frame staggered, and I was on him in an instant, driving one sai into the soft tissue beneath his ribs while the other sliced across his knee, forcing him down to one leg.

The demon swung wildly, but I was already moving, ducking under his heavy arm and landing a series of rapid, precise strikes along his back. The world around me blurred as I focused entirely on the fight, my senses heightened, my movements swift and deadly. Every slash and stab guided by something deeper than thought—something primal, something Herculean.

With one final roar, he collapsed. I stood over him, panting, the adrenaline still coursing through my veins, my mind catching up with what my body had just done. I stared at the baby tridents in my hands, the blood on the blades glistening in the moonlight. I wasn't sure if I was more terrified of Droopy Lips or of what I had just unlocked within myself.

I didn't have time to be grossed out. Paul needed me. I jumped over the body without even thinking and pushed into the fastest run I'd ever done in my life, asthma be damned.

☉☽ CHAPTER 15 ☾☉

Branches whipped against my arms and face as I tore through the underbrush. My lungs burned, but I pressed on, following the grunts ahead.

Night. Paul.

The words hammered in my head, louder with every step. Could he die? No, gods couldn't die—they were immortal. Right? But was a guardian different from a god? Cynthia's frenzied, wild eyes burned in my memory, sending a sudden spike of fear through me. It was the look of someone who knew they were about to lose something, or someone, irreplaceable. Paul's words from earlier echoed in my mind. When in human form, he doesn't have his full powers.

I hurdled over a fallen tree, my chest convulsing with a barrage of coughs. I'd never pushed my asthma this far. My lungs felt like they were on the verge of exploding. A thick branch suddenly slashed across my path, missing my face by inches. I dodged it just in time and spun toward the direction it came from.

"Hey!" I put as much strength as I could into my voice, relieved when it didn't come out as croaked and weak as I felt.

In the distance, someone collapsed, and two gigantic shadows turned my way. My legs trembled from lack of air. My head pounded, the faint light of night dimming. Everything blurred into shadowy blobs as I staggered forward, pushing through the pain, the suffocating lack of air, the relentless coughing and wheezing. I gripped my sais so tightly I was sure they'd leave bruises.

Then my eyes locked onto the figure sprawled in the grass. The person who'd fallen.

No.

No, no, no. This couldn't be happening. It couldn't be right. This was my fault. I should've stayed behind. Shouldn't have let him bring me here. My eyes stung, my throat knotted, choking me even more. I had nothing left. The giants were just steps away now. Everything slowed to the pace of my fading heartbeat.

I failed.

The thought of Paul's face, pale and lifeless, flashed in my mind. The idea of being all-powerful yet still losing fueled one last burst of strength. My lungs clamped shut, my ribs heaving as though trying to force air into a vacuum. The sharp edge of each breath scraped my throat raw. I raised my sais and, with no breath left, charged both demons.

One step, two steps—my grip tightened on my weapons, aimed for a single chest.

Three steps, darkness closed in.

Four steps, almost there.

Pain shredded through my chest, ripping me apart from the inside. If I did die, at least I wouldn't go down alone. I'd take one of these bastards with me. With the last of my energy, I thrust both blades into one of the giant's chest. I felt the crunch as my blades pierced through skin. Thick, knobby fingers seized my head, and I was hurled into the air.

The wind caught me, cradling me in my blindness. My body slammed into the ground, rolled a few times, and finally stopped. I curled into a ball. There was nothing left. No tears, no screams, no words. I forced my eyes open, fighting for just one breath. Through my blurred vision, I saw Paul lying inches from me, eyes closed, his sun-kissed skin eerily pale under the moonlight.

It felt like cement had pooled in every part of me, filling my lungs, crushing my bones, stopping my heart. I should've done something different. I could've saved him somehow. I knew I'd screw it up. I knew I couldn't do it. There was no way. Not me. Not ever.

As the last of my air hissed from my lips, strange noises filled the space around me. I struggled against my personal suffocation, trying to see through my blindness. The nearest tree uprooted and illuminated by the bright moonlight, transformed into... a lady? I was hallucinating from the lack of oxygen. She walked out of view, and my vision faded completely. My hearing was all I had left as the darkness closed in.

Someone shrieked. Trees rustled like a hurricane had blown through. A loud gasp of air followed, as if the world itself had taken a giant breath. But the sound that resonated most clearly in my ears was my name, called out in desperation.

"Jessa! Jessa, come on."

Electricity zapped my fingertips, and my body jerked and twisted. My lungs restarted with a jolt, and my back arched as I gasped for dry air. My eyes snapped open to find Paul huddled over me, his hands frantically moving from my shoulders to my hands, then to my arms in a desperate, rhythmic pattern. His touch was erratic, as if he couldn't settle, gripped by the fear that he'd lost me. Just as his hand moved to touch my cheek, our eyes met, and he froze, realizing I was alive.

He let out a gasp of relief and scooped me into an embrace. I wanted to return the favor, but my lame brain was too shocked to get my body to cooperate. He let go way too soon.

I swayed a little as he helped me sit back against a tree. Had it been there before? I blinked, trying to shake off the disorientation. Paul kneeled in front of me, his intense eyes locking onto mine. Relief washed over me. I was so incredibly glad he was okay, sitting there, looking at me as if waiting for me to keel over again.

"You're okay." My words were barely a whisper, and I wondered if he'd even heard me before the wind snatched them away.

He closed his eyes, sat all the way down, and nodded. I sighed and rested my head against the trunk. Heat radiated from the tree like a living, breathing creature. I glanced up at its branches. *Did it just wave at me? Nah, that's impossible.*

"How?" I asked, my gaze drifting back to Paul as I swallowed, trying to soothe my painfully dry throat.

He took another slow inhale before opening his eyes. "I was only stunned. For the moment, anyway. Would've been a lot worse off if you hadn't come along. And Cynthia."

She must've gotten the other giant. He noticed my searching eyes. "She's cleaning up the mess."

"Right." After that, I couldn't stop looking at him, memorizing each line on his face, the way his hair blew around his eyes. I wanted him to hold me again. The relief of him being okay was too much to admit out loud. I forced a grin instead. "So, we're even now?"

He laughed, soft and tired, playing with the long blades of grass between his fingers. "Almost."

"Aw, you had to save me again, didn't you?"

He smiled, a full teeth-showing smile, and I wished I had a camera. It was the kind of smile that made a shitty day perfect.

Cynthia walked up behind Paul, hands on her hips, and glanced between us. "What in father's name were you thinking?" Thank God, or the gods, her venom was targeted at Paul. But then I found myself getting defensive.

"It was my fault."

They both looked at me and I wished I had a shell to duck in.

Cynthia scrunched up her nose. "What?"

"It would've been fine if I could, well, you know, breathe on my own."

She rolled her eyes and turned back to Paul. "You shouldn't have brought her. That would've been another Potential killed, and then what? Another week for Hades to unfold whatever sadistic plan he has for the mortals."

"Wait, Hades?" I looked from one to the other, wondering when I'd be clued in on all this.

As usual, Cynthia ignored me, her finger stabbing the air toward Paul. "You're getting reckless again."

Paul's face hardened, and I could've sworn I heard his teeth grind.

"Are you trying to get yourself killed?" Cynthia's voice cracked like a whip. "Because if that's your plan, just let me know. I'd rather skip babysitting duty and watch it happen."

A fire that had nothing to do with my asthma flared up in my chest, and I got to my feet. "Hey, knock it off. How did you plan on training me, Cynthia?"

Her name on my lips seemed to catch her off guard. She turned her head my direction, nice and slow, eyes narrowing. But I wasn't about to let her steamroll me. I swallowed the rising nausea and pressed on. "Paul was trying to help. He's your brother. You really think he's gonna just turn his back? Sure, he could've come alone, but if the Underworld's about to make a play for my people, then it's about time I started kicking some demon ass myself. So maybe don't chew him out for trying to get me a little real-world experience."

The shade of her face turned pinker the more I went on. I stopped to take a breath, and she jumped on her chance.

"You know nothing, amateur." And her lethal stare down finished the rest of her words. She didn't feel the need to waste her breath explaining anything to me.

My fists tightened. Paul stood up, probably about to say something for himself. The anger burning my throat wouldn't cool, however, so I lifted my chin and gave her the best stink-eye I could manage. "You're such a bitch."

Her mouth fell open and I brushed past her before she could say anything. My entire body trembled in rage and fear, but the more I thought about it, the more I realized she couldn't do jack to me. I was a Demi. She was here to protect me, not beat the living shit out of me. Which, on further thought, I was pretty sure she wanted to do right about now.

I got to the edge of the trees, trying to ignore the heated discussion taking place between siblings. Some loose trash blew through the swings, and I closed my eyes and leaned against a tree.

I didn't turn at the crunch of leaves behind me. I wasn't sure exactly how I knew it was Paul. Maybe his smell, the gait of his walk, or something in my demigod powers.

"I'm sorry," I said. Crossing my arms over my chest, I followed the white plastic bag blowing around the park with my eyes.

"It's okay, she deserved it."

I laughed a little and found his face. We stayed like that for a long time, just watching and studying each other. I knew for sure now there was something between us—something from the present or something from the past. I still couldn't shake the feeling of his arms around me. And I couldn't shake the want for it to happen again, either.

"Paul..." I hesitated, but the thought of not having another chance like this to ask pushed me forward. "What is it we have between us?" I might as well use this random burst of courage before it fled and left me with the self-doubting version of me I was all too familiar with.

Paul's jaw tightened, his eyes darting away like he was searching the night for an escape. His silence was worse than any answer he could have given. I tried to convince myself he was gathering his thoughts, but the longer it stretched, the more obvious it became. This wasn't a pause. This was being flat-out ignored.

You're an idiot, repeated in my head like an anthem. I hated words couldn't be deleted like before sending a text. Or there wasn't some fancy internal editor device that could read your thoughts and send out a blaring alarm if you were about to say something stupid.

He shifted, leaning his shoulder against a tree, hands in his pockets. His sleeve was ripped, the broken material hanging limp with the still air around us. The silence was eating me alive.

"Say something." My voice sounded a little too pleading for my taste.

"You did good tonight."

My chest caved in on itself and I pulled my eyes back to the park. I gave a faint nod, something that told him I'd heard him, but otherwise said nothing.

That's right, Jessa, you are an idiot. God, I couldn't believe I'd even gone that route. I only had myself to blame for the crack in my heart at him totally ignoring the subject. Of course, he wasn't going to say anything... there was nothing for him to say. I'd probably made things between us even more awkward. My index finger nervously scratched at my thumb's cuticle. I tried making the sting in the back of my eyes go away. I wanted to pound my fist into the tree. At that, I swear, the tree seemed to shift away from me if just the slightest. I had to be going crazy.

I curled my fingers tight. Who was I kidding? It had to be obvious to him. I wasn't an actress. I was a singer. I wore my emotions like a neon sign flashing over my head. I pushed away from the tree and started walking.

Without a word, Paul kept pace by my side. I really wanted to go off on him, but I directed my rage inward instead. I'd already done a spectacular job of making myself look like a dumbass; no need to add to it.

I wasn't sure where Cynthia had disappeared to, and a million questions swirled in my mind about what had just happened with the giants and what Hades had to do with it. But the last thing I wanted right now was to talk to Paul. About anything.

He either didn't get the point or didn't care.

My phone chimed, and I let out a sigh of relief, grateful for the interruption. I fished my phone out of my pocket, miraculously still intact after the brawl with giants, and saw Lizzie's name flash on the screen. I answered quickly, trying to sound normal. Lizzie's laughter bubbled through the phone, carefree and full of life. It should've felt like home, but instead, it reminded me how far I'd drifted from normal. "Hey, what's up?"

"Jess! We're at Logan's, and guess what? Free Dr. Pepper for Richland Heights peeps!" Lizzie's voice was almost drowned out by laughter and music.

I heard Sam in the background asking if it was me. Another girl's voice, unfamiliar and teasing, cut in with something flirty. Lizzie squealed at whatever was said. "Hah! You're such a tramp!"

I subconsciously stopped walking. "Excuse me?"

"Oh!" She fell into a fit of laughter. "Not you! I was talking to Chloe. Come to Logan's, Jess!"

"They have plenty of Dr. Pepper!" yelled Sam.

I laughed, despite my mood, and glanced up to the street sign a few feet away. I was five miles from home, and Logan's was even further. "I'll see what I can do. How long you guys there for?"

"Who knows? Get your ass over!" Click.

I took a deep breath as I slid my phone back into my pocket. I glanced over at Paul, who was doing a horrible job acting like he hadn't been paying attention. I couldn't say anything, though. His silence told me enough. I started walking again.

When I turned the corner, he finally spoke up. "You going?"

"What's it to you?" So much for keeping my emotions in check. Every fiber in me tensed when he touched my shoulder. I kept walking, leaving his fingers grasping at the air.

"Want me to take you?"

That made me stop. "What?"

"It'd be a lot faster." Confidence seemed to spill out of every pore he had and I, now, hated him for it.

"I don't care. I'd rather walk." I turned and started up again before pausing mid-stride to add, "Alone."

I heard his sigh, and hoped I'd stabbed his confidence like he'd stabbed my heart. But only silence followed. It wasn't until the tingling sensation I'd grown accustomed to vanished that I glanced back. Paul had left.

I wanted to scream after him, but the words stuck in my throat. Good riddance, I told myself. But my chest ached, and it wasn't from the battle. It was the hollow ache of realizing that, for all my anger, I didn't actually want him to go.

☉☽ CHAPTER 16 ☾☉

The wind tangled through my hair, whipping it around while Sam's silver sedan tore down the streets. My arm hung lazily out the window, the summer air a small comfort against the rush of thoughts swirling in my head on our way back to Logan's.

"Thanks for picking me up."

Sam glanced over as she turned onto the next street. "So… why Addison Park? And what happened to you? You look like you wrestled a bear."

"Bear, bush, demon shrubbery," I muttered, then waved a hand. "Take your pick."

Sam raised an eyebrow. "Seriously."

"Seriously, I tripped over a root. Not my most graceful moment." I laughed it off, even though my chest tightened. "Nature: 1. Jessa: 0."

She frowned but let it drop, her focus shifting to the music. "Fine, but next time, call me before you go all Jungle Girl."

"Deal." I forced a grin, relieved when her attention turned to tapping her fingers on the steering wheel, stopping at a red light.

A part of me ached to spill everything to Sam, to let her in on the madness that had become my life, but I knew it would take more than a few sneaky shots from Logan's bar before I'd find the courage to open up again.

"How long you guys been up there?" I finally asked.

"An hour or so. Dawn and Mike already left." Sam revved her car when the light turned green, heading down Lawrence Street.

"Your mom's called me like, five times."

Crap, I totally forgot about her. I pulled out my phone. Ten missed texts and four missed calls. "Great."

Oh well, better enjoy tonight since the rest of my remaining summer would probably be spent on lockdown with mom breathing down my neck, grounding me into the next century. I sent a text letting her know I was still alive and wasn't surprised at the reply that said to come home immediately. I pocketed my phone.

Sam pulled into Logan's full parking lot, and I recognized most of the cars. I laughed at seeing Dawn's red convertible. "I thought they left?"

Sam noticed and scrunched her nose. "God, you'd think they'd get a room or something."

We got out of the car and headed up the steps. "Don't forget to breathe!" I yelled at Dawn and Mike swapping spit.

They jumped apart at my voice. Dawn let out an annoyed grunt and Mike waved, big grin and all. I laughed and waved back, pushing the door open. The sounds of the band, Erasers, pumped through the club-like atmosphere. Laughter, glasses clinking, people being way too loud... the sounds of normal life. No roaring giants or flying arrows or whooshing sounds of gods disappearing. My mood did a one-eighty.

The thumping bass and flashing lights wrapped around me like a shield, muffling the part of me still stuck in the chaos of Addison Park. I wanted to lose myself in the crowd, to drown in the noise, but every shadow shifting in the dark corners pulled at the edge of my attention. Normal had never felt so fragile. I needed a second to breathe, to pull myself together before facing anyone else.

"Gonna hit the bathroom real quick," I said, leaning in close to make sure she heard me over the noise.

Sam nodded, already eyeing a table where some of our friends had gathered.

I ducked into the bathroom, grateful for the relative quiet. The fluorescent lights buzzed overhead as I stepped in front of the mirror. I took a deep breath and finally looked at myself. My hair was a tangled mess, dirt streaked across my face, and a few scratches on my arms were already starting to scab over. There were smudges of dried blood on my hoodie, and I winced at the sight.

I couldn't face everyone looking like I'd just starred in a low-budget horror flick. Wet paper towels in hand, I scrubbed furiously, watching streaks of dirt and blood swirl down the drain. The stubborn stain on my hoodie refused to budge, taunting me like a reminder of the night I'd rather forget.

It was one of my favorites, but there was no salvaging it now. With a little pang of regret, I peeled it off and stuffed it into the trash. *Lucky I wore layers*, I thought, making a mental note to do the same more often, just in case. I groaned at my thoughts. Apparently, my subconscious was already drinking up this new reality, planning ahead like this was my life now.

Once I looked less like a wild gorgon fresh from a cave and more like a halfway functional human, I headed back out to join Sam. I skirted the pulse of the crowd, walking along the edge until I spotted her at a booth overflowing with half a dozen people from our senior class. My phone chirped as I approached. Mom. The wild part of me wanted to ignore it. The good girl in me didn't.

I put the phone to my ear. "Yeah?" I winced in anticipation of a well-deserved reaming.

"Where are you?" Each syllable was punctuated.

"Out with friends. I know it's passed curfew, that's fine. I'll deal with whatever consequences. I'll be home soon."

"No, you'll be home now."

I slid into the booth with Sam, a tall glass of Dr. Pepper already waiting for me. I twirled the straw between my lips and took a sip.

"Right. Be home soon." I hung up and powered it off. A squeamish feeling pressed against my ribcage. I'd never done stuff like this to my mom before but the last place I wanted to go right now was home. Especially my room, a place Paul tended to visit lately.

Another song started, electric guitar whining over our heads. Eddie, the lead singer of Erasers, just graduated from Hardin Christian Academy, Richland's rival. But he was cool in my book. Someone I'd often been inspired by before Mike and I started up our band.

Logan's was The Place to hang if you were between fifteen and eighteen on summer weeknights. With a pool hall and a row of video games on one half of the building, a full-service bar—that only served non-alcoholic beverages during Teen Night—and a kitchen on the other end, the place was a haven for anyone looking to escape the watchful eyes of parents. The dim lighting and loud music made it easy to lose yourself in the crowd, which was exactly what I needed tonight.

The stage gleamed under the scattered light of disco balls, the glittering shards a stark contrast to the raw, shadowy image of Droopy Lips burned into my memory. I blinked hard and redirected my thoughts.

This had been the first place where Mike, Lizzie, and I—otherwise known as The Purple Band-aids—had performed three years ago. We'd done a few more gigs this past year, but nothing quite as cool as the Erasers.

Sam shoulder-bumped me and I looked over at her. She smiled behind her straw. "You gonna tell me what's up with you?"

I smiled, but it wasn't genuine, and I was pretty sure she could tell. "Maybe you can come over tomorrow?" I twisted my lips at that thought. "Or, not. I'm probably grounded for the rest of the summer after tonight's rebellion. You can call me?"

"Assuming she doesn't take away your phone rights." She rolled her eyes and snatched a fry from the cheese fry basket in the center of the table.

Sam said something else, but her voice blurred under the sharp detail of my surroundings. The way the flickering light above the stage bounced off polished glasses, the slight crack in the bar counter, the dust particles dancing in the spotlight's beams. Everything was crisper, clearer, as if someone had turned the world into high definition. It made me dizzy.

Even as I forced myself to focus on Sam's words, rehashing some drama that had happened before I'd arrived, I kept scanning the room, my gaze darting to the exit signs, the too-dark corners of Logan's. Every flicker of movement caught my attention. I wasn't sure if I was paranoid or if something deep inside me was finally waking up.

Lizzie's squeal echoed across the entire place, rapidly tugging my focus back into the present. She bounced between people, hand in hand with a stunning girl whose long braids swayed with each step. She was effortlessly beautiful, her dark skin glowing under the lights. Lizzie beamed, clearly smitten. "Jessa! You made it! Did you see Eddie? Isn't he awesome?"

Lizzie grinned as she pulled the girl closer, her excitement barely contained. "Jessa, this is Chloe," she said, her eyes sparkling. "Chloe, this is my friend, Jessa. She's the one I've been telling you about all night."

Chloe smiled and waved. "Hey girl, it's great to finally meet you."

I waved back. "Nice to meet you, too." Lizzie grabbed my arm and tried pulling me up. Of course, I didn't even budge. Uh oh, was I going to have to start remembering to be normal and weak? I quickly made myself give a little, just enough to seem believable.

"Come on! He's playing 'Never Over You' next, you have to hear it." Lizzie's determination was impossible to resist, her excitement infectious. She tugged harder, and this time I let her pull me to my feet.

Lizzie looped her arm through Chloe's, and together they pretty much dragged me toward the stage. There was no stopping Lizzie when she was on a mission, and with Chloe by her side, it seemed like nothing could stand in their way.

"Want another one?" Sam called after me about a refill.

"Nah, got no cash."

She rolled her eyes and got up to head to the bar.

I did my best not to run into anybody, half afraid I'd stampede them or something with my Herculean strength. It was going to take the rest of my life to get this demigod thing down.

The people scrunched together at the front of the stage were pretty much all girls. Most of them were freshmen from Richland Heights, and the others probably from Hardin. Man, I wished I'd had this kind of turnout when we'd performed.

Eddie started singing his ballad. I tried to enjoy myself, swaying back and forth with the others, but my thoughts kept drifting back to Addison Park. The giants, Cynthia, and mostly Paul, circled through my mind. Halfway through the song, I caught sight of a familiar head of long, wavy golden hair to my right.

No. Way.

I craned my head a little to get a better look. My mouth hung open. If Ashlyn was here, that meant...

"Jessa?" Zach was pushing around people, more than likely to get to Ashlyn. He looked thoroughly surprised to see me.

I glanced at the two drinks in his hands and forced a casual, "Hey." My brain screamed for me to snatch one and toss it in his face, but my body had other plans. Instead of fury, a strange numbness crept over me, like my emotions had finally run out of steam.

"Hey, baby! Oh." Ashlyn glanced at me with a what-the-hell-are-you-doing-here look. "Well, come on! What took you so long?" She pulled on

Zach, guiding him back to her spot.

He followed along, but I didn't miss the glance. Could he finally be feeling guilty? Lizzie nudged me, and then poked me hard in the shoulder when I didn't respond. I couldn't stop watching Zach. Sam had been right. He looked very unlike himself. Unhappy. He'd never been into schedules, routine... servitude. And now with Ashlyn, it seemed all he was good for. Even though I dumped him because I knew he'd rather be with the two-faced Kim Kardashian wannabe, I still missed him.

#

Logan's closed at eleven, leaving us to either go home or have fun somewhere else despite skirting the town curfew. I really didn't want to go home. I followed the herd out into the parking lot. Mike and Dawn had returned earlier and walked with their arms hanging over each other's shoulders. Dawn made it a point to walk next to Sam.

Lizzie and Chloe spun circles in the street like drunken ballerinas. Drunk on life. The loud laughter behind us belonged to Ashlyn, Zach, some guy I forgot the name of, and the girl I knew by last name only, Garner.

"I didn't think they'd be here," said Sam under her breath.

I shrugged like it made no difference. Sam glanced back for me. She curled up her lip in disgust. "Don't worry, he still looks miserable."

I couldn't help myself and spared a look. To anyone who didn't know him well, he looked normal, maybe even happy. But I couldn't miss, there was something different about him.

"Have you guys talked at all since the parade?"

I shook my head, running a hand through my loose hair, flicking out a tiny twig… shit had that been there the whole time? I stopped with the others at Dawn's convertible.

"Everyone wanna come to my place? 'Rents are still out of town 'til Friday," Dawn said, her full attention on Sam.

I swallowed the grunt threatening to escape and forced a neutral expression. Dawn's house. Of course. She'd monopolize Sam the second we walked through the door, treating her like an audience for her endless updates on her *oh-so-dramatic* life. Just imagining it made my teeth ache.

Sam hesitated, her shoulder brushing mine as she glanced my way, the silent question hanging between us. I offered a tight smile. "Thanks, but my mom's already got her lecture locked and loaded. I'm not trying to be grounded until graduation."

Dawn sighed, loud and exaggerated, but before she could press, Ashlyn's syrupy voice cut through the night air. "Aw, come on, baby!"

I turned my head toward her car and immediately regretted it. There she was, half-hanging out of the driver-side window, clutching Zach's hand like he might float away. She tilted her head just so, her golden hair cascading perfectly over her shoulder, as if she'd stepped out of a magazine ad for toxic relationships.

I turned back, raising an eyebrow. "Anyone got a barf bag?"

Sam snorted, and Lizzie nearly choked on her soda. One by one, my friends cracked up until the whole group dissolved into laughter, carving through my irritation

My friends.

I wanted to tell them everything—about Paul, the giants, this thing I was becoming—but where would I even start? And how could I expect them to believe it? The thought alone made my shoulders tighten, like I was wearing chains only I could feel. I shifted my weight, wishing I could brush it all off as easily as the twig I'd flicked to the pavement.

I didn't want to look at what was going on between Zach and Ashlyn so made a point to be interested in Dawn's convertible. Mike and Lizzie blabbered on about Eddie's ballad and how we needed to come up with something like that, Chloe resting her head on Lizzie's shoulder.

"You sure you don't want to go?" asked Sam.

When I saw Ashlyn's car pull out of the parking lot without Zach inside, my heart did a little somersault.

"Jessa, come on! Don't be such a killjoy." Lizzie grinned. Crickets dotted the parking lot, skittering or hopping around. Another car peeled out onto the road. Sam was my ride home and I felt an obligation to go. Not that Dawn lived that far from me, but still.

"Did I hear there was a party at Dawn's place?" Zach's voice stilled my thoughts.

Everyone's faces seemed to drop at the same time. Most turned away from him, as if staring at him would be betraying me for whatever reason. I was ashamed to admit I liked it.

"No one said you were invited," said Dawn.

My lips parted to say something, but Dawn had sucked the breath right out of me. I forgot how loyal she could be when she was actually acting like a good friend. Zach's eyes lost their hopefulness. He looked defeated and I sort of felt sorry for him, which was stupid of me.

In that awkward, uncomfortable silence where no one knew exactly how to respond, I decided I'd be the first to speak. "Right, so..." I rocked back on my heels. "Sam, you mind dropping me off, first?"

"Seriously, Jessa?" Dawn frowned, disappointed. Maybe I owed it to her after that ballsy display of friendship, but my thirst for living wild and free had fled. I just wanted to go home and go to bed.

Sam wrapped an arm over my shoulder. "It's fine, I don't mind."

Zach walked around Dawn and made it a point to stand in front of me. "I could give you a lift. Heading home myself."

I blinked. And when no words could form on my tongue, I stared. It must've been contagious, because no one else said a word, either.

Zach laughed, nervous. "Seriously, guys, grow up. Jess and I are neighbors and... still friends." He looked at me for reassurance. "Right?"

My brow arched on its own. A flicker of mortification flashed across his face. As much as he deserved it, I couldn't embarrass him. "Sure."

Sam shifted uncomfortably. "You sure?"

I shrugged. "Yeah, I'll survive."

I still hadn't moved my gaze from Zach. Why was he here? I tried to figure it out by studying him. I think he wanted to talk to me. About what, I hadn't the slightest clue. What I did know was that it could be my only chance at vindication with him. I finally looked at Sam. "Call me tomorrow."

She smiled a little. "I'll try."

My mom had to work. There was only so much she could control, and we both knew my phone was probably the first thing to go. I gave a wave to my friends and followed Zach to his pickup truck.

☉☽ CHAPTER 17 ☾☉

Uncomfortable didn't begin to cover it. I leaned closer to the passenger window, the cool glass doing nothing to ease the tension twisting in my chest. Zach had one hand on the steering wheel, Green Day playing low over the stereo. Of course, he'd pick *our* band to play. Typical.

I crossed my arms, sneaking a glance at his profile. What had possessed me to think this ride was a good idea? The thought of my friends gawking at this bizarre reunion burned behind my eyes, humiliating.

"Why?" The question came out hot and venomous.

He shifted in his seat, his eyes flicking to me before darting back to the road. A small smile tugged at his lips. "Good to see you haven't changed much."

My anger spiked. "It took like, two days to replace me, asshole."

That smeared the smile right off his face. It was very possible he'd stop the truck and tell me to get out. I kind of hoped he would. I'd made a horrible choice. This ride would surely be more uncomfortable than having to break up with one of my mom's boyfriends for her again.

Zach rolled his shoulders, like he was trying to relax—or maybe psych himself up. "I dunno, just thought we'd try the whole friends thing again."

I faced him and hardened my jaw. "Don't you already have somebody for that?"

"What? Ashlyn?" He glanced my way. "She's just—"

"Your girlfriend."

His knuckles tightened over the steering wheel. It was sweet to make him uncomfortable like that. The jealousy and anger building in me for the past two months were ready to break through my mental dam and drown the asshole. Plus, I was pretty sure all the stress from the entire week was ready to burst free into some form of rage.

"You couldn't even wait," I snapped. "What was it, Zach? A week? Two? Before you went running to Ashlyn?"

"Jess—"

"No. You don't get to 'Jess' me," I said, trying to keep my voice steady. "The way you looked at her when you thought I wasn't paying attention, how you started finding ways to be around her? I'm not an idiot, Zach. You really thought this friends thing could work?"

He didn't answer. The silence made my chest ache, but I wasn't about to let him off the hook.

"Why?" My voice dropped, almost a growl. "Just tell me why." You killed me. Dug my heart out with a spork and tossed it on a butcher block.

His cheeks went hollow, a sure sign he was getting pissed off. Good. I craved it like Dr. Pepper after days without or my inhaler after sprinting from Death.

"Why, Zach?" I spat his name, hoping to ignite his temper, wanting him to feel as angry or hurt as I did.

"You're the one who broke up with me."

"Yeah, for obvious reasons." My hands flailed around as I spoke. "Everyone could see it, Zach. My friends saw it before I did. God, do you know how that made me feel? Stupid! Everyone knew it but me! So, I did what any heartbroken, good girlfriend would do, and I let you go." Pain replaced the rage burning in my chest, and my throat tightened.

His silence was a slap in the face, sharper than any words he could have thrown at me. It was like he'd sucked the air out of the truck, leaving me isolated with everything I'd just thrown at him. The Green Day song ended, its last notes fading into the heavy quiet. Zach slowed to a stop on the side of the road, put the truck in park, and turned to face me.

"I'm stupid, alright? I made a stupid choice, Jess." He turned off the radio before another song could play. "It's just, it ain't right without you."

"What?" This wasn't what I expected. Yelling, a curse word or two. But this?

Zach seemed to have lost his tongue.

"Zach. Speak." I snapped my fingers. The bitch thing was kind of fun.

Zach let out a breath, his hand sliding off the steering wheel as he turned to face me fully. The vulnerability in his eyes caught me off guard, like I was staring at a version of him I hadn't seen in years. His voice was softer than I expected when he finally spoke.

"It's just... every day without you, it felt wrong. Like I was missing something huge, something I couldn't replace no matter what I tried." He paused, his gaze dropping to his hands. "Ashlyn... she was just a distraction. A stupid, temporary distraction. But you? You're... you're everything, Jess."

The raw honesty in his words melted away my anger. Old feelings I'd tried so hard to bury resurfaced stronger than ever and I hated it. I wanted to be angry, to stay angry, but his words were like an axe to the carefully constructed wall I'd built around my heart.

"What are you saying?" I asked, afraid of the answer but more afraid of not hearing it.

Zach swallowed, his eyes locking onto mine with a yearning that made it impossible to look away. "I miss you, Jess. I miss us. I miss the way you used to look at me, the way we'd talk for hours about nothing and everything. I miss how you'd laugh at my stupid jokes, how you always knew exactly what I was thinking before I even said it." He hesitated, his voice dropping lower. "And I hate that I ruined it. I hate that I hurt you."

His sincerity made my chest ache. This was the Zach I'd fallen in love with, the Zach who had been my best friend, my confidant, my everything. And despite it all, a part of me still longed for that, still longed for him.

But then there was Paul. Mysterious, powerful, protective Paul, who made my heart race and my mind spin with possibilities I'd never even considered before. Paul, who had been there for me in ways Zach never could be, who understood me on a level that was almost terrifying in its depth.

Torn between the comfort of what I once knew and the thrill of something entirely new, I failed at words. I wanted to tell Zach that it was too late, that he'd had his chance, and he'd blown it. But instead, I just stared at him, my heart in a war with itself, unsure which side to take.

"Jess," Zach whispered, leaning closer. "I know I messed up. But I'm asking for another chance. A real one. Just... just tell me you don't feel anything for me anymore, and I'll walk away. I'll let you go. But if there's even a part of you that still feels something, anything, then please... don't push me away."

My throat tightened, the battle between what I wanted and what I knew I should do raging inside me. His words hung in the air, and I didn't know how to respond, didn't know if I even could.

Zach inched closer, his eyes locking onto mine, making my heart pound. The heat radiating from him brushed against my skin, his breath warm as it mingled with the space between our lips. Every alarm in my head went off, blaring warnings that this was a bad idea, that I couldn't go down this road again. But beneath the panic, there was also a yearning, a deep-seated desire for the familiar comfort of his kiss, the kind of kiss that used to make everything else disappear.

I was caught between the pull of old feelings and the knowledge that too much had changed. The closer he got, the more my thoughts scrambled, and the harder it became to think straight. I wanted to stop him, to say something, anything, but I couldn't.

Just as his lips brushed mine, a dark shadow streaked across the windshield, faster than any bird. My pulse slammed against my ribs, and I jerked back so hard my head hit the seat.

"What the hell was that?" Zach's voice cracked.

My mind raced, trying to process what I'd just seen, but all I could think about was the kiss that had almost happened... and the sudden, ominous interruption.

"Start the car," I said, all the earlier anger draining into something colder.

"What?" He squinted into the darkness outside, his confusion mixing with annoyance. "Jess—"

"Zach, drive. Now."

His cheeks were still flushed from the almost-kiss. I could see the hurt flash in his eyes, the way he was taking my words as rejection. He hesitated, as if trying to decide whether to push forward with what we'd almost done or listen to me.

"What's wrong?" His voice was tinged with disappointment, like he'd rather pretend nothing was out there and focus on the moment we'd nearly had.

I didn't have time to coddle his feelings. "Just trust me. Take me home."

Zach's shoulders slumped slightly, and I could tell he was reluctant. He turned the key, and the engine roared to life. We were halfway down the road when something darted across our path.

"What the fu—" Zach's voice cracked as the truck lurched over the thing darting across the street.

A leathery, gray, two-headed thing. With wings.

Every nerve in my body snapped to attention.

Zach slammed on the brakes. The tires screamed against the pavement as our seatbelts jerked us back in our seats.

"Keep going!"

"What?" His wild eyes darted to the rearview mirror before settling on me, his bangs falling over his flushed face.

"It was just a squirrel or something, go!" My fists clenched so tight my nails bit into my palms. Did he really see it?

"Seriously? Since when do squirrels have two heads?"

Yep, he saw it. I bit my lip, scanning the street. "Drive."

Instead, he unbuckled his seatbelt and twisted in his seat to look back.

"Come on!" I yelled, panic swelling as his face went slack, his eyes stretching wide.

The demon we'd run over staggered upright, its leathery wings dragging in the dirt, both heads bobbing in the air. Its ember-like eyes glowed in the dark. Without thinking, I shoved the clutch into drive, swung my leg over the console, and slammed my foot on the gas.

"Whoa!" Zach lunged forward, grabbing the wheel. "Jessa, what the hell?"

"Trust me!"

Zach hesitated, then took control of the pedal. I twisted around to check, but the two-headed thing was gone.

The truck screeched to another jarring stop, the tires shrieking like a wounded animal. My seatbelt slammed my body back against the seat, the impact stealing my breath in a choking gasp. A split second later, Zach's airbag exploded with a deafening *whoomp*, the deflated material smacking him square in the face. White fabric unfurled like a parachute, covering his chest and sending a cloud of chalky dust into the air.

Zach clawed at the airbag, shoving it aside with a frustrated grunt. His face was flushed, an angry red mark already blooming on his cheek. "What the hell?" he sputtered, coughing through the smokey dust.

"You good?" I rasped, rubbing the ache in my chest.

"Fine."

I opened my mouth to ask why we'd stopped when a shrill crack jerked my attention forward. Something hit the windshield, hard enough to splinter the glass. My stomach twisted as a shadow moved across the hood. Then claws—long, hooked, and razor-sharp—scraped down the glass with a screech that made my teeth ache.

"What *is* that?" Zach's voice wavered as he stared at the demon perched on the hood.

Its two heads jerked in opposite directions; four-foot wings stretched like they were ready to spring. Twin tongues flicked out, hissing, and its glowing red eyes bore into us. The cracks in the windshield spiderwebbed under its claws. It wasn't just scratching—it was breaking through. My breath hitched as I noticed movement behind it.

There were two of them.

"Drive!"

Zach slammed on the gas. The truck jolted forward. The beast scrambled, its claws skittering against the hood before it tumbled off with a screech. Relief barely had a chance to settle before a strange shadow loomed ahead.

"What—" Zach choked as another leathery, gray, two-headed demon flew straight toward us. Its wings flew open, and its snarling faces were the last thing I saw before the impact.

The truck slammed into the creature with a bone-jarring impact, sending it hurtling into the ditch with a sickening crunch. The windshield shattered under the force, spraying shards of glass into the cab like glittering shrapnel. I instinctively threw my arms up to shield my face as the truck screeched to a halt.

Dazed, I fumbled with my seatbelt, my chest aching like I'd been punched by one of the giants from earlier. "Zach?"

"I'm fine," he muttered, shoving the remnants of the airbag aside. His voice shook, and his wide green eyes flicked toward the shattered windshield.

"Come on," I said, my voice trembling as I pushed the door open. "We can't stay here."

We both stumbled out onto the road. The night air hit me like a slap, hot and muggy, against the adrenaline coursing through my veins.

"We hit it," he mumbled, his hand finding mine as he stared toward the ditch. "It's gotta be dead, right?"

The creature lay still, wings sprawled at odd angles, heads twisted unnaturally. I let out a shaky breath, a flicker of hope sparking in my chest. Maybe we'd gotten lucky. Maybe—

A low, guttural snarl turned my blood to ice and we both turned slowly to face the sound.

The first demon—the one that had tumbled off the hood—staggered toward us, wings dragging, both heads snapping in eerie synchronization. Its eyes burned brighter, locking onto us hungrily.

"Sweet cartwheeling Jesus," Zach squeaked under his breath.

Before I could form some plan of action, a rush of air whipped past us. I turned to see the second demon, revived from the ditch, flying crookedly over us. It perched on the hood with a clucking screech, its claws sinking into the dented metal.

I tightened my grip on Zach's hand, praying I wasn't breaking his fingers with my newfound strength. His face was pale, his terror mirroring my own.

"Stay behind me," I said, though I had no idea what I was going to do.

Somehow, I'd get him out of this alive. Somehow.

☉☽ CHAPTER 18 ☾☉

Zach's pickup idled in the middle of the road, its engine humming like it was the only thing keeping the darkness at bay. To our right, a dense thicket twisted in the breeze like clawed hands reaching out. On the left, the dark silhouette of an abandoned fast-food joint stood lifeless, its sign cracked and dim, casting eerie shadows across the empty street ahead. The traffic light blinked red, painting everything in a blood-colored glow that only deepened the sense of dread.

If I'd had a normal hand, it might've been broken by Zach's death grip. He stared at the demons, his chest heaving up and down. I hated that he could see them.

And they could see Zach.

They looked from him to me, then to each other. The beast on the roof made a low clucking noise, its split tongue slithering out with its hiss. They were stalling. Because of Zach? What did it matter? If I was going to do anything, now was my chance.

Centering the raw, unexplainable energy coursing through my veins, I grabbed Zach under his arms. "I'm sorry."

His wide, terrified eyes locked onto mine, his face shifting from confusion to outright horror. Before he could protest, I inhaled sharply, hoisting him like a stuffed animal, and flung him into the bushes. "Stay down!"

His startled scream cut through the night, followed by the rustle of leaves and a heavy thud as he landed somewhere in the thicket.

Better bruised than dead, I told myself, shoving aside the guilt that pricked at my chest. Clenching my fists, I turned back to the demons, my pulse thundering in my ears.

They spewed giant fireballs at my face.

I choked on my scream as flames roared toward me, their heat licking at my skin. I braced for agony... but nothing came. My eyes flew open. My arms were fine. I was fine. I stared at my fingers, my skin, my hairs...everything was fine. Not even a singe.

What the hell? I thought, flexing my fingers. The air around me shimmered with heat, but I was untouched. A laugh bubbled up from my chest. "Sweet."

With a renewed sense of strength, I glared up at the demon through my lashes and smirked. Its two heads glanced at each other, confused as to why I wasn't a heap of ashes. In a single flap of their wings, its needle-like claws struck my face.

I shrieked, trying to rip the beast off. The momentum hurled me onto the street, my head smacking hard against the pavement. My brain rattled inside my skull. My fingers scratched desperately, searching for anything to grab onto, anything to tear away.

I couldn't breathe. The demon's claws raked across my arms, my neck, my face, hot lines of pain tearing through me. Blood blurred my vision as I thrashed, desperate to break free. One talon pressed against my chest, pinning me like a butterfly. Its other head reared back, flames curling between its teeth. Ignoring the shredding pain ruling my body and the flames licking at my face, I kicked with everything I had, my sneaker connecting with its jaw.

The demon screeched, its body smashing into the truck with a deafening *thud.* Its partner lunged at me, wings slicing through the air like blades. I ducked low, my fingers clamping around one of its legs. With a surge of strength that was both terrifying and exhilarating, I twisted hard.

The demon thrashed, hissing and clawing at the air, but I held firm. My muscles burned as I spun it around—once, twice, three times—before releasing it with a roar.

It shot through the air like a missile, colliding mid-flight with the other demon just as it recovered to charge toward me. The two slammed into Zach's already battered truck, their combined weight crumpling the metal, leaving the vehicle sagging and steam hissing from under the hood as the demons struggled to disentangle themselves.

The wind stabbed at my raw face and arms. Blood was everywhere. My blood. No time to think about it.

I hunched over, gasping as my lungs felt like they were shrinking, every breath rasping against the tightness building in my chest. Panic flared hotter than the fire I'd just faced. I pressed a hand to my ribs, wheezing, the ragged sound filling my ears. I couldn't focus, couldn't even think past the suffocating grip of my asthma threatening to take me out before the demons could.

My trembling hands instinctively reached for my baby tridents—my only hope—but they weren't there. Lost somewhere in the chaos with the giants. My vision blurred, spots dancing at the edges.

No. I forced a shaky breath past the burning in my chest. *I can't stop.*

My empty fingers curled into fists. I had nothing to fight with. Nothing but my will to survive.

The air crackled behind me, a low hum that sent chills racing up my spine and my ears to pop from the change in pressure. I didn't need to turn around. About time my Greek friends showed up. Before I could see who'd just appeared, one of the dragons belched another ribbon of fire.

Stupid, ugly pieces of shit. Didn't they know fire couldn't hurt me?

Pushing through the searing pain radiating all over, I charged through the fire, the heat of the flames licking at my skin but doing little else. The dragon-demon heads chomped at me, but I sidestepped, planting my feet firmly and, with every ounce of strength I could muster, threw an uppercut straight into its jaw.

My fist connected with bone, the jarring impact snapping its head back like a whip. The crunch sent a tremor through my arm. The demon stumbled, wings flailing as it tried to recover.

My asthma robbed me of what should've been a triumphant moment. Each wheeze made my chest feel like it was collapsing inward. I stared at my trembling, blood-streaked hands, half-expecting to see melted flesh or charred skin. Still nothing. I wasn't crazy. Fire didn't hurt me. That should've been reassuring, but it was hard to feel invincible when every nerve in my body screamed in agony. I turned to whoever had materialized nearby.

Henry stood there, a staff in one hand, his eyes darting between the crippled dragon-demons and me. "Looks like you've got this handled," he said, but his forced smile faltered as his gaze landed on my face—or what was left of it.

The ground beneath me seemed to heave, and my legs buckled. I hit my knees, the jagged asphalt biting into my skin.

"Jessa!" Henry dropped beside me, gripping my shoulder. His words blurred as the searing pain swallowed me whole. Every nerve screamed, and all I wanted was for it to stop. To curl up and die.

He pressed something cold and hard against whatever was left of my tender cheek. I cried out. Henry braced me, pinning me down so I couldn't throw him off. A warm glow radiated next to my eyes, and I squinted through tears of pain, trying to see what was happening. Henry's staff was the cold, hard thing emanating the bright light. My sporadic breathing calmed. The pain in my face faded, as if blanketed by layers of warmth—or skin, probably. Hopefully.

Henry's staff did the same thing Paul could do on his own... heal.

Behind him, the two crippled demons moved. Henry pulled me up. "You can only kill them with your sais."

"Paul has them," I rasped, hoping I was right.

He tilted his head, his frown deepening. "He's not here?"

I shot him a look. "Do you see him around?"

His concern hardened, and I half-wondered if I should be worried, too, but the rustling in the dry bushes behind us, dragged my stomach into freefall.

"Zach." How could I have forgotten?

"What?"

"Zach! I threw him over there. I need to check if he's okay."

Henry's expression darkened. "You brought a mortal with you?" His voice was sharp, nearly a hiss.

I ignored him, already pivoting toward the thicket. My heart hammered, blood rushing in my ears. Zach had to be okay. He had to be.

I swallowed the knot down, glanced up, and froze.

A chill fell over me like a death shroud, freezing my bones to stillness. At the edge of the gnarled shrubs stood Thanatos, his sickly beautiful face twisted into a crude smile. His pale fingers curled around Zach's neck. Zach's head lolled forward, his eyes closed, body limp.

"If you would have cooperated earlier, you could've spared your friend," Thanatos said, his voice taunting.

"Let him go!"

Henry stepped next to me, and I swear he puffed out his chest like he was some big, bad bodyguard. "Leave the mortal out of this, Thanatos." The way he said it made it sound like Zach was still alive. I had to figure out a way to free him.

Thanatos didn't even glance at Henry. His captivating violet eyes were locked on mine, unblinking, as if trying to peel back every layer of my defenses. Half of his long white hair was pinned up, the rest streaming behind him like a ghostly banner in the wind.

"Come with me," he said, his voice smooth, almost coaxing. "And I'll let him go."

"What?" The word slipped out before I could stop it, confusion twisting my features. Since when did he care about deals? I shifted, catching the faint shuffle of claws and wings behind me. The dragon demons… sneaking closer.

"Henry, could you—"

"On it." He spun around and an array of screeches, flapping, and grunts followed as he went to fight off the beasts. I didn't look away from Thanatos.

Couldn't, actually.

He had some freakish hypnotic grip on me. As much as I tried to check on Henry, make sure I wasn't about to become shredded Jessa again, my body couldn't move. I wiggled my fingers. That was something.

His smug, arrogant smile widened as he watched me struggle. The moonlight danced in his eyes, making the violet hue shimmer like liquid gemstones. My pulse quickened, not from awe but from frustration. Where was Paul? Or Cynthia?

"Let him go," I said through gritted teeth.

"Come with me." He repeated it like it was the most reasonable request in the world.

I ground my teeth, flexed my fingers, and hoped I didn't have an asthma attack in front of him. Metal crunched behind me. I tried to move again, turn and check on Henry. My muscles were still locked in place. Thanatos smiled. Fine. Different tactics, then. Maybe I could stall until someone else showed up to help. I tried lifting a foot, but it was like my limbs were stuck in wet sand, every effort draining away as soon as I made it. No matter how hard I tried, it was useless, like the God of Death had sunk his claws into me, holding me captive in my own skin

"I'm not going anywhere, freak." Literally, but also definitely not to Hell with him.

Thanatos's smile faltered, the corners twitching. For a moment, his expression darkened, something dangerous flashing in his eyes. My breath caught as the details of his face came into unnerving clarity—the exact flecks of violet swirling with threads of black, the slight twitch of his jaw. It was as if I were seeing him through a magnifying glass.

My powers. If only I knew how to actually use them.

He jerked Zach higher into the air, his limp body swinging like a doll. My heart slammed against my ribs. "No!"

Thanatos tilted his head, that ghost of a smile returning. "Then stop playing games."

"Tell me where you're taking me." More scuffling behind me. I wanted to look so bad. Every thought was consumed by the fear that one move from Thanatos would make Zach disappear.

 Forever.

A bright, silver light arched overhead and passed me, a battle cry piercing the air.

Thanatos scowled and Zach's neck seemed to shrink beneath his grip. I couldn't spin around to see, but the crazy madwoman laughter gave Cynthia away.

"What took you so long?" I yelled, hopeful the odds would swing in my favor. My eyes were fixed on Zach. *Please be okay.*

"No time for chitchat, rookie!" she snapped. A familiar whistle sliced through the air behind me—Cynthia's arrow—followed by a demon's wail. I flinched at the screech, wishing I could cover my ears, hating the helplessness that came with having no control.

"Your little Guardians can't help you, Jessa." Thanatos's venomous voice slithered through the air. He tilted his chin and gave Zach a deliberate shake, his limp limbs swinging lifelessly, like a marionette abandoned mid-performance.

"Come to me, and I'll let him go," Thanatos continued, his words laced with cruel confidence.

"Stop!" I choked out. The sting of tears gave me away. I hated that I couldn't wipe they away as they slid down my cheeks. They weren't from fear anymore, but rage. Rage at having no control over anything...my body, my powers, Zach. "I'll kill you," I growled.

Thanatos's laugh cut off as the earth quaked under our feet. I stumbled back and braced myself, momentarily free from his hypnotic grip. Not that I did much moving after that, too stunned at what I saw.

The ground parted next to him. A nasty sewage smell gagged the air, and from the depths of what I guessed was the Underworld, two bodies catapulted out of the giant fissure like escapees from hell's worst prison riot. They slammed into the ground in a tangle of limbs, fists flying at breakneck speed.

Despite the blur of motion, my vision zeroed in, defining every detail like I'd hit some supernatural zoom button. Every flick of a fist, every shift in their expressions—I caught it all. My chest tightened as recognition slammed into me. Hypnos and Paul.

☉︎☽ CHAPTER 19 ☾☉︎

The sun god and sleep god shouted ancient Greek at each other, breaking apart when they realized they'd surfaced into the mortal world. Paul panted, gripping his side, his torn clothes and wild hair making him look like he'd just left a battlefield. His eyes found mine, and in a blink of mist, he appeared beside me.

Hypnos wasn't far behind, his yellow eyes pinning me in place. My muscles locked; my chest tightened… The Underworld brothers were working together now, binding me with their power. I couldn't even blink, my body trapped by invisible chains.

"I can't move," I whispered in bad ventriloquy.

Paul didn't answer, his stillness a quiet promise of a fight, and I was pretty sure he was glaring some golden-misty eyes at the god of death.

Thanatos sighed. "I've little patience. Come with me now or lose your friend."

Paul's sharp breath confirmed my fears. Whatever Thanatos was planning, it wasn't good. I tried to speak, but exhaustion hit like a wave, folding me into Paul's body. I was free, but too weak to move.

"Tired," I whispered, my eyelids drooping.

Paul held me up, his voice urgent. "Stay with me," he said, shaking me gently. "Thanatos, you can't do this!"

Another demon shrieked behind me, followed by Cynthia's

triumphant howl. For the moment, the two demons were out of commission. I forced my eyes open with tremendous effort, and it was worth it. Thanatos and Hypnos were backing up, their menacing smirks replaced by a flicker of uncertainty. Cynthia and Henry had moved to stand at our sides, with Paul steadying me. Four against two. Those were good odds. Well, three against two if I couldn't shake off this overwhelming urge to take a nap.

"You're done, Thanatos," said Henry. "Put the mortal down."

Thanatos sneered. "You think I can't call up more, Hermes? You think you're any match for me?"

My body involuntarily shuddered at the thought of more demons. Paul opened my fingers and placed something cold and metallic in my hand. Baby Trident.

"You're the only one who can send them back," he whispered, his healing warmth flooding through me, pushing back the panic with a wave of courage. But the drowsiness still clung to me, heavy and oppressive.

The earth hummed beneath my feet, and the grass suddenly seemed very inviting. *Just a little nap,* I told myself. A small rest, and then I could fight. The sweet scent of my mom's aromatherapy candles filled the air, lulling me further. My body felt like lead. I had to rest. I yawned and slunk down to Paul's feet.

"Jessa!" Paul yanked me upright by the arm. "Snap out of it!" He shook me so hard my teeth clattered, my brain sluggishly trying to keep up. The world spun, blurring with the echo of Hypnos's cackle and Thanatos muttering in Greek, his words like oil slicking over my ears. Above it all, the guttural roar of more demon dragons shook the air, their approach a drumbeat of doom.

I fought to open my eyes, to shove my body into action, but my limbs refused to obey. It was like being locked in my own skin, paralyzed while the chaos stormed around me.

The power under my skin pulsed, hotter and harder now, a steady drumbeat of its own. It was a wild, untamed thing thrashing to break free and I clung to it, desperately trying to channel it, to focus. It wasn't enough to feel it; I had to own it.

"Move," I commanded myself, the word ricocheting in my mind like a spark catching dry kindling. My breath hitched, the pressure behind my ribs building. It wasn't just adrenaline—it was something deeper, something stronger.

My eyes snapped open, and the leash holding that energy broke free. I was moving before I could think, my sai gripped tight in my hand, my body surging forward. The haze of sleepiness evaporated, replaced by blistering clarity. I zeroed in on Thanatos, every nerve in my body honed like a blade.

Hypnos leapt into my path with a growl, his shadowy form a blur. Paul lunged at him from the side, golden mist exploding around him like armor as he tackled the god of sleep.

The screeching demons whirled overhead, dropping like flies thanks to Cynthia's arrows and in less than a blink, the tip of my blade hovered under Thanatos's chin. I wanted to see his expression, to know if he was surprised or pissed, but I wasn't taking any chances on paralysis again. My eyes stayed fixed on his nose instead, my grip tightening on the handle.

"I don't bargain with people trying to kill me." I pushed the blade up, making him raise his chin. My powers snapped back to me like they'd been there all along, fighting for my attention. Once again, I felt the rush of adrenaline and the desire to kick some major ass.

Hypnos and Paul moved at warp speed behind Thanatos, hurtling each other into trees. The earth shook with each tree that cracked and fell. Paul struggled, the night making him weaker and I fought the part of me that wanted to jump into action and help. Zach needed me more, and Thanatos really needed to learn to leave me alone. Henry charged the fallen demons and Cynthia—

"Hey!" She appeared in the corner of my eye, speeding through the path of broken trees to Paul and Hypnos. In a flash of silver, a beam struck Hypnos square in the chest.

Thanatos curled up one corner of his lip. "Impressive. But can you actually follow through?"

Baby Trident quivered. Shit, was I really trembling? "I shouldn't have to. I have a pretty good feeling you shouldn't be doing whatever it is you're trying to do."

Something behind Thanatos caught my attention again. My focus zoomed in like a camera lens as the trees moved, their limbs raking down to tear at Hypnos's clothes. Glowing spirits clung to the trunks, guiding their movements. Tree nymphs? Man, this night was one helluva way to break me in.

Thanatos stepped into my blade, forcing my attention back to him. A thin ribbon of golden-red blood slid down his neck. "You have no idea what I'm doing."

I pressed the tip of Baby Trident's blade against the side of his neck. "Give me one good reason why I shouldn't skewer you right now."

"If it's your desire, I shan't keep you from it. But aren't you the least bit interested in your invitation?" His accented words piqued my curiosity.

"Invitation?" I let my eyebrows go all quirky. The god of death wasn't trying to kill me? Right, I'd forgotten.

He stepped closer, unfazed by the blood now dripping down his neck from the cut of my sai. Zach remained limp in his grip, feet dragging helplessly through the dirt.

"I have a feeling you still don't know about your past." The wind swept through Death's hair, silver from the glint of the moon, his voice a low, dangerous purr. "Have they told you yet?"

I swallowed hard, fully aware of his attempt to manipulate me, but unable to push away the doubt gnawing at the edges of my mind. Just as I steeled myself to square up with him, scorching claws dug into my wrists, forcing my fingers to spasm open. The blade slipped from my grip and hit the ground with a hollow clink.

The two dragon demons from earlier had reanimated, their talons digging deeper. I gritted my teeth, swallowing the scream clawing at my throat.

I shot a look past Thanatos to Paul and Cynthia. Hypnos still stood, probably half-naked right about now with all the trees tearing at him, but the new demons were shaking out of their stun and jumping back into action.

You're the only one who can send them back. Paul's words reverberated in my head.

Thanatos's voice, silky and insidious, pulled me back to him. "Have they?" He repeated his question about my past, a dark smile playing on his lips, as if he knew more about me than I did.

My past life had been one of those untouchable subjects with my so-called god friends. "No." I bit back the stabbing pain of the dragons. "But if this is your way of persuading me, you suck at it."

He laughed. "Of course they haven't told you, their precious Amara. *He* can tell you. Give you all the answers you desire."

"Who?"

"God of the Underworld, of course."

One short, sweet guffaw full of nervous energy escaped my lips. "Hades?" But I knew he wasn't joking.

In response, the dragons' claws dug even deeper into my tendons, sending white-hot pain coursing up my arms. This time, I couldn't hold back a cry, hating myself for showing weakness.

"Let him go," I said, my voice shaking despite my best effort to sound steady. Zach's unconscious body dangled in my line of tear-blurred sight, each second hammering the guilt deeper into my chest. "… and I'll consider it."

"It's a yes or no answer, Jessa." He smiled as he said it, like he knew I had no other choice.

I knew it was the wrong choice, but I couldn't let Zach die. I'd gotten him into this… it was on me to get him out. "Fine. Swear I'll come back."

"On my life," he said a little too chivalrous. The hand choking Zach let go, and he crumpled in a heap. With lightning speed, Thanatos placed his palm on the side of my head.

"Wait, now?" I whispered, unsure if he even heard me. Blood trickled down my hands. I tried to pull away, but a scream tore from my throat as claws ripped muscle, demons cuffing me with talons. My head swam, faintness threatening to take over with every drop of blood lost.

The god of death leaned in, his cold forehead pressing against mine, his amethyst eyes holding my gaze, and his hand cradled my cheek, sending a chilling wave through my entire body. "This won't hurt," he whispered.

He pulled away slowly, his too-pretty smile softening the edges of the moment—despite the desperate need for a breath mint. He tilted my chin, forcing me to meet his callous eyes again. The River Acheron churned there, dark and unrelenting. Something deep inside me twisted, a jagged pull as though a piece of my soul was being torn free.

A shout rang out, garbled and distant, like someone yelling through water. Muscular arms clamped around me, yanking me backward, the force crushing against my ribs. The world blurred. My legs gave way, and someone screamed.

The shadows swallowed me whole. My chest heaved as air was

squeezed from my lungs, crushing me from the inside out. Agony consumed every fiber of me as the darkness claimed its prize. I'd failed—Zach, Paul, my friends. All left behind. And now, I was his.

☉☽ CHAPTER 20 ☾☉

Light burst into focus as air rushed into my lungs, sharp and desperate, like I'd been drowning. My knees hit the ground hard, hands sinking into damp grass. Nausea followed fast, a tidal wave that left me retching before I could even blink.

Ignoring the cramps, I reached to wipe my mouth but froze. My hand was slick with blood. My blood. Trembling, I stared down at the cool, blood-covered grass beneath me. Not stone. Not ash. Not what I imagined I'd see in the Underworld.

"Can you sit up?" Paul's voice sent a tidal wave of relief over me. He was crouched beside me, one hand holding back my hair. I blinked, trying to make sense of how I was here—with him—and not in the hands of the God of Death.

Sitting back on my knees I closed my eyes and took a shaky breath. The realization of it all crashed into me: I wasn't in the Underworld. I wasn't dead. But I also wasn't whole. When I opened my eyes, they locked on my arms, my hands—blood everywhere, smeared and dripping like a grotesque painting I couldn't escape.

Paul's mouth moved, but the sound was muffled now, distant, barely audible. Cynthia appeared beside him, snapping her fingers in front of my face. The world slowly came back into focus.

"Think she's in shock?" Cynthia's voice echoed, still sounding miles away.

"Wouldn't doubt it." Henry approached, looking slightly winded.

The last image of Zach hit me like a slap in the face, ripping me from my daze. "Zach!" His name tore from my throat before I even realized I'd spoken, my brain finally clearing.

Henry answered first. "He's fine." He stepped to the side to reveal him.

Zach sat slumped on a bench, elbows on his knees, his eyes fixed on the grass. We were in another park. My mind stumbled over the realization we were far from the battle I'd just fought.

I swallowed hard against the sour taste in the back of my throat. "Is he... okay?"

"Sort of," Henry replied with a shrug. "When I saw Thanatos let him go, I grabbed him and ran."

Maybe Henry wasn't so bad after all. My body swayed, the wooziness pulling at me like an undertow. Paul's hand was still wrapped around mine, sticky with blood but steadying. He didn't let go. His touch grounded me, not because of his powers, but because it was him. Did he even realize what he did to me?

I turned back to Henry, forcing my scrambled thoughts into something resembling a coherent question. "What do you mean, sort of?"

"He still remembers what happened. But he can't see us right now."

His words hit me like a kick to the ribs and my eyes widened. Paul's grip tightened. God, poor Zach. "How did he see all of that?"

Henry shrugged like it was no big deal. "You were with him. Mortals can see what you see when they're with you. Which is why you have to be careful."

"I'm supposed to be careful?" My voice rose, sharp and accusing. "Like I knew those things would come after me!"

Paul's hand tightened, his voice calm but pointed. "That's why your visions matter. Normally, you'd know what's coming."

I wasn't sure if it was awkward to him, but I didn't let go of his hand, glad for the security. My mind flipped from the new information about visions to Zach and what he must be going through. "It would've been nice if you guys could've told me that, like, before now."

"Yeah, well, your situation is a little unique," said Cynthia with her normal snootiness. "Most Potentials don't have demons on their ass the day they become one, much less a god trying to kill them."

"You guys have really gotta stop keeping me in the dark about all this," I said angrily. My gaze drifted down to Paul's hand in mine—strong, olive-toned, faintly visible veins—and a stray thought tugged at me. How old was he, really? Did his hands hold centuries of stories I'd never know?

I looked up, drawn to his face. Concern was etched there, so still it felt ancient, like a statue carved with care. What did he really feel? Was this protectiveness just his duty as my Guardian, or was it something more?

The questions churned, each one more annoying than the last. Why hadn't they bothered to tell me I wasn't some run-of-the-mill Potential? Was that classified info? How much other crap were they hiding? Did I need to file a Freedom of Information request with the gods?

The secrets felt like a weighted blanket—except, you know, less cozy and more suffocating. I could practically feel the aneurysm forming if they didn't start spilling the truth soon.

Reluctantly, I let go of Paul's hand and held my stomach for fear I'd barf all over the place again and stared across the grass to where Zach sat. "Does he think I'm dead?"

Henry shrugged. "Not sure what he's thinking."

Curling my fists, I was ready to punch Henry right in the nose, back to not liking him. "Do you even care?" I pushed past him, determined to get to Zach and try explaining all this craziness to him.

Cynthia flew in front of me with her insane speed and crossed her arms. "What do you think you're doing?"

"Letting Zach know I'm okay." I didn't miss the lookover she gave me with her fierce green eyes. I couldn't even begin to imagine what I looked like. Soaked in my own blood, clothes half-torn and vomit covered. Paul had healed all my wounds. I wasn't in pain, but still. Cynthia had a point, even if she hadn't voiced it.

Her eyes softened, and she relaxed a little. "We can take care of him. You should go get cleaned up."

"What does that mean, take care of him?" I looked from her to Henry, who was now at her side.

Henry and Cynthia exchanged a look, the kind that screamed *united front*. Great. Like I didn't already feel outnumbered. Cynthia shrugged. "His memory. We can... adjust it."

"What? No, you're not touching him." The words shot out of me before the realization slammed into me. "Wait…" My hands clenched so tight my nails bit into my palms, a surge of heat flooding my chest. "You! You did this to Samantha!"

It wasn't Cynthia who flinched. Henry's expression tightened, a crack in his usual smug demeanor and I could practically smell the betrayal.

"That's how it works," he said.

I shook my head. "No. Not with me, it doesn't. Don't touch my friends." I jabbed a finger hard in Henry's chest.

He grabbed my wrist. Though it had healed, a raw ache flared from everything it had been through, and I grit my teeth, forcing myself not to react.

"It isn't up to you," he said, enunciating each consonant. I yanked my wrist free and leveled a glare at him, pouring every ounce of my contempt into it.

"Jessa, you're in shock. You don't know what you're talking about," Cynthia said.

Why did she have to be Paul's sister? It was like an extra layer of pressure to stay on her good side, just to make myself look better in front of him. Ugh, screw that. I couldn't keep bending over backward trying to decode Paul's thoughts—it was a one-way ticket to losing my mind. "Whatever, I know exactly what I'm talking about. And you two were a little late, doncha' think?"

Cynthia twisted her lips, obviously holding something back. "You weren't the only one with problems, rookie."

Paul finally spoke up, and my hopes flattened with each word he said. "Think about it, Jessa. Even you had a hard time grasping all of this. Imagine what it's going to do to him. Keeping this night in his memory?"

So much for him taking my side. I should've known, based on our "conversation" at Dawn's house.

I ran a bloody hand through my hair. "He'll be fine." He'd have to be. And then I wouldn't have to carry the secret with me for the rest of my life. I'd have someone normal to talk to about all the crazy stuff. He'd have to deal, and I'd be there to help him. Samantha would be next. It wasn't fair for me to keep this all to myself.

Cynthia let out a laugh that didn't reach her eyes. "He must be pretty important if you're willing to drag him into this." She paused to arch one eyebrow. "Or...maybe not."

"At least let me try," I insisted.

I felt a hand brush lightly against the small of my back. "We should go with you. Might help to explain things," Paul suggested.

"Or bring him back around after he faints from seeing Jessa like that," Cynthia added, her gaze flicking to where Paul's hand rested on me.

I let out a tense breath. "Thank you." I wiped my hands on my shorts, over the lump in my pocket that was my phone. I winced. My mom. This had to be the worst night of my life. "You all owe me a ton of answers after this."

I walked toward Zach with them, my brain playing ping-pong with everything that's happened in such a short span of time. It all felt heavy, scattered, and just out of reach—like trying to piece together a puzzle while someone kept swiping the edge pieces.

"By the way," said Cynthia, a smile tracing the edges of her lips. "Not a bad job, out there."

"Yeah, about that. How exactly did we get here?" I wasn't sure what park it was, but I knew it wasn't anywhere near where Zach stopped in the middle of the road.

"That little poofing thing we do," Paul answered. He came up to my left side but kept his eyes forward.

I stopped dead in my tracks. "Wait. I thought you said you didn't know if that would even work?" My stomach flipped. "You risked me coming back missing, like, a kidney or a leg or something?"

A biting silence fell over the group. I turned to Paul first. His eyes were fixed on his feet, like they might offer an escape from the weight of my stare. Cynthia, on the other hand, looked anything but guilty. Her smirk carried a hint of smugness, as if she knew something I didn't and was savoring it. And Henry looked everywhere but at me. The raw power in me sizzled, ready to erupt on my supposed allies and give them a good beating for taking a stupid risk.

Paul's voice doused my fire. "It was that or lose you again." He walked away.

Cynthia's smirk vanished, replaced by pure anger. I ignored her.

What did Paul mean? Like, at Charlie's Diner? I shot a desperate glance at Henry, silently begging for answers. He grimaced, caught off guard when our eyes met, then quickly turned away, muttering something under his breath as he hurried to catch up with Paul and Cynthia.

Okay, someone was going to have to fill me in and quick, or I was going to combust. But Zach first.

I hurried to Zach's bench, my pulse quickening when his eyes landed on me. The recognition in his expression sparked yet another question to hurl at my so-called godly "friends." Had I been invisible with them?

He lifted his head, spotted all the blood, and froze. I knelt in front of him, hands on his knees. "Hey."

His body twitched. "Jesus Christ, Jessa." He stared at my shirt, then my hands. "Am I in Hell?"

Breaking him in was going to be harder than I thought. "No. I'm okay, I swear. There's, um, something I need to tell you."

His eyes weren't quite focused. "Jessa," he started, faint and weak. Then he shook his head, as if unable to ask whatever he'd wanted to ask.

"Look at me," I said.

Eventually, he did. Not fully, though, like he was looking at me but mentally stuck somewhere in the past. I could make him okay. I could make this work. I held his hands and kept a firm hold on his gaze. "I'm okay." My stomach went all topsy-turvy on me, and I licked my lips. "I'm not, uh... a normal human. If I am one at all," I muttered the last part more to myself.

Zach blinked. I had his attention now.

My hands shook. Even my voice came out quivery. "Look, I can prove it." I wiped my face. The pasty blood proved hard to rub off. "My face, see? No scratches. My arms are fine, too. And I didn't die of an asthma attack."

He didn't say anything.

"I'm, um, sort of..." Okay, now I had a little sympathy for Paul when he broke the news to me. "Well, you know Hercules, right?"

"There's blood all over you." His voice shook and I was pretty sure he hadn't heard a word I'd said.

"No." I shook my head and tried for a smile. "No, I'm okay. Really. I can't get hurt. I mean, technically—"

He grabbed his head, shook it hard, and stood so fast I had to back up. "No. You're not okay. Those things... and you threw me. How? How'd you... no, it couldn't have happened. This is a nightmare. Some messed up dream. I'll wake up soon." He paced in front of the bench.

I reached for him. "Zach..."

He jerked away. "Just... don't."

None of it was going like I'd planned. He had to let me try and explain. I'd never seen him this shook up before. A barrage of flashbacks hit me at once: My scrolled handwriting of "Jessa London" all over my school folders, our first date together at the movies, our first kiss, his fingers brushing through my hair...

"Please let me explain."

He ran a hand through his dirt-covered hair. "Fine."

I took a deep breath and started again. "I'm half god."

That stopped his pacing. He shot me a sideways look, the kind you'd give someone who just confessed to hearing voices in their toaster. "What's wrong with you?" His words were cold, sharp, and they hit like a smack, leaving me frozen on the sidewalk. "You're joking about this? You hurled me across the street. And those things… what the hell were those things? You could've been hurt. This isn't—"

And that's when they decided to show themselves. I could only assume their visibility in front of mortals was a choice.

Zach fell back onto the bench. "What the fu—"

"Watch it now, lady in your presence," said Cynthia with a lopsided smile.

His eyes lingered much longer on Cynthia. Could I blame him? Decked out in a silver gown that molded to her body like skin and having the beauty of, well, a goddess? Maybe I was a little jealous, but she wasn't a threat. She'd eat him alive.

"Well, what's it going to be?" she asked. The I-told-you-so tone made me wish I had my baby tridents so I could swipe them at her out of spite.

Zach hung his mouth open and though surprised, looked way more confused than anything else. I wanted to say it would just take time; that he would come around and could keep our secret. But one more look at his haggard, terrified face and I knew I couldn't lie to myself. I was totally alone in this, and it hurt. It hurt worse than a broken heart, worse than being abandoned by a father, worse than Death nearly claiming me. I hugged myself and turned away, fighting once again for control. I couldn't cry in front of them. Crying while being scratched and clawed to death was one thing, but this? They'd never understand.

"Do what you have to," I said without a quiver in my voice, and started to walk away. "I'm going home."

Paul followed me. "Let me take you."

I felt too numb to argue. "Whatever." I stopped and let him cradle me in his arms. Not even that comforted me. Before he burst into his godly run, I looked over his shoulder to see Henry and Cynthia surrounding Zach.

If only he could've taken it better. If only he could've tried to understand. I closed my eyes and pressed my face against Paul's shoulder and a second later, wind ripped through my hair and snatched at my clothes. My life had officially turned into a living nightmare.

☉) CHAPTER 21 (☉

Entering through the front door wasn't an option with all the blood on me, let alone the fact I knew my mom was probably in the front room waiting to pounce. I scaled the lattice up the side of the house, reaching the roof's edge.

"Careful," Paul called from below. It was the first thing he'd said since we left Zach and the others. Not that there was much time for conversation when you're racing through town at breakneck speed. I glanced down, barely making out his shadow in the darkness. I'd insisted on making it inside on my own.

With a not-so-graceful grunt, I hauled myself onto the overhang. Crawling at a turtle's pace to my window, everything that happened tonight hit me all at once. I fought giants and mini dragons, almost died way too many times, nearly lost Paul and Zach, promised to visit the Underworld at some point, and now, I was completely alone in dealing with it all.

I pressed my palms hard against my eyes, trying to block it all out. Before slipping through my window, I shot a glance at the shadow lurking below. "I need some time alone."

After a beat, Paul responded. "Understood. Is there anything I can do?"

He got it, but then again, he didn't. He wasn't mortal. He didn't have to juggle a normal life, with family and friends, alongside all this supernatural insanity. He didn't have to deal with the secret of it all. I shook my head. "Just some time alone."

"As you wish."

I felt, more than I heard, his departure. A quiet whoosh of air and a shift in the atmosphere, the electric buzzing over my skin gone.

I crawled through my window, locked it, and stood there for a minute, letting everything sink in. My clothes were soaked in blood. I tossed them into the closet behind an old box of dolls and headed for the shower. I crossed to the bathroom door and glanced at my cluttered desk against the wall. It looked messier than usual. My stomach twisted. Mom.

With new urgency, I locked the door, turned the shower to scalding, and avoided the mirror. The last thing I needed was to see how bad I looked and pass out like some damsel in distress.

The hot water pounded my muscles, easing the tension. I scrubbed furiously until my skin was pink. The red tinted water swirled around the drain as I gingerly touched my face, half-expecting to find some left-over damage. The memory of that earlier searing pain? Yeah, not something I could just shrug off. Physically, I felt fine now. Mentally? Not so much.

Stupid. That's what I'd been. I went into tonight thinking I was some kind of superhero, and for a bit, I even felt like a badass. But now, all I wanted was someone to talk to. Someone real, someone who knew me and how messed up my life had become.

I sank to the bottom of the tub, the relentless spray of the shower pelting my head. My chest felt hollow, like someone had scooped everything out and left me with an aching cavity. I told myself to pull it together, to stand up and face whatever this was. But how do you strengthen yourself when the floor has crumbled into a pit and you're already halfway down?

My grip on everything slipped, and the reality of the night came crashing in. I buried my face against my knees, letting go of the pressure to pretend I was okay. Hot tears streamed down, lost in the pounding water, and I let every piercing, suffocating emotion pour out. The kind of crying you can't stop, the kind that leaves you emptied and raw, because for now, that was all I had left.

A hard knock on the bathroom door jolted me. I rubbed my eyes, trying to clear my vision as I fumbled for the towel bar to help me stand.

"Jessa!"

Shit.

"Jessa, get out here right now." Her voice shook with fury I'd never heard before.

"Coming." I took a few deep breaths to clear the quivering, turned off the shower, and stepped out. I wiped the fog from the mirror just enough to see that I looked normal, apart from the red eyes and puffiness.

I wrapped a towel around myself, tried to steady my trembling hands, and unlocked the door. It flew open before I could even turn the handle.

My mom stood there, an older reflection of me, eyes also red and puffy, glaring at me like she didn't recognize the person in front of her. "This is not okay, Jessa Noelle Whitley."

I felt like a little kid caught stealing cookies before dinner. I could only stand there, dumbstruck.

"Where have you been? I've been worried sick!" She paced back and forth, simmering with an intensity that made the room feel smaller. Her hair was disheveled, her face drawn tight with frustration—like a frazzled version of Cynthia, but without the goddess grace. She kept shaking her head, her voice rising with every word. "This isn't you. My Jessa doesn't just disappear like this." Her pacing grew faster, her footsteps erratic. "And you're not going to do it again." She stopped abruptly, a foot away from me, her glare boring straight into mine. "Ever."

I clutched the towel, guilt eating away at me for putting her through this. "I'm sorry."

"Sorry doesn't cut it!" She took a shaky breath, covering her mouth as if trying to hold back everything else she wanted to say. "I can't do this right now. I'm so angry with you." She ran her hands over her face, trying to reset, but it was useless—the anger and hurt were still there, etched into every feature.

"You don't just get to say 'sorry' and move on," she continued, voice tight. "Actions have consequences, Jessa, and you need to understand how serious this is."

I gripped the towel tighter and had the sudden urge to almost say everything. To lay it all out—gods, monsters, the mess that was my life now. Maybe, just maybe, she'd understand. But then Zach's face flashed in my mind—how he'd pulled back, eyes wide with terror and confusion. The thought of seeing that same look in my mom's eyes… I couldn't do it. Not to her. Not like this.

Mom crossed her arms, her gaze narrowing. "You can't just run off and expect me to—"

"I'm not running off!" I shot back, immediately regretting my tone. I took a deep breath, trying to reel it in. "I'm trying to handle things, but it isn't that simple. I'm dealing with... stuff. Things you wouldn't understand."

"I don't care what you're dealing with, Jessa. You don't get to disappear and leave me in the dark. You're grounded. And I mean it this time. No phone, no going out, no exceptions."

All fight had drained out of me, and I simply nodded. Her eyes searched mine for a moment, as if she was looking for some sign that I was really listening, really taking in what she said. Then she let out a long, tired sigh, the kind that made her look older than I'd ever seen her.

"Okay," she sighed, her voice finally losing that hard edge. "We'll talk more in the morning. Just... get some rest."

She turned slowly, her hand hovering over the doorknob as if she might say something else. But then she shook her head, probably more to herself than to me, and pulled the door open. The soft click of the door closing behind her echoed in the quiet room, leaving me alone with the heaviness of everything unsaid.

A familiar prickling sensation crept over my skin, and a spike of anger sliced through me. My fists clenched, heat rising in my cheeks. Was it too much to ask for five minutes to breathe without someone lurking?

Still wrapped in the towel, I stomped to the beaded curtain and yanked it aside. The dim orange glow from the bathroom spilled into my room, just enough to catch the three figures perched on my roof, blinking at me. "Can't this wait?"

Paul and Henry turned away like modesty meant anything at this point. Cynthia smirked. "No," she said simply.

I growled and spun around. It was nearly three in the morning. I grabbed some clothes from a drawer and changed in the bathroom. Okay, I couldn't help it... looking decent mattered, especially with Paul around. I smoothed down my wet hair, trying in vain to look halfway presentable.

My flannel pants swished as I went back to the window, threw aside the beads, and unlocked it. "Make this quick and quiet. I just got reamed by my mom, and if she hears anything, it's my funeral."

Paul stood by the window, unusually quiet, while Henry and Cynthia fielded my questions, occasionally throwing some my way. They filled me in on the obvious: Thanatos wasn't out to kill me now; he wanted to drag me to the Underworld instead. The big mystery, at least to me, was why? And as usual, they were holding back, only giving me half the story. I wondered just how strong my newfound Herculean strength was... maybe enough to shake some real answers out of them.

"Every potential in the past four months has been… killed within three days," Henry stated, pacing as if he intended to carve a trench into my floor, his blond curls a hue of orange from the bathroom light spilling in. He glanced at Cynthia, who was watching me like I was an experiment under a microscope.

"Good to know," I muttered. I wasn't in the mood to deal with them. I just wanted to go to bed.

"You should take this a little more seriously," Cynthia warned.

"Then maybe stop withholding shit," I shot back, folding my legs beneath me on the bed.

Her face hardened, but before she could fire back, Henry waved a hand. "We don't have time for this." He stopped in front of me, his expression dark. "You're the only potential that's lasted this long. Why? And why is Thanatos trying to bring you to Hades instead of just killing you?"

"Don't you think I'd tell you if I knew any of this? I'm not the one holding out on information," I replied, fiddling with a loose thread on my stuffed bunny.

Cynthia turned her back to me, thumbing through the papers strewn across my desk. Papers I'd gathered from the research I'd done a few days ago. All about them and everything involved with Greek mythology.

"Jessa." My heart skipped a beat when Paul's voice broke through the tension. I didn't look up as he approached. "Have you seen anything? Anything else that could help us figure this out?"

I tossed Bunny on the bed and stood. "I. Don't. Know!" I winced at the volume and lowered my voice to a fierce whisper. "Listen, in the past week I've been stalked, nearly killed multiple times, seen nightmarish creatures I never knew existed, almost lost a friend to one of them, and on top of all that, found out I'm some freakish half-mortal with visions of fire destroying the world."

I stopped in front of Paul, glaring up at him. "I've told you everything I know. Fire. Volcanoes. Lots of eyes. Lots of screaming and death. I don't know anything more than you guys, so stop expecting me to figure it all out for you!"

A muscle twitched in Paul's face, his eyes clouding over with that familiar stormy look he got when his temper flared, even though he was trying to hold it back.

"Now I have a few more questions I'd like answered," I demanded, crossing my arms.

Paul looked past me, refusing to meet my gaze. I sighed, long and exasperated, and turned to Henry and Cynthia. "Is Zach okay?"

Cynthia shrugged like it was no big deal. "He's a mortal. He'll be fine. As far as he knows, he dropped you off at home tonight. He's peacefully sleeping in his bed as we speak."

I rubbed my arms, glancing at Zach's closed blinds across the yard. "So, he doesn't remember anything?"

"Nothing," Henry answered, his tone colder than I liked.

"And what's stopping any of you from erasing my memory?"

Cynthia scoffed. "You still have a lot to learn, rookie. You're half us, remember? Doesn't work on you."

For some reason, that didn't make me feel any better. Maybe it was the tiny hope in the back of my mind that I could forget it all and just go back to a normal life. I stared at a pink bead on my curtain, focusing on how the bathroom light made it sparkle like a jewel. "So let me get this straight. Giants, two-headed dragons, and dryads exist. What else is out there I should know about?"

"Those weren't anything close to real dragons," Henry said casually. He slid his finger along the spines of my books on their shelf, mostly all about Greece and its mythology. "And if we were to tell you everything that existed in our world, it would take a lifetime to finish."

I sighed. "Okay, fine. I'll just assume I know it all already. Not like I haven't read anything about your mythology."

Cynthia snorted. "Please, whatever's in those books or on the internet is only the tip of Mount Olympus."

I pretended to ignore her remark. "And why exactly are these things after me? You mentioned that wasn't normal. And what's the point of having one of me if you guys are out there kicking demon ass way better?" I flopped back onto my bed, snatching Bunny again.

"We have a pretty good idea." My bed creaked as Paul sat next to me. I squeezed Bunny tight with one hand, my heart betraying me with its quickened pace. His nearness made it hard to breathe, and I hated that I cared so much about what he might be thinking. Did he even notice me the way I noticed him? Or was I just another responsibility?

"We're guessing since it's past the three-day mark, Hephaestus is getting desperate. Or Hades. We're not entirely sure who's behind your visions of the Apocalypse. The fact you've survived this long says something to them. You're powerful. It's taking too long to kill you in the mortal realm."

"Or she's just lucky," Cynthia said.

I barely registered her snide remark, too caught up in what Paul had just revealed. "Apocalypse?" My chest tightened, fear mixing with frustration. "You're telling me my visions are about the end of the world, and you're just now sharing this? How am I supposed to deal with all this when you keep me in the dark?" My voice rose, betraying the fear rising through my anger.

Paul finally looked at me, his expression unreadable. "It's the only thing that makes sense. Fire devouring the Earth, Hephaestus, Cerberus—"

I frowned, confusion cutting through my frustration. "Cerberus? When did I see Cerberus?" I searched my memory, trying to piece it all together.

"The three pairs of eyes," Paul answered quietly.

It clicked. Cerberus, the three-headed dog of Hades. But he was with Hephaestus instead. "Wait, he's not with Hades?"

"Exactly," Henry said, placing a book back on the shelf. Cerberus was only loyal to Hades, so seeing him in a vision with Hephaestus could be a sign the two were now working together.

Paul turned and looked at me, but I could only stare at the pink thread on Bunny. "So, Hephaestus is working with, or for, Hades," I said.

"Finally, your brain is starting to work," Cynthia said. "If Hades is behind this, we're in some serious trouble."

I didn't have the energy to throw a glare at her. The pieces of my visions were like shards of glass in my head, waiting for me to fit them together. Cerberus, Hades, Hephaestus, fire, death, the Apocalypse.

And then the biggest question of all slapped me in the face. I couldn't believe I'd forgotten to ask it. "Fire." I shot my eyes to Paul. "It doesn't burn me."

Henry nodded. "That's right, I forgot about that."

Silence hung in the air, stiff and uncomfortable. Without warning, Paul jumped to his feet. The wheels were definitely spinning in his head. "If she's resistant to fire, that means..."

All eyes turned to me, and I felt like shrinking. "What?" I asked. "What does that mean?"

Paul stared at the floor, lost in thought.

"Paul, what? What are you thinking?"

He addressed Cynthia. "I need to check something. Stay here, don't leave her for anything."

The air popped and he vanished.

I stood. "What is going on?"

"Just because we're Guardians doesn't mean we have the answers to everything," Henry said.

"But you have more answers than you've given me. I know you're holding something back."

I didn't miss the glance the two of them shared. My fingers curled into my palms. I had the distinct feeling they really didn't like me, and I had no clue as to why.

Henry decided to give in a little. "It would make our lives a lot easier if we knew the motives of every chthonic deity. But they change. Often. Hades is one of the three most powerful gods. He's been known to outsmart even his brothers. Plus, whether it is Hades, Hephaestus, or both, they have Thanatos."

I made a face at his name. "What does that mean?"

"Thanatos is like a living encyclopedia. He's taken every soul from here to the Underworld when it's their time."

That explained the whole kissing attempt. Kiss of Death. Ick.

But wait—Hermes was known for helping mortals to the Underworld after death, too. "What about you? Aren't you supposed to help with that?"

A strange sadness twisted Henry's face. "At one time I did. Things have changed." And that was that. His body language pretty much said the discussion was over.

Cynthia continued to go through my journals and papers. "Loyalties change. If one isn't a Guardian like us, they have free will to serve the

Underworld. For a lot of gods, it's a benefit to try and have humanity wiped clean. Or to start them over."

I rubbed my eyes, the bridge of my nose, my entire face. This was all way above my head, even if I thought I could grasp some of it. Maybe I wasn't giving myself enough credit, but I was tired. Exhausted. Beat.

With a disapproving look, Cynthia waved a dismissive hand at me. "Get some rest. Write down any visions you may have. We'll talk more in the morning."

"It is the morning," I mumbled over my hands.

"Then take a quick nap. It may be the last morning you see." She flashed a smile that sent my stomach into a bunch of knots not even the best Boy Scout could unravel. She couldn't be serious, could she? She towered over me by a good three inches or more, and I had to wonder if she actually wore heels while battling demons.

"One last question," I asked before they could do their poofing thing.

Cynthia relaxed her usual uptight face, revealing just how tired she was. "What?"

"What happened," I started, losing some of my courage to voice the scariest yet most intriguing question of all. I'd been waiting for Paul to be absent. I swallowed and tried again. "What happened in my other life? Why don't I trust you?" I looked pointedly at Henry. "And why do I feel I knew Paul then, too?"

Henry turned with an "Oooo," as if he'd spotted something way more interesting on my bookshelf than my question. Cynthia shot him a peeved glare.

She moved to the window. "Because you did. You were a Demi then, too. Only Paul can give you the specifics." Her voice was tight, like she was forcing out the words, revealing just enough without really saying anything. "Henry, stop acting like an idiot and get over here."

Henry begrudgingly obeyed, but he wouldn't meet my eyes, like I was something toxic he didn't want to see or touch.

"Why won't you guys tell me? I know you know."

"Because we promised we wouldn't," Cynthia said, her voice almost regretful.

"Promised who?" I already knew the answer, but I needed to hear it from them.

Henry moved to climb out the window. Cynthia followed, tossing back over her shoulder, "We'll be out here if you need anything."

I growled and I fought the urge to hurl Bunny at her retreating figure. "You're a bunch of jerks," I blurted as the beads clinked together, marking their exit.

I peered out the window, trying to catch a glimpse of them, but they'd gone invisible. I could still feel their presence, though. With a growl, I slapped the beads closed, spun around, and flung myself onto my bed.

Staring at the ceiling, my thoughts spun like a cyclone. It was too much—the secrecy, half-truths, the sense that I was a pawn in some game where no one bothered to explain the rules. Exhaustion tugged at me, loosening my fists, but the anger lingered, smoldering quietly beneath the surface. It wasn't fair. None of this was fair.

I hugged Bunny tighter, my fingers digging into the fur like it might keep me safe. Stupid, but it was better than feeling like I was slipping through the cracks of something I didn't understand. A part of me wanted to scream, to rage at the gods who had dragged me into their mess. Another part just wanted to shut my eyes and make it all disappear.

But there was no escape.

I turned onto my side, Bunny tucked under my chin. The ticking of the clock on my nightstand was the only sound in the room, each second driving home that time was moving forward, with or without me.

How was I supposed to deal with any of this? I'd been a high schooler—normal-ish—until all this mythic madness crashed into my life. Now I wasn't even sure who or what I was anymore.

Why me? Why was I the one who survived? Why did Paul always look like he was holding back some massive truth?

I pressed my lips together, shoving the questions into the back corner of my mind. Breaking down wasn't an option. Not now. If no one else was going to help me make sense of this mess, I'd figure it out myself.

But the exhaustion hit harder than I expected. As my eyes drifted shut, the weight of the unknown pressed down on me, crushing.

The world around me had grown bigger, darker, and far more dangerous than I'd ever imagined.

And I was basically navigating it alone.

☉︎☽ CHAPTER 22 ☾☉︎

Sleeping wasn't easy, no matter how exhausted my body was. I tossed and turned, clutching Bunny tighter, trying to drown out the voices and shadows outside my window. But every time I drifted off, the visions started, pulling me into a world of fire and darkness.

Flames leaped out of the void, and I walked straight into them, determined to bring back answers—answers about my past, my future, and the fate of humanity. Could I control my visions, steer them toward what I needed to know?

My courage faltered the second I saw something moving through the flames—a figure, tall and broad, stepping toward me with dark, tousled hair and eyes burning with the reflection of fire. His shirtless torso revealed a sculpted body, tan skin stretched tight over rock-hard abs and muscular arms. I tried to remind myself it was just a vision, but the thought fizzled as he came closer.

Behind him, a massive three-headed dog prowled, each head moving in sync with the others, eyes glowing a sickly yellow.

"Hello, Amara." The man's voice made the hairs on the back of my neck bristle.

Every muscle in my body tensed. I wanted to run, to escape my own mind, but the distance between us disappeared in an instant. The flames molded into his form, and I was frozen in place.

"My name is Jessa."

His smile was dark, beautiful, terrifying. I knew who he was, but my brain refused to accept it.

"I'm starting to feel a little put out. I've offered you a warm invitation, and you've yet to respond."

I struggled to find my voice, but when I did, it was barely a whisper, laced with fear. "What do you want from me, Hades?"

His smile didn't falter. He sighed and held out his hand. "To give you the answers you so desire."

His hand was flawless, inviting, and every part of me wanted to take it. Just like Thanatos, he drew me in, arousing something deep and unwanted inside me. I hated the pull he had on me. "I desire nothing from you."

"That isn't true." He turned his hand palm down but kept it extended, waiting. "They won't tell you the secrets of your past. I will. I see everything, know everything. And they don't trust you enough to share with you what you really are."

I bit the inside of my cheeks, trying to stay defiant. "I know what I am."

"Do you?"

His words planted doubt in my mind, eroding my confidence. "Yes." But even to me, it sounded uncertain.

He shook his head and tsked. "Dear Amara, they've kept the most important thing from you."

I swallowed hard, the heat drying my throat. "And what exactly is that?"

Any shred of distance evaporated in one step, his lips next to my ear and all I could do was hold my breath. "They failed to mention that you, Amara, were the first demigod after Hercules."

The three pairs of eyes behind him blinked slowly. Cerberus laid down like a monstrous guardian, each head resting in a posture that belied their deadly nature. My mind snagged on Hades' words—*first demigod after Hercules*—and the meaning of it pressed against my thoughts, demanding to be understood.

What did that mean? A thought tugged at the edges of my consciousness, a doubt that hadn't been there before. Why hadn't my soul been recycled before now? Was this question truly mine, or had he planted it, weaving his influence through my mind like a dark spell?

He pulled back slightly, but the space between us was still a mere breath, his presence overwhelming. I'd been close to so many men in the past few days, yet I still couldn't get used to it. It was as if gods didn't understand the concept of personal space—or maybe they just didn't care. The heat radiating from his body pressed against me, and despite myself, tingles of unwanted desire spread from my navel, curling lower, betraying every instinct to stay guarded.

"I can show you," he said, his voice smooth and coaxing, the closeness making it impossible to ignore the power he held. "Take my hand. I can show you the past."

I shook my head, trying to summon the strength to speak, but the words were choked by the smoky air. I managed a whisper, "How did I get here?"

"Dreams," he answered, his voice lyrical, almost mocking, each word wrapping around me like a spell.

With a wave of his hand, the flames dissolved into slithering smoke, leaving us in a cave of blackness that somehow still held light. His presence was an inescapable shadow, pressing against my will.

"So, none of this is real?" I dared to hope, clinging to the idea that waking up might be my escape.

"Oh, it's real, my dear. Unlike dreams, you'll remember every moment, every word spoken." His eyes roamed my face, and I couldn't help but wonder—did I look like her?

"But how?"

His voice slipped through the air, silky and dark, as he circled me, the cave transforming into a lush jungle, pulsing with unnatural life. The vibrant flowers leaned in as if they, too, were drawn to him.

"Your friends," he began, his tone both mocking and seductive, "would tell you to figure it out on your own. But I'm not like them. I'll give you all the answers you crave." He paused, letting the weight of his words sink in, daring me to take the bait.

I wanted to retort, to keep my wits about me, but his every movement, the way his eyes bore into mine, made it difficult to think straight.

Hades closed the distance between us again, his gaze locking onto mine with a piercing focus that momentarily stole the air from my lungs.

Slowly, almost tenderly, he reached out and traced the line of my jaw with his finger, the touch both electrifying and unsettling. "You know," he murmured, his voice dropping to a seductive whisper, "Hypnos has a son."

The sensation of his finger trailing along my skin sent a shiver down my spine, scattering my thoughts as I tried to focus. "Morpheus," I finally managed, the name slipping out as I recalled the god of dreams, the one who could twist reality within the bounds of sleep.

His lips curled into a knowing smile as his finger held my chin, tilting my head ever so slightly so I couldn't look away. "Yes, Morpheus," he purred, the word dripping with dark promise. "He's the one crafting this dream, shaping it to my will. But it's me who holds the reins, guiding you through this little journey. And trust me, this is only the beginning of what I can show you."

His touch was magnetic, drawing me closer to the edge of something dangerous, something I knew I should resist but found myself gravitating towards anyway. The line between desire and fear blurred as he held me there, the jungle around us continuing to pulse with an unnatural, almost hypnotic energy.

"Why?" I asked, my voice shaky, betraying the mix of fear and unwanted excitement pooling between my legs. "Why are you doing this?"

He paused, his hand moving to gently lift a strand of my hair, his touch sending low tingles. "Because, Jessa," he whispered, "I find you... fascinating. A soul as ancient as yours, with such power—it's a rare thing. I want to help you unlock that potential, to see you rise to what you were always meant to be."

The way he said my name was a stark reminder of who I was now, not the woman they claimed I had been. The thrill that ran through me at his words was undeniable, an unsettling mix of fear and desire. It was as if, in that moment, he saw me more clearly than I saw myself, and that realization both terrified and enticed me.

I swallowed hard, trying to ignore the way my body reacted to him, the way his voice seemed to wrap around my senses like a velvet ribbon. "And what do you get out of this?"

His smile was slow, seductive, as he let the strand of hair slip through his fingers. "I get to watch you. To see what choices you make when you have all the pieces of the puzzle. And maybe," he leaned in closer, his lips brushing my ear and sending a chill down my neck, "just maybe, you'll find that our interests align more than you think."

His words were tempting and perilous, and I hated how much they made me want to trust him. Deep down, I knew that trusting Hades would be the most dangerous thing I could do. Still, the jungle around us, the warmth of his presence, and the tantalizing offer of answers pulled at me like a tide I couldn't resist.

"Morpheus may be guiding your dreams," he continued, his hand hovering near mine, "but it's my will that shapes them. I can take you wherever you want to go, show you whatever you need to see. All you have to do is take my hand... Jessa."

The way he said my name sent a spark through me, and I found myself almost reaching out, almost letting my fingers brush against his. But at the last second, I pulled back, every instinct screaming at me to stay in control.

"You're lying," I whispered, more to myself than to him, trying to cling to whatever shred of reason I had left.

Hades chuckled, a low, rumbling sound that made the jungle tremble. "Perhaps," he teased, "but doesn't that make it all the more exciting?"

A cruel glimmer caught in his eyes. Without warning, he grabbed my arm, his grip like iron, and everything around us ripped away.

The jungle disappeared, replaced by roaring flames that shot up from the ground. Hades yanked me down, pulling me into a never-ending pit of darkness. His grip burned, searing my skin, and I tried to scream, but the sound was swallowed by the rushing wind and water that engulfed me.

I was drowning, tumbling through the abyss, cold water crashing against me, spinning me in every direction until I couldn't tell up from down. The dark, suffocating depths threatened to swallow me whole, every ounce of air forced from my lungs.

His voice cut through the chaos, a reminder that this wasn't real. "This was the end."

And then, as if watching a movie in reverse, the water receded, and the darkness peeled away. The world around me unfurled, the land rushing backward, trees shrinking into the earth, buildings crumbling and rebuilding in a blur. The sky above flipped between day and night in rapid succession, stars streaking across the heavens like time-lapsed comets. The scene slowed to a stop, and I found myself staring at a woman standing alone on a white sand shore, the endless ocean stretching out before her.

She stood at the edge, dressed in a flowing ivory gown with a golden sash, her sun-kissed hair blowing in the salty breeze. She looked familiar, but I couldn't place her. Behind her, massive white stone walls stretched into the distance, encircling a city of gold and stone I somehow knew.

The scene rewound again, and I fought to hold on. "No, wait!"

But Hades didn't listen. The next moment, I was on a balcony with the same woman, the sun setting over a pearl-studded horizon. A man appeared behind her, his golden-brown hair glowing in the light. My heart twisted at the sight. It was Paul, unchanged except for his ancient attire.

"What is it?" he asked, his voice full of urgency.

The woman buried her face in his chest, and jealousy burned in my stomach. "Water. Floods. He's going to drown everyone."

Paul held her close, kissed her hair, his voice tender. "I won't let it happen. Stay here, I'm going to find Hermes."

"No." She gripped his arms, and I could feel the strength in her hold, the same strength I possessed. He sighed, trying to pull away, but she wouldn't let him.

"I must." His voice was heavy with regret, and the look they shared was so full of love it made my chest ache.

Hades' voice cut through the moment, dripping with sarcasm. "Isn't that sweet."

I bit my lip, desperate not to lose the images. I needed to see, to know, to understand. But could I trust what I was seeing?

Paul rested his forehead against hers, closing his eyes. "Release me, Amara."

My breath caught in my throat. That was me?

I focused harder on them, on the intensity of their connection. The sounds of the world around them faded, leaving only their breathing, their heartbeat. Amara's fingers flexed, and she reluctantly let him go. Their gaze held for a long, heavy moment.

"Please," she whispered.

He held her hand, his voice thick with sorrow. "I'm sorry." He kissed her hand, and then he was gone, leaving a ghost of warmth on her skin.

Tears streamed down her face as she turned to the balcony, staring out at the ocean, at the walled city that seemed so familiar yet so distant. Before I could take it all in, the scene shifted again.

I braced myself as I was flung into the next memory, standing in a grand marble hall filled with golden machines and people in flowing robes. Paul walked with Henry beside him, both armed with weapons, both looking like the gods they were.

"It's started," Henry breathed.

Paul's face was flushed with anger, his eyes hard. "We'll need everyone's help."

"When is it to happen?"

"She doesn't know."

"We must act fast." Henry turned, but the details blurred as the memory started to fade. I fought to hold on, to see more.

"I'll get Amara," Paul said.

Henry stopped, his expression disapproving. "That's unacceptable."

"What?" Paul's face darkened.

"We've spoken of this already. She's a demigod, Apollo. You know it isn't allowed. Stay focused."

The hall dissolved into darkness, leaving only their glowing forms. "I am focused," Paul insisted, his voice sharp. "We need her."

Henry's eyes flickered past Paul, landing on something just behind him, and for a fleeting moment, it felt like he was looking right at me. His lips pressed together, a subtle sign of hesitation. It was as if he was wrestling with his words, struggling with what he had to say—or what he was choosing not to say. "Yes, we do. Which is why Artemis has been sent to retrieve her. She'll be at the battlefront."

Paul, trusting Henry, seemed to miss the flicker of uncertainty in his voice, but I didn't. My stomach twisted with the realization that Henry was keeping something from him, something important. Before I could process it, their figures blurred and then vanished, replaced by the balcony again, this time with Amara pacing, her expression frantic. The sounds of battle echoed in the distance, and she looked up, her face full of dread.

And then, I was her, or she was me. We were one, and I could feel everything she felt, hear everything she thought. I stood on the balcony, waiting for Artemis, just as I'd been told. But a gnawing unease settled in my gut. The sounds of battle grew louder, the world crumbling around me, and no one came. I waited, clinging to the hope that Artemis would appear, that Hermes's promise would hold true.

Deep down, I knew. The overwhelming fear of losing Apollo was suffocating. Darkness swallowed the sun, casting a shadow over the land as the first tremors of the rising wall of water shook the earth. I stood on the balcony, helpless, as the city—my beautiful city—was devoured by the oncoming torrent. White stone walls, once gleaming in the sunlight, crumbled like sand under the rush of the relentless wave. The streets below, bustling with life moments before, were now a churning, chaotic sea, dragging everything in its path into the abyss.

I watched in horror as the wave tore through the heart of the city, ripping apart buildings, uprooting trees, and swallowing whole families in its merciless grasp. The temples, the marketplaces, the homes… all gone, reduced to nothing in a matter of seconds. The cries of the people, once vibrant and full of life, were now drowned out by the roar of the water, a deafening cacophony that echoed the end of everything I'd ever known.

And still, the wave grew, building higher and higher, an unstoppable force closing in on me, as if the very wrath of the gods had been unleashed. The air grew heavy with salt and despair, and I could feel the moisture on my skin as the wave reached the walls of the palace, crashing through the gates and flooding the courtyards. The ground beneath me trembled, the force of the water shaking the very foundations of the world.

I held my breath as the wave reached the balcony, towering above me, casting its dark shadow over everything. There was no escape, no way to fight back. The end was inevitable, a force of nature that even the gods could no longer stop. The last remnants of the city disappeared beneath the swirling waters, and the waters loomed over me, ready to claim its final victim.

I closed my eyes, tears slipping down my cheeks, mingling with the spray of the wave. My thoughts of Apollo, of the life we had almost shared, the future that would never be. My heart ached with expansive emptiness, with the knowledge that I had failed.

"I'm sorry," I whispered, my voice barely audible against the roar of the wave. And then, with a final surge, the water crashed down, and I was lost to the darkness.

☉︎) CHAPTER 23 (☾︎☉︎

The waters took me in. Again. Seeing it was one thing, but living it all over again? Not something I was sure I'd endure. Pressure crushed against my ribs, toyed with my body like clothes spinning in a washing machine set on high, tangling my hair around my neck. If someone could die in a dream, I was pretty sure I was about to find out.

A hand reached out, grabbed my forearm, and pulled.

Suddenly, I was no longer weightless in water but stood on solid ground, dripping wet. A cold tremor coursed through me. I stared through the flames at Hades. I didn't know what to say, what to ask, what to do. What could I say after seeing that? Thanks? Not likely I was about to thank the god of the Underworld.

"Now you know," Hades said, his voice a mix of satisfaction and something darker.

Cerberus panted, drool hanging from one of his many fangs. Behind him, I noticed movement. A young boy, looking no older than ten or eleven, watched me from beneath a hooded cloak. The firelight illuminated his striking electric-blue eyes and black hair. Morpheus, god of dreams, I guessed. I wrapped my arms around myself, unable to stop shivering despite the overbearing heat. Hades waited, perhaps expecting gratitude I wasn't willing to give. His eyes danced over my wet body, lingering in a way that made my skin prickle. "I never did understand what he saw in you," he mused, his voice laced with curiosity and something more sinister.

I snorted, trying to hide my discomfort. "Yeah, I figure I can't be much to look at compared to your kind."

His smile widened, and instead of the creepiness I wanted to perceive, it looked... genuine. Not what I wanted to see. "You've made your point, can you let me go?" I tried to sound indifferent, but the burning heat of his hand against my arm made it hard to keep my voice steady.

"Not yet," he murmured, his tone shifting to something more intimate. "There's something else I must show you."

I sighed, trying to steady the conflicting emotions swirling inside me. The desire I'd felt before he'd plunged me into that ocean of memories, pun intended, had faded, but something more unsettling remained. "What now? I don't want to like you, and you've been trying to kill me. So why should I give you any more of my time?"

His fingers curled slightly over my forearm, his touch almost tender despite the underlying threat. He tilted his head, the light casting a sheen on his glistening neck. "Thanatos was right. You are a rather intriguing individual."

The mention of that name was a mistake. I jerked my arm back, grimacing as if I'd lost a layer of skin in the process. "I'm done with this dream."

Hades chuckled, a low, rumbling sound that sent all sorts of bad feelings through me. "You have no choice," he said, his voice wrapping around me, intoxicating. He reached out again, more gently this time, and despite myself, I didn't resist as he took my arm once more. "Come."

The fire shimmered like glitter, and when I blinked, I was no longer in the inferno. Instead, I stood in a vast throne room, the cavernous floor uneven beneath my feet. The smell of burning logs, dry ashes, and something reminiscent of a high school chemistry lab filled the air. Cerberus, now beside Hades, took three equally unsettling sniffs in my direction. If his enormous size didn't freak me out, his giant fangs did the trick.

"I thought Hercules killed you," I said to the oversized pet, trying to sound braver than I felt.

Each of Cerberus's three heads growled low in response. *Great job, Jessa,* I chided myself. *Piss off the three-headed monster and get ripped apart.* But then again, could I really be harmed here? I wasn't physically there—this was just a dream, right? *But if this is all a dream,* I thought, *then why does my skin feel like it's on fire? Why does it hurt so damn much?*

"Now, now, Cerberus," Hades cooed, "she's our guest."

The dog barked, three in a row, shaking the cavern's very foundations. He strutted over to a metal door with rod iron bars in a small window, like something out of a medieval dungeon.

"I'm giving you a choice, Jessa," Hades said, his tone suddenly shifting to something more serious.

I turned to face him, the sound of my name on his lips stirring something deep within me, a command I didn't want to obey. My throat tightened as I debated whether to move closer or stand my ground. "You just said I didn't have one."

He waved his hand dismissively. "Not about being here. About your life. Everything you know and love is slipping through your fingers before you can even digest what's going on around you, am I right?"

"Yeah, and you're also, like, the devil. Why should I trust you? Why do you even care?"

He smiled again, a slow, deliberate curve of his lips that sent my pulse racing. "A soul is much like a fingerprint—unique, unmistakable, and each line tells a story etched by time. Other than Hercules, you're the eldest soul of your kind. Which, as you've probably noticed, makes you rather difficult to kill. A bit of a nuisance, really, for those who've tried." He waved a hand again, as if the attempts on my life were mere trifles. "But when I discovered who you truly are, I knew I couldn't simply dispose of you like the others. Your soul is," he leaned in, his breath warm against my cheek, "...special."

He pulled back to meet my gaze. "So, I'm giving you a choice. You don't have to accept the fate that's been thrust upon you. You can renounce the title, walk away, and return to your ordinary life with your friends." He made way to his thrown, turned to me, and sat down while I mulled over his words.

Images of Samantha and Zach flickered through my mind, a sharp pang of longing following in their wake. Were these feelings truly mine, or were they twisted, manipulated by Morpheus? The kid still stood over there, his eyes not as disgusting as his father's, but just as creepy. I licked my chapped lips, searching desperately for a way out of this literal hell.

I started to feel something shift within me the more I dissected his words, a quiet certainty taking root in the chaos. "And just let you wreak havoc in my world? Not a chance." I crossed my arms, trying to reclaim a sliver of control in a situation where I had none.

"And who said anything about that?" Hades leaned forward, his elbows resting on his knees, his eyes never leaving mine. The torches on the walls flickered, casting a warm glow on his bare chest, making the sweat glisten like molten gold. He held out a finger, curling it towards himself in a gesture that was impossible to ignore. "Come, talk with me here."

Before I could resist, my body moved on its own, obeying his command until I was standing right in front of him. My breath hitched at the realization that he had complete control over me. The fear that had subsided came rushing back with a vengeance. "What are you trying to get at then? Why give me this choice? Why else if not to eliminate the one person who might get in the way of your plans?"

"And whoever said they were my plans?" His voice was a whisper, seductive and dangerous, as he leaned closer, his face inches from mine.

He had a point there. I hadn't seen Hades in any of my visions. But before I could answer, he leaned back, his expression turning serious again.

"Something to think about," he said, his voice more commanding. "But your choice expires. By the next sunset, you remain as you are."

I exhaled sharply through my nose, trying to hide my anxiety. "Sounds like something from a fairytale."

He tilted his head, watching me with an intensity that made the hair on my arms stand on end. "Sadly, this is no fairytale, Jessa. I do hope you make the right choice." He snapped his fingers.

The world around me rippled, the floor vanishing beneath my feet. My stomach lurched as I fell, a scream tearing from my throat as I plummeted into the abyss.

The scream jolted me awake. I was sitting up in bed, drenched in sweat instead of ocean water. My breaths came in shallow, rapid gasps, and I scrambled out of bed, my heart hammering in my chest.

Henry burst through my window, shards of glass flying everywhere. "Mother of Zeus, what happened?"

Ignoring him, I crawled across the floor, desperate to reach my desk drawer for my inhaler. The world was spinning, my vision going fuzzy as my chest tightened with each breath.

"Jessa?" Henry's voice held a note of concern, but I couldn't focus on him. My mind was a blur of fear and survival.

I clawed at the knobs of my bottom desk drawers, trying to pull myself up. "Cynthia!" Henry shouted.

"What?" Cynthia's annoyed tone only added to my frustration. The last thing I wanted was her help.

My superhuman strength worked against me again as the knobs crumbled in my hands. I stretched, reaching for the top drawer, my breath coming in ragged gasps. With a grunt, I yanked the drawer open and fumbled for my inhaler, pumping it to my lips.

Inhale. And again. And again.

When my vision finally cleared, the two blurry figures crouching in front of me sharpened into Henry and Cynthia.

"Another vision?" Henry asked.

I glared at him, my hatred burning hotter than ever. "You."

I'd hated people before. Zach for choosing Ashlyn over me, my eighth-grade geometry teacher for being a hard-ass, my dad for abandoning me… but this was different. This was a new level of hate, one that scorched any kindness or tolerance I had left for Henry.

His eyes widened, and he stood up, his expression wary. I stood with him, my body trembling with anger. "Get out of my room."

"What? Jessa—"

I threw my arm towards the shattered window. "Out! And fix your mess!"

Ignoring Cynthia, I glanced at the clock. They'd let me sleep in. It was a little past ten a.m. A folded note lay on the nightstand. Cynthia, for once, stayed quiet, but her glare bore into me.

"Jessa," she finally said, but it wasn't a question. I followed her gaze to where she was staring.

Across my right forearm was a large handprint, blackening the flesh as if burned or branded. The same arm Hades had gripped in my dream. I covered the mark with my other hand, my breathing became wild again. Seeing it meant it had really happened, right? That it hadn't been a vision, but something real. How could I even begin to process this?

My stomach twisted with anxiety. Where was Paul? Just thinking about him brought back vivid images of that place so long ago. He'd loved her, Amara, but hadn't taken control enough to save her. I longed for his touch, his reassurance, but it wasn't coming. Amara had been destroyed, and I wasn't trustworthy enough for him to tell me the truth.

Cynthia's face hardened, her stare like a knife slicing through my defenses. Finally, I gathered what little courage I had left and met her eyes.

"Mind telling me what that is," she growled through gritted teeth, her focus fixed on the arm I'd covered.

For some reason, tears burned in my eyes, but I couldn't let them fall. I couldn't tell her. Fear clamped my mouth shut.

Cynthia pressed her lips into a tight line, her stare making me shrink just a little. Even without her full power, those sharp green eyes of hers were enough to make me feel like I was being dissected. She hated me, and I couldn't understand why. But things were different now. She'd known me then, was supposed to find me, take me to the battlefront. She didn't. I'd been left to die, and I had to wonder if it had been on purpose.

"Jessa," she snapped. "What. Happened."

"Get out of my house." My voice trembled, but I managed to keep it steady enough.

"Jessa, you owe us an explanation."

I jumped to my feet and jabbed a finger into her shoulder. "I owe you nothing!"

Her eyes widened, the green depths swirling with silver mist. I'd never paid much attention to Cynthia before. She and her brother were so different, yet so alike. She grabbed my hand, her grip tight, and I glared at her, daring her to try anything. I didn't care anymore. I'd throw her out the window if I had to. They all owed me the truth, and they'd done nothing but keep it from me. Now I knew why.

"Go ahead," I said, low and defiant. "Rip my arm off. But after that, leave. I don't need your protection anymore."

"It was him, wasn't it?" she hissed, throwing my arm down. "Tell me."

"I'm not going to ask again."

She laughed, a short, bitter sound. "What? You going to throw me out?"

"If I have to."

Her smile vanished. "Have it your way." She turned and walked over the broken glass without so much as a flinch. Halfway out the window, she glanced back at me. "Paul won't like this."

I said nothing, but the knot in my stomach told me I cared more than I wanted to admit. I closed my eyes, listening to the glass squeak back into place, the beads stop swishing, and feeling Henry and Cynthia's presence vanish from the air.

Fifteen minutes passed before I got off my bed. I hated that I couldn't stop shaking, like my adrenaline was stuck on high and refused to calm down. I pulled open my closet door and pushed the clothes aside. Yanking off a long-sleeved white shirt, I realized I could see every dust particle in crisp focus. Even the tiny threads were clear, as if I were looking through a microscope. I blinked hard, trying to clear my mind. My eyes fell to the clump of bloody clothes on the floor. Ew.

Numbly, I changed into jeans and pulled a dark green Richland Heights shirt over the long sleeves. I grabbed the to-be-burned pile and salvaged my phone, slipping it into my pocket along with my inhaler, and took the rest downstairs to the fireplace.

☉☽ CHAPTER 24 ☾☉

The fire crackled and popped, burning my clothes to a crisp as I opened the windows, trying to air out the house before my mom came home. Her note sat untouched on the coffee table across from me, a reminder of her check-in call earlier.

I grabbed my phone, scrolling through the missed messages, bypassing my mom's texts. Sam had sent five, each one more urgent than the last, ranging from "r u home yet?" to "call me, worried," and this morning's "txt me asap wanna hang." Lizzie had also messaged, asking if I'd be going to Dawn's party tonight—apparently, it was the place to be.

I fired off a quick reply to Sam, then sank back into the couch. The sight of the flames brought a rush of memories—Hades, the dream, or whatever it had been—and I felt the familiar rush of nausea. I hadn't eaten dinner last night, and now the thought of breakfast made my stomach churn.

My phone chimed. Sam's reply flashed on the screen, and my frown deepened. She'd made plans with Dawn, since I never got back to her. I tossed the phone aside, letting my head fall back against the couch. Some friend.

What if I'd died?

I scoffed. Thanks to Henry and his memory-erasing tricks, I was still the same old Jessa—just a little less responsive. And grounded. No wonder she'd rather hang with Dawn.

Fine. I texted Lizzie a 'maybe'. With Death, Hades, and demons running loose in my city, I wasn't sure how accessible I'd be to anyone right about now. I stared at the flames again, my thoughts drifting to Paul. I hadn't seen him since the debrief in my bedroom.

Apparently, they hadn't let me sleep in... they just couldn't wake me up. After several unsuccessful tries, Paul had to leave to fend off nasties. At least, that's what Henry told me. Who knew what the truth was with him.

I hated needing Paul. I didn't want to need anyone. But those memories... they felt real. Maybe they were from a past life—or maybe they were just some twisted fabrication—but something deep in my gut told me they were more than just imagined. I'd always been wary of Henry, but now, it all started to make sense.

The image of Paul and Amara together on the balcony stirred a longing for what they had, something I clearly didn't. I had to remind myself that I'd only seen glimpses. I still didn't know the whole truth. Love like that couldn't really exist. If it did, Amara would've been saved.

I growled and threw myself back against the couch. Why did everything have to be so complicated? A stabbing pain in the center of my chest took me by surprise. God, it hurt, like a nail being hammered over and over through my heart. I leaned forward, clutching the side of my head, wishing there was an easy answer to everything. And it all hit me, square in the heart, deep in the gut.

Zach didn't want me anymore. Paul only wanted someone who didn't exist. Samantha had traded me in for a better friend, and I'd become the epitome of disappointment to my mom, if she didn't hate me already. Not to mention, my life had turned inside out. The abnormal was normal, and the normal was practically non-existent.

My phone chimed. I closed my eyes, dread seeping into my bones as I reached for it, the weight of everything pressing down on me. Lizzie's belated reply flashed on the screen: 'Just woke up. Don't worry, made other plans with Chloe.'

Anger, sharp and bitter, coiled in my chest, squeezing until it felt like I couldn't breathe. Without thinking, I hurled the phone at the wall. It shattered into pieces, a violent reminder of the strength I never asked for, never wanted.

I collapsed back into the couch pillows, my body trembling with the force of everything I'd been holding in. And then I broke. The tears came in a torrent, my sobs muffled by the fabric as if the pillows could somehow absorb the pain, take it away. But they couldn't. Nothing could. The more I cried, the deeper the ache grew, carving a hole in my chest that felt like it would never heal.

I was alone—completely alone—and the loneliness pressed in on me, suffocating, like I was drowning in it. Why me? Why was I the one cursed with this? Why couldn't Sam or Dawn be the ones caught in this nightmare?

No, I wouldn't wish this fate on anyone. It was impossible to have a normal life being this... thing. Whatever I was—this demigod, Hercules incarnate. The Guardians didn't trust me. Was I not good enough to trust? Why couldn't they tell me what Hades had? What was wrong with me? Why couldn't someone want me? Love me?

Save me.

My breath came in ragged gasps, each one tearing at my throat as though it were lined with shards of glass. I couldn't stop it, couldn't control it. The floodgates had opened, and the storm inside me was raging, relentless. Every sob that escaped felt like a piece of my soul breaking free, but instead of relief, it only deepened the void. My face was drenched, my vision blurred, and my throat was raw, strangled by the sobs that wouldn't stop.

I needed something—anything—to numb the pain, to quiet the storm. Ten shots of Jack Daniels might have done the trick, but even that seemed like a distant fantasy.

I slammed my fist into the pillow, the feathers bursting out like a cruel joke, sticking to my tear-soaked cheeks. All I wanted was to curl up, to shrink into myself and let the world fade away. I wanted to disappear, to retreat from both worlds—the mortal and the immortal—and become nothing, no one. My fingers dug into the ruined pillow, clinging to it as if it could fix me, but it was as hollow as I felt.

I needed him. Paul. His absence cut deeper than any blade. Why wasn't he here, holding me, telling me it would all be okay?

But it wouldn't be. It never would. There was no happily ever after for someone like me. Paul didn't care about me the way I foolishly hoped he might. If he did, he would've told me everything. He would've been there when I woke up from the nightmare Hades had plunged me into.

He would've kissed me by now.

I buried my face deeper in the pillow, teetering on the edge of suffocation, wishing it would all just end. I wanted to vanish, to run so far that even the gods couldn't find me. I'd take a lifetime of being Zach's ex, of competing for Sam's friendship, over the horror that had become my life.

Finally, the sobs began to subside, leaving me hollow and exhausted, my breath still coming in uneven, heavy hiccups. I turned onto my side, my wet lashes sticking to my eyelids as I stared blankly into the void.

I had until sunset to decide if I was willing to give it all up, to walk away from this mythic life, an experience old Jessa would've eagerly jumped at, to leave the powers, to leave Paul. The clock ticked forward, the choice shadowed over me like a bad punchline: give up Hercules and go back to a life where I was invisible, powerless, and unloved—or keep this cursed strength, this impossible existence, and stay stuck in a world that didn't want me. Either way, it felt like losing.

☉☽ CHAPTER 25 ☾☉

My skin prickled with a familiar icy chill, the kind that seeped into my bones and warned me of his presence before he even spoke.

"Jessa." Paul's voice was soft, a thread of concern woven through it. "Are you okay?"

I wiped my face hard, hoping to erase the tears, the snot, and the evidence that I'd completely lost control of myself. "Fine," I said, relieved that, for once, my voice didn't betray me.

Be careful what you wish for, my mom always said. She was right. Instead of feeling relief or comfort with Paul in my living room, I felt agitated, raw. This Paul, one who loved a woman that no longer existed, wasn't the Paul I wanted. The Paul I wanted was lost somewhere in time, bound to a past that didn't include me. Now, it was like I had no privacy, no space to even breathe.

I sat up from the couch, keeping my back to him, hoping he'd take the hint. But Paul wasn't one to be easily deterred. He moved in front of me, his presence a wall of seriousness and something else—something fierce. "Is it true?" His voice held a gravity that pulled at the edges of my control, threatening to unravel me completely.

Anger was the easiest emotion to draw on. I set my jaw and glared up at him. "What?"

He didn't break eye contact, even as his gaze flicked over my face, taking in the signs of my emotional breakdown. I could tell he wanted to ask if I was sure I was okay, but something stopped him. His eyes caught on the sleeve of my shirt, and before I could stop him, he grabbed my arm and yanked the fabric up, exposing the handprint branded into my skin.

His face paled, shifting from shock to anger, then to something I couldn't read. He threw my arm to the side, his expression hardening like a parent ready to scold a reckless child.

"What did you do?" His voice was accusatory, a tone that grated against every nerve in my body.

I was on my feet before I even realized it, the sting of frustration and hurt propelling me. "What's it to you?"

"Jessa, this isn't a game."

I stormed towards the staircase, intending to escape his lecture, but his hand clamped down on my other arm, holding me in place. "I'm serious. Tell me what happened. He saw you, didn't he?"

Every part of me froze at the mention of Hades. The Underworld, the memories, the things he'd shown me—all of it flooded back, making my blood run hot and thick with a mixture of fear and anger. Despite my thoughts of giving it all up, the last thing I wanted was to remember being there. And for Paul to be in my house, treating me like a child, grabbing my arm just like Hades had...

"Let. Go." My voice came out low, dark, and threatening in a way I didn't know I was capable of.

But he didn't let go. "Tell me what happened."

I jerked my arm free, spinning on him with all the pent-up emotion that had been boiling beneath the surface. With a hard shove, I sent him stumbling backward. "Tell you? Tell you? Like you've been telling me anything! Why did I have to find out from the god of the Underworld about my past? That should've been *you*."

Paul caught himself against the coffee table, his breath knocked out of him. He looked at me, stunned, like I'd just slapped him. Good. Maybe now he'd leave me alone. I took the opportunity to bolt, heading straight for the front door.

But in a gust of air, Paul zipped around me, blocking the exit. "Where are you going?"

"Not your business. Move." I screamed at myself for letting this happen. All I'd wanted was for Paul to show up and comfort me, but not like this. Not lecturing, condescending, keeping-everything-from-me Paul.

"No. What did he tell you? What happened? Jessa, talk to me." His voice was desperate, pleading. But the look in his eyes, that calm blue, didn't match his words. It was like he wasn't seeing me, but someone else. Someone from a past life. Recycled soul or not, I wasn't her.

"I owe you nothing. How's it feel to be kept in the dark?" I gathered every ounce of power I had and shoved him aside, watching as he slammed against the foyer wall. I practically flung myself out the front door, hoping to escape before I broke down completely.

I ran to my car, trying to keep my breath steady. *Please don't follow me. Please don't follow me.* But of course, he did. Paul stood in the driveway, arms crossed over his black t-shirt, looking like a fallen angel in the sunlight. Why did he have to wear black today of all days?

I stopped at the edge of the lawn, my fingers twitching with frustration. "Get off my property."

"Stop being unreasonable." He sounded tired, defeated, like he'd already given up on trying to reach me.

"Too late for that, Apollo." The words were bitter on my tongue, but I didn't care. "I don't want you here."

I watched as my words hit their mark. His face fell, his arms dropping in defeat. He stared at me for what felt like an eternity, the silence between us biting. "As you wish."

And then, just like that, he was gone. But there was no sense of victory, no rush of triumph. I felt like a total jerk. My chest tightened, the hole in my heart widening into a chasm. I still wanted him, hated hurting him. Damn it, I was so confused. It would be so much easier if I could just forget the whole Amara thing. But every time I saw even a flicker of concern in Paul's eyes, all I could think about was her.

Dragging my feet, I trudged back into the house. Maybe it was a good thing he left. It saved me from looking like an idiot trying to escape without my car keys. I may have acted like a jerk, but he could've tried harder if he really cared.

As the door clicked shut behind me, the phone rang, its shrill tone slicing through the heavy silence of the house. I hurried through the foyer to the kitchen counter, pausing just long enough to take a steadying breath before answering. "Hello?"

"I tried calling earlier, and no answer." My mom's voice brimmed with impatience.

Guilt tightened my chest. "Sorry. Is that all?"

"No. There's some leftover pasta in the fridge. Heat it up for dinner around four. I'm getting off work early so we can have a talk."

A knot formed in my stomach, twisting tighter with each word. This wasn't going to be just any talk. "Okay."

"Yes, ma'am," she corrected, her tone like a whip.

I flinched. "Yes, ma'am."

She hung up without another word. I clicked the phone off, my gaze drifting to the keys on the counter. I was going to have to give it all up. Greek mythology had been my one true passion, the obsession that shaped my life. And now, I was ready to walk away from it all.

Because how could I possibly have both? A normal life with Samantha, high school, a decent relationship with my mom, maybe even a shot at love—and still be the savior of humankind, constantly battling demons? It was too much to ask of anyone. I wished I could talk to Hercules, find out how he managed it all.

I needed to figure out how to get back to the Underworld, how to make my decision final. I closed my eyes and forced myself to think of Hades, trying to summon the courage to do what had to be done.

Okay, I've made my decision.

Something crashed upstairs, jolting me out of my thoughts. I jumped back, half-expecting Hades to stroll down the stairs. But it was something much worse—Cynthia, storming down with contempt in her eyes.

"What did you say to him?" She looked bloodthirsty, her red hair wild around her face, eyes narrowed into fierce slits.

I backed into the counter, feeling a surge of fear. "Back off, it's none of your business."

"The hell it isn't."

She was about to run right into me. I tensed, ready to defend myself, but she stopped inches from my face, her hands clenched into fists. "You're lucky he likes you, or I'd send you back to the Underworld myself."

"Really? You mean it? 'Cause I'm tired of this shit." I stepped closer, matching her fiery intensity. "Send away, bitch."

"Oh, you are such an asshole."

She punched my shoulder, and it felt like she'd nearly ripped it out of its socket. Gritting my teeth, I centered on what strength I had left and shoved her in the chest. She flew back into the staircase, crashing into Henry, who had just appeared out of nowhere.

Figures. Now I was outnumbered. "What's taking you so long, Cynthia? Get rid of me. Or should I say, betrayer? 'Cause that's what you are. You left me for dead."

She froze mid-stride, the fire in her eyes dimming as sadness flickered across her face. "He told you."

"If by 'he' you mean Hades, then yes." Breathing normally was impossible.

Henry remained at the bottom of the stairs, stiff and possibly in shock. When he finally spoke, his voice was barely audible. "You don't know the whole story."

"And whose fault is that, asshole? No wonder I don't trust you. You hated her. Amara. You wanted her out of the way for some reason. It doesn't matter why, all that matters is that you did. My soul. Out of the way. She was messing up some stupid plans, so let me make this easy for you."

I closed the distance between us with each word I spoke next. "I want to renounce my title." I locked eyes with Henry. "Take me there."

"What?" The word was full of air, barely audible. "No. I can't."

"Really? Sure fooled me. Seems like all I am to you guys is one giant untrustworthy burden."

"No, I mean, I *can't*."

Cynthia pulled herself together enough to join the conversation again. "Jessa, you don't know what you're doing." She moved next to Henry, the two of them standing like giant sentinels, ready to block my path.

I scoffed. "Well, this doesn't surprise me one bit. Artemis and Hermes working against me. Again."

Henry's face hardened, and for the first time, I saw a flicker of anger in his eyes, white swirls highlighting his irises. His neck muscles twitched, and he licked his lips as if trying to rein in his emotions. "Jessa, he's shown you exactly what he wants you to see."

"At least he showed me something, which is more than I can say for you."

"You can't just give up," Cynthia protested. "You're the last Potential."

"What?" I whispered, my anger now tinged with disbelief. They had kept so much from me, and now this? "I'm the last half-mortal on the planet, and you're only telling me this now? What the hell is wrong with you?"

Henry raised a hand, as if that could somehow ease the situation. "Things got complicated."

I shook my head, my vision blurring. I didn't know who to trust anymore, least of all them.

Cynthia placed gentle hands on my shoulders. "He's right, Jessa. You've got to believe us. You have to understand, they've picked through every demigod old enough to count. You don't know what that could mean. If you renounce your title, the next Potential to replace you could be a three-year-old, a baby, or non-existent."

Jessa.

The voice in my head wasn't mine. A cold shiver ran through me as I recognized who it belonged to.

Jessa, Thanatos said again. *I'm in your backyard. I've come to honor your request.*

☉︎☽ CHAPTER 26 ☾☉︎

Cynthia was the first to notice something was wrong. Her eyes locked onto mine, hands still gripping my shoulders. "What is it?"

My vocal cords refused to work. But this was what I wanted, right? Normalcy? I had made this choice. It wasn't theirs to make. It was mine. Right? Or was Hades manipulating me?

Cynthia shook me slightly, her voice more urgent. "Jessa, listen to me. He's up to no good. If Hephaestus is working with him, whatever they're promising you is a lie. Hercules—his soul was destroyed."

I remembered what Paul had said about Hephaestus destroying a soul, and I stared blankly, trying to wrap my mind around how something like that could even be possible.

Cynthia continued, her voice steady. "There are ways to kill a soul. Our father banished Hephaestus to Tartarus after he destroyed Hercules' soul, as revenge for being cast out of Mount Olympus. Hephaestus, angry at being the only disabled, disowned son, carried that resentment for years. But eventually, he was needed again and released from the pit."

Henry shifted uneasily. "Within the past four months, someone has systematically eliminated every demigod except you. We thought it was him again. Guardians couldn't reach the potentials in time to train or warn them. Within a day, three at the most, they were dead."

Cynthia glanced at the burn mark on my arm. "After recent events, we realize someone else is responsible."

A rock seemed to plunge into the pit of my stomach. I had a feeling I knew who, and their name started with an "H" and ended with "-ades."

"Hades," Henry confirmed.

If he could destroy a soul, then—

Remember, Hermes is a trickster. They'll say anything to keep you here. We want to give you your freedom, Jessa. Come, I'm tired of waiting. Thanatos's voice was musical, enticing. It tugged at my spirit, a pull I couldn't resist.

"Where are you going?" Cynthia's tone turned brutal again.

Where *was* I going? "It's time," I heard myself say. My feet moved on their own, ignoring my mind's desperate screams to stop. Panic clawed at my thoughts, but I could only watch helplessly as my body moved through the tiled kitchen hallway and into the dining room. This was worse than last night—being paralyzed by his gaze was one thing, but having him manipulate my body like a puppet?

Beyond the cherry wood dining table and six fancy chairs were the windows facing the backyard. I couldn't see him, but that didn't stop my feet or the longing in my soul.

"Jessa?" Henry's voice now.

I couldn't turn and look. Didn't want to. I had to get outside. I had to find him, see his eyes, watch the River Acheron ripple there. Nothing mattered anymore except satisfying the craving, getting to him before they could stop me. My fear no longer made sense. A gentle thought touched my mind—Thanatos would help. Everything would be okay.

My hand touched the cool metal of the doorknob, and I turned it, stepping outside. The center of the backyard was just grass, the short crape myrtle near the back fence fluttering pink blossoms to the ground. In a ripple of colors, Thanatos materialized, standing in the center of the grass. He looked like an angel, his white wings tinged with blue against the afternoon sun, spreading wide behind him. Silently, he called to me. I held my breath, feeling parts of my soul slipping out of my grasp. Numbness spread through me, distant and beautiful.

My focus sharpened like it had in battle. The flecks of his eyes shifted, misting over into a river. Deep blue, not the black of Acheron. Lethe, the river of forgetfulness.

Thanatos opened his arms, and the invisible rope tethering me to him tugged at my core. Whispers brushed the edges of my numb consciousness. Lethe would fill the emptiness. Everything would be okay. Come to Thanatos.

I heard Cynthia and Henry scrambling out the back door.

"What the hell is going on?" Cynthia snapped.

They couldn't see him? That made things easier, I guessed. I reached out to Thanatos.

I'll take away the hurt. You'll be normal again. A trip through the river, and you'll remember none of this. Your soul will be cleansed.

Cleansed. A cleansed soul sounded good. It'd be like waking up from a bad dream, but for real this time. No more gods hunting me down, no more monsters trying to tear me apart. No more juggling the fate of the world with a normal life. No more secrets from my mom and friends. No more Cynthia and Henry.

No more Paul.

My feet stopped. Would he just be a dream, stuffed away into my subconscious? Thanatos pulled again, like he'd lassoed my soul and wasn't going to let go that easily.

Paul. I closed my eyes, seeing him hold me, kiss the top of my head, pulling away to see my face in a timeless place full of golden sunlight, warmth, and eternal love.

But that didn't exist—not for me, anyway. It had existed for Amara. I was just a reminder of what Paul had lost. If he cared as much as he had in that vision, why had he left so easily? I let out what I expected to be my last breath on earth before Thanatos took me to the Underworld and opened my eyes. "I'm ready."

A blinding light exploded in the sky. It fell like a giant gold-flamed meteorite, streaking across the backyard and slamming into Thanatos. My soul snapped back into place. I gasped, staggering as my thoughts shattered the wall Thanatos had built around my mind.

Holy hell.

A raging headache pounded against my skull. I caught my breath and looked up. Within the brilliant ball of light, I saw him. Paul was back.

Everything happened at lightning speed. A burst of light struck Thanatos, sending him crashing through the fence. Cynthia and Henry rushed past me, leaping through the hole. Inch by inch, I lowered my arms, watching Paul spin in my direction. In a blur, he ran at me. I crossed my hands over my chest, bracing for impact. In one motion, Paul's body collided with mine, his arms binding me tight, and the world went black.

Pressure crushed my body in the vacuum of space. It squeezed my lungs, popped my ears, and suffocated me. But Paul's firm arms held me securely. My cheek pressed against his chest, his heavy breathing pulsing in my ear.

The black void tore away, and the ground slammed beneath my feet, sending me stumbling. Paul grabbed my waist, pulling me close. I kept my eyes closed, two thoughts repeating in my head like a broken record: Don't puke, and What had I just been about to do?

I took deep breaths, trying to stay calm, and folded into Paul's warm embrace. His fingers pressed into my back, his chin resting on my head. I swallowed down the nausea clawing at my throat, though it wasn't like I had anything in my stomach... the last meal I'd had was almost 24 hours ago.

"Stay here," he breathed.

My eyes flew open just in time to see the last of his form disappear into nothingness. Blinking, my eyes adjusted to the night after being surrounded by sunlight. I felt exposed, vulnerable, and really pissed at Paul for leaving. Heavy winds whipped my hair around my face, and that's when I smelled it, the city. It smelled like a mix of dirt and rocks, old and salty, fresh, cool, and clear.

Athens.

I turned around, my breath catching in my throat. Holy shit, was I standing on Mount Olympus? The moon shone behind me, casting a pale green haze over the thin streams of clouds. Over the edge, I could see the Parthenon lit up in all its glory. Goosebumps lined every inch of my skin. Since when did cities have a scent?

The air popped, and Cynthia blinked into existence next to the mountain wall. Her fists clenched at her sides as she stalked toward me, the moonlight casting her in a terrifying glow. Though my insides trembled, I stood my ground.

"You're such an idiot," she spat. "You could've ruined everything." Her breath came out in harsh, smoky puffs. "Again."

"You know, Cynthia, your attitude sucks." My eyes narrowed, my powers sharpened my vision until I could see the silver mist swirling in her green eyes and every detail of her perfect godly face, brightened by her moonglow aura.

"Where's Paul?" I demanded.

"Cleaning up your mess." She shook her head, her voice filled with frustration. "You just don't get it."

She kept invading my personal space, forcing me to back up until I was pressed against the mountain wall. The last thing I needed was to fall off the damn thing.

"No, I don't," I shot back. "Care to fill me in?"

"Yes," she said, her tone suddenly calm.

I blinked, caught off guard. "Wait, what?"

"You really think Hades would just return you to your normal life, Jessa?" She gave me an incredulous look. "Yes, I betrayed you."

My brain scrambled to process the answers I was finally getting. I didn't care about the poor timing.

Cynthia uncurled her fists and began to pace. "You have to understand, it wasn't easy. Paul is my brother, but back then, you were like a sister to me. I had to choose. I had to. There was no other way." Her words were tight, clipped behind gritted teeth.

"Just tell me what happened," I demanded.

She stopped and took a deep breath. "What you and he had... it's forbidden. But he didn't care. He was willing to become mortal, to give it all up, and I hated you for it. I hated you for making me have to choose. You were like a sister, Jessa, but he was—he is—my blood brother."

Her voice turned gentle, a tone I wasn't used to hearing from her. "The day of The Flood, when you finally gave the premonition, Henry and I saw it as the chance we had to keep Paul from making a stupid choice. Henry has always been a brother to us. Paul had no reason not to trust him. He told Paul I'd retrieve you before the waters came, but..." The wind carried away her last word, and she looked away.

Silence gnawed at the raw edges of my heart, assuming there was anything left of it. The truth was almost worse than not knowing.

Clouds of air swirled into Henry's form as he appeared, staggering. He didn't look too good. Gold-flecked blood smeared across his white linen shirt, but one look at Cynthia and his face fell.

"You left me for dead," I finally finished Cynthia's story.

She winced and nodded. Henry had a look on his face that said, 'Shit, my timing sucks.'

"He needs your help," he said to Cynthia.

Without hesitation, Cynthia disappeared. My heart, though shattered, found a way to pound in my chest. "Is he okay? Take me there. I'll help." The thought of Paul in trouble was like someone carving out my insides with a spatula.

Henry wore a sad smile as he shook his head. "No offense, but you being there won't help." He swallowed hard, his throat bobbing. "How are you holding up?"

Clutching my chest, I leaned against the mountain. "You mean about the truth or about Hades?"

"Pick."

"Finish the story," I said, my voice tinged with exhaustion.

☉☽ CHAPTER 27 ☾☉

Henry let out a long sigh, his blond curls shifting slightly in the cool Athenian breeze. He tilted his head back, studying the sky as though it might offer him the courage to finally spill the truth.

"Cynthia and I were foolish. And I wouldn't blame you if you never trust me again—"

"Good, 'cause that's very likely."

Henry inhaled sharply through his nose and turned away. He kept his back to me, eyes fixed on the city below as he continued speaking. "Paul was never the same after that. We thought we were saving him, but we were selfish. We couldn't imagine him becoming mortal." He paused, turning to give me a long, meaningful stare. "We still can't."

A long, ominous silence hung between us before he continued, his voice breaking slightly. "You think humans know how to hold a grudge? Paul didn't speak to me for five hundred and sixty-one years. He went off the grid for a while. Even Cynthia didn't know where he'd gone. But we'd hear about things—things only Apollo, only Paul, could do. So, we knew he was still out there, he just chose to have nothing to do with us."

I wrapped my arms around myself, trying to shake off the cold creeping into my bones. The tragedy his words carried settled over me like a heavy fog. My mind strained to grasp a love so eternal, so devastating. The realization that my soul had once been part of something so eternal coursed through me, leaving a throbbing ache in its path.

Before I could fully process Henry's words, the empty space next to him was suddenly occupied by Paul. He gripped a bulging rock to keep from falling over, his face pale and strained.

I was at his side before my brain could catch up to my feet. "My God, are you okay?"

He managed a smile, but the tightness in his eyes betrayed the pain he was trying to hide. His hand pressed to his side, where blood was seeping through his fingers. "Fine. And technically, I'm not your God."

A half-laugh, half-sob escaped my lips, the sound more desperate than amused. "Nice."

My hand trembled as I reached toward his wound, needing to do something, anything to help. But the sight of his blood, shimmering with that eerie, otherworldly glow, stopped me in my tracks. Blood shouldn't be beautiful, but somehow, in this twisted reality, it was. Vibrant and sparkling like gold-flecked rubies, it was a cruel reminder of the power flowing through his veins—power that I could never fully understand, let alone control.

Okay, I was officially losing it, thinking about blood like that. I turned to Henry, but he was gone. Paul and I were alone. "What happened? Is Thanatos... has he been dealt with?"

Paul still leaned against the mountain wall, catching his breath as if he was working on some internal healing. He shook his head. "Thanatos is hard to kill. That's sort of his thing."

"Oh, right." That was a bummer. How did you defeat a god if he was undefeatable?

"He's taken care of for now, but he's the least of our worries." Paul finally straightened up, letting out a refreshed breath. "Cynthia and Henry are making things normal again at your place."

His light-hearted tone rubbed off on me, and I clung to it, knowing the conversation would turn serious any second. "Good, 'cause the last thing I need is for my mom to have any more reasons to kick me out."

He laughed softly, but there was a sadness to it that tugged at my heart. Some silence stretched between us. "What exactly were you trying to do, Jessa?"

And there it was—the shift to seriousness.

I tried to hide my discomfort, but I knew I wasn't doing a great job.

Pushing aside the hair flapping into my face, I wrapped my arms around my stomach, feeling cold, and not just on the outside. "I don't know. Become normal?"

The words were out before I could think them through, and I immediately regretted it. I didn't want Paul to misunderstand, to think I was rejecting him and everything he represented. I just... didn't know what I wanted anymore.

Paul started to respond but stopped himself, his mouth closing, lips pressed tight. Something like recognition flickered in his dark blue eyes, and for once, I thought I understood him.

At one time, he must have wanted to do the same thing—to become normal for Amara. Was that what he was thinking about now? I couldn't meet his gaze, my eyes drifting down, tracing the spiderweb cracks in the rocky surface beneath us.

"I'm sorry," he breathed, his voice tinged with regret. Beneath his words, I heard the unspoken plea: Please, look at me.

I fought to calm the crazy jitters in my stomach that spread to my chest, and I finally looked at him.

He reached out, touching my cheek. "I should have told you." His hand brushed up my skin, fingers threading through my hair before resting on my shoulder. Tiny prickles of electricity danced across my skin, like touching one of those electro-globes in science class. I hadn't realized how much I craved his touch until it was happening.

Nervous, I shuffled my feet. I didn't want to talk about my past anymore. I was afraid I wouldn't measure up to what Paul wanted, to what he had lost. "Why did you bring me here?"

"It's the safest place for now. The last place they'd expect you."

I closed my eyes, savoring the strong winds rushing into my face. The air smelled like him, with just a hint of the sea. "They want to destroy my soul, don't they?"

"Yes." His voice cracked, and I opened my eyes to see him looking away toward the horizon.

"Because I'm one of the strongest Potentials, and maybe the last real threat to them and their plans?"

"Yes." He sighed through his nose, his hands finding either side of my face. "I'm not going to stall anymore. I'll tell you everything. Just don't ever do anything that reckless again."

I laughed, though it came out as a pathetic, high-pitched sound. He took the breath right out of me. My brain couldn't focus on what it should—like the impending Apocalypse. Instead, all I could think about was his touch and how it drove me crazy and calmed me all at once.

His thumbs traced the edges of my ears. "What do you want to know from me?"

Everything, I wanted to say. But that felt like too much to ask, so I settled on something simple. "Can Hades make me see things that aren't real?"

"No. But he can choose what not to show you. Can you tell me what you saw?"

The clouds seemed to race across the sky, lights from Athens blinking at me in the distance. "A place. I thought it was Greece at first. A woman... Amara." I paused, looking over his shoulder, unable to hold his gaze. "You." My palms rested against his chest, feeling the hard muscles beneath and seeing the visions as if they were playing on the inside of my eyelids. I could fast-forward, rewind, relive each scene, each moment, over and over. "I saw you two together."

My breath came out shaky. The mark on my arm seemed to burn the more I thought about what Hades had shown me. I licked my lips, swallowed, needing to move past it. "Henry and you. You told him about my vision—the world underwater. You wanted to stay with me; he wouldn't allow it. Cynthia was supposed to get me." Each word brought back the memory and the emotions that came with it. My soul was waking up, remembering that life from eons ago. I felt everything Amara had felt that day: pain, loss, failure, betrayal. Total helplessness.

Paul's hands slid down to my arms, though his chest went rigid. "The place was Atlantis." He struggled with the memory. I hated seeing the pain in his eyes. And with all the weirdness that had become my life in the past week, my brain didn't even stumble over the fact that Atlantis had been real.

He continued, "Poseidon was the enemy. He and a few others believed the blessings they'd bestowed upon humans had been taken for granted. Humans had failed in their eyes. Contempt, hatred, bloodshed had all become the ways of the Atlanteans. They'd become too egotistical, self-centered. My father had already turned his back after losing Hercules long before." He paused, his brows furrowing as he wrestled with something internally. "Hercules was my father's favorite son. Nothing was ever the same with the Pantheon after Hephaestus destroyed his soul."

"But Hephaestus was framed?"

He searched my face as if he hadn't expected me to know that. He nodded, taking a deep breath, his eyes distant. "You... Amara had been seeing visions for weeks, but they planned it well. Each god only knew part of the plan. The day it happened was the day you figured it out."

My shoulders slumped. I *had* been a failure.

He shook his head. "It was a wonder you figured it out at all. I doubt even Hercules could've been as quick as you."

"Quick? Almost the entire human race was wiped out thanks to her inability to act in time."

He kept shaking his head. "You can't blame yourself. I should've been there to protect you. I won't let that happen again. Ever."

The passion in his voice made my heart race. "I'm not her, Paul." He had to know that. I didn't want him to love a ghost. I wanted him to love me, Jessa Whitley, current demon-slayer-in-training.

He held my gaze, his hands still gripping my arms. He couldn't say it. He couldn't say he knew I was right, that I wasn't her. Because, as Apollo, he couldn't lie. The knot in my throat hurt, and I didn't have the strength to speak. I couldn't do this. I needed him. All of him.

Pressure built between my eyes, and I fought it back, not wanting to cry in front of him. I wanted him to want me, need me, crave me like I craved him. And I needed to know I could do what was asked of me and not fail. I couldn't fail. Not again.

Again. The word echoed in my mind like I'd been there, like it had been me. But it had been Amara. Yet it was my soul. I shook my head as my thoughts went in circles, like a giant spotlight had centered on this truth, illuminating it from the depths and shadows of my comprehension.

Amara and I were linked, forever a part of each other. Those memories were becoming permanently threaded into the fabric of my mind. I was her, and she was me. We were one and the same.

My breath fogged the air, and I watched it stream from my lips. There was a reason I'd had those visions on the bleachers. There was a reason I felt this strange magnetic pull to Paul, that I needed his approval, wanted his touch.

My thoughts crumbled the moment he touched my waist and pulled me close. "You're different people, Jessa. I know that."

Every part of me tensed, but it wasn't from fear. He was close enough that I could feel his warm breath when he spoke, every word dripping with an intense passion he'd never shown so strongly before. "But I'll always be connected to that soul, Jessa. Your soul. I'll always protect it. You. You've always been a part of me. Understand that, Jessa." He kept saying my name, as if to emphasize that he knew exactly who I was.

One of his hands moved to the small of my back, and my brain totally shut down. My heart felt like a dozen sparklers had lit up inside. Heat radiated between us as he pressed closer. We practically shared the same air now. My body relaxed, going limp as my head swam with yearning I couldn't control.

"If you want your space, I can learn to understand that. I don't want to suffocate you or make your life more difficult. I don't want to be..." He paused, his jaw tightening. "In your way."

My shoulders trembled as a rush of emotions coursed through me. I swallowed, my lips parting as I imagined how this closeness could play out. "And I don't want you to think I'm someone I'm not."

"I don't."

I stared up at him, my palms still pressed against his chest, my voice barely above a whisper. "Then kiss me already."

A slow smile curved up his lips, and I melted in his arms. His arm wrapped around my waist, and I felt a rush of anticipation, my stomach flipping as the moment built. His other hand cupped my cheek, his touch gentle and warm, full of energy yet careful, as if afraid he'd break me. In one smooth motion, he pressed his lips to mine.

He tasted of salt and something inexplicably familiar, like he was meant to be mine all along. My soul lifted, a cascade of sparks igniting into a full-blown Fourth of July display in my chest. My arms slid around his back, fingers tracing the ridges of his muscles as if they were carved just for me. His kiss wasn't just a kiss—it was a revelation, a rediscovery of something I'd somehow always known. His tongue moved with mine, leading me through a dance so ancient it felt like instinct, like we'd done this a thousand times before.

My body sizzled as he pulled me tighter, his hands moving behind my head, through my hair, fingers tangling in the strands before they trailed down my shoulders and pressed against the small of my back again, pulling me into him. His other hand cradled my head, and he let out a low groan.

Warmth spread everywhere, almost more than I could handle, but I was okay with the idea of letting the kiss consume me completely. I couldn't get close enough despite our already tight embrace, my fingers digging into his back. Heat was an understatement now. I wanted to fuse with him. I wanted all of him. And I didn't even need to gasp for air—it flowed through me as if he were the source.

Screw the apocalypse.

He broke the kiss for a fraction of a second, only to whisper my name—*my* name, not hers—and then pressed his lips against mine even harder, his hands buried in my hair, gently pulling. Never in my life had I felt so cherished, so wanted, needed, desired. It had to be the strongest power ever. I crawled my hands to the back of his neck, feeling the tip of his hair tickling my fingertips. I didn't want to stop. Wouldn't. As far as I was concerned, I could go on kissing him right through the Apocalypse.

A gust of wind hit my back. The sound of flapping material swished in the air, and the familiar scent of woods and medicine made me wrinkle my nose. Paul pulled away slowly, still too quick for my liking. My eyes fluttered open, and I smiled. He wasn't looking anywhere but at me, even with an audience, and he rubbed his thumb along my jawline. I leaned on him, unsure if I could stand on my own after that perfect, glorious kiss.

"Well, this is déjà vu," Cynthia said, her voice laced with amusement.

Paul gave a lopsided grin. I turned but made sure to keep as close to him as possible. Cynthia looked a little flushed and out of breath. Henry's hair had gone full puffball, and they all shared a glance before settling their eyes on me. Great. Nothing like being the center of attention. I had to wonder if they still felt the same as they did back then. Did they hate me for loving Paul, or for Paul loving me? Once this apocalypse was dealt with, I planned on figuring out why in Zeus's name it was forbidden for us to love each other. As appealing as it sounded, I wasn't sure I was ready to let Paul give up his immortality for me, either.

The four of us peered over Mount Olympus, watching the sleeping city of Athens twinkle below. It was beyond weird thinking how getting here was a twenty-something hour trip by plane, but with Paul? More like a twentieth of a second.

"I knew it was Athens before I even saw it. I could smell it. How?"

Paul wrapped an arm around my waist. "It's part of what you are. Your adrenaline heightens your senses."

"Sweet." That explained my ability to see people's eyes in microscopic detail. "So, uh," I hated to crash the surreal moment, "how do we stop this whole apocalypse thing?"

Cynthia and Henry exchanged a glance, which I hated. They were thinking the same thing, and I had no clue what it was, but I knew it had something to do with me. Paul squeezed my side. His hand brushed my hip as he let go and turned to face me.

"There's something else I have to tell you." Judging by his tone, the 'something' wasn't a good something.

I took a deep breath, let it out slowly, and said, "Alright."

"You know how you're immune to fire?"

I frowned, my brows knitting together. "Yeah?"

Paul laid his hands on my shoulders, a sure sign this wasn't good news. "That's because of who your father is."

Damn, knowing everything was starting to suck. I let his words roll around in my brain. Immunity. Fire. Father. Holy mother of Zeus.

"Hephaestus is my father?" My breath caught in my throat. Instinctively, I reached for the inhaler in my pocket. My fingers curled around it but stopped.

Hello, Paul was touching me. No wonder. Pulling my hand back out, I closed my eyes. If only the apocalypse could wait one more day so I could digest everything. Or an entire year, for that matter.

"So, what does that mean? He's the one doing all of this, right? He has to be. And now I'm the one who has to stop him. Gee, what a family reunion this oughta' be."

Cynthia crossed in front of Henry and stopped at my side. "You'll have our help."

"Yeah?" I felt a tug on my lips, but it wasn't a happy smile. "Should you have to, though?"

"To be fair, you sort of skipped your training," Henry said. He'd been avoiding eye contact the entire time he'd been back. Was he avoiding me because I hadn't yet forgiven him? 'Cause I hadn't. If only I could live five hundred and sixty-two years to put Paul's record to shame.

I shook my head. "Why would Hephaestus help Hades after being framed by him?"

Paul sighed. "This is recent news. It wasn't until—" His eyes moved to my arm, the one branded by Hades, and then quickly looked away.

"Hades' visit. Right. Won't your dad do something to stop him? Can't we tell him?"

"We can try. If he'll listen."

Light brightened the sky, and we all looked up. My hand found Paul's in an instant. Dozens of flaming rocks rained down on Athens.

His fingers laced between mine. "And so it begins."

☉︎☽ CHAPTER 28 ☾☉︎

Freaking out didn't even come close to how I felt. Meteors rained down in a blazing streak, but my mind couldn't catch up. I blinked hard, hoping to clear the haze, but the flames didn't flicker or fade. They burned the horizon like the end of everything. This wasn't a vision. It was terrifyingly real.

For miles, the sky was ablaze, a hellish inferno stretching as far as I could see. My eyes, enhanced by whatever strange powers I had, zoomed in on the devastation. Beyond Athens, past the shore, across the Aegean Sea, flames devoured everything in their path—forests, streets, buildings.

No matter which direction I glanced, it was all ablaze.

"Paul," I said, my voice catching in my throat. "It's everywhere. Tell me it's not everywhere."

"Panicking won't help," Cynthia's voice cut in, but my eyes stayed glued to the apocalyptic scene unfolding before us.

The air beside Cynthia shimmered, and when I blinked again, two figures materialized—a man and a woman, both exuding a god-like presence. The man had a bow and a quiver of arrows strapped across his chest.

"Eron," Henry greeted him, a note of surprise in his voice.

Eron nodded, his dark blond hair tied back. "It's begun," he said, his French accent heavy with acceptance. His eyes fell on me, and I suddenly wished I could disappear.

"Is this..." He trailed off, staring at me more intently. He glanced at Paul, then Cynthia, and finally Henry. "The Demi?"

His reaction seemed off, unsettling. I shifted uneasily and turned my gaze to the dark-haired woman beside him. She smiled, an oddly warm gesture given the circumstances.

"Yes," Paul answered, still holding my hand. "Jessa, meet Eron and Sy, better known as Eros and Psyche."

No. Way.

Eros and Psyche were legends—one of the greatest love stories in mythology. But any thrill I might have felt at meeting them was crushed by the screams rising from Athens. I knew I needed to do something, but what?

The others talked, their words fading into the background while my anxiety spiked at the thought of me being responsible for stopping all of this. What was I supposed to do? How could I possibly stop this? Even with the help of gods, it felt impossible.

Sy stepped toward me and placed a gentle hand on my arm.

"It's going to be alright," she said, her words soothing, breathing a glimmer of hope into my frayed nerves.

Her calmness helped me catch fragments of the conversation. Elder. Help. Warn. I snapped out of my daze.

"Tell me what to do," I demanded, my voice shaky but determined.

Everyone turned to look at me, and I swallowed hard.

Cynthia bolted past me, leaping off the edge of the mountain. I gasped, running to the precipice, only to see nothing but darkness below.

"Show off," Henry muttered before vanishing in a blur of movement.

Eron and Sy clasped hands again. "We'll alert the Elders," Eron said, his eyes meeting mine. "Are you certain of your prophecy?"

I looked to Paul for reassurance, and when he nodded, I did too. "Yes?"

Sy's smile was kind, almost disarming. Her short bob shifted with the breeze, its ends catching the moonlight as they danced.

Eron raised an eyebrow. "Well, that's reassuring, mon ami." He gave me a long, searching look before adding, "Bonne chance, Jessa. We'll be out there, helping." Then they dissolved into swirls of pink and dark blue mist.

I turned to Paul. "What do I do?"

He shrugged, pulling out my belt holding two familiar weapons. "First, stop losing these. You'll need them to take down the bad guys."

"Right." I took the belt holding my baby tridents and strapped it above my hips. "Where did Cynthia and Henry go?"

"To fend off the bad guys," Paul said, wrapping an arm around my waist and readjusting one sheath.

Taking this brief second of calm, I locked in every detail of his face, imprinting it in my memory—the way his hair moved in the wind, the deep blue of his eyes, the shape of his lips. Just in case.

"Hold on," he said.

I clung to Paul, my fingers digging into his shirt as the world kaleidoscoped into a dizzying mess. Pressure pushed against my chest, darkness encroached the edges of my vision, and my ears pounded with a relentless drumbeat.

The blur blinked away in a flash, and the ground under my feet tilted. My stomach twisted violently, a warning I refused to give in to. I bit down hard, forcing the nausea to stay where it belonged—anywhere but out.

Paul's grip steadied me, pulling me upright. "Stay sharp."

The wind tore at us, carrying the sharp tang of salt from the ocean. Cool droplets hit my ankles as. I edged forward through the sand, every nerve screaming, the dark water behind me stealing away any sense of safety.

It was impossibly hot, worse than one of the hottest days in a Texas summer, and streaks of fire raked across the sky above, bathing everything in a surreal, fiery glow.

Then I saw him. Across the shore, a man stood tall on a jagged outcrop of rock, his silhouette outlined by the hellish glow. Flames coiled and danced around him, not random but precise, like they were obeying his commands. Every flicker, every flare, was his doing, and he looked like he was enjoying the show.

"We're on Lemnos," Paul breathed.

The island of Hephaestus. My grip tightened around my sais. I wasn't ready to meet my father, especially not under these circumstances, but I wasn't about to back down, either.

"Am I going to have to kill him?" I whispered.

"By your definition, yes."

"What's that supposed to mean?"

"With immortals, the soul returns without waiting for the Fates. We're reborn again."

"But souls can be destroyed."

Paul's posture stiffened. "Yes."

As we moved closer, the heat became unbearable, my lungs burning with every breath. I squinted through the heat waves.

"Is Hell this hot?" I asked, trying to ease the tension.

"No. Hell is worse. You should know. You've been there."

"Not technically." I didn't like his tone. "And it's not like I wanted to go." I wheezed, feeling the dry air scalding my throat.

Paul grabbed my hand, replenishing my strength and air as we moved forward. Suddenly, he stopped us, throwing an arm across my path to hold me back. A low growl rumbled through the air, and six glowing eyes blinked at me from the shadows.

The massive form of Cerberus blocked our path. Each of its three heads growled in perfect discord; their glowing yellow eyes fixed on us. I tightened my grip on the sais as I shot Paul a look that said to wait.

"Hey, big guy. Remember me?"

Cerberus lowered his heads, lips curling back in a snarl.

"Guess that's a yes." I sighed. "It doesn't have to be this way. Let us pass, and I promise not to hurt you."

Cerberus answered—three clipped, mocking barks.

"He's laughing at me, isn't he?" I asked dryly.

"Yep," Paul confirmed, still focused on the beast.

Cerberus's growl deepened, and he lunged. Paul's palm shot up, a bolt of sunlight slamming into the beast's chest. Cerberus yelped, Paul's light searing off fur and blistering skin, but it wasn't enough to stop him.

Cerberus zeroed in on me, all three heads snapping and snarling as he charged. I darted forward, twisting and slashing with my sais. One blade glanced off his teeth with a sharp clang, the other nicking his lip. He jerked back with a guttural growl, a spray of snot shooting from his middle head and splattering disgustingly close.

"Gross," I muttered, tightening my grip.

Paul stood firm, golden arrows flying into the beast's neck, slowing him but not stopping him. My stomach dropped. This fight was mine to finish.

Cerberus lunged, his teeth grazing my arm. A fiery burn streaked through the cut, but I shoved the pain aside. Gritting my teeth, I growled right back and rushed him, ignoring the blood dripping from my arm.

Paul's arrows kept one head distracted, but the other two were locked on me. Ducking and weaving, I sucked in ragged breaths, my focus razor-sharp as I stayed just ahead of the snapping jaws. Heat radiated from the beast as I darted beneath him, both sais clenched tight. Twisting sharply, I drove one blade into his belly, the force vibrating up my arms.

Cerberus let out a deafening roar, thrashing violently. I rolled to avoid his legs and teeth, every motion fueled by adrenaline and sheer will.

Springing to my feet, I gripped Baby Tridents tighter and bolted for his side. With everything I had, I leapt onto his flank, my sais digging deep into his hide to anchor me as I climbed. Cerberus bucked and shook, trying to throw me like I was nothing more than a stubborn flea.

I reached the base of his neck, sweat slicking my palms as his roars rattled my body. One head snapped at me, jaws slicing through the air just inches away. Climbing with sais was about as fun as it sounded. Sheathing them, I latched onto the thick, matted fur instead, scrambling higher.

My stomach slammed into his spine as I leapt for the middle neck, the impact knocking the air from my lungs. Hanging on by sheer grit, I clawed at folds of skin and fur, dangling as Cerberus thrashed and whined.

Paul's arrows zipped past, hitting their mark and stunning one head until it slumped, jaws slack. Cerberus staggered, and just as my strength began to fail, Paul was suddenly there, a blur of godly speed.

His arm locked around my waist, his golden aura surging through me. The pain in my arm vanished, my lungs filled, and strength rushed back like a wave. Without hesitation, I slid out a sai, straddled the middle neck, and focused on the energy churning in my core.

"Sleep!" I roared, raising the hilt high and slamming it down with everything I had into the back of his neck.

Paul held me steady as Cerberus let out a final, anguished whine. The beast stumbled, swayed, and collapsed with a ground-shaking thud.

The drumming of my heart slowly eased, and I became aware of Paul behind me, his chest pressed against my back, rising and falling as he caught his breath. My own breaths came hard and uneven as Baby Trident slipped from my grip. I staggered away from the unconscious beast.

Paul was at my side in an instant, steadying my arm as he handed me the weapon. "You didn't kill him." His tone carried a flicker of surprise.

"Wasn't trying to." I swallowed, struggling to catch my breath.

He nodded, the faintest hint of a smile breaking through the tension. "Good. Now let's finish this."

With a quick glance at each other, we bolted toward the inferno, weapons in hand, ready to take on whatever nightmare awaited us.

☉☽ CHAPTER 29 ☾☉

The flames flickered wildly ahead, shadows leaping across the shore like they were alive as Paul and I ran. I swallowed hard, my mind spinning with questions I couldn't outrun. There were gods—actual gods—who hated humans to the point of extinction. Why? What made us so detestable? And why had I been chosen as a demigod, and the last one left at that? I wanted to accept it, to embrace the power and purpose that came with it, but the reality was a little harder to swallow.

I was seventeen….and a quarter. A high schooler. I should be stressing over prom dresses and SAT scores, not fighting mythical creatures or questioning the survival of humanity. The thoughts pooled in the pit of my gut, bubbling and hissing like an angry cauldron.

And then there was the truth I couldn't ignore. I was about to meet him. My father. An actual god. But not just any god. Of all the celestial beings that could have shared their DNA with me, it had to be the one orchestrating the apocalypse. I wasn't just navigating an impossible fate—I was about to face it head-on.

"Watch out!" Paul pushed my head down mid run, a large rock hurdling over us.

We both watched it career into the ground, a plume of sand erupting on impact, and whipped our heads back forward. "Does Hephaestus know about me?" I wheezed, trying to dodge small boulders scattered randomly on the shore.

"No." His curt reply matched the rhythm of our frantic pace.

I hadn't expected that answer. How could he not know? We skirted around large rocks, and I winced at the ache in my lungs. Each breath was a battle against the hot, smoky air.

Paul's hand shot out, gripping mine with firm commitment. His touch sent relief rushing through me—like he'd become my personal inhaler, supporting me and pulling me forward as the fire raged around us.

A deep rumble echoed ahead, the sun just breaking through the horizon. I couldn't tell if it was a creature, a machine, or the sky collapsing. I flinched as a searing light engulfed the area and squeezed my eyes shut. The air around us vibrated, warmth radiating against my skin, and I risked a glance. The glow wasn't from the horizon—it came from Paul, his golden aura blazing like a fragment of the star.

"You're beautiful," I whispered.

But there was no time for his response. We were spotted. A hulking figure towered ahead, broad-shouldered and heavily built. Hephaestus. The god of fire, his face twisted and scarred, sneered down at us.

"You can't stop me," he growled, his voice rough like gravel. "It's already begun."

So, he'd been expecting me. But he didn't know who I was beyond "The Demi." I took a breath and readied myself.

"Is this him?" I asked Paul, loud enough for Hephaestus to hear.

Paul only nodded, his entire body coiled like a spring ready to strike.

Hephaestus waved a hand, and the ground beneath me cracked open with a thunderous roar. I yelped, stumbling as the earth threatened to swallow me whole. Reflexes I still wasn't used to kicked in, and I leaped across the widening gap, landing in a crouch. My heart hammered against my ribs as I blew a strand of hair out of my face and glared up at him.

"Is that any way to treat your daughter, Heph?" I quipped.

The wind howled, whipping at my clothes and stinging my skin like it wanted to peel me apart. Hephaestus laughed, apparently entertained at my lame attempt. His face was a harsh landscape of scars, his crooked nose and dark eyes burning with molten rage. He was the only god known for his ugliness, and he wore it like armor.

"Jeez. I guess it's a good thing I got my mom's looks," I muttered, turning to Paul. "You sure this guy's my dad?"

Paul's body shifted slightly, positioning himself between me and the god of fire without a word, his aura pulsing like a star on the verge of eruption, radiant and impossible to look away from. Hephaestus's sneer deepened, his eyes glowing with the flames that surrounded him. That fire wouldn't protect him from me.

"I have no children from this century," Hephaestus scoffed. He flexed his massive arms, the muscles bulging under his skin. "No one would want this."

I kept moving toward him, unflinching. "Yeah? Well, it's a good thing I've got the god of truth with me."

His sneer turned into a snarl, and with a flick of his wrist, a massive hammer flew toward me. I barely dodged it, throwing myself to the ground as it whooshed past, close enough that I could feel the wind from its force. The earth cracked again, the gap widening between us.

I spit out a mouthful of sand, my anger flaring. With a growl, I hurled one sai at his chest. Hephaestus swatted it away like a toy, sending it flying into the sky.

He laughed, a sound that grated on my nerves. "You rookies are all the same."

He raised his arm, calling forth something dark and menacing. The earth rumbled beneath me. Teeth snapped in the distance, followed by low, growling breaths. Four oversized dogs, their bodies engulfed in fire, leaped through the inferno.

Hell hounds.

The first one lunged at me, its fiery form tearing through the air. An arrow zipped past me, burying itself in the hound's chest. It hit the ground with a sickening thud, whimpering as its flames sputtered, leaving behind the acrid stench of burned flesh and singed fur.

Paul moved in front of me, but I shoved him back. "I got this."

The remaining three hell hounds circled me, their eyes glowing with nasty intention. Two charged at once with ferocious snarls. The first hellhound lunged, its flaming jaws snapping inches from my face. Ignoring the searing heat, I caught its head and twisted hard, hurling its massive body into the second one. The collision sent a spray of embers into the air, and the ground quaked as they hit the earth, flames extinguished in an instant.

"See? Fire does nothing! Shouldn't that tell you something?" I shouted, the adrenaline coursing through me like a drug.

Paul's gaze flicked toward me, his expression unreadable, but his grip on the bow tightened, the knuckles white against the wood. The last hound charged, its eyes locked on mine, fangs bared. I sprinted forward, my muscles fueled by raw, primal energy. We leaped at each other, meeting in midair. My fist collided with its flaming skull, and I felt the bone shatter beneath my knuckles. Blood sprayed, hot and metallic, as the hound cried.

I landed lightly on my feet, spinning around to watch the hell hound crash into a tree, splintering it on impact. I smirked, the blood on my hand dripping down my arm as I faced Hephaestus. "That all you got? Now come on, stop trying to kill me and listen."

Paul had retrieved my lost sai. He held it out to me, his hand steady on my arm, ready to heal me if needed. "Jessa, you are certifiably insa—"

"Hush, Paul." I took Baby Trident and gripped it tightly. "I have a plan."

Paul's eyes were sharp, but I saw a flicker of something softer—a hint of a smile, maybe. He let go of my arm but stayed close, his entire body rigid.

"Heph, Apollo can't lie. Ask him if it's true. Despite this whole ending-the-human-race thing you've got going on, you wouldn't want to kill me, right? Not if I was your daughter?"

I was grasping at straws, but I had to keep him talking. Keep him distracted.

Hephaestus hesitated, confusion flickering in his eyes. "It doesn't matter who you are. What's done is done."

Another hammer soared toward me with lightning speed. I dropped beside Paul, my chest heaving, hammer skirting just above our heads. The impact bruised my body but I scrambled back to my feet, ready to charge through the fire and take him down myself. "Is this seriously how you plan to get rid of me?"

"Enough!" His bellow shook the earth, but his eyes betrayed him. He was confused, maybe even curious.

Around us, the rain of fire ceased, and the sky began to lighten, turning a dark shade of blue. Dawn was breaking. Paul stepped forward, his aura blazing as he spoke.

His voice carried a melodic, almost hypnotic tone as he began, "Hephaestus, there's no running from the truth, no matter how deeply you've tried to bury it. Let me remind you of a past that still haunts you, a past you've never truly escaped."

"There was a mortal woman, Jennifer Whitley," Paul began, "Her beauty captivated you in a way you hadn't expected, hadn't wanted to believe was possible. But you knew, deep down, that no mortal could love you for who you are… as you are."

Hephaestus's fists clenched, the world trembling beneath us as though responding to his simmering rage.

Paul didn't falter. "So, you did the unthinkable. You stole one of Eros's arrows, twisting Jennifer's heart, bending her will to yours, making her love you as desperately as you wished she would."

His words hung heavy in the air, each one a deliberate strike. Hephaestus's expression wavered, his fingers flexing, but he let Paul continue.

Paul's tone changed, almost entrancing, drawing Hephaestus deeper into the memory. "For a time, she did love you. She loved you with a passion that consumed you both. But that love wasn't real, and you knew it. When Eros discovered your crime, he broke the spell, leaving Jennifer confused and heartbroken, wondering why the man she thought she loved had suddenly vanished. Because you didn't stay to see her confusion."

For a second, I swore I saw a flicker of regret cross his face. I was as riveted as he was, picturing the story as Paul went on.

"You fled, ashamed of what you were, afraid of what she would see if she looked at you without the veil of enchantment."

Paul's words echoed like a haunting refrain as he continued. "But what you never knew, what you couldn't have known, was that Jennifer was carrying your child. She was left with nothing but her broken heart and unanswered questions, never realizing the true depth of what had happened."

As Paul spoke, I squinted against the piercing glow of his aura, amplified by the rising sun. The light was overwhelming, almost too bright to handle, but through the glare, I couldn't help but stare. He didn't just look strong—he looked extraordinary. Ethereal. Like he belonged to a world far beyond mine, a god stepping out of myth and into reality. The golden light framed him, stretching shadows across the sand like the universe itself was bending to him. The warmth of the sun seeped into my skin, but it couldn't touch the icy knot tightening in my chest with every word he said.

"And now, Hephaestus, that child—your daughter—stands before you, carrying the legacy of a love that was doomed from the start." Paul's voice faded, leaving his conclusion to dissolve in the thick, firelit air.

A storm of emotions brewed inside me, each one colliding in a tangled mess. I'd wanted answers to make sense of it all, but now that the truth was out, all I felt was a sharp, hollow ache. No relief. No clarity. Just emptiness.

Hearing what Hephaestus did—how he ran, how he left my mom—struck too close to home. Not even a day ago, I wanted to do the same. Run from the powers, the danger, the responsibility. I couldn't run. Not now, not after hearing his story. I wasn't ready, but I wouldn't be like him. And let's be real... running was not my best skill set, anyway. Aside from the asthma, I'd probably trip over my own feet.

"Here." Paul extended his hand, and I took it. Instantly, the pain in my body faded, my strength flooding back. Hephaestus stood motionless, his gaze distant, his expression unreadable as he processed the truth.

Paul finally broke the silence, his voice almost gentle. "Hades sent Cerberus to protect you."

Hephaestus's focus snapped back to me, his eyes scanning my face like he was searching for someone else in my features. My mom, probably. "Understand why I'm doing this," he said, his gravelly voice heavy with emotion I couldn't name. "They've destroyed everything. They turned the gifts I gave them into weapons against each other."

Paul ignored his justifications and went for the kill. "Hades framed you for destroying Hercules's soul," he said with barely contained anger. "He's been playing this game for centuries, and you walked right into it."

Every muscle in Hephaestus's body locked as the wall of fire surrounding him wavered, lowering in uneven flickers. His eyes widened, burning with a mix of fury and something else... hesitation. His expression hardened, nostrils flaring as if he were trying to sniff out a lie. The only sound was the faint crackle of embers and the low rumble of his breathing as Paul and I stood waiting.

Paul's fingers tightened around mine, slick with sweat, his usual calm fading just enough for me to notice. If I weren't immune to fire, my hand would've probably been scorched by the heat in his.

"Hades and Thanatos have been on a soul-destroying spree," Paul broke the silence again. "They've been wiping out the half-mortals, one by one. Jessa is the last Potential of age left, and she's your daughter. Her soul, the oldest remaining since Hercules's destruction, and her immunity to fire are the only things that have kept her alive this long."

He stepped forward, daring Hephaestus to meet his gaze. "Hades is using you," Paul pressed. "You're just a pawn in his game."

"I'm not weak-minded!" Hephaestus roared, his fury sending a torrent of fire racing up the mountainside. Out of the corner of my eye, one of the hellhounds twitched, flames flickering back to life along its scorched body. But before I could warn Paul, something splintered in my mind.

Zach's face—twisted in terror, tears streaking his cheeks—seared itself into my thoughts. Invisible hands yanked him backward, his screams piercing through the walls of my skull, embedding itself in my brain.

Another image ripped through before I could catch my breath. My mom, her skin pallid, lips stained an unnatural blue. Her lifeless eyes stared into nothing, and in the distance, white wings flashed… a stark, cruel contrast to the darkness.

No.

Zach again, clawing at stone, his fingernails snapping as blood trailed across the ground beneath him. The sickening crack of each break echoed in my head, his struggle replaying in an unending loop of agony. I knew that place—the barren cliffs, the flicker of torches casting sinister shadows.

The Underworld.

The visions ripped away, leaving behind an ache so raw it felt like my heart had been pulverized.

"No!" The scream tore free, guttural and unhinged, as I collapsed to my knees. My fingers dug into the coarse sand as the onslaught of images burned into my consciousness, an inferno carving its way through me. My chest heaved with the effort to hold it back, my pulse a relentless throbbing in my ears. The rage swelled into a firestorm threatening to consume all of me.

My mom, Zach, his screams, the sickening crack of nails against rock. It was too much.

The fury overtook me, clawing its way out of the pit of my stomach until it seized every inch. The air itself seemed to ripple with the force of my anger, hotter than the flames surrounding us, hotter than I thought I could withstand. It was too much—too big, too feral for my body to contain.

I staggered to my feet, shoving Paul's hand away when he tried to help me, the motion more desperate than defiant. Tears blurred my vision, their heat matching the fire in my veins. My voice cracked as I finally forced the words out.

"My mom." My throat tightened, but I pushed through, my breath hitching with barely contained rage. "Zach. He has them."

Swallowing hard, I crushed the lump in my throat, inhaling deeply to find enough breath to make my demand. "You have to take me there." My voice came out like a blade forged in fury. "Now."

☉☽ CHAPTER 30 ☾☉

The image of my mom's lifeless face branded itself into my mind, and a sick feeling settled in my gut. This was on me. Whatever I was—half-immortal, demon slayer, chosen pawn—it had painted a target on her. If I hadn't been this... thing, she'd be safe.

"Take me there," I demanded, my breath coming in shallow gasps as I fought the tears threatening to break free. I couldn't fall apart. Not here. Not in front of these gods. My feet refused to stay still—bouncing, pacing, spinning in frantic circles, like motion could shake off the guilt and anxiety crushing my ribs.

I glanced between father and soulmate, two impossibly powerful beings, and found only unreadable faces. They just stood there, the silence unbearable. Their calm made me feel small, like I was flailing in a storm they could withstand without blinking. Exposed. Helpless.

"Take me now," I roared, "or I swear to God I'll drown myself to get there."

The fury tearing through me was something new… consuming, wild, a virus taking over my entire system. My breath hissed through my teeth as my chest heaved, my vision blurred with unshed tears, and my pacing turned erratic, like a caged animal. I had to go. Time was slipping away. Was she really dead? No. It had to be a trick. Thanatos couldn't do this, couldn't kill my mom, couldn't take Zach. It wasn't their time. It couldn't be.

I did this. I brought this danger into their lives.

My grip tightened around the sais. When had I unsheathed them? I didn't know. All I knew was the urge to strike someone, anyone. Maybe even myself. I'd definitely get a trip to the Underworld doing that.

A darker side of me that I never knew existed broke through the surface, breaking down my rational thought. I couldn't handle it. The thought of them doing something to my mom, destroying her soul, anything... it rushed a madness through me that would destroy me if I didn't act on it.

"Calm down. What did you see?" But Paul's words only enraged me more.

"Just take me there." My voice shook, dark, rough and hoarse.

"Whatever you saw doesn't mean it's happening now. It's a ploy. They want you down there."

I looked from Paul to Heph, who wore an expression caught somewhere between worry and confusion. "Listen to him," he said, like he was suddenly trying on the whole fatherly role for size.

Seriously? After trying to kill me, now he wanted to play Dad?

It didn't matter if it was a ploy, I had to know. I couldn't take the chance. "Forget it." I spun on my heels, stuck my sais back in their holder, and marched towards the ocean, ready to end it all.

"Wait!" Paul grabbed me and spun me to face him. "Hold on." He wrapped his arms around me in an embrace. I buried my face in his chest, the thrum of his heartbeat cutting through the whirlwind inside me. For a moment, the world stopped spinning. For a moment, I could breathe.

His shirt bunched between my curled fingers, and I waited for the world to spin my insides upside down. He held me tighter than he ever had before, not afraid of breaking me, suffocating me. I wanted to get through this nightmare. I wanted to open my eyes and still be in my bedroom at home, with Mom and Zach safe.

The air shifted, cooler now, tinged with salt, olive trees, and something ancient. I blinked. Columns rose around me, cracked and bleached by endless sunlight. The sun blazed too high in the sky, blinding and wrong. This wasn't home. This wasn't anywhere I'd been before. I didn't want to let go of Paul and waited for my nausea to subside. Hatred continued to burn beneath my skin, boiling through my veins. "I'm going to kill him," I said through clenched teeth, my venom aimed at Thanatos.

Paul pulled back slightly and took my hand. Behind him stood a ruined temple. His beautiful aura melded with the sunlight, casting an ethereal glow over the crumbling structure.

"Where—"

"Tell me what you saw," Paul said as he guided me up a set of broken steps.

I hesitated, peaks of a distant mountain catching my gaze. "Where are we?"

"The Temple of Delphi," he replied, glancing back at me.

The weight of his words hit me, and for a moment, the hatred ebbed. A marble altar stood ahead, its surface streaked with time and the promise of forgotten power. This was his temple. Paul's. I swallowed at the realization of where he'd taken me, but my anger flared again, pulling me back to the visions.

"My mom…" My voice cracked, my brain grasping for rationalization. "Dead. Zach—he's—Thanatos…" My heart raced, and I forced the rest out in one breath. "He's dragging Zach into the Underworld." Even with Paul holding my hand, the hysteria tightened its grip, squeezing out what little air I could manage. My vision blurred, not from tears, but from the realization that nothing, not even his touch, could fix this.

Lost to the torment of my visions, I hadn't realized he'd led me toward his altar, its black-and-white marble gleaming under the midday sun. Paul stopped, turned to me, and gripped my shoulders with a forceful urgency that jarred me back to reality. I looked up at him and, for the first time I could recall, saw fear crack through his calm exterior.

"Jessa." His voice broke in a way I'd never heard before, almost pleading. "You must trust me. Please. This is a trap."

Tears burned in the corners of my eyes. I couldn't hold them back much longer. "Then I'll find a way out of it. I have to save them."

Paul's jaw flexed like he was biting back everything he wanted to say. The heat of his emotions thrummed through the air between us. His eyes, golden flecks burning brighter than ever, locked onto mine with a fire that mirrored my own. "They want you to go down there. Don't you get it? He wants to destroy you."

"I won't let that happen. You don't understand." I felt like I was back on the shore of Lemnos—beyond desperate and willing to burn bridges and kill myself if it meant saving them.

But Paul's expression didn't waver. He wasn't going to let me face this alone, no matter what it cost him. I gripped his arms, my fingers digging into the solid strength beneath them.

"I have to save them. I have to stop this." The words came out more a vow to myself than anything else.

Paul cupped my face, his hands gentle despite the storm I could feel radiating from him. His thumbs swept away the tears that had finally escaped, tracing the curve of my jawline with a touch so fleeting it made my chest ache. His eyes softened, the tempest within them giving way to something unfiltered and bleeding with despair.

"No," he said, his voice barely above a whisper, his thumb hovering just above my bottom lip. "I don't understand."

Before I could respond, he pulled me into him, his arms wrapping around me with a firmness that felt like both a shield and a promise. His embrace was secure, protective, as if he could hold me there forever and keep me safe from everything threatening to tear me apart. He kissed the top of my head, and I closed my eyes, cherishing the warmth it brought.

"But if I can't talk sense into you," he murmured, his breath brushing against my hair, "I won't try and stop you."

I squeezed him tight. "Thank you." I tried another deep breath, hoping to clear the shakes from my voice. "For trusting me."

He brushed some of my hair behind my ear and carefully swept me into a cradle. I knew the drill. I looped my arms around his neck and buried my face against the crook of his shoulder. And then we were moving. Fast. The world blurred until the wind snapped still. My face stung from its harsh bitterness as Paul set me down in a new place.

The room was shadowy and cool, its walls carved with timeless precision. Polished bronze plates hung at intervals, catching faint lamplight and casting a diffused golden glow that melded with Paul's. In the center stood a broken chair. At first glance, it looked like a three-legged chair, squat and unassuming, but the reflective gleam from the bronze made it seem far more deliberate—like the focal point of a forgotten ritual.

My brow furrowed and I tilted my head, that tiny, irrational voice in the back of my mind whispering doubt. Where had he taken me, and how could it help me save my mom and Zach?

Paul was the god of truth—trusting him should've been instinctual, automatic, not to mention he was like, my literal soulmate. And yet, like an unwelcome splinter, the thought poked at me: what if this wasn't the answer? What if I'd misjudged everything? It was ridiculous, I knew that. But once the thought was there, it was like giving a weed room to grow.

I pushed the doubt aside, focusing instead on the tripod in front of me. Not a chair… a tripod. My inner mythology nerd groaned in realization. Tripods weren't just décor in ancient Greece. They were sacred, used for sacrifices, offerings, even as seats for oracles. This one practically radiated importance, clearly belonging to Apollo, who was standing right next to me, glowing like he'd been lit from the inside with celestial fire.

This tripod wasn't just a relic—it was a connection. A tether between mortals and gods. And now it was standing in front of me, a question mark made of bronze, waiting for me to figure out how it fit into saving the two people I couldn't lose. Beneath the tripod, a thin crack traced a broken line across the floor, leading my eyes to a stone that stood out from the rest.

"Omphalos," Paul answered cautiously.

Exhaustion muddled my thoughts, making it harder to connect the dots. I used to know these scraps of mythology as instinctively as the way Zach's hand had fit into mine. The Omphalos…the navel of the world.

A glorified rock with a god complex. That's what the books always made it sound like. But now, standing here, staring at it, the intricate carvings etched into its surface like a knotted net holding something at bay, I couldn't shrug it off as just another ancient myth.

Omphalos hummed. Not a sound, but a vibration, faint and insistent, tugging at my chest like it was syncing with my heartbeat. My fingers twitched at my sides, instinct screaming at me to touch it while common sense begged me to stay back.

Paul moved to the other side of the chamber, watching me watching Omphalos. His silence carried more weight than any warning, his gaze shifting between me and the ancient stone like he expected it to spring to life at any second. And then a kind of realization broke through my tired brain.

Adyton.

The name floated to the surface of my mind, unearthed from hazy memories of mythology class and bedtime stories. The inner sanctum of Delphi—where mortals came begging for answers, clinging to whatever scraps the divine chose to throw their way.

Adyton was a gateway.

My breath caught as I looked down. The jagged crack beneath the Omphalos was a path, an open wound in the world itself. Cold, bitter air seeped out, coiling around my ankles like it had fingers. I didn't need Paul to confirm it. I knew exactly where this led.

The Underworld.

The thought landed heavy in my chest, not with panic, but with a suffocating clarity that left no room for doubt. My mom, dead. Zach, screaming, dragged into the darkness. The vision replayed in my head like a bad movie I couldn't shut off, each scene more vivid than the last.

This was it. The thing I had begged for, raged for, been willing to die for. But now? Standing here, staring at the crack that led straight to everything I'd sworn to fight, I thought I'd feel relief. Instead, a cold, hollow dread opened inside me. What if I wasn't enough? What if I failed?

Paul shifted, still standing on the other side of the chamber, continuing to observe me. His steady presence reminding me of what I'd already survived. My pulse hammered in my ears, drowning out the hum of the stone and I tightened my fists, forcing my feet to stay planted even though every instinct screamed at me to turn and run.

Because for some crazy reason, the Fates had chosen me.

Me. A girl who couldn't run up a flight of stairs without her inhaler. A girl who had to psych herself up just to look over a balcony. A girl who'd been anything but heroic her whole life.

And yet, here I was. The new Hercules. And I'd be damned if I let the Underworld take those closest to me.

I squared my shoulders, forcing my knees to stop trembling, my breath to steady. Fear wasn't going to stop me—not anymore.

"This leads to the Underworld, doesn't it?"

Paul's jaw tightened, and though he didn't say a word, the tension radiating from him was answer enough. I planned on asking exactly how it would work, but a faint tremor started, timpani beneath my feet.

At first, I thought it was me, trembling under the weight of what lay ahead. But the ground shuddered violently, loose pebbles dancing as a low groan rumbled through the chamber. The crack split wider, exhaling a cold, sulfuric breath that stung my lungs.

Within the curling fumes, a shape emerged—tall, white, and winged.

Paul moved, a golden blur racing toward me, but Thanatos was faster. His hand clamped around my wrist, and with a harsh pull, dragged me into the gaping void.

Paul's scream vanished as the fissure sealed behind us with a venomous hiss. Darkness swallowed me, thick and suffocating, while Thanatos locked his arm around my stomach like a steel band. My head spun, and it took a disorienting moment to realize we were descending—gradually, deliberately—with each beat of his wings.

This was definitely not how I'd planned to reach the Underworld. My nails clawed at his arm, desperation overtaking reason as I scrabbled against his grip. His fingers tightened, crushing against my ribs in warning. Below us, the chasm yawned endlessly, the depth shredding any fragile remnants of logic. My thoughts flickered like dying sparks, impossible to hold.

He leaned in, his voice brushing against my ear like a taunt. "I told you. You'll be his ruin."

I jerked, twisting against his hold, my fury flaring hotter beneath my panic. His calm only fanned it further, each slow beat of his wings punctuating his words. "He was ignorant to bring you there. And now, I'll have you both out of the way. Any god who sides with your kind forfeits the right to call themselves divine. You made this too easy."

I ground my teeth and drove my heel up between his legs. His grip faltered for a fraction of a second, but he only laughed. "Your naivety will be the death of you—and everyone else, for that matter."

"I'll kill you," I snarled, grabbing a fistful of his white hair and yanking hard.

He growled, swiping at my hand with his free arm, broken feathers scattering around us. Twisting in his loosened grip, I raked my nails across his face. His descent faltered, spinning dangerously out of control.

Thanatos clamped down on my arm, white-hot pain surging through me as his crushing grip took hold. I bit back a cry and drove my free elbow into his throat. He choked—a harsh, satisfying sound—and I seized the hilt of Baby Trident, relieved I hadn't lost it.

With a wrenching motion, I tore it free. Thanatos hissed…

…and then let go.

My scream ricocheted off the walls as I plunged straight down into the abyss, the drop so sudden my stomach was still somewhere up above. Baby Trident slipped from my grip, spinning out of reach and vanishing into the void.

Flashes of every dream or vision I'd ever had erupted behind my eyes, a chaotic montage I couldn't escape. My brain skidded straight past panic into full-blown hysteria. Free falling into some unknown depth of doom wasn't just traumatic—it was terrifying. I clawed at the air, desperate for something, anything, to grab onto. There was nothing. Just the endless plunge, the kind that turned nightmares into cuddly bedtime stories.

They say facing your fear is how you conquer it.

They lie.

My shoulder slammed into the ground, the crunch of impact twisting through my bones. Pain exploded down my arm, my scream stealing my breath, raw and guttural. I curled inward, barely processing the throbbing ache radiating through my body. Disappearing into the floor felt like a solid option.

No time.

A pair of boots slammed onto the stone ground in front of me. Before I could scramble away, Thanatos's hand clamped around my neck and hauled me up, my feet dangling. "Why do you always make things so difficult?"

I tore at his grip, my nails scraping uselessly against his hand. "Thought you said it was too easy," I croaked.

He sneered and dropped me. I crumpled, clutching my ribs as I gasped for breath. My fingers brushed the hilt of my second Baby Trident, still in its sheath at my waist. Hope flared—then sputtered out as Thanatos grabbed my bad arm and yanked me to my feet.

A cry ripped from my throat as unbearable pain scorched through me, threatening to pull me into unconsciousness. He dragged me behind him, each stumble over the uneven ground jolting my body with fresh waves of searing agony. My hand ached to reach the weapon that now felt impossibly far away.

Praying wasn't my thing, but right now? I'd try anything. For the pain to ease. For Paul to find me. For a miracle—or maybe just one good shot at fighting back.

☉︎☽ CHAPTER 31 ☾☉︎

When I opened my eyes, Thanatos's wings had gone invisible, and a sharp, chemical smell tickled my nose like a botched chemistry experiment. He dragged me by the elbow along a narrow ledge, the dark river far below roaring like a caged beast.

Every muscle in my body locked in terror, my thoughts consumed by the fear of being hurled into the depths. Thanatos snickered. "He has a much better plan for you, darling demi."

But the river wasn't as terrifying as the dead. Luminescent spirits drifted along the ledges spiraling around the rocky columns that held up the Underworld. Their blank eyes fixed on me with haunting intensity. Echoes of distorted voices filled the cavern, a chorus of lost souls that burrowed under my skin.

I tried to jerk my elbow free, but his hold was ironclad. The only reward for my effort was a fresh wave of pain searing through my battered body. If I had been a normal human, I wouldn't have been able to walk, let alone withstand the agony. No… I'd be dead by now.

"You never answered my question," I hissed through gritted teeth, forcing the words through the anguish.

"Who says I have to?" he asked, indifferent.

"You're not supposed to be doing this. Your job is to cross people over when it's their time. Not to decide it for yourself."

"Time changes everything. Humanity evolves, yet the cycle remains unbroken—round and round, full circle. Now, it is our time once more, not for the tainted blood of half-mortals, and certainly not for the fleeting lives of humans. This era belongs to us." He pulled me around a jagged bend, his last words echoing in the cavern as he stopped at an ominous opening.

Through the threshold, the dimly lit chamber stretched out before me. And there he was.

Hades, standing at the center, his presence commanding every corner of the room. The torchlight carved shadows across his muscular chest, every sinew gleaming with an otherworldly strength. His olive-toned skin absorbed the dim light, while his dark, tousled hair fell just over his sharp eyes—eyes so deep and magnetic, they felt like they could strip me bare. His face was an intoxicating mix of allure and danger, promising power and despair in equal measures.

Thanatos shoved me forward, and I stumbled into the room, Hades's gaze crashing into me like a physical force. The ache in my shoulder flared unbearably—I wanted to rip my own arm off just to make it stop. I staggered forward, barely staying upright.

"Where are they?" The words tore out of me as a snarl, my nails biting into my palms so hard I thought they'd draw blood. My lungs burned like I was inhaling fire, my panic tangling with my anger, clouding every ounce of logic. "If you've done anything to them, I swear—"

Laughter echoed off the stone walls, a low, dark sound that twisted through the air and sent my anxiety spiraling. Paul had told me it was a ploy—that the vision of my mom dead and Zach being dragged into the Underworld was a trick meant to break me. I'd wanted to believe him. I'd clung to that hope, even as Thanatos hauled me into the depths.

But now, standing here, doubt seeped into my thoughts, spreading like a stain I couldn't scrub away. Was I too late? Had they already taken my mom or Zach?

My heart pounded as Hades approached, every step he took drawing the breath from my lungs, leaving me gasping for air. He stopped just before me, his presence suffocating, his eyes locking onto mine.

"I'm here, Hades," I forced out, my voice trembling with desperation I couldn't hide. "You've got what you want. Just let them go."

Hades moved closer, exuding a force that seemed to draw me in, stripping me of any control. His voice was smooth, almost hypnotic, as he said, "I'll never fully understand the strengths of human emotion. But you shouldn't worry." Instead of dismissing my fears, his fingers brushed against my jawline, a fleeting touch that sent a shiver skittering across my skin—a mix of cold fear and something dangerously alluring. "Your mother and friend aren't here."

My heart stuttered as his wicked grin twisted across his face, the kind of smile that could make you question everything. Relief should've flooded me, but instead, a strange mix of fear and something else, something darkly enticing, tightened every muscle in my body. My instincts screamed to stay away, yet I found myself leaning into his touch, unable to resist the pull he had over me.

I swallowed hard, forcing air into my lungs, and let my powers rise, infusing me with a false sense of invincibility. I had to focus, had to push through the haze he was weaving around me. "Good," I managed to say, meeting his gaze with defiance, "otherwise, I'd really have to kick your ass."

He chuckled. "It's a pity things have to be this way. You're rather entertaining." Hades tilted his head, inspecting me with a magnetism that made my skin flush. I could feel his eyes traveling over me, as if I were an irresistible mystery he was hungry to unravel.

"And why do things have to be this way? What, you get bored so you decide an Apocalypse is in order?"

He leaned in, almost nose to nose. "Among other things," he said, his gaze searching mine. "Don't take it personally, Amara. You're just in the way."

Then he straightened, clasping his hands behind his back, and walked off as if he'd finished enjoying the evening's entertainment.

"Jessa," I corrected, my voice tight with a mix of fury and something else, something that made my heart race. "My name is Jessa, you idiot. Kind of embarrassing for the god of the Underworld to be this bad with names, don't you think?"

I rasped for air, despite my smugness. I'd been holding off using the inhaler—saving that last pump for when I really needed it. Apparently, that moment had arrived. With my good arm, I reached into my pocket, pulled it out, and used up the last of its contents, the taste of the medicine thick on my tongue.

Hades's eyes darkened, the earlier amusement slipping away. "Jessa," he repeated, rolling the name over his tongue like he was savoring it, though the edge in his voice was unmistakable. The seductive power he'd wielded moments before was still there, but now it was laced with something far more dangerous. Something that promised torment.

He smirked and shrugged. "It doesn't really matter now, does it?"

I threw the inhaler at his feet. "So, what, you think you can just destroy my soul and wipe out humanity because it's 'your time'? Whatever that means. You're a jerk." My rage throbbed against my ribs, swirling in my core like a storm with nowhere to go. I clenched my good arm to keep from cradling my injured shoulder.

"You try having a dead-end job for an eternity. No promotions, no career advancement, just the same thing, day in, day out," he said as he closed the distance between us again. His eyes burned with purpose. "Unless, of course, you start over. And then there's you." He grabbed my chin.

I jerked it free. "Don't touch me."

Thanatos shoved me forward, and I nearly stumbled. I'd almost forgotten he was behind me. My jaw clicked as I rammed my heel down on the tip of his boot. He hissed and retaliated, digging his fingers into my bad shoulder. Gritting my teeth, I refused to cry out, but my eyes betrayed me, tears slipping free.

Hades circled us, his gaze intent, searching my face, likely trying to figure out how best to break me. "Why the others feel any sort of attraction to mortals has always eluded me. It's time they stopped polluting our bloodline, creating things like you."

Desperation clawed at me. I had no chance against one god, let alone two, if this turned into a fight. "Zeus won't be happy."

His laugh twisted my stomach. "You think he cares? It's high time he stepped down anyway." Bitterness coated his words, like a spoiled child jealous of his older brother.

"My lord, we're wasting time," Thanatos said, his grip finally leaving my shoulder.

I tried not to show too much relief, but my shoulder still screamed in protest. A whole bottle of painkillers would've been nice right about now— not that I had time to down one before whatever nightmare came next.

With lightning speed, Hades's hand snapped around my branded arm. I tried to pull free, but the space around me warped, disappearing and reassembling into something new.

Another cavernous room. Circular, with a domed ceiling lined in stalactites and flaming torches bolted to the walls. But the walls weren't made of rock or stone. I swallowed the bile rising in the back of my throat. Human bones. White, gray, chipped, some disturbingly intact, stacked and layered to form the entire chamber.

Hades released my arm and walked toward one of the walls, his back to me. "Of course, *Jessa*," he said, over-enunciating my name like he was correcting himself. He turned around, his eyes gleaming. "If you fail to cooperate, I'll allow Thanatos to follow through with your mother and friend."

"Leave them out of this. They have nothing to do with this. They're mortal," I snapped. Of course, I had no clue how a god destroyed a soul, and I really wasn't planning on finding out.

"Exactly. So, they have everything to do with this." His dark smile twisted deeper. "But don't worry. I'm sure their souls will find their way to the Asphodel Meadows."

I glared, every muscle tensing as he gestured lazily toward Thanatos, who had silently followed us in. "Now come," Hades said, his tone almost bored. "Let's get this over with. I'll make it quick and painless."

I snorted. "Too late for that." My hand cradled my throbbing shoulder as my thoughts unraveled. My mom. My friends. Zach. Trees, the wind, sunlight, coffee, Dr. Pepper, music, singing, school.

Everything. Gone.

Because these bastards were bored. Because they didn't like mixed blood. Because they were on some horribly disillusioned power trip.

I'd failed before. I wouldn't fail again.

I glared up at Hades, letting the energy in me build, rushing through my veins like a current I didn't want controlled. I wasn't stupid enough to think I could win alone, but I wasn't going to make it easy for him.

"Tell me," I taunted, "how exactly do you destroy a soul?"

"Why don't you come here and find out?" Thanatos's voice prowled from somewhere behind me.

"Too afraid to do it yourself, Hades?"

Hades's glare darkened, but I smirked. My instincts fired all at once, cutting through my fear, and I launched myself at him.

White wings flared in my face, and a fist slammed into my jaw, sending me crashing into the wall of bones. The brittle cracks rang in my ears as I hit the ground.

Ow.

I snapped my head up, narrowing my eyes at Thanatos as he waved two fingers at me in a mocking 'come and get me' gesture. My body screamed in protest, every nerve alight with fire, but adrenaline numbed the burn as I launched at him like a flying rabid bull.

One beat of his wings, and he met me midair. I tucked my legs and kicked him square in the chest, sending him torpedoing into the opposite wall. Bones clattered to the floor, scattering in an erratic cascade.

I didn't let up. I tackled him, punching and pinning him to the ground. I curled my firsts tight over his, ignoring the agony stabbing me all over. My strength still startled me. I could crush his bones in an instant if I wanted to. He cried out as I squeezed, and then dug my knee into his ribs, and I savored the sound. He thrashed, slamming his head into mine.

Holy hell, that hurt.

Black spots ate at my vision, and in the split second I faltered, he threw me off. My head struck the ground, the impact reverberating like a hollow drum, and my vision blurred as Thanatos straddled me.

The pain in my skull pulsed like metal clamps squeezing my head, and the taste of copper filled my mouth from my busted lip. He grabbed my face, his nails biting into my skin, and leaned in for a kiss.

The kiss of death.

The kiss that would steal my soul and deliver it to Hades.

Hades loomed nearby, waiting.

I seized Thanatos's throat with both hands and squeezed. He didn't stop, pressing closer even as I tightened my hold. I fought for the energy buried deep inside, channeling it into my grip with everything I had. With a surge of strength, I shoved him off and rolled to the side.

Thanatos wheezed, clutching his neck, but I didn't give him a chance to recover. I shot to my feet and lunged. My hands latched onto one of his wings, and with every ounce of Herculean strength I had, I hurled him across the room.

He slammed into the wall, snuffing out a torch in the process. More bones rained down, their white dust choking the air and stinging my eyes. Before I could react, Hades grabbed my hair and yanked me backward.

"Ow!" I shrieked, swatting at his hands. "Let go!"

He, unfortunately, obeyed. With ease, he spun me around and released me. I sailed into the jagged rocks, my body slamming against the wall before collapsing to the ground.

My arms gave out, and I crumpled, gasping.

A brilliant light illuminated everything. Peering through the strands of hair plastered to my face with blood and sweat, I watched as a figure materialized, faint golden light spilling off him and driving the shadows into retreat.

My heart stuttered, then found its rhythm.

Paul.

"Enough, Uncle."

He didn't just look like Paul. He looked every bit the god Apollo, the way I'd always imagined him in books—radiant, powerful, and untouchable.

Cynthia appeared through a swirl of silver mist behind her brother. Hope flared, fragile and flickering like a cheap candle in a hurricane. I closed my eyes, trying to steady my erratic breathing. I wanted Paul to come to me, to heal me, to make it all better. To tell me he was okay. That I'd be okay. That somehow, everyone would be okay.

But then someone else walked in.

She had dark, wavy hair that spilled down her back like a river of shadows, her skin so pale it could've rivaled Thanatos. She was breathtakingly beautiful in that deadly, goddess kind of way that made you feel like garbage just existing in the same room as her.

Persephone. Queen of the Underworld. Hades's wife. She had to be. If Hades was here, of course his better half would be too.

And then all hell broke loose in Hell.

In a blur, Persephone launched herself at Cynthia. Paul turned toward me but was intercepted by Thanatos.

Which left me with Hades. Of course.

I gritted my teeth and grabbed at the pockmarks in the bone wall, forcing myself to stand. Hades, for once, looked... conflicted. His gaze kept darting between me and his wife. Whatever internal debate Hades had, it didn't last long. He made his move with a fierce wave of his hand.

"No!" My scream came out raw, tearing at my throat.

Cynthia went spiraling across the room, thrown by Hades's invisible force. But impossibly, she twisted midair and landed squarely on her feet, whipping her auburn hair back like she'd just stepped off a roller coaster. Not a scratch.

She so had to teach me that.

Paul and Thanatos were an obscure mix of gold and black in their elemental forms, their movements too fast to follow. I barely caught Paul's flick of his wrist and, in the glint of the torchlight, saw something shiny streaking toward me.

Without thinking, I snatched it midair with reflexes I kept forgetting I possessed.

Baby Trident.

A smile tugged at my lips as I spun it in my hand. Paul. Always finding my sais.

Henry, in his usual impeccable timing, materialized at the entrance to the bone room, throwing himself into the fray with reckless abandon, going straight for Hades.

The scene before me was a surreal nightmare. They moved so fast, their divine forms streaking with the speed of their attacks, yet somehow, I could see every movement in excruciating detail. Persephone's hands clamped around Cynthia's throat and Cynthia fought back with everything she had—knees, nails, hair-pulling—but Persephone didn't even flinch. Across the room, Henry darted around Hades with unmatched speed, dodging sledgehammer-like blows by millimeters. Paul was back on Thanatos, relentless despite the growing odds. Paul tore through his wings with savage precision, feathers scattering across the room. Thanatos twisted and evaded, bashing Paul's face into the unforgiving stone wall.

I'd grown up with stories about these gods, but this...this was something else entirely. It was chaos incarnate, divine beings tearing each other apart with a ferocity that was both awe-inspiring and horrifying. The beauty and grace I'd once associated with them was shattered, replaced by a brutal reality where survival was all that mattered. How could something so magnificent, so powerful, be so completely horrific?

This had to stop. My brain struggled to calculate who to attack, which god to focus on to bring some balance to this nightmare, but my heart had other plans. I sprinted toward Paul and Thanatos, my focus narrowing to a single goal.

As if sensing me, Thanatos twisted, dodging Paul's swing, and in one swift motion, grabbed Paul by the neck and hoisted him effortlessly into the air. His eyes locked onto mine, a cruel glint playing in their depths.

Paul's face contorted, his hands clawing uselessly at Thanatos's grip. Thanatos was too strong, his powers amplified by his domain, his evil purpose driving him like a relentless force. And deep down, I knew the truth: Paul was weaker here, in the Underworld. Without the sun, he fought at a disadvantage.

The sight of Paul, *my* Paul, helpless and vulnerable, ripped through me. The thought of losing him, of Thanatos threatening to take him from me—like he had with my mom and Zach—ignited something dark inside.

Rage. Raw, unrelenting, all-consuming.

The infernal power I'd never fully understood broke loose, wild and untamed. My hand flew to the second sai strapped to my belt. With both weapons in hand and a feral growl, I launched myself at a speed almost rivaling Paul's.

Thanatos didn't see it coming.

I swung the first sai at his wing, the blade cutting deep enough to scrape bone. Thanatos roared, but I didn't hesitate. My second swing came fast and furious, slicing through the joint. It wasn't a clean break. Bone crunched under the force of my blade, the wing twisting unnaturally as his golden ichor sprayed the air.

His scream shook the chamber, rattling bones from the walls. He reeled back, his mutilated wing hanging by what looked like threads of sinew. I stumbled away, staring at the magnificent, godly blood dripping from my blades, the weight of what I'd just done crashing down on me. My knees buckled, and I hit the ground hard.

Despite everything he'd endured, Paul's first instinct was to get to me. With swift, almost desperate determination, he ignored his injuries and placed his hand on the first thing he could reach, my head, warm and soothing. A rush of blessed air filled my lungs, and the ache in my body disappeared, his healing power wrapping around me like a shield.

Thanatos shoved Paul away, his movements sluggish and unsteady. The room, once deafening with the clash of gods, fell into an eerie silence, the kind that made the hairs on the back of my neck rise.

I forced myself to my feet, my arm trembling as I pointed one sai at Thanatos. The other stayed poised for whoever thought they'd take the next shot. My breath came hard and fast, my eyes darting between the mayhem unraveling around me. Cynthia. Henry. Persephone.

Paul's focus shifted, his head snapping toward his sister. A faint ball of light flared in his palm, its glow pulsing brighter as his jaw tightened. In a blink, he vanished from beside me, reappearing in an instant at Cynthia's side.

Persephone's hands remained locked around Cynthia's throat, her fingers pressing deeper with the slow precision of someone savoring the act. Hades, meanwhile, had Henry in—what else?—a chokehold.

Seriously. Was there a divine handbook that mandated chokeholds as their go-to move? Because it was getting old.

I gripped my sais tighter, my breath shaky, taking it all in.

This was a freaking Mexican stand-off.

Hades sneered at the guardians. "Interfering was your first mistake. Assuming you could win will be your last."

Cynthia and Henry were too preoccupied being strangled to respond, leaving Paul as the only one able to say anything. He didn't need words.

For the first time since I'd known him, Paul's swirling amber eyes burned with something deeper. It wasn't just anger. It was wrath, a god's unfiltered fury.

Hades kept a firm hold on Henry as he raised his free arm toward the walls, the ground trembling. A grinding crunch followed as the bones lining the walls shifted, scraping together in chaotic unity. Fragments of ribs, skulls, and limbs fused into skeletons armed with rusted relics of battle. Shields of fractured spines, swords of sharpened femurs, and brittle armor pieced from bone shards and decayed metal clattered against their frames. The wall transformed into an army of the dead, hollow eyes locking onto me with unnerving focus, as if they already knew how this would end.

I shifted my stance, my mind racing. How was I supposed to fend off an army of bones and free my guardians at the same time? The odds didn't matter. I'd find a way… or die trying.

☉︎☽ CHAPTER 32 ☾☉︎

The walls stood silent now, skeletal guards lined in rigid formation, blocking any hope of escape. Beyond them stretched the abyss of the Underworld, vast and endless, its darkness swallowing the edges of the chamber.

No way out. Trapped.

A slow, ominous rush of water drew my attention downward. Below the uneven ledge, the River Lethe wound through the shadows, its currents thick and sluggish. Spirits churned beneath the surface, gray-blue forms shifting and writhing, their hooded faces straining upward as if the river itself refused to let them go.

I swallowed hard, the thought slamming into me like a fist. What if they were there? My mom. Zach. What if they were among the endless, drifting souls? My head spun with possibilities I didn't want to believe. No. It wasn't real. It couldn't be real. They were safe. They had to be.

But the world didn't slow down for my fears.

The chamber erupted into mayhem. Gold and silver arrows sliced through the air, glinting in the torchlight. Skeletons clashed with the guardians in a whirlwind of bone and madness. Two skeletal guards seized my arms. I thrashed one off, shattering it to pieces. The other's head rolled across the floor as I clipped its collarbone. Their brittle frames were no match for my immense strength, but there were too many, never-ending. Copy. Paste. Repeat.

I spun just in time to see Thanatos charging at me. His hand clamped around my neck, lifted me, and hurled me through the air. My body tore through a dozen skeletons, scattering them like pins, before slamming onto my side. My sais flew from my grip, clattering somewhere out of reach as I skidded to a stop, one arm dangling over the ledge.

The scrapes burning across my arm and stomach were nothing compared to the dark, ghostly water waiting below, ready to devour me.

My fear of heights momentarily paralyzed me, and I pressed my eyes shut. I had to focus.   If I fell, I'd be lost—just another soul swallowed by the river. My identity, my memories, my will—all of it stripped away. For what? Because I wasn't strong enough? Because I couldn't finish what I started? Because I was too afraid of heights?

A flash of memory ripped through me: the first time I faced Thanatos in my kitchen, the terror that gripped me as his power nearly crushed me into submission. I remembered the helplessness, the way I relied on Cynthia, Henry, and Paul to pull me through. But I survived. I fought back, even then. And now, here I was—alone, but stronger. I could do this. I had to.

The chamber roared back to life—shouts, clashes, the crash of destruction. I forced myself to my feet, my body screaming in protest. Thanatos was already there, a feral gleam in his now inky black eyes. His wings invisible again, the composed god I'd first faced was gone. He was wild, unhinged, like an animal that had tasted blood, his white hair falling in loose, tangled strands around his pale face. His once-pristine white robes were smeared with the remnants of our earlier fights, a patchwork of dirt, blood, and ash.

And now he had a sword.

The blade gleamed in the torchlight, long and elegant, its silver edge etched with delicate, swirling patterns. I blinked, the image sparking a memory from mythology books: Thanatos, the peaceful bringer of death, ushering souls to the afterlife with gentle grace.

Right. Peaceful. Because hurling me across the room and swinging a death blade at my head was totally serene.

He arced his sword and swung. I snatched a random bone from the ground, barely blocking the strike. The blade shattered it in half, the force rattling up my arms, but it bought me enough time to roll out of the way and hop to my feet.

He swung again. I ducked, straightening just in time to drive a kick into his chest. He flew back into a pile of bones. My sais. I spotted them just feet away and dove for them, swiping them up before spinning to face him. A quick glance confirmed my fears—the skeletal guards were multiplying, cutting me off from Paul and the others. I was on my own.

The weight of the sais in my hands steadied me, though my knuckles ached from gripping too hard. Paul had shown me some basics, but nothing could prepare me for going blade-to-blade with the god of Death.

Thanatos shot to his feet, his sword gleaming as he leveled it at me. His grin twisted into a mix of rage and sadistic glee. The way he moved— fast, erratic—kept my pulse hammering. The enjoyment faded from his face, replaced by something darker, something primal.

He wasn't toying with me anymore. He wanted this to end. Now.

Was it because I'd almost taken his wing off? Pride? Or maybe I was just a bigger pain in the ass than he'd expected. Either way, it didn't matter. One thing was clear: Thanatos wasn't following Hades's orders anymore. He wanted this personal.

He lunged. I parried, crossing both sais to deflect his blade. I twisted my wrists and shoved his sword aside. Another strike. I ducked low, slashing upward toward his torso. He dodged, spinning back with a counterattack that I hardly managed to block.

The fight blurred—his sword slashing, my sais deflecting and countering, redirecting his momentum at every turn. The blades felt like extensions of my arms as I struck, forcing him to shift his footing. He snarled, his swings heavier, more irregular, but I held my ground, stunned I'd lasted this long.

I didn't have time to think about the asthma creeping into my chest or the bloody scrapes on my stomach, or how dangerously close I was to the river's edge. Thanatos charged again, and I swung my sais to meet his blade. The clash of metal reverberated through me, but I focused on summoning the raw energy in my core, willing it into my arms, into the sais—anything to match his strength.

He twisted, swinging again. I barely managed to parry, each blow forcing me back. My foot slipped near the ledge, and I forced myself to keep my eyes on him, not on the River Lethe rushing below. I had to find a way around him.

He stabbed at my side, but my powers guided my reflexes, allowing me to sidestep and knock his sword away with Baby Trident. I seized the opening, moving away from the deadly drop.

"Thanatos, keep her alive!" Hades's voice was winded. Good—at least someone else was struggling. But those words only confirmed what I'd already guessed: Thanatos wasn't listening. He didn't care about Hades's plan.

Hades needed me alive to destroy my soul. Thanatos just wanted me dead.

A deafening roar shook the chamber. Paul's voice rang out in a sharp shout, followed by Cynthia's unmistakable string of curses. What the hell was over there with them?

The need to get to my guardians, to make sure they were okay, chipped at my concentration. My arms shook uncontrollably as I tried to brace them. Each wheezing breath scratched at my ears, a brutal reminder of my own limits. I hated it.

Hades's words meant nothing to Thanatos. His face twisted with seething rage. Godly speed. Overwhelming force. Swing after swing, thrust after thrust. I blocked, parried, dodged—barely keeping up. My powers whispered, guiding my instincts, but one wrong move, one slip, and it would be over.

My foot caught on a pile of bones, and my heart lurched as I fell back. Thanatos's sword descended, a streak of death. I rolled and the blade slammed into the rock where my head had been. My body felt like an overstretched rubber band, ready to snap. My chest burned with every gasping breath, and the raw flesh on my stomach throbbed like an open wound.

"Is this all you've got?" he sneered, spinning his sword like a baton. His twisted grin stretched wider, then he lunged again.

I shoved myself flat on my back, my sais crossed in front of me as Thanatos's sword hammered down, over and over. Each strike reverberated through my arms, forcing the blades closer to my face. The bone-strewn ground beneath me offered no traction, and my muscles burned under the relentless barrage.

Thanatos towered above me, his pale face carved with ruthless intent, his wild, white hair streaked with grime and blood. His strikes were deliberate, heavier and faster than the last, calculated to break me. "I am a god," he hissed, his voice curling with disdain. "You are nothing."

My arms shook like they were about to give out, my grip slipping against the crushing weight of his blade. I had to move. Had to escape. I hesitated, knowing one way to get the upper hand. I had no choice. Gritting my teeth, I let it one sai from my hand and planted my palm against the slick ground, pushing to the side just as his next swing came slicing down.

The strike cleaved into the stone where I'd been, shattering bone and scattering shards. I reached for my abandoned sai, but Thanatos moved faster. His sword arced down again, clashing with my remaining Baby Trident as I blocked. The impact rattled up my arm, and I gritted my teeth, swallowing a cry.

Movement flickered in the corner of my vision—Paul's golden aura, subtly blazing as he vaulted over a heap of skeletons. My focus splintered for just a second, my eyes snapping to him before I could stop myself.

I shouldn't have looked.

Thanatos didn't miss it. With a savage swing, his sword caught my sai, ripping it from my hand and sending it spinning into the shadows. His eyes gleamed with swirling black triumph as he raised his blade again, poised for the final strike.

Frantic, I fumbled for something—anything—to defend myself. My hand closed around a flat, solid object. I swung it up just in time, his blade glancing off the makeshift skeleton shield. Bone crumbs rained down my arm, but it held. Still flat on my back, I swung my leg out, hooking it around his and yanked with everything I had left.

Thanatos hit the ground with a heavy thud. I scrambled to my feet, my lungs screaming for air. I should've been keeled over from an asthma attack by now. Adrenaline must be one hell of a drug.

I leaped at him, slamming his sword arm down with one hand and swinging a punch at his face with the other. He moved faster than I expected, kicking me off with enough force to send me flying. Somehow— miraculously—I landed on my feet, the momentum of his force sliding my back a few inches.

Before he could recover, I rushed him, driving a hard palm strike into his chest. The force sent him tripping backwards over scattered bones as his sword slipped from his grasp, sliding out of reach.

"Nothing, huh? Nothing is kicking your ass." My voice was a ragged croak.

I spotted a bone on the ground, snatched it up, and hurled it at him. It smacked against the side of his head with a satisfying crack. His ebony eyes blazed, the intensity rolling off him like heat from the bowels of Hell.

Where the hell were my sais?

In a blind fury, Thanatos charged. There was no calculation in his movements, just raw, unbridled aggression. He wasn't thinking anymore. Maybe he believed I was too weak, too untrained, or that my asthma would finally take me down before he had the chance.

Time dragged, every second expanding endlessly. Thanatos, the very embodiment of death, came at me with a rabid look in his eyes. My strange powers sizzled within me. My arms tingled, my ears throbbed with the echo of every bone and rock he crushed underfoot. Then, he was on me. His face twisted in ferocity, his eyes black as ink, his skeletal fingers clawing for my arm.

My foot brushed against something solid. My sai. Without hesitation, I kicked it up into the air, catching it mid-fall. In that fleeting second, I saw his expression shift—wrath giving way to something else. Fear. His black eyes flickered, fading back to their original violet.

A wave of strength tore through me, overpowering his grip on my wrist. With a desperate, powerful motion, I drove the sai into his neck.

I closed my eyes, unwilling to witness the aftermath. Doubts chipped away at the edges of my mind. Had I really done it? Was he gone, or was this just another cruel trick?

The memory of him pinning me to the kitchen wall resurfaced. His body pressing against mine in a savage claim, his lips stealing my soul with that kiss of death. The hopelessness, the crushing weight of his power. I wasn't ready to feel that again.

My fingers tightened around the sai still in my hand, slick with blood. My body trembled, every breath catching in my chest. I wasn't sure if I'd won… or if I was only seconds away from being destroyed.

☉☽ CHAPTER 33 ☾☉

Before I opened my eyes, a gust of searing heat blasted my face, forcing me to shield myself. The flames roared like they had a mind of their own, their suffocating heat squeezing the air from my chest and leaving a metallic tang on my tongue. I squinted against the inferno that disintegrated the skeletal guards into ash. Where had all this fire come from?

I turned my gaze, and there he lay. Thanatos, sprawled on the ground, his once-invisible wings stretched wide—one pristine, the other broken. Gold-flecked blood mixed with crimson on his white feathers, pooling around him in an almost hypnotic contrast against the ash-streaked floor. For all his rage, he looked peaceful now, like a fallen angel finally at rest.

I should've looked away, but I couldn't. The fight, the chaos… all of it faded into the background. A single thought took its place, heavy and cold: it could've been me lying there, lifeless and broken.

Through the billowing smoke, I glimpsed a monstrous giant lumbering toward Cynthia and Paul. The immortal siblings were battered, their bodies streaked with shimmering god blood, their clothes torn and singed. Paul looked worse, barely recognizable beneath the grime and exhaustion. My heart lurched. Where was Henry?

Every instinct screamed at me to charge through the fire, to knock the giant back and shield them. "Hey!" I shouted, my voice cracking—a feeble attempt to distract the monster and give the guardians a chance.

Bad idea. The moment I opened my mouth, thick smoke poured in, searing my lungs and shriveling them into useless husks. The Cyclops turned at the sound of my rasping voice, its single, massive eye narrowing as it locked onto me. It roared, raising its spiked club high as my knees buckled. I collapsed, Baby Trident slipping from my hand and clattering to the ground with a hollow thunk.

Gripping my chest, I searched desperately for air that wouldn't come… drowning in the smoky haze. The world blurred. Flames twisted into a vortex of orange and red. I fell, curled next to Thanatos, my vision wavering, tears spilling from the sting in my eyes. I couldn't breathe. Couldn't move. Couldn't fight.

A shadow burst through the flames, landing in front of me. *Please be Paul, please be Paul.*

A hand clamped down on my shoulder—cold, hard, relentless. Fear knifed through my gut. This wasn't Paul. I squeezed my eyes shut, blocking out the terror, holding on to the last shred of breath I had.

"Fix her!" Hades's voice boomed next to me.

But as I kept my eyes shut, the turmoil began to dissolve. The inferno, the smoke, the clash of battle… it all ebbed into nothingness. In their place, a vivid blue sky stretched endlessly above me. The sounds of the Underworld slipped away, replaced by the soft rustle of wheat fields swaying in a gentle breeze.

Memories floated to the surface, vibrant and bittersweet: my mom pressing a band-aid to my scraped knee, my first nerve-wracking day of junior high, Zach's lips brushing mine during our first kiss. Giddy laughter from a pillow fight with Samantha. Ice cream with my mom, its sweetness comforting and familiar. Quiet rooftop talks with Paul, his presence solid, endless, and full of unspoken meaning.

Each memory shone with clarity, only to blur and fade moments later, slipping through my grasp like grains of sand.

A voice—distant, muffled—called my name, tugging me back. It took every ounce of willpower to open my eyes. When I did, the serene image of the Asphodel Fields, the resting place of souls to be reborn, dissolved into the grim reality of the Underworld. Glowing stalactites loomed above me, and the faint whispers of lost souls echoed from the River Lethe far below.

The rocky floor no longer pressed against me. The blistering heat of the fire had vanished, leaving behind a chill that crawled up my skin. A familiar warmth melted the ice that had taken over my entire body.

Shapes blurred and swam until my vision slowly focused. I gasped a ragged breath. And another. And one more, just to be sure.

Paul's face hovered above me, emerging from the haze as clarity returned. His hand moved away from my chest after pulling me from the brink of death, but his expression wasn't relieved. Not even close.

That's when I realized my feet weren't touching the ground. The crushing pressure on my throat, cutting off my breath again, was Hades. A choked gasp escaped me as Hades tightened his grip on my throat. The sense of déjà vu hit hard—another damn chokehold. Did these gods have no creativity?

His glare was full of the kind of hatred I was getting used to seeing from these Underworld gods. I had no idea what had gone down with Paul and the others while I was battling Thanatos, but it didn't look good. Persephone had Cynthia's arms twisted and pinned behind her back, forcing her into a helpless, bent position like a criminal being restrained. And as for Paul...

"Come any closer, and I'll crush her," Hades snarled.

Paul stood motionless, every muscle in his body taut with tension. He looked like the statue of him I'd seen in a museum—except darker, battle-worn, and lethal. I could only assume Hades had forced him to drag me back from dying just so he could try destroying my soul all over again.

His grip was firm as he started dragging me along. My nails scraped uselessly against his arm, my feet thrashing in a desperate, wild bid to break free.

A sudden crack split the air. I twisted, just in time to see a whip of fire lash out behind Hades. The lord of the dead hissed, spinning around and dragging me with him. My body flailed with the motion, his grip tightening as I struggled to free myself.

Hephaestus stood in the smoke, his presence like a forge come to life, glowing with power. The flaming whip in his hand curled back to him. Behind him, the Cyclops lay in a smoldering heap, the acrid stench of burning flesh choking the space between us.

"Let her go, Hades," Hephaestus said, his voice as threatening as the fire encircling him.

"You're outnumbered," Cynthia said, her voice daring despite the odds.

Hades's lifted me higher. My neck burned and my fingers curled around his hand, desperate to loosen the crushing hold. Each ragged breath scraped against the shrinking air, tears spilling before I could stop them.

"I'll do it," Hades growled, his voice low and edged with finality. That's when I realized he was holding me over the River Lethe.

A booming voice shook the chamber, the floor beneath us trembling. "What in the name of Gaia is going on here?"

My hair had fallen into my face, blocking my view, but I didn't need to see to feel the shift in the atmosphere. The air turned brittle, sharp enough to slice. Even Hades seemed to pause, his grip on my throat loosening slightly, as if he were holding his breath.

"Hades, put her down," commanded the new voice, calm yet carrying a weight that demanded obedience. Whoever this was, he seemed to be on my side.

Hades hesitated, but I didn't. The moment his grip slackened, I twisted and kicked until my feet hit the ground. His hand still hovered at my neck, but now I could see across the chasm holding the River Lethe.

Standing on the other side was a man radiating sheer authority—his silver hair glinted in the low light, his spiraled beard framing a face carved from marble, and piercing blue eyes locked onto me as if he could see every secret I'd ever kept.

My mouth dropped open. Holy mother, was that Zeus?

Henry stood beside Zeus, his chest heaving as he fought to catch his breath. Had he gone to fetch the king of the gods himself? Behind them, a frail old man stood. Charon, the guide of the Underworld. His hollow eyes met mine for a fleeting moment, sending an icy shiver through me. A stark reminder of just how deep into enemy territory we were.

Hades's grip tightened around my throat again. "You can't stop me," he growled, his voice low and menacing. And he wasn't wrong. Everyone knew the ancient pact between the three brothers—sky, sea, and underworld. They were forbidden from interfering in each other's realms.

But Zeus didn't seem to care. If anything, he looked pissed. "What exactly are you trying to do?"

Zeus's words were calm, but a storm churned beneath them. The air around him seemed to crackle with restrained power, his gray robes rippling as if caught in an unseen wind. He looked every bit the god he was—regal, imposing, like he'd stepped straight out of one of my books.

"Since when have you cared?" Hades spat.

The silence that followed caused an ache in my ears. I had to figure out how to break free. There was no way I was going to kick and flail like an idiot in front of Zeus. I needed to be cool, calculated. I needed to be badass.

Zeus's voice finally cut through the silence, answering Hades. "Since you brought my children into this." The entire Underworld seemed to vibrate with the weight of his words.

Hades's nails dug into my skin, a fresh wave of pain making my vision blur with tears. I could feel Paul and Cynthia behind me somewhere, their presence a small comfort. But Hades, ever the tactician, dragged me backward, ensuring that the other gods were in his line of sight. He wasn't about to let them make a move while he had me in his grasp. Bluffing wasn't his style.

"*They* brought themselves into this," Hades hissed. "We don't need these half-bloods to do a god's job, Zeus."

He shook me like a ragdoll to hammer his point home. My body felt limp, my strength slipping with every second. Breathing was a losing battle, every gasp sharp and shallow. I hated my asthma more than I ever had—useless, cruel, and always there at the worst possible time. But I didn't cry out. I wouldn't give him the satisfaction.

"You turned your back on humans long ago," Hades continued, his voice like poison. "You don't care about them. Let me finish the job."

Out of the corner of my eye, I caught a glimpse of Paul. His chest rose and fell with labored breaths, his fists clenched tight at his sides, golden eyes blazing with barely contained fury. I could see it—he wanted to attack, to take Hades down. But he couldn't, not without risking my life.

And I hated it. Hated that I was the reason they couldn't stop this monster.

"Humans, yes. Jessa isn't human."

Holy shit, Zeus knew my name.

He continued, "And what job would that be, brother?" Zeus's voice was smooth, cunning even.

He was onto him. The lord of the underworld was screwed now.

Hades stiffened, his smirk twitching at the edges.

Zeus tilted his head slightly, his expression as unreadable as stone. "You've been awfully quiet about Hercules's soul all these years. Strange, isn't it, how Hephaestus got all the blame?"

Hades's jaw shifted as if he were grinding his teeth. He didn't answer. He didn't need to. The tips of my shoes scraped against the ground as he dragged me closer to the edge. Panic roiled in my gut, threatening to shatter the mask of defiance I clung to. Hades didn't care. Zeus, bound by ancient laws, wouldn't stop him.

Hades couldn't destroy my soul now—not without Thanatos—but he didn't need to. He could cast me into the abyss, remove me as a threat, and bide his time until my soul returned, vulnerable and defenseless. The thought of him finding me again, when I was too young or too weak to fight back, dropped a heavy nauseousness in my gut.

Hades dangled me over the chasm, the black waters below taunting me, eager to consume. It wasn't fear of drowning that ate away at me... I'd never even learned to swim, always too afraid of the water. No, it was this river, ready to erase me, to strip away everything I was and leave nothing but a hollowed soul.

"You can't stop me." Hades didn't need to confess. His arrogance oozed from every word, his triumph practically radiating. He thought he'd already won.

In my peripheral, I saw Paul and Cynthia exchange a glance. Something unspoken passed between them, a plan hatching in a single moment. Cynthia, her arms twisted and locked behind her by Persephone, suddenly threw her head back into Persephone's face. The crack of bone on bone sent Persephone reeling, her grip faltering as she staggered back.

Paul moved in an instant, bolting toward me, while Cynthia spun around, slamming Persephone to the ground.

It was too late.

Hades let go.

My scream ripped through the cavern, echoing off the bone walls as I plummeted. Instinct took over. My body twisted in mid-air, arms grasping for anything solid. The cliff wall rushed past me, scraping my face and shredding my nails. Then—impact.

My hand caught on a sharp rock jutting out, the jolt slamming through my entire body. I dangled there, my arm trembling as the weight of my body tested my grip. Blood streaked the jagged surface where my fingers clung, making it slippery. Somehow, I'd stopped the fall. Somehow, I'd saved myself. Again.

Just as I started to pull myself up, I froze. Bare feet hovered over my fingertips. Hades stood there, a demonic smirk twisting his face as he stared down at me. "I'll see you soon," he promised, lifting his foot to crush my fingers.

Instinct took over. I grabbed his ankle just as he raised it and yanked. Shock flashed across his face as he lurched forward off the ledge.

But he wasn't going alone.

His hand shot out mid-fall, latching onto my leg and nearly ripping me from the rock. My fingers dug into the bloodied ledge. I held on with everything I had, but it wasn't enough. I couldn't carry both of us. My fingers began to slip.

Tiny rocks broke free and tumbled down my arms, stinging my face. A raw, guttural scream tore from my throat, as if sheer willpower could somehow keep me hanging on as I tried to pull both of us up.

But it wasn't enough. My grip failed, and my hand slipped free.

The drop yawned below me, terror exploding in my gut.

Someone grabbed my wrist.

I craned my neck to see Paul, his face flushed, veins bulging, planted firmly on his chest as he fought to pull both me and Hades up. Rocks scraped against my raw, bleeding stomach as he dragged me back onto the ledge. Behind me, Hades went wild, clawing at my back, trying to climb up me and reach Paul.

A burst of faint light flared from Paul's hand and the crushing weight vanished.

Hades's scream—an agonized wail that would haunt me for months—echoed through the cavern before the River Lethe swallowed him whole. The lord of the underworld, undone by the waters of forgetfulness. How poetic. He'd return someday, no doubt, but he wouldn't even remember why he wanted to destroy me, let alone all of humanity.

I found myself in Paul's arms, his warmth instantly dissolving the pain that had been tearing through my body. Every throb, every ache, every slice of agony faded away as I clung to him, desperately soaking in the comfort and strength he provided. We simply stayed there, wrapped in each other's embrace, too exhausted to move, too drained to do anything but hold on.

His heartbeat pounded, steady and strong, and I matched my breath to its rhythm, finding a fragile sense of calm I didn't want to let go. The world outside this moment didn't exist. It was just us, holding on as if the connection alone could hold back everything waiting in the shadows.

Eventually, he stirred. His grip loosened, but his fingers reluctantly lingered against my skin. Slowly, he pulled back, his eyes searching mine like he needed proof I was still here—that we'd made it through.

"We're okay," he whispered, but it sounded more like he was trying to convince himself.

I forced myself to meet his gaze. He was studying me, his eyes scanning my face like it held answers to questions he hadn't dared to ask. He looked... normal. Mortal, even. His skin was streaked with scratches and dried blood, his hair a mess, dirt and grime covering every inch of him. And he looked exhausted—not just tired, but completely drained, like he'd given everything he had and then some.

We stared at each other, breathless and trembling. My whole body shook from fatigue, and for a second, I wanted nothing more than to collapse back into his arms and stay there, unconscious, for about a year.

"Good job," he finally said.

I snorted, wiping the ashes and crusty blood from my face. "Yeah. Right."

☉☽ CHAPTER 34 ☾☉

Apparently, being the protector of all mankind didn't exempt me from the most epic to-do list known to humanity. My mom's attempt at grounding me before senior year started meant cleaning, organizing, and basically not having a life. And honestly? I didn't mind. After everything that had happened, being stuck in my room with a normal list of chores felt like a gift. Well, except for the sais hidden behind a box in my closet—that wasn't exactly normal.

My mom cracked the door open, peeking in. "Did you want any dessert?"

I laughed under my breath, lying on my bed with my arms stretched behind my head. "You give me a list of chores a mile long and then offer me cookies? What kind of mom are you?"

"I'll take that as a no, then." She started to close the door.

I shot up. "Wait, no, I'll have some."

The door opened again, and she walked in, balancing a plate of freshly baked chocolate chip cookies. She sat on the edge of my bed and patted my legs. "Listen, I know I may not be the greatest mom in the world, and you probably hate me for treating you like a child."

So, I'd gotten her looks and her dramatics. "I don't hate you." The last few days had given me a lot of perspective. Not that I ever hated my mom, but still. Coming home to see her waiting for me, furious because I'd missed curfew, was the best moment of my life. She wasn't stuck in the Underworld. She was here, alive, safe.

"Someone has to keep me in line." I winked.

She pursed her lips into that familiar smile I knew too well and handed me a cookie. It was moments like these that made me cherish the ordinary. "I know about Dawn's house party. I'd hate for you to miss out. Am I being too lenient letting that be the only thing you get to do this month?"

I beamed. "Seriously? You mean it?"

"That depends on your answer."

Biting into the cookie, I savored the way the chocolate melted on my tongue, warm and sticky. The little things I used to take for granted felt sharper now, like they'd been waiting to be noticed all along. "I'm going to need a glass of milk," I said between chews. "And, yeah, maybe a little lenient. But cool. Cool mom is good, right?"

She ran a hand over my head, probably fixing a strand of hair that was out of place. Normally, that would've annoyed me, but for once, I didn't mind. "I suppose so. Just no more staying out past curfew, okay? And no more ignoring my texts or not answering phone calls."

"You got it. I'll be home whenever you want me to be."

"How does eleven-thirty sound? You can take my old flip phone until your new one gets here."

"Perfect." Even if the party didn't start until nine, it was better than nothing. I slightly mourned the loss of my phone, though. Shattered by my own strength—that had been a fun story to spin for my mom.

"Alright, well, I'm heading to bed. Lights off in an hour?"

I munched the last of the cookie and gave a mock salute. "Sure thing."

She got up, doing a quick sweep of the room like she was mentally cataloging tomorrow's cleaning list, then left. I flopped back onto my pillow and closed my eyes. Exhaustion pulled at me, but sleep felt dangerous.

Instead, I replayed yesterday in my head, sorting through everything I'd learned during the debrief. The details felt heavier now, sinking in piece by piece.

Apparently, it took an almost-Elder and a pissed-off messenger god to convince the big bosses to listen. While Henry raced mid-battle to drag

Zeus into the fray, Eron and Sy teamed up with Hephaestus to make sure the Elders actually took us seriously. I guess it helps to have an Olympian tag team when you're trying to save the world.

As for my dad, I still hadn't worked up the nerve to talk to him about everything. He went to the Elders for help, which spared him from facing Lethe's consequences, but what he'd say to me now? That was a conversation I wasn't ready for. Eventually, yeah. Just… not yet.

While we were busy duking it out in the Underworld, Immortal Guardians everywhere fought their own battles—some wounded, some killed. That one still stung. I couldn't imagine anything taking down an immortal, but apparently, it happens.

Part of me wished I'd met more Guardians like Eron and Sy, but considering I was still here, still the Demi Guardian, I figured it was just a matter of time before that would happen.

As for me, Jessa Whitley, demon-slayer still in training, Zeus decided my "brave deeds" warranted a gift. Pneuma—or, in English, breath. I'd refused, obviously. I mean, wasn't protecting all mankind kind of my job? But he insisted. And really, who's going to argue with Zeus?

The scar of Hades's handprint on my arm hadn't disappeared. Not even Paul could heal it. I hated the thought of suffering through Texan August in long sleeves, but the alternative was explaining the big, black handprint branded into my skin.

What really got me, though—more than the scar, more than the gods and their meddling—was that I was lying here in my room, enjoying the last crumbs of a chocolate chip cookie. Not trapped millions of levels below in the Underworld.

In the old myths, no one got out of the Underworld. That was the rule.

My smile tugged at my lips, feeling strange, like I shouldn't be smiling—but I couldn't help it. I didn't know all the stories that weren't written down, but I did know this: the only other half-immortal to make it out alive was Hercules.

And now, me.

With the happy, maybe a little too proud, smile still stuck on my face, I rolled over and stared out my window. The beaded curtains were pulled to one side, giving me a clear view of Zach's room—my hundredth check tonight.

He sat at his desk, the glow of his computer the only light in his room. Probably playing some video game. I wanted to call him, but my shattered phone was long gone, swept up and thrown in the trash. And my mom's ancient flip phone? No clue if his number was even in there.

Still, I couldn't stop checking, couldn't stop making sure he was really there. Some part of me kept fearing I'd imagined it—that Thanatos had taken him after all, that he was still trapped in the Underworld, tormented and screaming.

But there he was. Totally fine. Normal. Unphased.

It still hurt that he didn't know… that he hadn't been willing to believe the truth about what I'd become. That pain sat heavy in the crack in my heart, the one that seemed to widen with every beat.

And yet, with the pain came a flicker of hope. Determination, maybe. That one day, I'd find someone I could share my secrets with.

I rubbed my eyes and sank back into the comfort of my pillows, cuddling Bunny. The events of the past week whirled in my head, refusing to settle. Things would never be the same.

Obviously, Jessa. What a stupid thing to think.

It left me missing part of what life had been like before all of this and wondering what it would look like after tonight. With Demi Guardian training ramping up, school starting, and keeping this secret from everyone… I wasn't sure how my life would unravel. Taking it one day at a time seemed like the only plan I could manage.

Mid-yawn, a strange awareness prickled through me. The hairs on my arms stood on end. I crawled out of bed, wincing at every sore muscle protesting the movement. Pushing the window open, I stuck my head out and caught sight of Paul sitting with his back against the siding of my house.

"Hey," he said, offering a smile. Not his usual Paul-smile, though. This one seemed… off.

"Hey," I said, climbing out and settling crisscross beside him, my back against the frame of my window. "Everything okay?"

"Oh, yeah. No demons out yet since you patched everything up."

"We," I corrected, my gaze lingering on his profile. Something was different about him, and I hated that I couldn't put my finger on it.

Paul ran a hand through his hair, glancing at me from the corner of his eye. The air between us felt wrong, like another big secret was pulling us apart.

"What's wrong?" I asked, leaning closer as if that would close the emotional space between us.

He didn't answer. Which meant something was wrong. Being the god of truth and all, if there wasn't a problem, he would've said so.

I locked my fingers together, flexing them absentmindedly, watching the skin on my knuckles wrinkle and smooth with each motion. My gaze darted to Paul. Still staring into the distance, still refusing to answer. I popped my knuckles, folding my hands in my lap, and glanced at Zach's window. His blinds were closed now. I wondered if he'd looked out before shutting them, and if so, what he'd seen—just me sitting there, or Paul, who could make himself invisible at will.

Maybe a new approach would work. "Can I ask you something?"

"Would it matter if I said no?" His tone was light, and he smiled, almost grateful for the change in topic. Not for long.

"Why didn't you guys just tell me everything from the start? Would've saved us a lot of trouble."

Silence. I sighed, annoyed. "Paul, please talk. The silent treatment isn't exactly my favorite."

He pulled his knees up, resting his hands on top and fidgeting with his thumbs. Was the god of the sun… nervous?

"Hades and Thanatos may be out of the way for now," he said finally, "but they were just the foothills of Mount Olympus."

I placed a hand on his knee, trying to reassure him. "Hey, don't stress. We'll start my training ASAP. We'll keep the demons under control and…" My words faltered as a dark thought crept in. Hypnos. He hadn't shown up during the last battle, and the realization planted a cold knot of fear in my chest. He knew where I lived.

"And Hypnos… we'll find him and stop whatever vengeful plot he's brewing." I forced the words out, hoping they'd bury the rising dread. Paul's silence, his faraway expression, made it harder to believe them.

"Hypnos will be dealt with when the time comes," he said softly, his eyes fixed somewhere beyond me. "But that's not what I'm worried about."

My fingers froze on his knuckles, the silence stretching longer than I wanted. What did he mean? What could possibly be worse than Hypnos? The question churned in my mind, heavy and unwelcome, like a shadow creeping into a room I'd thought was safe.

I looked away, my throat tightening. "You've changed your mind."

It wasn't a question. The fragile stitches holding my heart together unraveled, anger and the sting of heartbreak colliding in a sharp ache. Throw me into the Underworld to battle gods—that I could survive. But being dumped twice in one year? That was a wound I wasn't sure would ever heal.

"Changed my mind about what?"

"About us." I stared at the ground far below, the words tumbling out before I could stop them. "I mean, after almost letting humanity end, why wouldn't you? And I'm not her. I'll never be her. She was beautiful, and I'm just..." I swallowed hard, my throat burning. "I get it, okay? I really do."

Each word felt like ripping open an old scar. The doubts I'd buried ever since I learned about Amara, about the love they'd shared, came pouring out, raw and exposed, tearing through me in a way I couldn't stop.

But I wouldn't hate him for it. I couldn't. Not an option.

Paul turned to face me. "Jessa—"

"—and Cynthia, she hates me. I know she does, and she's your sister, so of course—"

"Jessa." He placed a gentle finger on my lips, cutting off my rambling. It worked. His hands wrapped around mine, grounding me in a way that felt almost magical. The cicadas in the trees strummed their endless tune, mingling with the soft evening breeze. It was like a concert, beautiful and soothing. Was Paul doing that?

"It was my fault we didn't tell you everything," he said. "I thought, for some stupid reason, it would keep you safe. I couldn't stand the thought of losing you again."

Then he smiled—the saddest smile I'd ever seen. "I love you."

My heart leaped. "Yeah?"

He nodded. "Yeah."

I exhaled, brushing my lips over his knuckles. "Well, that's good, 'cause I love you too."

The jitters in my chest were like a bunch of Lizzie's on speed, and for a second, everything felt perfect. There was first love, and then there was true love. And Paul? He was my true love. My literal soulmate.

But his smile—dark and hurting—remained. It chipped away at the fragile joy I'd been holding onto, an unwanted reality creeping in.

"Something's wrong."

He let out a slow breath and looked away. "The laws haven't changed, Jessa."

I blinked, the words not registering. "What?"

"The reason Henry and Cynthia did what they did back then... to Amara. The same problem still exists."

When he looked at me, those gorgeous blue eyes full of anguish, everything inside me crumbled. All the happiness I'd just felt melted into a cold, dull ache.

"We're not supposed to be together," I finished for him.

Paul shook his head, and the sight of him looking so miserable hurt more than I could bear. "But why? It's a stupid law. That was thousands of years ago. Can't we change their minds? Isn't there someone I can talk to?"

He shook his head again, pulling me closer. "Things might change after what happened today, but Zeus... my father doesn't change old laws easily." His hand moved to my shoulder, his touch sending tingles down my spine as I closed my eyes. "If I could lie, Jessa, I would. I'd find a way to make it work without anyone knowing, but I can't. Physically, I can't lie."

"I wouldn't want you to." My voice was soft as I pressed my forehead to his chin.

He held me tighter. "I don't think anyone else knows yet—besides Henry and Cynthia. For now, they haven't said anything, but I'm not sure they'll let me train you, knowing the risks."

The idea of Henry and Cynthia keeping Paul from me sent a fresh wave of anger through my chest. "What, you mean forcing you to choose mortality? I'd never make you do that. I'd never make you choose anything."

"I know," he said, his hand rubbing my shoulder. "But that doesn't mean I can't choose for myself."

I pulled back, staring at him. The thought of Paul giving up his immortality, his status as Apollo, to be with me, made my chest tighten. Would the sun still rise? Would someone take his place? A million questions rushed through my mind, but one truth drowned them all out.

He'd give it all up for me.

To be with me, Jessa Whitley. A girl who, just a week ago, was a human high schooler relying on her inhaler whenever life got too intense.

Could I let him do that? Give up everything that made him Apollo, just to be with me? The idea poisoned what I thought our love should be. As much as I loved Paul, I could never put my desires above everything else. I wasn't like Dawn, always twisting situations to suit her, no matter who got hurt in the process.

Paul's hand slid down my cheek, his thumb brushing my jaw before he tucked a loose strand of hair behind my ear. His fingers stayed, tracing the curve of my ear with a deliberate slowness that made my breath hitch. I knew what he was doing—distracting me, softening the edges of my spiraling thoughts—and I let him. The heat of his touch, the faint electricity it sent skimming down my spine, was too much to resist, anyway.

"Right now," he murmured, his voice low enough to vibrate through me, "we should celebrate the fact that you—Jessa Whitley—took care of Thanatos and Hades, two very powerful gods, without any proper training. If that doesn't give us hope for the future, I don't know what will."

His lips curved into a sly smile as his hand slid down to rest lightly on my shoulder, his thumb brushing the fabric of my shirt in soft circles. The closeness, the way he tilted his head just slightly toward me, made it impossible to think about anything but him.

And that wink? That wicked, playful wink that left me feeling like the only girl in the world? It sealed the deal. Whatever he was doing to keep my mind from unraveling, it was working. He pulled me tighter against him, and I couldn't help but sink into the warmth of his embrace.

"We," I said, determined to fix his perspective. "We took care of them."

His soft laughter was warm and rich, like the low hum of a bass guitar before the first note hit. It smoothed out the static in my brain, quieting everything for just a moment.

"Alright, *we* did," he said, his tone carrying a smile of its own.

But the peace was fleeting. Thanks to Paul, me, and the others, there would be a tomorrow. But what good was it if Paul wasn't part of it?

I closed my eyes and swallowed the harsh reality. Tomorrow would bring the hard choices and impossible plans, like convincing the gods to rewrite laws they'd clung to for millennia. For now, I let Paul hold me, fitting against his body like light that belongs to the sun, and pretending I wasn't afraid of what tomorrow might bring.

"Come here," Paul whispered, a command wrapped in warmth. His hands cradled my face, his thumbs brushing along my jawline with deliberate, featherlight strokes that sent a slow heat curling through me. His touch wasn't just electric… it was magnetic, pulling me closer until there was no space left between us.

Our lips met, soft at first, like a secret shared in the dark. Then it deepened, deliberate and consuming, igniting something I seem to always forget was there, an ache that burned brighter with every second. His fingers slid passionately to the back of my neck, tangling in my hair as he tilted my head, drawing me closer, deeper, until I drowned in him.

If not for my gift of breath, he'd have stolen it without even trying.

The kiss saturated me, pulling me into a world where nothing else mattered—no gods, no laws, no demons. Just us. Just this moment.

But then, the wind shifted. The hum of cicadas stilled, and the air grew dense, charged with an energy that zinged along my skin like a warning. His kiss lingered, a phantom warmth on my lips, blurring the edges of everything else. But reality pushed its way in, dragging a thunderstorm with it, stirring to life in the air around us.

"Paul…" My voice wavered. "What's happening?"

His hands held my face a second longer, his touch a mix of comfort and devastation, before they fell away. "I'm sorry." His words were nearly lost to the rising wind.

I searched his expression, desperate to piece together what he wasn't saying. Then it started… an all too familiar glow around him, flickering like the last light of a dying star.

"He knows." His voice carried regret, sadness… finality. His form began to dissolve, breaking into fragments of light that scattered into the air. He was leaving, piece by piece, and no matter how hard I tried to hold onto him, I couldn't stop it.

"Don't!" I surged forward, gripping his shirt, trying to hold him here, to anchor him to me. His hands covered mine, their warmth a fleeting reassurance.

"Jessa," he whispered my name heavy with everything he couldn't say. And then he was gone.

The golden light swirled into mist, evaporating into nothingness. My hands clutched the space where he'd been, and I sat there stunned, my chest hollow and aching. The storm pressed closer, the wind tugging at my hair, but I barely felt it. A thousand emotions warred inside me—grief, anger, defiance—but one thought cut through it all like Baby Trident.

Zeus.

He had taken Paul from me. No. This wasn't how it would end.

I dragged a trembling hand across my face, brushing away tears I didn't remember shedding. My gaze lifted to the sky, where thunderheads swirled like an ink spill, lightning splintering at their edges as if the heavens themselves were breaking apart.

"This won't change *anything*," I whispered, my words bitter but unshaken, fueling the fire burning in my chest.

The wind howled in response, but I didn't flinch. Tomorrow, I'd figure out how to fight for Paul, how to defy Zeus, how to tear apart the gods' laws if I had to.

Because if they thought I'd let them decide my fate, they'd underestimated the wrong girl.